A NOVEL

MARILYN BRANT

The Road to You
Twelfth Night Books
© 2013 by Marilyn B. Weigel
Cover © 2013 by Sarah Hansen, Okay Creations
Interior Formatting by E.M. Tippetts

Wish I May Excerpt © 2013 by Lexi Ryan

This is a work of fiction. Names, characters, places, brands, media and incidents are either the product of the author's imagination or are used fictitiously. Any resemblance to actual events, locales, organizations, businesses or persons, living or dead, is entirely coincidental.

ISBN: 978-0-9893-1604-0

For my dear writing friends—Karen Dale Harris, Lisa Laing and Laura Moore—I'm so thankful to all of you for your thoughtful feedback on this novel, for your longstanding encouragement of my writing career and, most of all, for your friendship.

And, of course, for Andrew—this book was yours from the beginning.

"All journeys have secret destinations of which the traveler is unaware."

~Martin Buber

A Note to Readers

I spent a large portion of my childhood in the 1970s, and I remember that decade with fondness if, perhaps, with a bit too much disco, oddly patterned clothing and kitchen appliances that were painted a disturbing shade of "mustard."

But that time period wasn't really *so* long ago...although, sometimes, it does seem like a galaxy far, far away. An alternate universe where the people of Earth did not have cell phones. Or GPS devices. Or even wireless Internet access.

It proved quite a challenge for me to write a story about missing teens set in an age when, if a family member disappeared, he or she couldn't be tracked by the technological or forensic methods so commonplace today. An era when finding an unoccupied payphone was the only way to contact someone if you were away from home. When folded-paper maps were the main tool you had in figuring out directions on the road. And when, if there was research on a topic to be done, the public library would be your best bet for getting the resources you needed.

We have so much information available at our fingertips now, but that not-so-distant decade still holds plenty of unique gifts in its treasure box. The music back then could be pretty amazing—if you knew who to listen to on your LP turntable, 8-track player or cassette deck. It was a known fact that there were some really cool cars on the highway. And, well, the Force was with us all...

Thanks for reading this story. I hope it brings you the joy of romance, the intrigue of mystery and the sheer thrill of adventure.

~Marilyn

"There are only two mistakes one can make along the road to the truth; not going all the way, and not starting."
~Buddha

Chapter One

Chameleon Lake, Minnesota ~ Thursday, June 8, 1978

MY HANDS trembled as I unlocked the cedar box in the tool shed. I listened for the distinctive click, lifted the lid and peered inside, not knowing what I'd find in its shadowy depths.

I half expected to see my old diary resting at the bottom, even though I knew it was safely back in my room. I used to hide it in here years ago, before the key to the box was lost. A key that mysteriously resurfaced this week.

But it wasn't my diary.

Instead, I found a different book. The small brown-leather journal that had once belonged to my older brother Gideon. My only sibling. The one who'd disappeared two years ago. The one everyone said was dead.

I bit back the usual sob that always rose up in my throat when I remember him, then stared at the medium-sized box and its contents, almost afraid to touch anything. To my eye, my brother's book seemed to have been conjured there, as if by magic. I hadn't seen Gideon's journal since the day he'd gone missing... What was written in it? And why, all of a sudden, had it reappeared—much like the key to this box—here, now?

Before I could talk myself out of it, I snatched up the journal and began to examine it.

1

Funny, even with the impression of a delicate butterfly stamped on the front cover, the book still managed to be tinged with Gideon's masculinity. To an outsider, it probably looked like it contained some kid's observations on nature. Something safe, simple, innocent.

And the first few pages really were ordinary. So typical of my big brother that I caught myself in a sigh, missing him. I still missed him so damned much—with every breath, every memory.

Like the way he'd grin at me whenever I saw him scribbling in it. Even if I teased him about the butterfly or keeping secrets or writing notes about his girlfriends, he'd just laugh.

"Aurora, I love butterflies and secrets...*and* girls," he'd tell me, amused and so self-confident.

But here I was, skimming through a dozen pages, and I hadn't found any dating exploits yet. Just details about cars and engines cluttering the first third of the journal. I spotted a step-by-step flowchart for performing an oil change. Something about the testing of transmission fluid. A procedure for fixing a leaky head gasket and the supplies needed to do so:

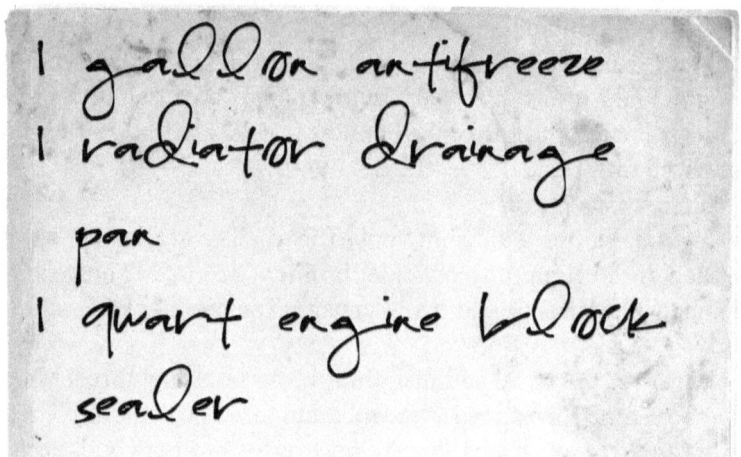

...and so on.

Looked kind of like a recipe to me.

Lists of standard adjustable wrenches (*8"/203mm, 10"/254mm, 12"/305mm*) and screwdrivers (*Torx #15, Phillips #00*) followed. I squinted at them all. For a girly, bookish seventeen-year-old like me, this was about as riveting as reading an old J.C. Penney catalog.

I kept reading anyway, my heart pounding as I traced my brother's words with my fingertip. The familiar raw ache twisted deeper.

On the page, Gideon was going on for an eternity and a half, specifying the differences between long nose pliers and nippers but, truth was, I didn't care. I knew the only reason I continued to flip the jaundiced, grease-stained pages was because this journal had once belonged to *him*. Just seeing that curious cramped script of his—far less even and so much smaller than my own—made me feel as though he were standing next to me, instructing me on something yet again. And Gideon had liked to teach lessons...when he was alive.

I shoved back at least fifty memories of my warm, funny, clever big brother, grasping for the emotional anesthesia that I knew cool over-analysis would bring—my default setting ever since he'd been gone. The same questions kept running through my head, but I didn't have any answers.

Why was this journal here? Why was I finding it now?

But then I turned the page once more and read a line that made me stop short.

The strangeness of what I saw left me struggling to inhale the musty air of the tool shed, and I felt tiny shivers sweep like lightning crackles across my skin.

The date somewhere in the middle of the page was from April 1976, but notated in the upper right-hand corner was a much more recent date: *Monday, May 29, 1978.*

Memorial Day. Less than two weeks ago.

I checked and double checked the numbers, almost positive my eyesight was playing tricks on me in the dim light. I had to be misreading this. It *couldn't* be real.

A few months after Gideon disappeared, the cops told us he must be dead. Insisted it had to be true. And due to the force of *everyone's* conviction, my parents and I had been persuaded to accept the police's assessment...although, I could never quite squelch the flicker of hope that lurked in my heart and flared up at the oddest moments. I could never really stop believing that *everyone* might just be wrong.

And now I had this.

Underneath the recent date were the words: *Start here. G.*

Logical or not, it was as if this were a message written just for me. Oh, God. Could it be?

My brain swam in a soup of questions and possibilities, a mix of elements and matter. Whos, hows and whens. Origins and endings. My hidden flicker of hope burst into flame.

There had been a lot of strangers filtering through our town over Memorial Day Weekend—visitors from places nearby, friends and relatives of residents, the occasional herd of curious wildlife—for the annual Chameleon Fest. Three days of hastily assembled carnival rides, taste tests, fireworks in the evening. A weekend of some small excitement in our otherwise sleepy lakeside village.

And then the key to the cedar box reappeared.

It had been lost for ages but, out of nowhere, it materialized again. In my room. In my desk. In my plastic paperclip tray.

Gideon used to tease me about how much I loved personalized stationery and office supplies. All of my neatly stacked notepads. My smooth-writing Bic pens. My colored bulletin-board tacks. For a couple of days, I tried to dismiss my discovery. I tried to convince myself I'd just overlooked the key in my numbness of the past two years.

But the jab of peculiarity pressed upon my senses and only grew stronger.

It was *too* strange to have found the key there, buried beneath a sea of paperclips, since I knew I'd replenished them just a few weeks ago. Even in grief, I wasn't someone who'd forget something like that. And I couldn't keep denying my instincts.

Standing here in the middle of the tool shed and holding Gideon's journal, I knew for sure that finding this key couldn't have been accidental. Like the trajectory of a pinball, if you were to hit the metal flapper so it connected with the ball in just the right, sweet spot, it would send the orb rolling with a smack, straight into the diamond center and—*bing, bing, bing, bing, bing*—you'd get the 10,000-point bonus.

The person who put the key in my paperclip bin *knew* I'd eventually find it, recognize it and head to the tool shed to hunt down the cedar box.

The person who put the key in my paperclip bin *knew* how organized I was, how much of a puzzle solver I'd always been and that I wouldn't stop looking until I'd found the box, opened it and discovered the journal resting there.

And the *only* someone who would know these things about me was my brother.

Somehow, Gideon must have come into town on Memorial Day Weekend, snuck into the house while we were away and left the key for me, knowing the path he'd set me on.

Bing, bing, bing, bing, bing.

I felt myself slam into the 10,000-point bonus, my mind reeling. I tried to shake the mental machine hard enough to clear my head. *Flash. Bing. Tilt.*

But it was too late. My world had already tilted and, suddenly, I knew I was playing a very different game.

I WANDERED back to our house, my brain still swirling and Gideon's voice—loud and insistent—in my mind.

"You *can't* tell," I could almost hear him say. A line from our childhood that he'd used more than once when he was doing something dangerous.

"Mom and Dad will freak," he'd add. Then he'd laugh and try to reassure me.

"Oh, stop worrying, Sis. They don't have to know everything all the time."

"We're not kids anymore. We can handle this."

"Trust me, it'll be fine. Really."

And it usually was...until it wasn't. Until, one day, he was gone.

Any normal person would've ignored the pleading voice from the past and run, not walked, to the telephone, to call her still-grieving parents. To give them a surge of hope that their missing son might be alive after all. Because, oh, God—I didn't want to witness even another minute of my parents' pain. Not if it was within my power to stop it.

But I wasn't a totally normal person. I knew intuitively—with a mysterious certainty I'd come to expect and rely on—that this wasn't what Gideon wanted. He didn't want my parents to find the journal. He wanted *me* to find it.

Me alone.

Otherwise, he would have left it in the middle of the dining room table, the place he'd always tossed his school notes when we were little kids, his car keys as we got older, his wallet and, sometimes, an empty beer can or Twinkie wrapper. It was *his* spot. Mine was the edge of the kitchen counter, just beneath Granny's Bavarian cuckoo clock. Nonverbal signals that we were home.

So, I didn't tell Mom or Dad.

Instead, I took the journal to my room—a deceptively cheery place I hadn't bothered to alter since Gideon's disappearance. It still held the relics of my life from two years ago. All of my interests frozen at fifteen.

My poster of David Cassidy was the cheeriest item of all, although I'd finally gotten over my crush on him. I now preferred men who weren't teen heartthrobs. Who were older, cooler and more serious. Like Harrison Ford.

I flopped onto my tie-dyed bedspread, took a half dozen deep breaths and flipped further through the journal. It was all written in Gideon's distinctive scrawl. Really, no forger could ever replicate those peculiar loops and lines.

"It's practically illegible," I'd told him mockingly once. I, Aurora Gray, the superior younger sister in matters of penmanship.

He flicked his eyes toward the ceiling. "Maybe I don't want just *anyone* to be able to read it," he retorted. "Maybe content is more important than style. Ever consider that, Miss Straight-A Student?" Then he winked at me and went back to whatever he was doing. Good-natured as always, though secretive. Delighting too much in his cageyness.

I read through every single page in the book, but my brother's notes didn't make much sense to me. Cities, sometimes states, with a handful of names listed, usually an equation or two. More car parts, chemical fluids, a smattering of tools. It was like a crash course in auto mechanics with an extra-credit seminar in geography—all in code.

Thanks a lot, Gideon. How useful.

My pulse raced at what this all might mean, though. And, again, my brother's corner note kept me looking, studying, scrutinizing.

"Start here."

Start here…what? Start reading? Start traveling to these places? Start piecing together a way to find him? If so, why would he have made this so hard for me? Sure, we used to play at codes a lot as kids, but did he really think games would be necessary now?

I heard a set of heavy footsteps in the far hall, shuffling in a way that signaled a thump of recognition low on my spine. Dad was home.

A so-so work day at the post office. I exhaled in relief. There were never *good* days any more. Gloomy was normal, and tolerable was the new excellent. How long had it been since we'd stopped expecting anything above barely okay?

Long.

"Hello, Aurora," he called to me, his voice tired, slightly hoarse.

"Hi, Dad," I called back and then waited, on high alert, until my father had walked past my room without coming in. Mom wasn't expected home for another half hour from her secretarial job, so I had a little more time. I intended to use it.

I scanned another page of Gideon's journal—just as cryptic as the rest, but this time I noticed a reference to "J." This, too, sent my mind rolling in a prescribed direction.

The "J," I knew, stood for "Jeremy," as in the younger of the two McCafferty brothers. He and Gideon were best friends, and they would both be twenty years old right now if they were, in fact, wandering any part of the planet jointly or separately. They'd disappeared together on that same day.

My heartbeat picked up the pace as I flipped back to the *Start here* page and reread it, more carefully this time. Slipped in between the gauges and chemical substances I couldn't identify was the date: *Monday, April 19, 1976.* Just a few months before they'd gone missing. And this was followed by the words: *J. & I drove to Crescent Cove.*

Where the hell was Crescent Cove?

I whipped out the dog-eared U.S. atlas from under my bed, brushing the threads of a spider's web off the cover and coughing as the dust particles swirled around me. Then I studied the state map of Minnesota. Looked in the city index, too, but I couldn't find any place with that name. There was a La Crescent, a Crescent Beach, a Crescent Bay…

But, as I was about to toss the book away, I saw it at the edge of the page. It was there in nearly microscopic print, just across the Wisconsin border, near the Saint Croix Chippewa Indian Reservation. About three and a half hours away. If I got in my car and started driving eastward, I'd get there by nine tonight.

And then…do what?

I turned back to the journal, inspecting it for hints. Clues. Anything to tell me the correct next step.

I had no trouble catching vibes off people, and I'd read Gideon's expressions well enough when he was here. His journal, however, couldn't gesture frantically or blink in surprise. It couldn't tell me any of the three thousand things other people said with their fidgety fingers, raised eyebrows and bitten bottom lips. It was just a collection of words on old paper.

But it was a collection of words that was branded in ink, probably by my brother, as recently as ten days ago. And if it was proof that Gideon was still alive—and if my instincts about him having left our town for a reason had been right all along—then Jeremy might be alive, too. Was that possible?

I could almost feel the pinball of connectivity rolling between the different centers of knowledge and recognition in my brain, leading inevitably to the *one other person* who not only had an immediate, strong and highly personal stake in the outcome of this question, but who also had a solid mechanical background. Somebody who might be able to draw secret understandings from words that, to me, resembled a form of hieroglyphic gibberish.

That would be Jeremy's older brother, Donovan.

Oh, crap.

I COULD count on one hand the things I knew were true about Donovan McCafferty:

He was twenty-three—just over five years older than I was.

He'd escaped into the Army at age eighteen and, except for a few quick but memorable visits, hadn't returned to Minnesota until this past winter.

He had an excellent mechanical mind.

And he made me very nervous.

Underneath my skin, every nerve fiber was fast twitching. Just thinking about Donovan always did that to me but, this time, it was also about the trip.

I couldn't have been more impatient to get on the road to Crescent Cove, and I really didn't want to make a stop at Donovan's workplace. But, awkward though it would be, he knew a few things I didn't. And he just might signal to me (whether he realized it or not) some very useful directions.

I waited until after dinner, biding my time. Made the three of us broiled chicken, mashed potatoes, broccoli. Boring, yes, but it wasn't like anyone cared.

Then I excused myself from the usual watching of TV news and Thursday-night shows—they were repeat episodes anyway—and drove to the only auto repair shop and gas station in town. The one I avoided like the plague whenever possible, preferring to fill up in places where no one knew me, like Alexandria or St. Cloud. Places where Donovan McCafferty...wasn't.

It was 7:05 p.m. by the time I got to the shop, and I parked a fair distance from the entrance. They closed at seven, but the work light in the back was on and two out of the three garage doors were still open. I knew he was in there. Not because I'd caught even one glimpse of Mr. Tall, Dark and Intense yet, but because the only other car in the lot was a crimson Trans Am with the giant Firebird decal in black and gold across the hood. His, of course.

I pushed open my car door, grabbed my tote bag with Gideon's journal tucked safely inside and inhaled several lungfuls of the cloying summer air. So early in June and already every breath was wrapped in sticky-sweet bugginess.

I didn't make it more than five steps before Donovan came out. A solid, broad-shouldered, six-foot-two mass of frequently impenetrable emotions. Not impenetrable enough this time, though.

Even at a distance of half a parking lot, I detected two powerful sensations that crashed, one after the other, into my awareness:

One, he was hugely curious about why I was here.

And, two, he very much wished I hadn't been.

He walked up to me and cleared his throat. "Car trouble, Aurora?" He glanced at my hand-me-down, smoke-blue, five-year-old Buick Century, which had done nothing but purr contentedly during my drives around town. Donovan was the type to have noticed this, so I could tell he knew it wasn't the car.

I shook my head. "I need to show you something," I told him. "Privately."

A small flash of amusement quirked one corner of his mouth upward. I was surprised he allowed me to read this, especially since he knew I could. Surprised he was letting me see that one of his possible explanations for my presence was flirtatious in origin—even as he immediately dismissed the idea.

I rolled my eyes. "It's not like that," I murmured.

He pressed his lips together, but the amusement still simmered just beneath the surface. "Too bad. 'We're both *young* and *inconspicuous*,'" he said, parroting the hideously embarrassing words I'd said to him one night when I was a sophomore and had snuck into our brothers' secret high-school graduation party with my best friend Betsy. The guys had held it forty minutes away in St. Cloud so none of our parents would know.

I fought a blush. "We're not *that* young," I told him, trying to stand straighter and look older. "And we're not inconspicuous *here*."

"Ain't that the truth." He turned and motioned for me to follow him inside, clicking the shop's cool new garage-door opener so the second of the three garage doors came down behind us, rattling until it touched the concrete.

He led me into the back office and ushered me in. "You want me to close this door, too? Snap the blinds shut?" He was mocking me, but there was a layer of concern beneath it. He knew something serious was up. In a town of 2,485 people, where you'd run into the majority of the residents a handful of times each week, I'd spoken with Donovan McCafferty in private exactly six times in the past five years.

Here's to lucky number seven.

"Yes to the door," I said. "No to the blinds."

He did as I asked and then leaned against the smudged once-white wall, crossed his arms and studied me. "What's this all about, Aurora?"

I nodded and pulled Gideon's journal out of my bag.

"I found this," I told him, explaining the odd circumstances of my discovery, and watched as his dark eyes narrowed. The curiosity of a few minutes before became heavily spiked with suspicion. He flipped through several pages of the journal, silent. He was processing all of this, I knew, but he didn't quite seem to get it. To be able—or willing—to take the appropriate intuitive leap. To allow himself to follow the fated path of the pinball.

So, I pointed again to the recently dated page and to Gideon's words on it, scrutinizing Donovan's face as he read it a second time. I saw every nuance of his reaction. Couldn't miss the two major transitions, shifting his expressions in slow motion like tectonic plates made visible. Incredulity hardening into doubt. Hope melding into anger.

"What makes you think this new date written down is even real?" he growled at me. "Your brother could've just scribbled it in the corner two years ago as a note for himself. Or somebody else could have written it. There are a hundred possible explanations. Finding this journal all of a sudden doesn't prove anything."

"I think it does," I said quickly, but very cautiously.

Insight into a guy's emotions was no guarantee I'd correctly predict his behavior. In Donovan's case, he was a human knot of tension and anger. I had no earthly idea what he'd do next, so I did my best to come across as super calm.

"I know this is probably difficult to accept," I said, "but I'm almost positive Gideon wrote in this recently and that he brought it back to Chameleon Lake himself."

Still, Donovan didn't believe me.

"Your brother is *dead*, Aurora. And so is Jeremy. You know that. We *all* know that. Otherwise, they would've come back by now." For a second, his voice broke, giving away the anguish behind the words. He tried to cover it up. "You show this thing to anyone and they'll think you're crazy. 'Oh, look, my brother wrote me notes from the grave,'" he said with full-on sarcasm. "'And, hey, sometimes he visits me at my house, too.' Yeah. Have fun convincing anybody of that."

"I'm not showing it to anyone else, at least not until I have an idea of what it all means," I snapped. "But try to imagine I'm right. Just *try*. You knew your brother best. Is there anything here that jumps out at you a little? Makes sense to you? Especially those technical terms. Can you figure out what they were working on?"

Donovan wasn't a person who took orders willingly, at least not from someone he didn't consider his direct superior, so, of course, he didn't answer any of my questions.

"Tell me *exactly* what you're planning to do with this." He held up the journal.

I shrugged. "I'm just trying to understand it." This was mostly truthful.

Donovan stared at me—his face moving closer to mine as he searched for whatever clue he was looking for in my expression. It was precisely *this* uncomfortable sensation of being so carefully observed that made me keep my distance from the guy. I was used to analyzing the minute movements, body language and facial changes of others. It was not, however, my idea of a good time to be the subject of such scrutiny myself. Thankfully, that rarely happened.

I knew Donovan didn't make a habit of reading reactions like I did, but he seemed to enjoy turning the tables on me whenever possible. He was one of the only people I'd ever met who instinctively knew from Day One that I possessed this heightened perceptiveness. A natural gift and, alternately, a curse. I'd been only twelve years old the first time we spoke, but he was guarded with me even then.

"Just read the page. Please." I motioned to the journal. "I looked up some of the words in an encyclopedia but, aside from figuring out that they're chemicals, they don't mean anything to me."

Ethylene glycol
Propylene glycol
Sulfuric acid
Sodium nitrate
Strontium nitrate
Atomized spherical
aluminum
Bismuth subcarbonate
Ammonium nitrate

Sodium hypochlorite
Aluminum
Manganese dioxide
Sodium silicate
Zirconium powdery $+$ 2
($+$ 0)
Monday, April 19, 1976
J. & I drove to
Crescent Cove
Potassium perchlorate
Sulfur
Antimony sulfide
M $+$ 1 ($+$ 0), D $+$ 10
($+$ 0)

He read each of these hard-to-pronounce compounds aloud, along with the numbers and the mention of Jeremy and Gideon going to

Crescent Cove. He shook his head. "This doesn't make sense. I don't know why they'd need most of it at all. A few of these are used for car engines, like the propylene glycol, so they might have needed that, but the others are common oxidizers."

I squinted at him. "In English, please?"

"Chemicals that blow things up. Potassium perchlorate and sodium nitrate are used as fuels for things like fireworks," he explained. "They're not hard to find. If our brothers wanted to get their hands on them, they wouldn't have had to drive three hours to Wisconsin. They could find them in St. Cloud. So, if they went to Crescent Cove two summers ago, it must have been for a different reason. To meet somebody, maybe."

Yes! And that was why I'd come here, risking sheer mortification and that pit-of-my-stomach unease, just to ask Donovan that question. I figured he'd know about stuff like this. And I could work with his conclusion. I could *do* something now... I only wished we'd had this clue two years ago.

But in my excitement, I made a stupid tactical mistake. "I can't wait to talk to that person," I murmured, realizing my error the instant the words were in midair. I tried to cover it up by smiling and shuffling my feet. Unfortunately, Donovan wasn't fooled.

His dark eyebrows rose slowly. "You're *going* there? When?"

I took a step back, regretting having requested the closed office door. We did not, perhaps, need *this* much privacy after all.

"Um," I said, shrugging and reaching for the journal. "It's not really set..."

Okay, this was a blatant lie. I had my excursion all planned, right down to my alibi for the weekend. No one would mind or even really notice. Not unless, like my brother, I happened to go missing the summer after *my* high-school graduation, too.

This worrisome thought distracted me. It was only for a second, but that was long enough for Donovan to snatch the journal from my grasp and say again, "Aurora, *when* are you going?"

Much as I preferred to keep him and everyone else out of it, maybe it would be wise to tell at least one person my real whereabouts. Just in case.

I sighed. "Tomorrow at noon. After I'm done with my shift at work."

"At the Grocery Mart?"

I nodded, not surprised he remembered that was where I had my part-time job. I'd felt his eyes track me when we were out in public. I knew he'd been aware of me all this time, just as I'd been aware of him. Unfortunately, the foolish crush I had on him only went one way. "I won't be gone long. Two days, at most."

In my mind, I'd already begun formulating the questions I wanted to ask in Crescent Cove. Seemingly innocent things that might draw out the responses I needed. I was sure if I asked just the right question to just the right person, the truth would be spontaneously revealed to me—by their hands, their eyes, their vocal tone, their posture. I didn't need their words. Soon, I'd know what happened to my brother and his best friend, and then this deadening sense of helplessness would have to stop.

Donovan was shaking his head again. With his Army buzz-cut long gone, his dark hair grazed the back of his black crewneck t-shirt—a faded tribute to The Who.

Appropriate band for him. *Who are you...Donovan McCafferty? Who? Who?*

He flipped through a few more journal pages and glanced at the wall calendar, stroking one of his sideburns in thought. *"June's Muscle Car Babe!"* the calendar proclaimed, showing a tanned blonde, her hair feathered à la Farrah Fawcett-Majors, clad in a skimpy cherry-red bikini and leaning like a slutty go-go dancer across the hood of an equally cherry-red Ford Mustang. I gagged a little.

"Do you know Johansen's Diner in Alexandria?" he said suddenly.

"Sure," I replied. Everyone knew it. The owners served some of the better Norwegian specialties in the area.

"Good. There aren't many spaces out in front, but they have that free public parking garage across the street. Park on the second level. I'll meet you there at one p.m. tomorrow, and we'll drive to Crescent Cove together. "

"What? No," I said, my irritation rising. "I'm not going there with *you*. I'm not going with *anyone*."

He stared at me for a very long moment. Opened the office door and motioned me out. He followed, locked up behind us and led me to the parking lot while clicking closed the third and last garage door. Then he pulled out his car keys and strode over to his Trans Am, turning to me a second before hopping in. "You sure as hell are, Aurora."

Too late, I realized he was still holding the journal. I broke into a run after him. "Donovan! Give me the—"

But he'd already started the engine and was partway to the street. He rolled his window down and added, "I need to read it tonight. You'll get it back tomorrow in Alexandria. Be there at one."

Then he sped away.

Chapter Two

Friday, June 9

"It's a birthday party for Betsy's cousin, Ruth Ann," I lied, pretty damn believably, I thought, to my mom. "She's in St. Cloud for the weekend."

"How old is she? And where did you say she was from, dear?" Mom asked, even though I'd told her these details twice before.

"Nineteen," I said. "And she goes to school in Valparaiso, Indiana now."

This part was true. Betsy, my best friend from high school, did, in fact, have an older cousin who was road-tripping back home from Indiana and visiting her family in the area, and Betsy had invited me to the girls-only birthday bash.

Betsy was leaving that night and staying in St. Cloud for the weekend at her aunt's house. Her aunt—Ruth Ann's mother—was totally on the hippyish side. Tie-dyed shirts, bandanas, crystal necklaces and slim marijuana cigarettes rolled up in her pockets. The whole look. So things were going to get wild. Too wild for my absence to be noticed by anyone except, maybe, by Betsy, and she'd cover for me if I asked.

"That's nice that you girls are going to do something together," Mom said absently, accepting, as I'd expected, the explanation without question. There was a haunting hollowness in my mother's eyes, even as she tried to smile. Gideon and Jeremy used to get together for parties all the time, many held out of town. Just hearing about this type of event had to be dredging up Mom's memories of them.

Of course, it was hard to escape the claustrophobia of remembrance anywhere in my parents' house, or even in central Minnesota. Gideon had a way of forever altering whatever environment he came into contact with—tinting it, like a droplet of dark-blue food coloring in a shallow pan of water.

I put my arms around Mom's shoulders, feeling the indentations with my fingertips where there had once been flesh but now was nothing but bone and more hollowness.

"I'm going to work," I told her, "and I'll leave for St. Cloud from there. But I'll call you tonight, okay?"

She nodded. I was just about to make my escape when she added, "You'll be back on Sunday, right? Before dinnertime?" Oppressive worry, always on the fringes of her voice.

"Yes," I said, projecting confidence, reassurance, permanence. "Don't worry, Mom. I'll be back." *And, hopefully, with some helpful news. Unless what derailed Gideon is as successful in derailing me.*

Mom lifted her hand in a slight wave and let me go. I strode away from the house as if it were just another normal morning, threw my overnight bag in the trunk of my car and cursed Donovan a time or two under my breath. Then I drove to my job and clocked in for my obligatory four hours at Dale's Grocery Mart.

To put it plainly, working there sucked. But I knew when I first started the job last summer that it wasn't a place anyone with half a brain looked to for career advancement.

My boss—Dale Geiger—was a paunchy, combed-over, fifty-something northern redneck and penny pincher, who tended to nod at me dismissively when I walked through the door, as if I were leaving not just arriving. We tolerated each other from eight a.m. to noon every weekday during vacations (I'd worked the deadly dull afternoon shift during the school year) because he needed someone who could stock shelves correctly and who could quickly calm complaining customers. I was more than competent at both, and he owed me a few favors as a result.

For me, I needed a place to go that was out of the house, plus a paycheck of some sort so I could put gas in my car and save money for "my future." Whatever that might be.

I spent the morning trapped between my coworker Sandy, who

was bitching about her boyfriend Kevin on one side of me, and an endless supply of canned tuna on the other side.

"He promised he'd take me to the movies last night. We were going to drive to the theater in St. Cloud because they're showing 'Corvette Summer' over there, and I've been waiting to see it all week, you know? Mark Hamill just makes my heart flutter," Sandy said, pausing and putting her hand on her chest.

She'd seen "Star Wars" over thirty times since it came out last year and had loved Luke Skywalker so much that she was now a card-carrying Mark Hamill Fan Club member.

"But we were too late leaving town because he was shooting pool with his stupid friend Jake, so we missed the show."

Box one: Chicken of the Sea brand tuna.

I wrinkled my nose and started unpacking it. "Sorry to hear that. You must've been disappointed," I said to her.

"I am. I hate Jake. He's so lazy. So...laidback. And slow! It takes him a half hour to cross the room. He walks like this." Sandy imitated Jake with such precision and with that distinctive heightened color in her cheeks that I knew Sandy liked him. A lot. (Though maybe not as much as Mark Hamill.) But she just didn't want to admit this to herself. Poor boyfriend Kevin.

Box two: Bumble Bee brand tuna.

"Oh, and don't get me started on his bad jokes. I could shoot Jake and Kevin both." She waved her pricing gun in the air. "Especially when they get going on their *blond* humor. They think they're so funny."

Sandy was blond.

"Sorry to hear about that, too," I said.

Box three: StarKist brand tuna.

Sandy shrugged. "What'cha gonna do? A guy's a guy." She stuck her tongue out at the four still-unopened boxes of tuna in front of us and lowered her voice so Dale wouldn't hear. "And a job's a job."

"Yeah," I murmured back. It would have been so much easier if I'd been able to follow my original career plan, which had been to graduate from high school and immediately go off to college at U of M, in the Twin Cities, a good ninety miles away. To study *what*, I didn't know, but at least I'd have been out of this myopic little town.

A whisper of long-buried discontent resurfaced and swirled up around me as Sandy and I unpackaged, priced and shelved those final boxes. This was a sensation I hadn't felt in nearly two years. Like an appendage that had fallen asleep, I had to shake off the prickles of pain that accompanied it. While I'd believed Gideon to be dead, I hadn't allowed myself to resent him or my humdrum life here, but now... now...

The hours didn't exactly fly by, but at least they were predictable. When it came time for me to leave, I didn't look back for a second. I hung my ugly puce-colored Grocery Mart apron on its hook in the back room, grabbed my car keys and headed out of town—toward Alexandria, not St. Cloud.

As I drove down the main—and only—drag, I found myself looking at Chameleon Lake like the out-of-towners visiting over Memorial Day must've seen it. Like the way *I* always saw it after a weekend away somewhere.

Homespun and mostly harmless.

With a corner grocery store stocked with beer (and a God-awful *lot* of tuna) and a tiny post office where my dad and everyone in it knew your name after you'd been in there once.

A local garage/gas station where the workers fixed up cars, flatbed trucks or tractors and gave the ladies full-service fill-ups, all while listening to hard rock on the FM radio.

A town where Viking football was big, NHL hockey was even bigger and bowling in the alley on the outskirts of town was considered a recognized pastime.

Where guys would take off school or work to go deer hunting in the fall and everyone had ice skated in winter on the lake, grabbed a Super-Tastee burger in summer and dreamed of spending spring break somewhere—anywhere—warm.

Where most of the residents had gone to see the one and only featured movie showing in the Main Street Cinema, which was wedged between an eggs-and-sausage diner and a local bar known for its "Half-Price Tuesday" beer specials.

Welcome to Hometown, Midwestern America.

Had Gideon cataloged all of these things as he drove away two years ago? Since his car was missing, the police had a theory that it might have been stolen—maybe even with him in it—but no vehicle was ever found. They even dragged the lake for his 1974 Galaxie. Nothing. It still hurt like hell to think about it.

Maybe he was unconscious or blindfolded. Unable to notice the buildings as he left. But he must have been fully aware when he returned to hide the journal. What was he thinking when he saw our little town again? Did he feel stabs of sentimentality, missing it? Or, much as it squeezed by heart to even consider it, was he glad on some level to have escaped?

I couldn't shake the feeling that I was saying goodbye to Chameleon Lake, too. At least for now. I had an undeniable hunch—and I'd learned to trust my instincts—that the discoveries of the coming weekend might just change everything.

TWENTY-FIVE MILES of Minnesota farmland later, I drove into the covered garage in Alexandria, parked on the second level and scanned for Donovan's Trans Am. I didn't see it, which meant I'd gotten there first. Good. That was my plan, and I'd been kind of speeding to make sure of it.

I checked my watch—12:36—rolled down the window and slouched in the driver's seat, waiting. My mind slid between memories like water around rocks in a ravine.

Gideon and Jeremy in the driveway.

Laughing.

Drinking bottles of Old Style beer.

Working on their cars.

Talking about girls they'd liked…or dated…or gotten frisky with at a party somewhere.

I used to eavesdrop on them all the time. Despite their incredible mechanical skills and strong general intelligence, neither one had immediate plans for college. Once, when I'd asked them why not, they'd shrugged and mumbled something about "not wanting to sell out." Then they snickered at my innocent questions and my girly-ness, certain there was no way I'd ever understand how their boy brains operated.

They were right. No matter how naturally perceptive I was, I never could crack the code on how or why they'd disappeared. I knew there *had* to be a good reason and, for months, I just couldn't bring myself to believe they'd really died.

Everyone around me slowly but surely lost hope in their return or recovery and, eventually, I got tired of trying to defend my intuition. But I wouldn't be able to forgive myself for whatever puzzle pieces I'd overlooked until the day I finally figured out what *really* happened.

I squeezed my eyes closed to force back the tears that had risen up behind them. God knew, I'd already cried enough to fill up all of the Mississippi River and one or two of the Great Lakes...but a knock on the hood of my car had me jumping half out of my seat.

"You awake?" Donovan asked, peering at me through my open window, his dark eyes taking in more than I wanted him to see.

"Of course," I said, irritated and not trying to hide it. I could've been an hour down the road to Wisconsin if it weren't for him. I reached over to unlock the passenger's side door. "Well, hop in," I told him. "I want to get going."

He laughed. "We're not taking *your* car." He studied the body of my Buick and smirked.

His Trans Am was parked a few spaces away and, with the parking garage's neon overhead fixtures slanting a shaft of light upon it, his choice of vehicle couldn't have looked more like an obscenely red beacon of obviousness.

"Everyone will notice your car, Donovan. Everyone who sees it will remember it. I'd like to be not quite *so* conspicuous when we're asking people questions." I crossed my arms. I didn't know what skills he'd learned during his Army training but, clearly, basic covert operations didn't top the list.

One glance at his expression, though, told me I'd be an idiot to say this aloud.

"Being *inconspicuous* is really big with you," he said. "Why is that?"

Oh, I could think of a thousand reasons—the better to observe people, for one—but he didn't give me a chance to say anything. He just tapped on the hood of my car again and said, "C'mon." Then he waved Gideon's journal at me, tauntingly, and he took several steps back from my Buick. None of those steps happened to be in the direction of his Trans Am.

I sighed, loudly enough to make sure he heard, then I got out. "Where do you think you're going?"

"To the diner. We need to talk."

"Wha—*talk?* Jesus, Donovan! We can *talk* in the car. We've got almost four hours of driving ahead. Don't you just want to get—"

"I'm hungry," he said. "I want lunch."

With a couple of flicks of his first two fingers, he motioned for me to follow him, turning his back on me with the certainty that I would.

And, damn him, I did. I couldn't help how drawn I was to him. Like an unwilling magnet, I seemed to have no choice in the matter.

He strode ahead of me, his dark hair and dark shirt both catching the wind and dancing with it, until we were right in front of Johansen's. Then he paused and held the door open for me when I got there. Such a show of being a gentleman.

As I breezed past him, he said, "Ask for a booth in the back."

I shot him the evil eye and was about to tell him to ask for it himself, but the greeter guy was already there, looking expectantly at me.

When we were seated with menus in our hands, the waitress, who looked older than me by a few years, placed a bread basket in front of us and glanced at Donovan, then at me, then back at Donovan. She licked her lips and smoothed down one side of her strawberry-blond hair.

I tried to keep from openly scowling and just ordered a cup of their fish chowder and a Coke. I'd had this here once before, thought it tasted okay and knew it wouldn't be too expensive. Donovan had snitched the journal and insisted we meet at this place, he could sure as hell buy me lunch for $1.09.

Donovan raised an amused eyebrow at my modest choices and ordered a Coke as well, plus a sausage rolled in thin lefse with potato dumplings and homemade gravy…and a cup of Sandvik's stew…and a side of Norwegian meatballs…*and* a piece of lingonberry cake.

I stared at him.

When the waitress left, I hissed, "There are restaurants and grocery stores in Wisconsin, you know. You won't starve there."

He grabbed a sesame roll from the basket, took a big bite and pointedly ignored me.

"Fine." I fiddled with the glass sugar dispenser at the edge of the table. "But you said you wanted to talk, so let's talk."

He held up his finger, waiting until the waitress brought out our food, and he insisted on paying up immediately. He slipped her a handful of dollar bills while scanning her nametag. "Thanks, Debbie," he said with a wink. "Keep the change."

She smiled prettily at him, scribbled a receipt and handed that to him in exchange. "Just let me know if you need *anything* else."

He nodded, glanced at the receipt as she sauntered away and grinned.

I recognized that expression from somewhere. It took me several seconds to place it, but I finally remembered when I'd seen it last and who was wearing it. His brother Jeremy. Looking as proud as a Stanley Cup winner as he told Gideon about some cheerleader he'd felt up under the ice rink bleachers after a hockey game a few months before they graduated.

"She gave you her number?" I blurted to Donovan. "Already?"

He studied me with one of his assessing looks, which never failed to make me feel like I was twelve again and he was the big high-school senior—nearly a man—that I'd first met those long years ago. Too much of a child for him to trifle with…almost.

"Debbie's off at six," he informed me, pocketing the receipt. "But we'll be in Wisconsin by then, won't we?"

"Maybe," I said. "Or maybe I'll still just go by myself." I reached for the journal he held hostage on his side of the table.

He grabbed it and put it on the seat next to him. *Hmm. Fast reflexes.*

"Just give me a chance, Aurora," he whispered. "Okay?" The grin was gone and, in its place, a grimace laced with sorrow. If I read it right, a hint of fear mingled there, too.

"Okay," I whispered back.

He poked a little at his meatballs with a fork as I blew on my chowder. "I read the journal three times last night," he said in a low voice. "Cover to cover. There was nothing that jumped out at me until I got to the page you first told me about. The one with the two dates." He paused, stabbed at another meatball and, finally, ate one. "I'm sure you noticed the city names slipped in between the various chemical compounds."

I nodded.

"Except for Crescent Cove, all of them are south of us. And I didn't find any city in the journal further east than Chicago. So, your brother, and maybe mine, too, seemed to be keeping tabs on something in the Midwest and West. What it is—or was—I don't know."

In a rush, I was reminded of Donovan's stake in this. How close he and Jeremy had been. In his own way, delay tactics and all, I knew how much he cared about the outcome, and I could tell he'd spent some time trying to piece the unknowns of this puzzle together.

He might be skeptical of my conclusions and afraid of getting his hopes up, but I was certain he was just as haunted by our brothers' disappearance as I was. Maybe even more so, though I didn't understand why I was getting that impression so strongly. He had the look of someone about to set foot in a confessional.

"Any idea what they were trying to do with the chemicals?" I asked.

He scrunched up his forehead and downed a few scoops of mashed potatoes and a bite of lefse-wrapped sausage before answering. My chowder had cooled enough for me to have a few spoonfuls, but I couldn't have been less hungry for it.

"I have a partial theory," he said, "given the dates they went to Wisconsin. For one thing, I think they went there twice. It was the only city that seemed to be repeated, although it was abbreviated the second time. See?"

He opened the journal and flipped a few pages past the first mention of Crescent Cove—which had been on Monday, April 19, 1976—and pointed to an entry on Monday, May 10, 1976 that listed various chemicals and car parts but, also, in Gideon's tight scrawl, included the letters: "J & I —> C.C."

"So, in the spring of '76, they went there and then, three weeks later, they returned. Maybe they ordered something from somebody and then had to go back to pick it up?" I suggested.

"That's what I was thinking." He shook his head, as if trying to shake loose the direction of his thoughts. "Look, this is nuts. I don't know what to make of it. And I think it's way too farfetched to believe this journal means anything, but there's something else you need to know." He hesitated, slurped some Coke and shifted in his seat. "April nineteenth didn't ring a bell when I read it, but the May date did. Two years ago, May tenth was the day after Mother's Day."

"And that's memorable to you…why?"

"Because Jeremy wrote me a letter that day," he explained. "I got it later that week, but I remembered the date. I was stationed out at Fort Monroe in Hampton, Virginia then, but I'd sent Mom a card for Mother's Day, and Jeremy told me she'd gotten it in time. That she'd been really excited to hear from me." He stopped talking and massaged his temples.

"Oh, God, Donovan. Do you have the letter with you? What else did he say?"

I watched as he exhaled a long stream of air. "I wish I'd kept it, Aurora. I've wished that for two years," he admitted, bitterness in his voice. "It was the last letter I ever got from my brother—and I threw it out."

He closed his eyes and shoved back whatever emotion he didn't yet want to share with me. "But I remember it was just a short note. There was that little bit about Mom. Then he was bragging about some Wendy person he thought was real foxy. And, finally, there were a couple of lines about your brother."

Donovan opened his eyes and looked up at me. Held my gaze in his, and I caught my breath at the intensity of it.

"He said the two of them had something 'fun' planned for the summer. Something they were working on. At the time, I didn't think anything of it. I thought he'd meant their secret graduation party up in St. Cloud. Since I was taking three days' leave in June to come home for his ceremony, I figured Jeremy would fill me in then, but—" A troubled expression washed over his face, revealing the worry lines etched at the corners of his eyes and the tight brackets on each side of his mouth.

"But he didn't?"

"No," Donovan whispered. "I mentioned his 'fun thing' when Jeremy was driving me back to the airport. Told him the party had been great and congratulated him again. But he just laughed. He said what he'd been talking about had nothing to do with graduation at all. That he'd write and tell me about it 'next month.' In July."

The month our brothers disappeared.

I left the words unspoken because, of course, both of us knew the timeline.

"You didn't tell the cops about that when they were investigating?" I asked.

He shrugged. "I tried to, but it was a pretty weak statement. They didn't take it seriously, and I had no other info then. Nothing to tie it to the disappearance until you showed me the journal yesterday. When the cops called the base to ask me questions, they wanted to know about major things—unusual behaviors or anything strange or out of character that I'd picked up on when I last saw Jeremy or heard from him. But I honestly hadn't noticed a single thing at the time that was different. Maybe I wasn't looking closely enough. Or listening hard enough."

Or maybe the cops were the ones not looking and listening.

I still wanted to strangle the police for their lousy investigation. Difficult to imagine a more ineffective one. Even more difficult to imagine me working jointly with Donovan on anything. Our approaches couldn't have been less similar, our temperaments weren't exactly complementary and, God, just being around him made me jumpy.

But on this very first step…well, pairing up with him might not only be helpful, it might also be necessary.

"So, our brothers were involved with something that—at least initially—they both thought would be really fun," I said. "And what they were doing was premeditated. Weeks in the making. Lots of planning. Something that may have had its origins in Crescent Cove."

I flipped back to the first Crescent Cove mention on April 19, 1976 and Gideon's note in the upper right-hand corner of that page, dated Monday, May 29, 1978.

Start here. G.

"Sure as hell seems that way," Donovan muttered.

We both managed to finish about half of our meals, though mostly in silence after that. At one point he pushed the small plate with the lingonberry cake toward me and said, "I got this for you. Eat some of it."

And, because it was easier than talking, I took a few bites. It was sweet and moist, but it tasted like paste in my mouth.

As we walked back to the parking garage afterward (he slowed his pace enough for me to keep up this time), I studied the planes of his face, his shoulders and his chest. He looked every bit of his five years older than me. Every ounce of him was masculine, Army tough and uncompromising. I knew, even if I put up a fuss, I was going to lose the battle of who'd get to drive.

I also knew there was no point in worrying about being inconspicuous. Not only was it futile, it was irrelevant. No matter which car we took to Wisconsin, people were going to remember Donovan McCafferty. It was pure foolishness to think otherwise.

In the garage, he pointed at my old Buick. "You got a bag in there?" he asked.

I boosted my tan-and-white overnighter out of the trunk. He took it from me and tossed it effortlessly into the backseat of his Trans Am, next to his camouflage-colored Army duffle. Then he opened the passenger door for me, and I slid inside.

When we were safely out on the open road, the whispering wind whipping through the windows and ruffling our hair, Led Zeppelin blaring on the radio and the golden summer sun beating down on us—heating our skin and threatening a burn if we left our arms exposed for too long—I felt an object being pressed onto my lap.

Gideon's journal.

I ran my fingertips across the leather cover, tracing the butterfly, then I shuffled the pages in time with "Stairway to Heaven." Yeah. Sometimes words *did* have two meanings.

"You can have it back," Donovan said, the first specter of a smile crossing his lips in over an hour. "For now."

I laughed at that, almost under my breath, but not quite. He almost laughed back.

And, while the boys on the radio may have disagreed on this, I sensed that, no, there wasn't any time to change the road we were on. The piper had called us, and we'd chosen our path.

In that expectant space between silence and melody, our trip began.

Chapter Three

Crescent Cove, Wisconsin

AFTER WHAT might have been the longest three hours and forty-seven minutes of my entire life, the Trans Am crossed the state line into Wisconsin.

I eyed Donovan warily. He'd uttered aloud only a handful of syllables on the drive, letting the rock on the car radio speak for him.

But, while Wings, the Eagles and Crosby, Stills and Nash gave voice to his love of the fast lane and general discontent with society, the increasing tension in his body called out to me like a scream. I could feel the vibrations of his stress in the claw-like grip he had on the steering wheel, the pale cast to his knuckles, the way he punched the buttons to change stations when one radio signal grew too weak, the ropy tautness of his neck and the steely intensity riveting his eyes to the pavement.

Donovan flicked off the radio finally. "We're almost there," he informed me.

I opened my mouth to say, "Thank God, it's about time," but something in his tone and the set of his jaw stopped me. He was not only anxious, I realized, he was angry.

Very angry.

Even knowing this anger wasn't directed at me but at the Crescent Cove city limits sign ("Population 949") wasn't much consolation. It shimmered off of him like light on a lake, and I was sure those waters were deep with danger.

"What do you want to do first?" I asked him, trying to come across as reasonable, accommodating and not likely to piss him off. "Once we drive through town, that is."

He turned his dark brown eyes in my direction, taking them off the road only long enough to blink and say, "Let's see what we see there."

Yeah, that *sounded* simple enough, but it wasn't. Donovan was glaring at everything in Crescent Cove through his own increasingly frustrated lens. We wouldn't be able to figure out anything that way. I knew we were going to have to view the place through Gideon and Jeremy's open and optimistic perspective instead. But both of us were out of practice being upbeat, and trying to tell Donovan what to do would get me exactly nowhere. I'd asked him once on the road if we should, maybe, stop for gas and the look he gave me would've made the Incredible Hulk cower in fright.

"Let's just consider how our brothers might have seen everything here," I suggested carefully, glancing at the one-street, two-stop-sign town, which was significantly smaller than even Chameleon Lake.

Donovan narrowed his eyes and pulled into a farmhouse driveway on the edge of the town so he could turn his Trans Am around and go down the main drag once again. This time more slowly.

"This place is a bunch of rubble in the road," he pronounced after taking an especially long look at the vendor lineup on the left side of the street: Bar with burnt-out neon lights, brownish brick corner store, paint-chipped post office, ramshackle bar, hardware store with taped-up window, shuttered empty store front, yet another bar... "What the hell were they doing in this dump?" he muttered.

I had to admit, I was almost as mystified.

Had our brothers liked hanging out at one of the bars? It seemed too long of a drive from Chameleon Lake just to come up for a beer, though the drinking age in Wisconsin was only eighteen while, in Minnesota, it was nineteen. That was reason enough for a lot of my old high-school friends to cross the state line.

But my parents had never been strict about stuff like that. Once Gideon and Jeremy got to high school, Mom and Dad let them drink a bottle or two of beer at the house without batting an eyelash. Dad even fixed us all—me included—whiskey sours one New Year's Eve. I remembered how quickly I got a buzz from it.

I also remembered how funny Jeremy had been that night, laughing with us as Gideon pulled Mom into a crazy waltz in the middle of the living room. "Dance With Me" by Orleans had been playing on the radio. Jeremy turned the volume up even higher and suddenly said, "Well, c'mon, Aurora. We can't let 'em show us up, can we?" So, I took his hand and he spun me around and around, until we both finally collapsed on the shag carpet from too much giggling and dizziness and, maybe, the whiskey.

Had Gideon and Jeremy danced with anyone here in Crescent Cove? Could it have been that one of them had a crush on a chick he'd met at a bar up here? Maybe. With so little information, it was hard to rule out anything...

But, while they'd both dated casually quite a bit, I didn't think either guy had been serious about a girlfriend two years ago. At their graduation party, they'd each been flirting outrageously with the girls in the hotel room, and I would've bet money they both got laid that night. But there were no longstanding relationships afterward. Not that I knew of, that was for sure.

"Could there be some other section of the town?" I asked Donovan. "There has to be a church here somewhere. A school. A library, maybe."

He looked at me like I was schizo. "Aurora, they don't even have a *gas station* in this stinkin' hell pit. You really think they'd have a *library?*"

He shook his head and went back to glaring at the handful of rundown buildings again, this time the ones on the right side of the street. A couple of local boys, who'd seen us zip down and back, eyed Donovan's car curiously, no doubt recognizing a pair of out-of-towners when they saw some.

Donovan abruptly turned the car down a narrow country lane. "You wanna look for a church? A school? A library?" he asked me. "Let's just go for a little spin around these parts and take in the diversity."

Hard to miss the sarcasm in his voice.

We cut a wide square driving through the surrounding farmland but, as Donovan had predicted, there were no signs of any large public buildings anywhere in the vicinity. We did, however, see a smallish lake.

"Behold, the Cove," Donovan said in full mocking mode.

There was also an entrance to one of the Saint Croix Chippewa Reservation Communities (know-it-all Donovan informed me that there were several tribal lands in the area) and a dark-green sign pointing in the direction of Ashburn Falls, a town thirteen miles away.

Donovan pulled off the pavement and onto the gravel, grabbing his road atlas from under the seat and locating the place.

"That might be our best bet for a motel," he told me. "Ashburn Falls has got a population of almost six thousand, so that's probably where the nearest school and church are. And your library," he added drily.

I had to agree on the prospects of the new town, although I forced all thoughts of a motel stay with Donovan out of my mind for now—I just couldn't let myself imagine *that!* Besides, our work in Crescent Cove wasn't done yet. Not by a long shot.

"Gideon and Jeremy never mentioned Ashburn Falls in the journal," I told him. "Gideon specifically wrote about Crescent Cove, though. So, there's something right here that is…or was…important to them." Not that I had any idea what that might be. "We need to park the car and go down that main street again—this time on foot. I think we should walk into some of these bars and little shops. Get a feel for them."

He nodded. "I know," he said, like he'd been fighting against it. Like doing this was going to cost him something.

He parallel-parked in front of the tiny post office and the two of us began strolling down the sidewalk, peeking into the various storefronts as if we were window shopping.

Since it was nearly six p.m., many of the places were already closed, including the corner grocery, which had a poster of Wonder Bread in the window and an orange sign next to it that read: "Sale on Peanut Butter!"

Bar #1 (with the burnt-out neon lights) was doing brisk business, though.

"You got an ID?" Donovan asked.

I grimaced, knowing what was coming. "I've got my driver's license with me, yeah. But it says my real birth date."

"What? No fake ID?" he asked, surprised.

I shook my head. Yeah, yeah, I knew it was odd. *Everyone* had a fake ID but me. I didn't go out much.

"How long 'til you're legal?"

"In this state? Three weeks," I admitted. I'd be eighteen on July first.

He shot me a glance that said he didn't believe I was that close to adulthood, dug into his jeans pocket and pulled out a rubber band. "Here." He held it out to me. "Put your hair up with this. Might make you look a little older."

I finger-combed my straight hair upward, fashioning a loose bun, and secured it with the band. I thought I did a pretty good job considering I only had a shop window as a mirror. "Better?"

He studied me for a long moment, looking more displeased than approving. But then he shrugged and said, "Close enough." And he pushed open the door to Bar #1.

The pungent aroma of cigarette smoke floated up at us, immediately making my nose twitch, as Donovan led me toward a table halfway to the bar. There were a handful of unoccupied tables nearby, but this one had the advantage of being mostly clean.

I swiped a few potato-chip crumbs off my chair before sitting down and scanned my surroundings. Dark wood paneling. Smudged windows. Low overhead lighting but a fair bit of neon. The pervasive scent of beer. And Boston's "More Than a Feeling" playing a little louder than it needed to be.

About a dozen people were already working toward various states of drunkenness, including a group of laughing thirty-something women, a few old men, a trio of guys playing pool in the back and a middle-aged couple sitting at the bar, drinking side-by-side but in silence.

I was about to ask Donovan if he'd seen a bartender or a waitress anywhere—because I sure hadn't spotted one—when I got to witness a remarkable transformation in his expression.

Turned out, a waitress was headed straight for our table. Tall and willowy with long, sleek, black hair, the girl reminded me of a twenty-two-year-old Cher. But what was far more interesting was Donovan's face, which seemed to lose its angry intensity and adopt the look of a reckless charmer. More astonishing still was the way he turned a magnetic smile on the waitress before she even reached our table. It was as if he'd been waiting all his life for someone like her.

"Hey, there, folks," the Cher-lookalike said brightly. "I'm Kim. What can I get 'cha to drink?"

"You got Budweiser on tap?" he asked.

"Sure do."

"We'll take two of those and—" He paused, glancing at the laminated card on the table with the bar's limited food options. "You hungry for a sandwich, uh…Sis?" he asked me.

My mouth dropped open.

Sis?!

But he was nodding at me and encouraging me to nod right back. So I did—mutely—as Donovan kept smiling that weirdly sensual grin at the waitress, managing to give off the vibe that, while he might be visiting town with *his sister,* he was still very much open to a little frolicking adventure with one of the locals.

"We got tuna, ham-n-Swiss, roast beef or egg salad. All sandwiches are served with potato chips and a pickle. Coleslaw is an extra twenty cents," the waitress said, smiling back at Donovan. "Where are ya two from?"

"St. Paul," he answered quickly. "You always lived here in Crescent Cove…Kim?"

She shook her dark head. "Oh, no. I grew up in Ripon, but I've been up here for three years now. I moved on account of my boyfriend, but then—" She lifted her slim shoulders in a shrug. "Well, Hal was a trucker. He left town."

"Sorry to hear that. Nice place, though," he said conversationally. "Real quiet."

She laughed. "Too quiet. Nothin' much happens."

He leaned closer, the pull of his charismatic sensuality—a trait he could turn on and off like a light switch—drawing the waitress nearer as well. "Really?" he whispered to her. "Nothing exciting? No infidelities, murders or mysterious disappearances?"

She laughed again but then lowered her voice to match his. "Just the old explosion near the Indian Rez a couple of years ago. Blew up Sammy Bonner's scrap-metal mill. And the usual gossip about the fire chief's wife and that American history teacher in Ashburn Falls."

Kim raised her eyebrows in the direction of the couple sitting at the bar and murmured, "Rob over there is the fire chief's brother and Stella used to be best friends with the wife. They're not speakin' to that side of the family anymore."

I gave a cursory glance to the pair at the bar but refused to stare at them the way the waitress did. I remembered all too well the gossip that swirled around me and my parents in the months that followed Gideon's disappearance. Gossip that *still* swirled, sometimes. I wasn't going to inflict the same punishment on someone else. And Donovan, I noticed, didn't look at them for long either.

"And, well, Officer Mendelsson's daughter, Ronelle, ran away with some big-city business guy. He looked like Burt Reynolds and drove a new Camaro. Nothin' mysterious about that disappearance," she said, sounding wistful. And in that second I knew this was *exactly* what Kim was hoping would happen to her someday. Knew she was looking Donovan over as if he might just be her Burt Reynolds.

I found my voice. "Do you get a lot of out-of-towners visiting? Guys driving through, picking up local girls?" I asked sweetly.

Donovan narrowed his eyes at me.

Kim seemed surprised to hear me talk. Probably had forgotten I was there, what with all that ogling of Donovan and all his flirting back. It seemed I couldn't take him anywhere without him making passes at the wait staff.

"Not all that often," she said, leaning away from the table and scribbling something on her order pad. "Did you say you wanted sandwiches?"

"Oh, yeah," Donovan said. "Ham-n-Swiss for me, with the coleslaw." He poked at my forearm, and none too gently. "You, too?"

"That's fine. Anything but tuna," I said, sitting back and crossing my arms. As if I gave a fig about the food.

The waitress made a few more notes on her order pad. "Be back with your beers in a sec. Sandwiches'll take about ten minutes, okay?"

"Thanks, Kim," Donovan said affably.

She smiled again at him, ducked her head almost shyly and headed for the counter.

When Kim's back was finally turned, I smacked his arm with the back of my hand. "What. Are. You. Doing?" I murmured.

Donovan's smile didn't dim one iota. He radiated confidence, warmth and raw sexuality. But, deep in his eyes, I saw something hard and angry still lingering there. "Just. Play. Along," he murmured back. "I'm gathering information. Don't throw any roadblocks up."

Kim returned with our beers and, a few minutes later, with our sandwiches and sides. "Here you go," she said. "And, um, here are some napkins, if you want. Anything else I can get you two?"

I smiled tightly at her but said nothing.

Donovan took a long, slow sip of his beer and licked his lips. "No, this is great. Just what we needed." His eyes twinkled when he glanced up at the waitress. No sign of hardness in them.

I was just beginning to understand what a skilled actor he could be and why, perhaps, I couldn't read his reactions half as easily as I did with most people.

"Hey," he said, "this may be a while ago, probably two years or so, but you seem to have a great…um, memory." The way he gave Kim the compliment made it sound like he was telling her she had great tits.

The waitress blushed. "Oh, thanks."

He lifted the pickle wedge from his plate and bit off the end like it was a cigar. "You ever see a couple of guys hanging around town who drove a two-tone, late-model Ford Galaxie? Had a white hardtop, a real nice royal blue body and Minnesota plates. They'd be about your age, I'd say."

Kim squinted off into the distance. "I remember seeing a car or two like that, sure, but it could've been anybody's. Those guys friends of yours?"

"Friends of friends," Donovan said easily. "We haven't run into them in long time, but I know they liked Crescent Cove and I thought, maybe, they lived in the area now. They said it had a lotta good things for a town its size." His sexy grin implied Kim might have been one of those good things.

I studied the waitress's body language and knew if Kim had even the slightest recollection of Gideon and Jeremy she would have said so, if only to please an attractive out-of-towner. But she didn't.

"Do you maybe have a picture or anything?" the woman asked.

He stroked one dark sideburn then tapped his lips with his index finger. He kept drawing attention to his mouth, something that could hardly have escaped our waitress's notice. "You know, I don't think—"

"I do," I interrupted.

I opened my purse and began rummaging through it. "Yes. Here's one of the guys." I pointed to a photo I'd taken of Gideon, posing with about six other boys on their graduation day. Jeremy was standing next to my brother in the picture. "And the other guy is to his left."

"Do they look familiar to you now?" Donovan asked her.

"Kinda," Kim said, nodding.

I did everything I could not to roll my eyes. No way had she ever seen either guy before in her life.

I motioned with a quick head tilt toward the bartender, hoping Donovan would get the message. I was pleased when he asked Kim, "Think anybody else might recognize them? The bartender, maybe?"

"Nah. He's from out East somewhere. Massachusetts, I think," Kim said. "He's only been in the area since March."

I thought about the music in the bar. The bartender wasn't playing a radio station but, instead, Boston's debut album—in its entirety. I'd listened to it all the way through at Betsy's house and liked it. A lot. But it'd been released just a few weeks after Gideon disappeared, and in a gut-punching way, it always reminded me of him. These were my brother's kind of songs. Roll-the-car-windows-down and turn-the-volume-up songs of the open road. Strains of "Hitch a Ride," faded as another tune began.

Kim wandered off again and, since Donovan had turned suddenly silent while devouring his ham-n-Swiss sandwich, I nibbled at my coleslaw and watched Kim make the rounds.

The waitress was over by the pool players within moments, flirting with one of them and letting a tall, scraggly-looking man put his arm around her and run his chalky fingers down the length of her side, from shoulder to hip. Was she hoping this spectacle would make Donovan jealous? If so, it was wasted effort. Looked like Donovan only had eyes for his sandwich.

More people had filtered into the bar, but I kept a watch on our waitress, unable to stop observing her desperate attempts at connecting with some guy. She was as easy to read as a kindergartener. I could tell Kim was the type to have barely squeaked through high school. She reminded me a lot of Sandy from work. Nice enough, but not exactly the sharpest tool in the box.

I sensed Kim's decision to relocate to the wilds of western Wisconsin for a trucker named Hal had been an impulsive one. That every night at the bar was another opportunity to meet a new man and, hopefully, make her escape again. But with a happier ending this time.

I also more than suspected that Kim both pitied and envied me. Pitied me because, in her eyes, I was every bit the uninteresting kid sister that Donovan had painted me to be. And, yet, she envied me, too, because, however platonic the relationship, I'd be the one leaving with him. Or, maybe, it was as simple as the fact that I'd be *leaving*—period.

With "Let Me Take You Home Tonight" playing loud and ironically, a second waitress came into the bar, stopped to chat with Kim and the bartender and, then, grabbed her order pad and got to work. It wasn't long before Kim dragged the new waitress over to our table, glad to have another excuse to chitchat with Donovan.

"Hey, this is Cindy," Kim said of her friend, who looked like a slightly older version of Kim, but with lighter hair and less of an air of hopefulness. "She's worked here for longer than me and also at Jacky's, the bar halfway down the block. Maybe she knows those guys you were looking for."

Donovan cranked up the charm level with his grin again, and even the older waitress wasn't immune to it.

"These guys in any kind of trouble?" Cindy asked when I handed her the photo, showing she was brighter than her fellow waitress.

Donovan shook his head. "Not that I know of," he lied convincingly. "Haven't seen them since a party we were all at a couple of years ago, and I thought they might be traveling together. Maybe through the area."

Cindy looked relieved. She also looked at the picture with far more genuine recognition than Kim had, I realized, but she was holding her tongue.

I tried to help her along. "They were so funny," I gushed, faking the kind of girlish laugh that my best friend Betsy did so well. "It'd be really cool to catch up with them again."

Donovan bobbed his head heartily.

"I'm pretty sure they were in town before," Cindy admitted. "I remember this one in the middle real well." She pointed to Gideon. "Speedy white and blue car, right? Taped up back window?"

I saw Donovan's Adam's apple slide up and down a few times before he could compose himself enough to answer. "That's right."

He sent me a careful, knowing look. Kim might have told Cindy about the colors of Gideon's car, but no one had said *anything* about the broken window. It had been a detail even I hadn't thought to mention until that moment.

"Yeah. Those two stood out. Had to be about two years back, though," Cindy said. "Pretty sure they were here a couple of times with Ben Rainwater, God rest his soul."

Donovan shot her a very sharp look. "Who is...or *was* Ben Rainwater?"

Cindy sighed. "He was from the Rez. A nice guy, I always thought. Sad story, though. He died in an accident. We still miss him 'round here."

"What *kind* of an accident?" Donovan asked.

"The Bonner Mill explosion," Cindy said.

"You brought that up earlier, didn't you?" Donovan said, directing his question at Kim. "When, uh...when did that happen?"

Kim looked pleased to be asked. "Two summers ago."

"Fourth of July weekend," Cindy added. "The night before the Bicentennial."

Donovan caught my eye, but I wasn't able to breathe—let alone speak—after hearing this news. This was the same time frame, the same time frame *exactly*, that Gideon and Jeremy had disappeared. What were our brothers doing in this town? What were they doing with a man who died the *same* weekend they disappeared? Was it just some strange coincidence? Had they gotten caught in the same explosion as Ben Rainwater?

Or—an almost inconceivable thought—were they the ones who'd *caused* it?

I finally recovered my voice, though it was shaky and soft. "That's... so sad. Does Ben have any relatives nearby?"

Cindy and Kim exchanged a look. "Just his cousin Ronny," Kim said. "His mom and sister moved away."

"Ronny?" Donovan parroted.

"Ronny Lee Wolf," Cindy said. "He owns the corner grocery store. Works there ten a.m. to five p.m. every day. Even weekends."

I knew, whether Donovan liked it or not, that we'd need to have a little conversation with Ronny tomorrow.

"Hey, Kim! Where's my beer?" one of the pool-playing guys bellowed across the room.

"I'm comin', Jesse!" the younger waitress bellowed back. She raced toward the bar to grab what he needed.

Cindy, older than her coworker by eight, maybe ten, years, glanced at the pool players for a moment, thoughtfully, then said, "I gotta get back to work. Y'all let me know if you have any other questions. I hope you find your friends."

"Thanks," Donovan murmured. "Appreciate your help." As soon as she was gone, though, he pushed himself to standing and said, "Let's get out of here."

I caught one last look at Cindy taking orders on the other side of the room while Donovan shoved some cash at the bartender to cover our bill and a tip for Kim. Despite our age difference of a decade, Cindy reminded me more of myself than Kim did. And I wondered if that sense of hopelessness I read in her gestures would be my fate someday, too—especially if I kept working at Dale's Grocery Mart, kept living with my parents in Chameleon Lake, kept postponing my dreams indefinitely.

I recognized something particular in Cindy's gaze. Sensed she knew Kim had limited time to make her escape. Knew her own days of doing so were probably closing in behind her. And I felt a warning in Cindy's wistful expression that led me to thoughts of college again.

It wouldn't be easy for either me or my parents if I finally applied to a college and moved away, but I wasn't helping them by remaining frozen in time in Minnesota. Leaving would be better than numbness, better than becoming yet another disillusioned girl who wrote eloquently about topics like women's lib and equal rights in my high-school history papers but hoped some white knight would ride into town in his King Cobra and rescue me.

And, God, if Gideon and Jeremy *were* still alive, not only might I get to see them and make our families whole again, but I could be free. Really and truly free.

When we walked out into the night, it had turned darkish, past twilight, and I remembered with a sudden panic that I hadn't yet called home.

"I need to find a payphone," I told Donovan.

"Why?" He looked frustrated by what we'd just learned, and I could see the anger inside him simmering again, burning hot enough to leave beads of sweat on his skin.

"I promised my mother I'd call her tonight."

He stared at me. "Why?" he repeated. "What are you gonna tell her?"

"Just that I'm fine and that the party's going well." My mom might barely notice my movements back at home, but her parental worry kicked into high gear when I was away.

"The party? Where does she think you are?" Donovan spit out.

"*Not* here," I spit back. "And *not* with you." He'd horned in on my weekend research expedition. I didn't owe him any damn explanations.

He blew the air slowly out of his mouth, as if trying to control the flow and sizzle of his temper. Recognizing, I suspected, on some more mature level that I wasn't the person he was actually mad at that night.

"The bartender back there, Mike, said there's a decent motel in Ashburn Falls. They'll have a phone."

I glanced at my watch. "I can't wait that long. She must be worried already."

"Fine." That he didn't argue with me about this was proof he'd witnessed his own mother's unbearable pain of loss. Knew it was an emotional hole that could never be filled, no matter how many reassurances followed.

Crescent Cove may have been a town without a gas station, but it did at least have a glass-sided phone booth, even if it was hidden in the shadows, around the corner in an alley, near the last bar on the street.

Donovan insisted on standing right next to me as I dropped my coins into the box. He scowled through the entire phone call as I fibbed to my mother about how much fun I was having at the birthday party for Betsy's cousin. After a minute, I actually had to turn my back on him so I wouldn't have to face his expression of disapproval.

"Well, what did you expect me to tell her?" I said to him, once I'd hung up. "The truth? Hmm? *You* try explaining that."

He gritted his teeth, but I knew he didn't have a good answer to these questions, which was why I didn't call him on it when he said instead, "Are we free to go now?"

"Yeah," I told him.

Technically, this was true. However, lost momentarily in the tension over my phone call home was the fact that we'd discovered some new information about events surrounding the time of our brothers' disappearance. Aside from Gideon's journal, this was the first real lead we'd had in *two years!* Just wondering what we'd learn at the little store the next day made my stomach churn with anxiety.

Then again, I had yet another reason to be nervous.

Although I'd managed to avoid thinking about spending the night with Donovan until we were on the road to Ashburn Falls, once we were actually in the Nite Lite Inn's parking lot, I couldn't ignore the reality of it.

Crap.

When he killed the engine on the Trans Am, he stared hard out the window before abruptly pulling his duffle bag up to the front seat. I watched as he began digging through it, eventually retrieving a thin gold ring that looked a lot like a wedding band.

"What's that for?" I blurted.

He thrust it at me. "Put this on your left hand, at least while we're checking in."

I thrust it right back at him, too shocked to even bother trying to disguise it. "Are you joking, Donovan? Back at the bar, you said I was your *sister*. Now you need for us to pretend to be *married*? That's ridiculous! It's not the 1800s. It's 1978. Couples check into motel rooms all the time now without even being engaged and, besides, no one knows us here."

Donovan glanced between my face and the flashing neon lights of the motel's "Welcome" sign and, for a moment, I was touched that this big Army guy was so interested in propriety and preserving my good reputation, even among strangers, that he'd come up with such an absurd idea. That he'd actually *planned* for it while packing...

But he didn't take back the ring, and he was not at all joking.

"Small-town business owners tend to be old-fashioned, Aurora," he said. "Anyone with decent eyesight can tell you're not my sister. We don't have any of the same features. Kim at the bar wanted to believe that, but no hotel manager will think so. There'll be fewer questions, and we'll be *less conspicuous* this way." A small smile replaced the words but there was no mistaking the seriousness of his command. Especially after he added, "Put it on and size it to fit."

In examining the ring more closely, I could see it wasn't real gold. It was kind of like a Cracker Jack prize and had a slice in it so it could be adjusted with an easy squeeze.

Sighing, I did as he requested, pressing the gold-colored band just hard enough to keep it firmly on my ring finger. Then I held up my left hand and waved it at him. "Happy now?"

He grunted something that sounded like "happiness is overrated," but I wasn't completely sure because he'd already jumped out of the car.

I trailed him into the motel's office unit and hung a step or two back as the lady owner greeted us coolly, shuffled some paperwork around and made Donovan fill out a few registration sheets.

"It'll be twelve dollars for a double bed," she informed us, eyeing my 'wedding' band with undisguised curiosity. "You two newlyweds?"

"Very much so," I told her, forcing a smile. *Like as of three minutes ago.*

"Congratulations," the woman said with almost no emotion. Definitely not a romantic. "From around here?"

I shook my head and Donovan said, "Nope." He pointed to something he'd written on the first sheet. "St. Paul," he told her, ignoring both my sharp glance and the ten-dollar bill and two ones that I tried to hand him. "I got this…honey," he said firmly as the older lady took a step back to snatch our room key.

"Number Nine." The woman sniffed as she dropped the key in Donovan's palm, and then she gestured toward a bright yellow sign hanging near the counter. "No smokin' in bed. No, uh, real loud noises—"

Donovan raised his eyebrows at her.

"Like TV, yellin' and…such," she clarified. But there was no denying the suggestiveness of her words.

I fought a blush and studied the dirty tile floor as Donovan handed over the cash.

"Checkout time's eleven a.m. tomorrow," the woman added. "You can park your car out in front of your unit, and there's a drop box for your key just by the office door, if you don't have to pay for any extras, like phone calls, in the morning."

He nodded once and swiveled toward the door. "Thanks," he said over his shoulder, as he strode outside. As usual, I followed him. Then he repositioned his Trans Am in front of "9" and grabbed our bags.

When we were safely in the privacy of our room, I whispered, "Why do you keep telling everyone we're from St. Paul?"

"Because people here wanna think we're big-city folks. They let their guard down with us more when we seem to be just what they expect. Human nature."

I shook my head. "It's human nature to be more comfortable around people who are *similar* to you. We should be pretending we're from a town as small as theirs. It's not like we have to try all that hard, Donovan. Chameleon Lake is miniscule."

He snickered. "You'd be right if the people here would believe that, but you're not as small-town as you think you are." He gave me look that bordered on condescending. "And I'm sure not."

He dumped our bags on a nubby orange armchair, flipped on the TV and adjusted the antennas. "The Rockford Files" was on. As we watched actor James Garner puzzle through a case, Donovan got more comfortable in the room, kicking off his sneakers, propping up a few pillows against the headboard, stretching out on the side of the double bed with his arms folded up and resting behind his neck.

If it'd been math class and there'd been a line intersecting the bed longitudinally, dividing it into halves, he would not have been charged with crossing over the midpoint. I'd give him full credit for geometric fairness, and I knew he'd keep a chaste distance from me all night, too. But I couldn't deny how imposing he was, lounging there on the mattress, filling up such a large amount of space without even trying.

I sat awkwardly on the other side of the bed, struggling to keep myself from remembering our brothers' graduation party and how once—very briefly—I'd felt Donovan's big body up against mine. How I had been temporarily sandwiched between his hard torso and a hotel-room wall...

Weird to be so close to him, having that whole scene play out again in my memory, like a movie of someone else's life. Focusing on the feelings hurt too much, though. There was always that low, jagged ache whenever I remembered my early attraction to Donovan (a.k.a. the "older mystery man" that I'd been so drawn to back then), or whenever I let myself inhale for a split second the happy silliness of summertime. The lusty, breezy freedom of it. I couldn't help but associate those feelings with the trauma that came later.

But when I just let myself get caught up in the mental motion-picture screening of that night, it was a different experience. Easier. I could be detached from that former me, from living in a time and an emotional state that no longer existed, because it was as if I'd just been an ordinary character in an ordinary film.

And that ordinary character had been gazing at Donovan *all* during the grad party.

Admittedly, I'd felt a lot like an actress that night. For one thing, I wasn't remotely as reserved as usual, thanks to being away from home and, also, being a little buzzed. At one point, the bourbon and the careless abandon of summer made me kind of bold, and I walked up to him when he was alone in the kitchenette part of the suite.

"Hey, Donovan," I murmured, standing much closer to him than I ever would have normally. But I was nearly a high-school junior then. I thought I was almost cool.

"Aurora," he whispered, watching me with a rare inquisitive look as I smiled at him and leaned against the mauve-colored wall. That glint of interest in his gaze gave me courage.

I reached out to stroke his chest—firm against my fingertips—and I grabbed a handful of his t-shirt because I liked the sensation of it. It was deep red, newish and much softer than I'd expected. Somehow, it made sense to me in that moment to tug him close, my fingers letting go of his shirt's front and reaching all the way around him. Caressing his back and pressing him to me. I raised my head to kiss him and noticed he was holding his breath.

For a second, he let me touch his lips with mine. Just that one single time. Then he stepped away, abruptly, and with an apology.

"Been drinking," he said, glancing to either side of us, not that anyone else was looking. "Sorry."

At first I didn't know if he'd been talking about my drinking or his. I sort of laughed. "*Everyone's* been drinking. Half the people in the other room are passed out." I shrugged. "Nobody's, um...watching us."

I knew Betsy was making out with some townie in the hall. My brother was on the sofa—a blonde sprawled languorously on top of him. Jeremy was smoking weed with a few people in the bathroom. I could smell it. Hear them laughing.

"You're too young," Donovan said simply.

I was almost sixteen then and, in my expert opinion, at least as mature as a twenty-nine year old. He'd just turned twenty-one and had to be going on about thirty-five. But I liked older men. Well, specifically, *this* man. He was just five years older, really. And, anyway, if he had a point, I wasn't about to admit it.

"We're *both* young and inconspicuous," I stated. "I like it that way, Donovan."

He squinted at me. "Hmm. You don't want to be the center of attention, do you?"

"No. Not usually. I'm an observer. I watch people. I know you know that." I grinned at him, feeling the strange high of being so direct and honest with someone I was attracted to. Someone I desperately wanted to touch again with my fingertips, my palms, my arms and more. I inched closer to him. "I want to get out of this bucolic little place and see the world. Anonymously."

"*Boo*—what?" He stepped back to restore the distance between us and chuckled at my phrase. "Anyone ever tell you that you use too many big words?"

I didn't answer. Alcohol made some people giddily drunk. For me, it had the primary effect of making me more introspective. And, apparently, it strengthened my vocabulary.

He exhaled, pecked a light kiss on my forehead and said, "Don't rush things, Aurora. It'll all happen for you." Then, with those patronizing words still hanging in the air between us, he raised his palm in a parting wave and marched himself out of the hotel suite.

I slumped against the kitchenette wall and grimaced, hoping he'd come back—wishing and almost praying for it—but knowing he wouldn't.

A half hour later, when Betsy stumbled in the room without the St. Cloud townie (he was snoring in the hallway), she said to me, "I'm tired. Can we go?"

So she and I left. I thought it would be years before I saw Donovan McCafferty again...but it turned out to be much sooner than that. Just a little over a month later, he came home briefly for a week, during the missing persons' investigation. And everything that had happened between us before that just seemed frivolous, embarrassing and improbable.

I never would have predicted that we'd ever be in a motel room together again. That I'd be studying him like this as he sat on the bed with me, acting like he owned it, while he faked the appearance of being calm.

What a lie. He couldn't have been more wound up if he'd been a yo-yo.

During the TV commercials, I tried to get him to strategize with me about the next day. Discuss what we'd do when we went to the corner store and found this Ronny guy. What we'd ask him.

"I don't want to talk right now, Aurora. I don't want to overanalyze anything. And I sure as hell don't want to plan what I'm gonna say *twelve hours* from now," he snapped. "I just want to relax, okay?" He underscored this statement by yawning loudly, stretching out even more and gluing his eyes to Jim Rockford.

Intellectually, I understood this was his way of resisting change, and I was starting to get a sense of what, exactly, fueled his anger.

I remembered beyond the investigation, even beyond the "funeral" services our parents had held for our brothers. In the early days, Donovan had been hopeful, so sure we'd find the answers quickly, much like a couple of lead actors in a detective show.

But he didn't deal well with ambiguity. Didn't like all the "I don't knows" that lingered. And, so, he'd made a choice. A choice to slam the door on all hope. To reopen that door could be potentially very painful and undoubtedly very frightening.

Donovan, I realized, wasn't a man who'd easily admit to fear. Anger, of course, was an acceptable emotion.

Sometime before the end of the show, he fell asleep on top of the bed, fully clothed—the TV crime still unsolved and me still watching him, thinking about how to get him to see the world a little more like I did. Get him to perceive a few more impulses, so he'd understand the complexity.

Not only of the situation, but of *me*.

Chapter Four

Saturday, June 10

DONOVAN AND I waited until a respectable ten a.m. before checking out of the motel and driving back to Crescent Cove.

During a lazy weekend morning, the town looked different than it had the night before. Not that the prior evening had been "bustling" by any stretch of the imagination, but there had, in fact, been people visible on Friday. Awake. Drinking. Wandering about the town and such. On a Saturday, midmorning, it was like the sun shining on a corpse—brightly lit but dead.

As we pushed our way through the corner store's torn-screen front door, I couldn't help but make comparisons again between Dale's Grocery Mart and this place. This store was even smaller and mustier than where I worked, but that depressing, end-of-the-line feeling I got just crossing the threshold was identical.

Only two people were in the store—the clerk, who was a twenty-something, very fair-haired male, and an old lady, who wore a thin print dress and was coughing up half a lung into her handkerchief.

I didn't have a problem with the old-lady shopper. I'd served an endless stream of customers like that. Always on a strict budget. Always a little sick with something. Almost always alone.

The clerk, however, gave me a distinctly negative vibe, especially when the very first time he glanced at us he shot us a look so irritated you would've thought we'd interrupted him in the middle of his lunch break.

Donovan drew in a surprised breath next to me when he spotted the clerk, and I knew why. We'd both been expecting Ronny Lee Wolf to be a Native American.

But this dude looked more Scandinavian than anything else, with eyebrows so blond they disappeared into his pale skin, and none of the traditional Chippewa facial features. Forget the "Wolf" surname, if he had even a drop of Native American blood I would have been surprised. Apparently, he was Ben Rainwater's "cousin," although maybe that term was used loosely. We knew for a fact that Ben had lived on the tribal lands when he was alive.

Unless the clerk *wasn't* Ben's cousin. Unless he was somebody else entirely—someone filling in for the cousin.

I couldn't shake the hope that this cold, creepy guy might not be Ronny. That the real Ronny would be someone else. Someone more approachable. Someone who wouldn't make my senses tingle with the absolute certainty that we couldn't trust him.

"You two need anything?" the clerk asked, a hard edge to his voice.

For a moment, Donovan looked as if he might stare the guy down, but then he seemed to remember his role and, instead, broke into a sloppy grin. "Just a couple of supplies, man. We'll find 'em." He grabbed a loaf of bread. To help, I snatched a jar of peanut butter and held it up like a prop.

The clerk grunted but continued to eye us suspiciously. Every tiny hair on my body rose when he looked in our direction.

The old lady coughed some more in that unhealthy, croaking way. Hunched over her little plastic basket with just a few items in it, she said, "Ronny, are you out of tomato soup? I don't see none here."

"Might be a few cans in the back, Ms. Ida," the clerk—who *was* Ronny, oh, damn—called out to her, his voice softening a little when he said her name. "I'll check for ya quick."

He disappeared for a minute, and Donovan, whose first thought actually mirrored mine for a change, murmured, "Shit. That's *him*."

I nodded and sighed.

Donovan sniffed the air and gazed down the aisles. "Something just smells funny about this place," he whispered, almost inaudibly. "I think he's selling more than Wonder Bread and Jif."

"Weed?" I mouthed.

"Maybe…or maybe something stronger," he mouthed back. "Acid. Angel dust. Cocaine. I don't know."

Ronny returned and handed over one soup can to the older lady. "This is all we've got for now. I'll get an order put in for more this week."

The Ida woman shuffled to the register, purchased her few items and left. Then, unfortunately, the clerk's full attention was on us.

Donovan swung into action, turning up his laidback charm-o-meter and finally putting to use some of the information he'd collected last night. He grinned again at the clerk. "So, man, you're Ronny Lee Wolf, right?"

"What's it to you?" Ronny threaded his fingers through his fine blond hair, which was longish in the back and stringy, like the way some stoner in a rock band would wear it.

"Just wanted to make sure I had the boss, you know, the big man."

How Donovan managed to make that line sound sincere was beyond me, but it seemed effective in buttering up Ronny, at least a little. The clerk shrugged. "Okay, yeah. So, what do you want?"

Donovan sidled up to the register, put the bread and the jar of peanut butter on the counter and glanced (a bit too obviously, in my opinion) around the store, as if sweeping for eavesdroppers.

"I didn't wanna say anything while the little old lady was in here, but we just came into town last night to visit some friends, and they told us about you." Donovan paused. Leaned forward. "Said you had, you know, extra *provisions*…" He let the thought trail off and smiled knowingly at the clerk.

This was a big gamble on Donovan's part. I tried to look relaxed and natural, but the edges of worry cut lines of anxiety into my gut. It was a dangerous game, playing on a hunch like that. Not only implying that Ronny was some kind of dealer, but that we knew intimately anyone at all in Crescent Cove, a town not much larger than some extended families.

My fears grew deeper when Ronny asked, "Which friends are those?"

I studied the clerk's face for tells. Caught the way his glance shifted for a split second toward the backroom. The way he flinched then forced his features into an approximation of a smile. The way his hands hovered just above the counter and trembled ever so slightly from the effort it took to keep from grabbing something—a weapon, maybe—from below the register.

"Kim and Cindy at the bar," Donovan said easily, pointing vaguely in the direction of the place we were at last night. "And we got to talking to Mike, too. You know, the bartender?" He fiddled with a stick of beef jerky on the counter. "They said you could, uh…help us out."

I forced myself not to hold my breath. It would take Ronny only one conversation with any of the people Donovan had just name-dropped to unveil the truth. Donovan had just put a ticking clock on our stay in Crescent Cove.

Ronny's eyes narrowed. "Where're you from?"

"St. Paul," Donovan said, his now-standard response.

A smirk graced the clerk's face that gave me the most uneasy feeling imaginable. "How much money you people got?" he asked.

"How much stuff is in a bag?" Donovan shot back, still grinning languidly.

"Little bag, ten bucks. Big bag, twenty. Cash only."

Donovan plucked a twenty-dollar bill out of his wallet and passed it to Ronny.

The clerk licked his lips, scanned the doors and windows for peeping eyes, snatched the bill and pocketed it. "Hang on," he said, as he walked into the backroom and emerged in under fifteen seconds with a largish, unmarked, brown-paper sack with the top rolled shut. "Careful with this. You don't want to shake it too much. And keep it dry."

Donovan unrolled the top and peered inside. His expression betrayed nothing, but the stillness of his body told me he hadn't gotten what he'd expected.

"Thanks, man," he said to Ronny in that same pseudo-relaxed voice. The two guys nodded to each other before Donovan nudged me out the door with an urgency that was surprising.

"What's in there?" I whispered when we were on the sidewalk, several yards away from the store and near enough to the Trans Am to make a quick escape. "That's an awfully large bag for drugs."

"Get in the car," he said grimly, "and I'll show you."

When we were inside, he slowly opened the bag and let me look. It wasn't drugs. No, it was fireworks. Unlabeled. Not uniform in size or shape. Without any typical commercial packaging. In other words, the illegal kind.

"Oh," I said. "Do you think that's all he sells?"

Donovan shook his head. "I wouldn't put drugs or firearms past him, but this is bad enough. Possession of this kind of stash could land him in almost as much trouble." He looked warily at the brown-paper sack. "Us, too, if we get caught holding this."

"Wonderful."

"Yeah." He set the bag gently on the backseat and put the car into gear. "I want to take a closer look at these. Somewhere private, though. And I want to check your brother's journal again, too."

We drove down one of the long country roads, headed in the direction of the St. Croix Chippewa Tribal Lands.

"We should poke around the Reservation area," I said. "And check out the site of this Bonner Mill, too." The more we looked around, the more people I could talk to face to face, the more subtle information I'd be able to pick up.

"First we go through everything in this bag. Then," he said, "we'll see."

After about a mile or so, he pulled the car into the driveway of an abandoned farmhouse, parked in the shade and began rifling through the contents of the sack—very gingerly.

As he studied each of the fireworks, he sniffed them, looked at their wicks and their casings, tested their weight in his palms and gently set them down on the dashboard, until he'd lined most of them up like a ragtag band of soldiers.

"Jesus Christ," he said under his breath as he held up a pair of red-tube firecrackers, each one not even two inches long, but they had a stiff fuse sticking out of their middles and paper end caps covering their sides like little bonnets.

To me, they looked kind of like those fake bombs you might see on a kids' cartoon. The ones poor Wile E. Coyote used to try to blow the Roadrunner up with—again and again.

Donovan wasn't laughing, though. "These are M-80s, Aurora. They might look harmless to you but, if they're what I think they are, they've got about sixty *times* more flash powder in each tube than is legal in the U.S.A. And there are cherry bombs in here and…oh, shit." He pulled something silvery out of the bag. "Original quarter sticks."

"What's that mean?" I asked.

My brother was the kind of kid who was always building models or experimenting with chemistry sets, taking apart old clocks or connecting electrical circuits—none of which I'd had any personal interest in growing up. I'd only played with sparklers on the Fourth of July and the occasional child-friendly Roman candle our dad had gotten for Gideon and me at the local drugstore.

To my inexperienced eye, the cherry bombs didn't look all that different from the smoke bombs I saw my brother and some of the neighbor boys fooling around with when we were kids, but Donovan was staring in horror at the silver tube in his hand. It was, maybe, four-inches long but he was looking at it like it was a lethal weapon.

He let out a long, slow breath. "It means if we get caught with this, we'll get one hell of a fine."

He shook his head, careful not to jostle the firecracker too much as he scrutinized it from every angle, looking for markings, touching the green fuse with just the tip of his index finger and wincing as if it hurt him to have to hold it.

"Legal quarter sticks can only have fifty milligrams of flash powder," Donovan explained. "Too many people got injured using originals like these, so they outlawed them. But this particular firecracker was either made a dozen years ago, before the ban, or it was made recently and in secret. From the size and heft to it, it most likely has ten *grams* of flash powder. That's two hundred times more than the legal limit. Enough to blow off a hand and, possibly, even kill a man."

Scary.

I leaned as far away from it as I could get in the passenger's seat. "Do you think Ronny makes them himself?" I asked. "Or, maybe, it's something they assemble together on the Reservation. Maybe it's not illegal there."

"Maybe, maybe not, but I can tell you it's illegal everywhere else. I spent four years in the U.S. Army, and I did some demolition work for a while. The M in M-80 stands for 'Military.' These are low explosives. Not as destructive as dynamite with high-explosive material like nitroglycerine and picric acid, but it's no plaything either. One spark of static electricity in the wrong place and *boom!*"

I flinched.

"Would you open up the journal, Aurora? Go to that 'start here' page."

I flipped to it for him and saw again all the chemicals listed there. He read each one carefully.

"Potassium perchlorate, huh?" he said. "I wonder if our brothers were helping to make these fireworks…"

He grabbed the journal from me and looked more closely at the scrawled chemical list on that page with the dual dates—April 19, 1976 and May 29, 1978. Then he flipped to the next page, dated Monday, May 10, 1976 and, since the car was shadowed by the shade of an unkempt sugar maple tree, he stepped out into the driveway to look at both pages again in the bright sunlight.

"Come out here," he commanded suddenly. "Take a look at this."

At first I didn't understand what he was pointing to—it looked like he was stabbing his finger at the words *potassium perchlorate* over and over again—but then I saw it. "The ink…" I whispered. "It's different at the bottom."

Beads of sweat formed on his brow and flew off in little droplets as he nodded. "The difference in shade is slight. I never noticed it until we were out here, with the sun shining directly on the page like that. Maybe it means something."

Of course it did.

"If that's the case then—" I began. I could feel the puzzle pieces connecting in my mind and, for a second, I could see a flash of the final image it might make, even though the puzzle remained unfinished.

"Then what?" he asked.

"Then Gideon added the last few lines of each entry at a later date," I finished. "At least for these first ones. Is every entry like that?"

"Think so." He flipped through several more pages of the journal and pointed to the spot on each one where the ink subtly changed color. It was always just the last three or four lines and, in almost every case, the newer part contained some kind of addition or subtraction equation using the variables D and M.

What were you and Jeremy doing, Gideon? What were you trying to tell me?

I took hold of the journal myself and studied the pages preceding the 'start here' part. There was only one kind of ink there. "I think this is actually a parallel record. Sort of like a secretive journal, though hidden in plain sight."

"What makes you say that?"

"What we're piecing together can't be pure coincidence." I began ticking items off on my fingers. "One, the journal has chemicals listed in it that are used to make fireworks and explosives. Two, the man they came to see here in Crescent Cove died in an explosion two years ago—the same weekend our brothers disappeared. Three, the cousin of the guy that died sells illegal fireworks out of his store." I held up my palms. "There's no way these things aren't connected somehow."

And, though I didn't mention this to Donovan, I suspected that what linked these three facts was probably a really obvious thread, or it *would be* obvious once we had more information. More contact with the people Gideon and Jeremy had interacted with two years ago. More nonverbal communication.

I felt an odd mix of feelings that kept alternating: A burgeoning sense of hopefulness that, after all this time, closure might be possible. Answers might be found. And our brothers—wherever the hell they were—might be alive with a logical explanation for having disappeared.

But there was also the other side—the dread and the fear that whatever explanation we discovered might cast our brothers in a less than a moral and righteous light.

Donovan was looking at me strangely.

"What?" I asked him. "Don't you think I'm right?"

"I'm not sure what to think," he admitted. "I'm not saying you're wrong, but aren't you overreaching here? Moving a little too fast. We can't just take leaps of logic like that." And Donovan, giving voice to my fears, added, "We know Jeremy and Gideon had knowledge of pyrotechnics. Without much effort those two could've easily built a box of bootleg fireworks. Or homemade bombs."

He gulped a few breaths before continuing. "A man our brothers knew died, and it happened the same weekend as our brothers' disappearance two years ago. Those are the facts. The only thing I'd for sure agree with you about is that this has to be bigger than it seems. Too big for us. I think we're in over our heads."

Who were our brothers? Were they good guys...or not?

I didn't like the questions suddenly bubbling on the edges of my awareness. I also didn't like having to justify my ability to reach conclusions about our discoveries.

"Do the lines at the bottom of each page add up to anything that you can tell?" I asked him, trying to direct the conversation away from this ridiculous notion that we couldn't handle what we were learning. "Is there a pattern?"

He reread the lines listed after the ink change on the *Start here* page. "Potassium perchlorate, sulfur and antimony sulfide are the last three listed, and they're the same three ingredients used in making a cherry bomb. But, how powerful a firecracker like that is depends entirely on the amounts used. Then there's that equation-like thing at the bottom: M + 1 (+ 0), D + 10 (+ 0). Don't know what that means."

"Could it be the proportion of the substance?" I wondered aloud. "Maybe the 'M' stands for milligram?"

"Possible. And maybe the 'D' is for the diameter of the shell casing." He looked at the list for moment longer. "Not sure in what unit, though. Millimeters? Inches or centimeters would be too long."

"Maybe 'D' is for density," I suggested. "Or it could be something totally different, like a tally of who owes them *money,* the 'M.' Or who they've made *deliveries* to, the 'D.' Something we're not even thinking about yet. That's why we need to get more information than we have now."

I'd worry later about how and where to get it. And what, exactly, I'd tell Donovan about how I found it. Because I sensed there would be a lot that I'd have to do on my own if I wanted to get any real answers.

I glanced inside the car where all the fireworks were still resting on the dashboard. "Is there any way we could get rid of these?" I asked. "Aside from being illegal, they're…kind of dangerous."

He agreed. "I just don't know where to put them yet. To take them with us is asking for trouble, but to leave them anywhere would be like planting a bunch of landmines on some civilian's lawn."

I considered this. "What if we went somewhere—somewhere isolated—and just exploded them? Then we'd know how powerful they are, but we wouldn't have to keep them."

"Maybe." He squinted at me, a smile twisting the corners of his lips upward. "This is a weird conversation. Never would've imagined talking about stuff like this with *you.*"

Before I could ask what he meant, he turned away, slipped back into the car and began carefully putting every one of the fireworks back into the paper bag, wrapping many of them up in dry plastic first, torn from an old garbage bag he'd had stashed in his backseat. Then he put the whole thing in the trunk, containing it in a small cardboard box.

"Should be pretty safe stored like that," he said. "And it's better than having them in the car with us."

I noticed that when he started up the Trans Am again, though, he drove slower than he had in the past twenty-four hours.

WE HEADED in the direction of the nearest area of land set aside for the St. Croix Chippewa tribe. When we got to the entrance, we expected to be able to just drive right through.

Turned out, we expected wrong.

An older, weathered man, who'd been sitting on a bench at the entrance, took one look at Donovan's car and stopped us. "Who are you here to see?"

Donovan cleared his throat. "Ben Rainwater's family. To pay our respects. We just found out last night that he'd died."

An odd expression crossed the man's face. "You people knew Ben?"

Donovan nodded slowly, then said, "Well, he was a friend of a friend. We hadn't seen him in a couple of years." He smiled that charming, laidback grin he liked to fake, trying to win over the old man. The old man was having none of it.

"It was a tragedy that Ben died. Went to live with the Great Spirit too soon. Only twenty-five years old." The elder tapped the hood of Donovan's car in a gesture of dismissal. "I'll pass your respects along to his cousin when he returns home. Thank you for visiting."

I thought I might be able to help. "We just spoke with Ronny at the store. Isn't there any other family in the area?"

If Donovan's tactics had fallen flat, my attempt at charm was even worse. The old man looked at us more guardedly than before and replied, "Family is gone. Moved away to Chicago, and there is no easy hunting of anyone there in the big city. Again, your thoughtfulness is appreciated."

Then, to make sure there was no mistaking his intention, he added, "You can turn your car around in this spot here." He pointed to a short, dead-end dirt road just to our right. "Goodbye."

We had little choice but to obey.

I blew out the breath I'd been holding as soon as we were a half mile down the pavement again. "It wasn't exactly the wellspring of information I'd hoped for, but we did learn a few things at least," I said.

"Like what?"

"Ben's age and that the place his family moved was Chicago...one of the places mentioned in the journal. And, also, how even someone in Ronny's own tribe dislikes him."

"How do you figure?"

"Didn't you see the man's face when I mentioned we'd talked to Ronny?" I asked. "The way his eyes narrowed and his jaw tensed? The way his grip on your window tightened? The way he looked at us like we were the enemy? Ben's cousin is not Mr. Popularity. At least not with that tribe elder."

"So what? Everybody's entitled to dislike somebody. There were a few men I wasn't all that fond of back in my unit in Virginia, and I couldn't stand half the guys in our high school. I'm pretty sure the feeling was mutual. So, I don't think that means anything."

Though the subject of school popularity had never been discussed between us before, I knew this was true. Donovan, unlike his brother Jeremy, was not a laidback, fun-loving joiner, even if he was fairly skilled at mimicking someone like that. He had a presence other guys tended to respect—sometimes grudgingly—and girls were often drawn to him, but I'd never gotten the sense that he was "popular" in the traditional way of his brother or mine.

Then again, neither was I.

We hadn't been driving for long when Donovan spotted a bent sign for Bonner Mill, just a half mile away, and he followed an even smaller country road directly to the site.

When we got there, though, it was more than an abandoned old mill—it was a burned out one. It captured my attention more for what it *wasn't* than for what it *was*. It wasn't actually much of a mill anymore, not of scrap metal (which was what the old sign claimed it to be) or of anything, really. It was in an even greater state of ruin than that old farmhouse we'd stopped at earlier or that dilapidated bar on the main street in town.

"Must have been some explosion," I murmured.

Donovan studied the broken-down wooden slats and gnarly old railings, the rusted window ledges with the glass blown out and the fire-tinged edges of what had once been the building's frame.

"No matter how many grams of flash powder over the legal limit were in Ronny's bootleg fireworks, it would've taken even more than that to blow up a place this bad. Dynamite, maybe." He shook his head. "I'm not sure what kind of trouble our brothers were in or what they were up to with Ben Rainwater, but there had to be more going on here to cause this than just a little mishap with too many hot fireworks."

Even knowing far less about the world of explosives than Donovan did, I had to agree. "I have an idea about how we might learn more," I said. "Although, you might not like it."

He regarded me with his usual half-suspicious, half-amused gaze, which never failed to make my breath hitch and my heart rate speed up. "What is it?"

"Well, first, we need to go back to Ashburn Falls. And, um, second, we need to find that library."

He rolled his eyes but, given that he didn't seem to have any bright new ideas of his own, he agreed to go there.

By the time we got to the Ashburn Falls Public Library, we had only an hour left before closing—the library shut its doors at three p.m. on Saturdays—but if we played our cards right, that would be just enough time to dig up a little background on Bonner Mill and Ben Rainwater.

"Stay over here by the magazines. Let *me* handle this," I told Donovan before grabbing a few pieces of scratch paper and a pencil from on top of the card catalog and approaching the reference librarian.

I could tell at least a dozen things about the woman from her posture (not overly confident), her facial expression (not easily humored), her direct gaze (not one to suffer fools willingly) and more. I would be respectful, serious and intellectual. That should put her at ease.

"May I help you?" the librarian lady asked.

"Yes, thank you. I have a research paper I need to complete on regional industries, and I want to do a really good job," I said, trying to sound like a grade-conscious teen. "Do you have any information on Bonner Mill? Newspapers or microfilm, maybe? I know it's no longer in operation, but I was hoping to learn a little more about what it used to produce and why it was closed a couple of years ago."

The librarian jotted down a few notes on the slim pad in front of her. "You're not from around here then, are you?"

I shook my head. "My family's from, um, St. Paul."

The librarian nodded. "School is still in session there?"

The woman was nosy and sharp but, after hearing her speak, I didn't sense that she was at all mean. Just very curious. I sent her a sheepish smile. "It's for a summer school project I have to finish and turn in. I got this one really bad grade in social studies, so…" I feigned an embarrassed shrug and waited.

It worked.

"I see," the librarian said kindly. She pulled off the top sheet from her notepad. "I'll gather a few documents together for you. I think the newspapers from before last year have already been archived on microfilm, and the mill, as you already know, was closed before then."

"Yes," I said, pretending to consult my scratch-paper notes. "I was told there was a big fire or something there two summers ago. Around the Fourth of July, right?"

"You could say that," the older woman said. "The first firefighter who arrived at the scene speculated it was a series of bombs, but…" She let that thought trail off.

I wanted her to keep talking. "But…what?"

The librarian cleared her throat. "It seemed to get cleared up by the police awfully quickly, is all. The state was never called in to investigate, and I don't know any more than that." She adjusted her eyeglasses and strode away with the air of someone who didn't trust herself with a secret.

She returned about three minutes later with a spool of microfilm and a couple of sections of newspaper. "You can return these to the cart by the wall when you're done." She pointed to a half-filled rolling cart near the reference desk. "And the microfilm readers are just over there." She pointed again, this time to a couple of sectioned-off desks near the back of the room.

"Great," I said. "Thanks so much."

The librarian took a few strides away, then paused and looked at me again, more closely this time. "Hope you get a good grade on your paper."

I forced a smile. "Me, too." Then I all but sprinted to a booth with an open reader.

As soon as I'd threaded the microfilm into the reader and turned it on, I motioned Donovan over. The two of us huddled together and studied the magnified type on the screen. He quickly took over the task of forwarding through the articles, racing past January, February,

March and April of 1976 to get to May, June and July. Then he slowed and we scanned each page for any headlines about Bonner Mill.

Not only did we find a few, but what was most interesting of all was when the articles were written.

Donovan tapped the screen near one date: *Wednesday, June 16, 1976*. A couple of weeks before our brothers disappeared. He pointed to the headline: *"Mill Mishap."* A grainy picture showing a burnt-out hole in the wall with the caption "Safety of Bonner Mill called into question by authorities" was front and center. There were a few lines about a faulty heating and exhaust system and how that likely played a part in the small blast.

"So, the explosion over the Fourth of July weekend wasn't the first one," Donovan murmured. "There'd been problems already, just not quite as large or as massively destructive."

This was confirmed by other articles we read in the paper on the days following—inspectors checking the facility for any other safety violations, the Bonner family dealing with legal issues and dissent from the various unions, interviews with people in the local white population and on the Rez—both communities expressing concerns about continuing mill operations.

Then, when there was the second, larger blast the night before Independence Day—attributed this time to a furnace explosion—it seemed so obvious, so cut and dried that of course the mill would cease to run its scrap-metal operation until these safety issues were cleared up. But the Bonners were in hot water legally and quickly came to be in debt, so the family didn't bother to make repairs. They just closed up shop.

And the Bonners' troubles were complicated even further by Ben Rainwater's death. Partly because he wasn't a worker there, he just happened to be in the wrong place at the wrong time—or so said the authorities—but, also, because he wasn't the only one who died there.

An unidentified man perished the same night as well. His name was a mystery because his human remains were so badly charred he had no fingerprints (they'd been burned off his hands), and his teeth didn't match any dental records of missing persons that the police had on file.

Donovan, who wasn't someone prone to a whole lot of intuitive leaping, at least not that I'd seen, jumped to a conclusion just then that really upset him. I saw it happening. Watched as he flipped through

Gideon's journal in panic, the blood seeping from his face as he scanned the second half of the book.

I knew right away what he was looking for, so I waited—letting him test his theory, holding my breath and hoping my memory of the entries was accurate.

"I'm sure I saw a reference to 'J' at least once in those later pages," I whispered after a moment. I didn't think *Jeremy* was the one to die in the explosion along with Ben. It couldn't have been him. And, whether or not Donovan believed me, I *knew* it wasn't Gideon.

No.

I watched as a hint of color returned to Donovan's cheeks. He ran the tip of his index finger underneath the phrase "J & I in Chicago" and nodded at me in obvious relief. Then, for good measure, he flipped a few pages further into the journal, hunting for additional "J"s, one of which he found in the vicinity of another handwritten city name: Tulsa.

"Oklahoma?" he said. "Any idea why there?"

I shook my head. "But, Donovan, I know, somehow, all of this is connected. I just *know* it. Is there any other city mentioned before Chicago?"

"No. There's only one entry between the 'Start here' page and the 'Chicago' one. It's got just one date on it—Monday, May 10, 1976, when Jeremy and Gideon went to Crescent Cove the second time—and another list of supplies, mostly chemicals."

I scanned a few more screens on the microfilm reader, articles in the paper following the Fourth of July explosion. There wasn't much else that referred to either Bonner Mill or Ben Rainwater, aside from some photographs of them both. (Ben definitely had the darker features of his tribe members, I noticed, which made me all the more curious about his relationship to Ronny.) But, as the librarian had insinuated, the incident seemed to be brushed under the rug very quickly. Too quickly.

Donovan had set the journal aside and was sifting through the sections of print paper, dated from late last year, and finding only a handful of columns referencing the closing of the mill. No new details. Nothing we hadn't already seen before.

"We need to go to Chicago," I told him.

Donovan looked up from the newspaper. "No," he said. Then

lowering his voice to barely audible, he added, "I came with you here. You got to see everything for yourself. And now you need to stop acting like Nancy Drew. This is where we bring the police in, if we want things to go further, Aurora. We have more evidence now. Maybe they could use it to reopen the case."

"They won't do it," I said, as certain of this as I was of my own name. And I was equally certain that however much Donovan pretended to be willing to have our brothers' case reopened, he wasn't committed to it.

"...if we want things to go further..."

He was angry at the guys for leaving in the first place, and he'd decided they must be dead or they would have come back. It was too big of a betrayal otherwise. He did *not* want to know the truth at all costs. Nor did he want to have to challenge the memory he had of his brother. And I knew he was going to fight me on every step, even as he tried to humor me. Even as he told me all the right words.

But I missed Gideon—and Jeremy, too. I couldn't let them down. I *wouldn't*.

Donovan leaned in close. I could feel his insistence in the heat of his breath as he spoke. "We're going to go back and talk to Officer James. He's a good guy, and the department has better resources for stuff like this than we do. They'll help us. Don't worry."

I unthreaded the spool of microfilm, turned off the reader and gathered the newspaper pages. "I don't like Officer James, and I'm not all that fond of the other two Chameleon Lake police officers either," I hissed. "They didn't solve any part of this last time, and the case has been all but closed for a year and a half. Reopening it now won't be a priority for them, but it's a priority for us."

I motioned for Donovan to follow me out of the library, putting the materials on the cart on the way and waving a goodbye to the librarian, who was thankfully too busy with another patron to ask any follow-up questions.

When we were outside the building, I turned to Donovan. "Gideon didn't want the authorities involved—that much I know. He chose to give the journal to *me*." I paused, making sure this sank in, and then I held up the journal I'd collected from the table back when I was picking up the reference material.

"I want to go to Chicago...and I'm *going* to go. With you or without you," I said. "And if you breathe a word of this to Officer James or to anyone, I'll light that bag of fireworks in the trunk of your car myself, and we'll just see what it does to your groovy Trans Am."

At this he actually laughed.

"Just hold on, hold on. Slow down and stop making threats." He sighed. "Though, you're kinda funny when you're angry. We need—"

I glared at him. "Donovan, I'm telling you—"

"Jesus, let me finish," he said. "We can't tell our folks, 'Hey, we're going to Chicago.' It's not logical for us to just up and leave like that, and it's not safe for you to do it on your own. You're smart, Aurora, I know, but you're not even eighteen. And you're going to do what? Act like an amateur sleuth? Just follow your hunches around the country? Go to every city your brother jotted down in his journal?" He shrugged this off like it was ludicrous.

I'd reached the frayed end of my rope. "Maybe that doesn't seem logical to you, but to me, that's the *only* thing that feels right."

I looked him in the eye and didn't blink. He could damn well try, but I knew he couldn't talk me out of this by brushing me off and calling me names. *Nancy Drew?* Screw him.

"Just look at what we've managed to pick up in only twenty-four hours," I reminded him. "By going to only *one* place Gideon wrote about in the journal. I know there's more we'll find—in Chicago, in Tulsa, in a half dozen other cities. I remember Gideon mentioned a few Southwestern states and, at one point, the city of Pasadena…"

"*California?*" His jaw dropped. "That's not somewhere we can just drive to for a weekend so you can test out your people-reading skills," he said, mockery coloring his voice. "You aren't going to be able to lie to your mom about *that* trip and get away with it."

He shook his head. "No. This is crazy. We go back home. We talk about this. And I think you'll realize, after a good night's sleep or two, telling the cops about what we found here will be the best way." He crossed his arms—a show of resistance, defiance and pointed unwillingness to participate in my plan.

Fine, Donovan. Have it your way.

"That's not how it's going to happen," I said, adamant. "I've already spent two years wondering what went wrong in their investigation. Why they didn't find anything. Why they shut the case down so quickly."

I poked him in the direction of his car and waited until we'd both gotten in, feeling that maddening jolt of powerlessness that I hated so much. Remembering how my questions had been dismissed by the cops because I was "just a kid"…"just a girl." I wasn't putting up with that shit again. Not from the police, and sure as hell not from Jeremy's older brother.

"This is *not* some simple case," I told him. "Our brothers didn't disappear for *no reason*. They didn't get themselves killed somewhere because they were 'high on drugs,' like that one cop suspected. They weren't 'secret homosexual lovers' who ran away together, like that other cop said. Both of us know that."

I shot him a significant look, remembering how Donovan had bristled silently at this particular insinuation a couple of years ago because it had showed such a lack of knowledge about both guys. Anyone who knew Jeremy or Gideon, even casually, knew they were straight. And, yeah, they both liked to party. They drank booze and smoked a joint every once in a while, but they weren't druggies.

"They may have been kidnapped or they may have committed a crime and gone into hiding," I said. "I don't know for sure, but I'm positive there's more to this than what we've been led to believe. More than the police either know or are willing to tell."

I paused and studied his face for a long, slow moment. Watched the tiny flicker of agreement in his eyes. Watched him try to blink it away, unsuccessfully. "You know I'm right," I said with conviction.

He swallowed, refusing to admit aloud the truth of it, of course, but the fact that he didn't immediately contradict me was enough.

"Well, there's nothing left to do around here," he said instead.

I didn't disagree.

"So, let's head back. No reason to stay another night in Wisconsin just because we can." He glanced at his watch. "We're going to have a lot to figure out in the next few days, so we might as well go home and get to it."

I knew I'd earned the right to boast winning one battle against him, but I stayed silent because there was a full-scale war ahead. I needed to save my energy so I could win that, too.

Donovan filled the car up with gas—sixty-one cents per gallon out in Ashburn Falls, a whole two cents cheaper than in Chameleon Lake, it was *that* remote—and we began the drive toward Minnesota.

I noticed his anger was more directed this time. Less of a simmering general malevolence than a laser-focused frustration.

Something else was different, too. Unlike the ride up, there were fewer pockets of silence on the way back. This time he actually initiated a few conversations. One in particular surprised me.

"Do you think our brothers were lying to us? To everyone?" he asked over the low crooning of Journey's "Wheel in the Sky" on the radio. "Do you think they were trying to get away with something illegal? I know they were capable of it. It's just—do you think they'd actually *do* it?"

I'd wondered about this. Over and over again I'd wondered.

"I don't know," I answered honestly. "I hope not. My sense is that they wouldn't do something really bad on purpose but, maybe... maybe, accidentally..."

"Yeah, that's what I thought, too."

"You know, there's a lot of risk in going to the police, Donovan. Not only might they botch up the investigation again, but if they find out something bad about our brothers, they'd expose them both. Our parents don't need that kind of heartbreak. Not on top of everything else."

He nodded, saying nothing but just running his fingers through his dark hair. I could see a tremor in them as he did it. Just one. Then he pulled the fingers of that hand into a tight fist and clenched the steering wheel with the other.

In the parking lot in Alexandra, he dropped me off alongside my car, getting out to put my bag into the backseat of the Buick for me. I dug out my keys and stood in the distance between our two vehicles for a minute, remembering something. The ring.

I tugged it off my hand and ceremoniously returned it to him— making a face as I did it and trying to get him to smile just a little after the seriousness of our conversation on the drive.

He did smile, and he pocketed the dorky golden band. "Too much of a women's libber for a ring, huh?"

"Maybe, maybe not," I said, trying to sound casual and sophisticated. At least that's how I hoped he'd interpret my words. "But, in any case, I won't need it here."

"Fair enough. And I'll let you have your way with the journal, since I'm not going to wrestle it away from you," he said, the smile mutating into a smirk because I'd been holding onto Gideon's leather book with a death grip, like it was my passport to get out of a foreign land.

"We need to talk in a few days and really figure out what we're going to do next," I said.

Donovan grimaced. "I've got to work this week, and I think you do, too."

I agreed. I'd probably need the week to come up with a good excuse for taking off some time from Dale's Grocery Mart. Not sure what, exactly, I'd say to my boss. And then, of course, there were my parents. Hmm, that could be difficult. But I'd deal with one problem at a time.

"How about we meet on Tuesday night?" I suggested. "It'll give us three days to mull over some ideas on our own, then we can run a few possibilities back and forth. About Chicago." I paused to gauge his reaction. "And, maybe…beyond Chicago."

His reaction was nearly nonexistent, his face devoid of all emotion. But, after a long moment, he consented with a short nod.

"Okay, so, Tuesday night then," I said. "Should I come to the auto shop?"

"Yeah. Make it seven p.m. And Aurora?"

"Yeah?"

"Don't run off before then," he said, slipping into the Trans Am with a wave and a tight grin that bordered on threatening. "I'll be watching around town for you."

Chapter Five

Chameleon Lake, Minnesota ~ Sunday, June 11

So as not to *entirely* lie to my mother, I drove to St. Cloud after Donovan dropped me off—to hang out with Betsy for the evening and to pretend this was just another event in a normal teenage girl's life.

Though surprised to see me, Betsy had dedicated herself to a weekend of heavy partying, and nothing was going to deter her from her agenda.

She just thrust a bottle of Old Style at me Saturday night and then loudly introduced me to the gang before returning to the sofa, where she was wedged between a lava lamp and a beefy looking guy named Stan.

The next morning, though, my friend's curiosity returned.

"Why did it take you so long to get here?" Betsy asked for the third time, attempting to rub away a hangover with the pads of her fingers. She winced. "Were you with a guy?"

I didn't trust myself to answer this directly, so I shook my head. "I just needed to research something without my parents wondering where I was."

"Research what?"

"Um…colleges," I blurted. I didn't know why I said that, but it seemed to be a reasonable response. A normal teenage girl kind of explanation. Versus the truth, which was not exactly *normal*.

My friend raised an eyebrow in surprise. "You're back to maybe going to the Twin Cities in the fall?"

Betsy and I had planned to go to college together in our early years of high school. Before the disappearance. Then my plans for the future had stalled. Betsy's hadn't.

"I doubt I could get in for the fall," I told her, trying to be honest whenever I could. "I may have already missed the application deadline. But I'm thinking of maybe trying to register for the second semester." I forced a smile. "That'd be fun, right?"

Betsy agreed right away, but I wasn't blind. Hangover or not, there was a flash of guardedness in my friend's eyes. A sudden crease in the middle of her forehead that she smoothed away—just not fast enough.

It was clear she'd already begun to construct her upcoming college experience without the tragic story of her high-school best friend. Someone whose personal drama would, no doubt, draw attention away from her lightness and add an unwanted shadow to an otherwise fresh, new adventure.

Not that Betsy would ever admit to this. I knew she cared about me and our friendship. Had stood by me through all of my stages of grief. I could even understand why she'd appreciate a little natural distance between us.

Still, the realization that my best friend had been hoping to cut ties...*hurt*. Made me wish I couldn't so often guess what people were thinking.

"Nothing is for sure," I said with a shrug. "I figured my parents wouldn't be thrilled about the idea, so I just wanted to have time to get some info without them suspecting anything. I'll probably need to wait a year or two to go anywhere anyway."

"Well, keep me posted," she said, the urgency in her voice tinged with relief. Then she sort of laughed. "So, there's really no secret guy?"

"Of course not." I laughed, too. "If there was one, wouldn't I tell you?"

"Yeah," Betsy said, although her tone actually said, *"Probably."*

As I was getting ready to leave and, finally, return home, my friend asked if I wanted to get together on Friday night. "Maybe see the movie that's coming to town?" she suggested. "I keep hearing about 'Grease,' but I don't know if it'll be any good."

"Sure," I replied, fully intending to cancel in a few days. I'd likely be spending the night getting ready for the trip—with or without Donovan. Either way, I was headed to Chicago no later than Saturday morning. "It looked kind of silly in the previews—all those poodle skirts and Fifties songs—but I bet it'll be fun." *For someone else.*

"Great!" Betsy said, seeming happy to be on such a neutral, easy subject. "See you then, if not before."

I waved goodbye and drove home, the sheer commitment of what I'd planned to do the following weekend settling on my shoulders like lead weights.

With my parents both otherwise occupied, I snuck in the backdoor and stole up to my room. Mom would soon notice the Buick back in the driveway again and feel relief at my return. Dad would be glad to have me home but even gladder to see his wife's jitteriness lessen for a little while. And, later, we'd all just pretend that we were still a normal family. Normal, in spite of everything.

There was something decidedly abnormal about that.

On Monday morning, I found myself back at work with Sandy, who was babbling about finally having gone to see "Corvette Summer" in St. Cloud over the weekend. *(Ohhh, Mark Hamill! Love, love, love!)*

Sandy was chitchatting about wanting to watch "Grease" soon, too. *(It looks so cute! And you should just see John Travolta dancing! It's going to be even bigger than "Saturday Night Fever"…)*

Yeah, right.

That feeling of being like the older waitress—like Cindy at that Crescent Cove bar—kept coming back to me. That sense of being trapped at the Grocery Mart for the next decade with Sandy, Dale and the occasional shopper looking for Hamburger Helper. It was too depressing a fate to keep imagining.

When I finally got a break, I cornered my boss in the backroom.

"Dale, I'm sorry to ask you this on short notice, but I'm going to need to take off work next week."

He shot me the withering look of someone convinced of his self importance. "Vacations need to be put in at least a month ahead of time."

I nodded. I knew this. But he owed me a few favors and I was going to get my way. Period.

"I'm not going on vacation. I'm going on a college scouting trip," I said, mentally commanding him to hear the determination in my voice. "The admissions offices already have shorter hours and they'll be closed once the summer-school sessions are over." Not sure if that was really true but, hey, it sounded good. "So, I really have to go *now*."

"You couldn't have decided this last month?"

"No, Dale. I couldn't have."

I stood still and faced him. Looked into those beady, bloodshot eyes of his and willed him to remember how my intuitive skills kept his store from being robbed by a couple of grimy thugs in the early spring. I'd warned Dale about them. Said they were big-city hoods who were up to no good. Pointed out how they were casing the place. And, in response, he'd called in Officer Cleary for backup. Major crisis averted.

After a moment of glaring at me, Dale exhaled—a longsuffering stream of hot air and irritation. "You really need *all* of next week off?"

"At least. Maybe we should make it a week and a half."

His squirminess told me that I was pushing it, but Dale was a coward. He gave in out of fear of confrontation rather than out of any sense of compassion or desire to help.

"One week," he muttered with a scowl and a dismissive huff, then he headed into the back alley for a smoke.

I smiled grimly to myself. My victory was small but important.

One battle down, two to go.

IT TOOK all of seven minutes on Tuesday night for Donovan to start picking a fight with me.

"You need to think about this," Donovan insisted when I informed him I'd gotten a week off from work for the trip. "Do we really need to rush into it?"

"*Rush?*" I stared at him. "Your concept of time is seriously warped. Being two years late is hardly *rushing*."

I could hear the exasperation in my voice, but I wasn't backing down. And, besides, in my not very humble opinion, I'd already won this damned argument.

"You were standing right next to me in Crescent Cove, weren't you?" I said. "We got more leads in twenty-four hours than the cops had managed to track down in a month, and that's even with their tromping all over our houses and putting out missing persons bulletins."

I shook my head, remembering Officer James and Officer Cleary tearing apart Gideon's bedroom, asking if he "always listened to disturbing music" (he owned a few KISS albums) or "looked at a lot of dark art" (he had *one* Van Gogh poster up on his wall) or "frequently read Commie literature" (someone gave him a book by Karl Marx, but I'm pretty sure he never cracked it open).

To some extent, I appreciated what the police were trying to do: Establish his patterns of behavior before the disappearance, determine what was or wasn't in character, check to see if there were other suspicious activities dotting his past—any juvie criminal records, disabilities that might impair judgment, indications of burgeoning mental illness, drug or gambling habits.

I'd overheard Officer James making some comment about "solvability factors" to his partner as they sifted through Gideon's old school notebooks, hunting for hints about why someone else might want to abduct him or why he might feel the need to either kill himself or disappear indefinitely.

But they couldn't find anything obvious.

No missing favorite things from his bedroom. No money trail. No suicide notes tucked inside his LP liners. Apparently, listening to "Rock and Roll All Nite" from KISS's *Alive!* album over and over again was not quite enough evidence to qualify an eighteen-year-old male as "troubled," although the cops called into question his musical taste more than once.

Donovan made a face and started digging around in a desk drawer for something. "What did you tell Old Man Geiger you'd be doing anyway?" he asked.

"College scouting," I replied. "Can't you tell your boss you're doing that, too?"

He stopped fiddling around and leveled an odd look at me. "Um," he said, which I took to mean, *Yes…yes, he could, but he wasn't sure he wanted to.*

I was aware he'd been in the Army long enough to pay for four years of college, thanks to the GI Bill, but he hadn't started taking any classes yet—at least not as far as I knew.

Deciding to push my luck, I said, "That's what we could tell everyone. The explanation for why we're leaving town together for a week. We're both just looking at a few colleges. That sounds reasonable enough, right?"

He cleared his throat. "Um," he said again. "I just…I don't know."

I sighed. There were a bunch of things I could do in Chicago by myself, and I would, but Donovan had been more help in Crescent Cove than I'd wanted to admit. It wasn't like I could force him to come with me, though. (He was a lot stronger than me.) But there was also no way he could force me to stay home. "It's okay," I said, and I meant it. "I can take it from here."

He shot me a look of disbelief and went back to scrounging through the desk drawer until he retrieved a stack of stapled sheets of yellow paper and a pen. He walked over to the Muscle-Car Babe calendar and studied the dates beneath the red Mustang and the too-perky blonde, comparing them to whatever was written on one of the yellow sheets. He exhaled slowly and jotted down a few notes on the calendar and then a few more on the paper.

My excitement began to rise at the sight. He was doing it. He was blocking off the time. He was going to go with me to Chicago.

I smothered a grin, knowing that—in Donovan's case—the only obstacle to his departure was work-related. Unlike me, he didn't have to clear anything with his parents. Both his real dad and his stepdad were out of the picture, and his mom, while still very much in his life, had her own house.

Donovan had been living in a small apartment on his own since he'd gotten back from the Army and, though of course he was always respectful of his mother, he didn't have to answer to anybody. Not even his boss at the garage, really. Everyone knew they needed him there more than the other way around.

"Stop looking so pleased with yourself," he growled at me. "Listen, I'm taking next week off, but that's it. We'll drive to Chicago and, maybe, another city or two in Illinois, but then we're coming back home."

He shot me the stern look of an elder brother, which seemed an act calculated to provoke me, even before he said, "Now you'd better get permission from your parents. I don't want you sneaking around behind their backs, and I really don't want them calling the cops on me and accusing me of kidnapping you."

I gaped at him. He couldn't be serious. "That's not funny."

"No shit, Aurora," he said without a trace of humor in his voice.

I crossed my arms. "Fine. I'll talk with them tomorrow, I promise. My plan was to leave on Saturday morning, but we could take off even earlier. Friday night. Betsy wanted to see some new movie, that Fifties musical, but I'd rather skip it and just—"

"No, you should go," he interrupted. "You know how people talk in this dinky little town." Impossible to miss the bitterness that clung to his words. "We need to use that to our advantage. You know we can't *both* be gone from here for more than a day or two and not have people notice. Or *speculate*."

He wrinkled his nose and paced the length of the office and back. "Friday night would be a good chance for us to spread your rumor about where we're going. I can plan to run into you and Betsy by the theater. If we talk about that college-scouting crap on the street for five minutes, there'll be enough people eavesdropping that maybe we won't have to deal with gossip about us being a couple or running away together or anything stupid like that."

I bit my lip to keep from spouting off a self-incriminating, completely embarrassing response to this. His dismissal of me as not being someone even worthy of dating *gossip* needled me to no end, but it wasn't like I could argue with him over it. What would I say?

Oh, c'mon! Why shouldn't they think we're a couple?

Wouldn't it be great if everyone talked about how we'd skipped town together to go on a wild road trip? That we were just irresponsible kids with loose morals, who'd probably even break the law a time or two?

That plan would be a hard sell with Donovan...and it wouldn't help me convince my parents to let me drive with him to Chicago either.

I shrugged. "Okay. Betsy and I will go to the show in town. Seven-thirty on Friday night. See you on the sidewalk afterwards."

I swiveled on my sneaker toe to leave—I couldn't get out of that cramped office fast enough—but he stopped me by gently grabbing my upper arm and tugging me toward him. "Hang on," he said. "There's something else we have to do tonight."

My pulse thrummed at the spot where he touched me, and I wished desperately that I didn't like the sensation. I snatched my arm away. "What?"

He flashed one of his grins at me, leaned close until his nose was just a couple of inches from mine and whispered, "Boom." Then he pointed toward the parking lot. "We got some bootleg fireworks to blow up."

Oh, yeah. We did.

He drove us out beyond the Chameleon Lake city limits, through the rolling countryside and halfway to St. Cloud, before he pulled the Trans Am onto the shoulder of the road. He nodded at the mostly open field to our right, sprinkled only with a few large maple-tree clusters.

With the crunch of gravel beneath our feet and the sun just starting to dip down to tree level, we made our way to the field, each of us having grabbed a decent sampling of fireworks from the cardboard box in the trunk.

"Let's just try this bunch first," Donovan said. "No telling how powerful they'll be."

Using a small, dried branch he picked up off the ground, he lit the stick with his cigarette lighter and, being careful to keep the lit branch away from the fireworks, took just one cherry bomb with him to the most open part of the field.

"Stay behind the tree," he commanded, and I didn't dare disobey.

He set the firecracker down on a rock and, then, using the branch to give himself a little distance, lit the cherry bomb with the tip of the flaming stick—arm outstretched, eyes shielded—and when the wick caught fire, he ran like hell back to where I was standing.

Like a mini snake, it hissed as though about to strike, and then…

Boom!

It went off, shooting sound waves and angry dust particles into the still-bright sky.

He glanced at me, a grin tugging his lips upward. "They're a little stronger than the county-fair variety." He reached for the M-80 next. "I'm almost afraid to light this one."

But light it he did. It sparked a hot, bright flash and sounded like the detonation of a cannon.

The two of us looked at each other and started laughing, so instinctively, so uncontrollably, at the sheer power of these small objects, it verged on hysteria.

"Good thing we're alone out here," I commented, wiping away a stray tear from the corner of my eye and handing Donovan one of the quarter sticks. "I wouldn't want to have to explain to anybody what we're doing."

"Me neither," he said, glancing at the empty road. "Sounds like we're trying to level the entire field."

We lit the remainder of our first batch, then Donovan went back to the Trans Am to retrieve another couple of handfuls from the box. After a few cars went by, he lit those one at a time as well.

We were laughing again at the spark and sound of a particularly deafening quarter stick when I asked, "How many more do we have left?" just a second before a male voice behind us asked, "What have you got there, kids?"

I gasped and pivoted toward the voice

And Donovan swung around so fast he looked like one of those cartoon whirling dervishes. "Uh, Officer James," he said. "We, uh, didn't hear you."

The young cop smiled indulgently at us. "Well, it was a little noisy down here, wasn't it?"

He had a thick head of reddish-brown hair that he tended to run his left hand through whenever he grinned. It was a casual, easygoing motion that seemed oddly paired—a connection of face and limb. Out of uniform, as he was just then, and dressed in jeans and a clean blue t-shirt, he appeared even younger than his early thirties. More like a peer than an authority figure. More like one of us.

Donovan and I didn't say anything, although we both shot a quick glance at the base of the maple tree where he'd been stashing the fireworks. I didn't see any left. Of course, I knew there were still some in his trunk.

"Celebrating the Fourth of July a little early, aren't you two?" the officer asked.

I watched Donovan swallow and nod. "A guy at the shop gave me a few of these, and I just wanted to see if they were any good."

Officer James raised an eyebrow. "One of your coworkers?"

"No," Donovan said quickly. "Just a guy who was passing through. Needed a little work done on his back bumper and an oil change. He was from out of town."

I studied the cop's expression as the cop, in turn, studied Donovan's, and I knew we were in trouble. Officer James wasn't buying this explanation.

"This guy from out of town, he just *gave* you a bunch of—" The officer waved his palm in the air. "What would you call them? *Specialty* fireworks?" He grinned some more and ran that same palm through his hair again, catching his fingers up in the chestnut strands like a spider dancing through a web.

Donovan winced. "I didn't know what they were for sure," he lied. "They did look a little, uh, different from the usual ones we get."

At that, the officer laughed. He may have been a small-town cop, but he was nobody's fool.

He clasped Donovan's shoulder with his wide hand and glanced between the two of us. "Well, son, I'm off duty, so you're in luck. When I saw your car by the side of the road, I thought you might've just had some engine trouble. Glad to hear that's not the case."

He gave each of us a significant look and let go of Donovan to examine the spot where the fireworks had been lit. Little bits of burnt black wadding remained at the scene, although, thankfully, most of the objects in question had been blown to bits.

Donovan muttered something under his breath when Officer James picked up a slip of smoky, blackened wadding paper—a remnant from one of the cherry bombs.

The cop's suspicious expression said it all but, for good measure, he added, "Thought with your military background you might know better, Mr. McCafferty."

But then, after an interminable pause, he broke into yet another smile, raking his fingers through his thick hair once more. "I remember these from when I was a kid. They used to pack a lot more punch back then. I'm not sure who, er...*designed* the ones you had in your possession but, from the look and sound of them, they were made the old-fashioned way."

I couldn't help but notice that, while Officer James glanced at me from time to time, he'd pretty much dismissed me from the start. There was no thought on the cop's part of my having been involved in the acquisition of the fireworks. No sense that I might have any pyrotechnic knowledge, however minimal. Nothing out of the ordinary about me that would require him to look at me with any real scrutiny.

It had been much the same during the missing persons' investigation. Not that I had been in any way involved with Gideon's disappearance, but shouldn't a good cop consider every possible angle?

Addressing Donovan, Officer James said, "You're not within the boundaries of the town of Chameleon Lake and, even if you were, I'm not on duty again until tomorrow morning. So, I won't be checking your pockets or your car right now, and I trust there'd be no unexploded evidence for me to find anywhere, would there?"

"No, sir," Donovan answered solemnly. I was reminded yet again how smoothly he could lie when motivated.

"Good." The cop laughed and steered us back away from the scene and toward the road. "Well, then I guess there's nothing to report. This time. But I wouldn't recommend that you pick up any more of those special fireworks from anywhere, you hear?"

"Yes, sir," Donovan replied, his tone respectful but with a hint of his trademark charm. Playing the game. Maybe even enjoying it.

I couldn't quite bring myself to act playful, but I tried to appear appropriately compliant. Because as jovial as the coolest, hippest cop in Chameleon Lake seemed at the moment, I remembered Officer William James well from the time of the investigation. Knew what a hard ass he could be when he wanted to. I wasn't inclined to get on his bad side.

Since he seemed to like me best when I played the part of the meek, easy-to-direct schoolgirl, I just kept quiet and let him think what he wanted.

Thing was, no offense to the good officer and his buddies at the police station but, as of two years ago, I hated all cops. Every last one of them. And I'd never trust them again.

When we got up to the road, Officer James jumped into his snazzy yellow VW Bug with a wave, but he insisted that Donovan drive ahead of him. So, of course, Donovan pulled out first and had to drive under the speed limit the whole way back into town. It wasn't until the cop turned left onto a side street that we could finally breathe deeply again.

"What are we going to do with the rest of the fireworks?" I asked. "There's still some in the trunk, right?"

Donovan shrugged as he pulled into the auto shop's parking lot next to my Buick. "Yeah, we've got five or six left. We'll take them with us, I guess. Maybe find a larger, more remote area when we're on the way to Chicago and light them there. We've got to be more careful out of state. Lucky it was Officer James who saw us tonight and not someone who didn't know us. Like some hardnosed cop from St. Cloud or another town."

"Yeah. Very lucky," I murmured.

He didn't catch my sarcasm and, at least for the moment, he didn't seem plagued with worrisome questions about our brothers' possible involvement in the building of these types of fireworks. Or, maybe, he just didn't want to tell me his thoughts. He was so irritatingly practical. So one-day-at-a-time focused.

I could scarcely keep myself from grimacing when he said, "Okay. I'll meet you by the movie theater on Friday night. Try not to get yourself into any trouble before then."

"No one ever suspects *me* of getting into trouble," I shot back and had the satisfaction of seeing him squint at me for a second in consideration.

"Well, then, I guess people are underestimating you, Aurora." He grinned. "I'm not that dumb. Or, at least, not as dumb as you think." He got out of his car, slammed the door behind him and walked toward the office. "Go home," he said over his shoulder. "Talk to your parents. We're not going anywhere unless they say it's okay."

He didn't even turn back to wave. But I didn't need to get in the last word. I'd accomplished two out of my three missions for the week. Dale—*check*. Donovan—*check*. Only one more to go.

WEDNESDAY NIGHT, it was finally time for that conversation with my parents. I presented the idea to them casually, over a dinner I'd made of beef stew and Bisquick rolls.

"So, Donovan and I got to talking this week, and we both thought it'd probably be a good idea to take a look at a few colleges. We haven't seen many, and—"

"I always thought you wanted to go to school up here when you were ready for it," Mom said, instantly defensive. "In the Twin Cities. We've already shown you that campus."

And they had. With Gideon, during the fall of his senior year, in an unsuccessful attempt to convince him to apply to college.

"Oh, I know," I said, using my most soothing voice. "I guess, after hearing Betsy talk about it at the party over the weekend, I just wondered about some other places nearby. U of M still seems the best, but I just want to make sure, you know? I never even questioned it."

This happened to be one-hundred-percent true, so I was positive my delivery held the ring of sincerity, but my mother had that ever-present look of concern on her face, and I could see flashes of pain in her eyes at the memories of Gideon that such talk of university campuses always dredged up. One of the million reasons why I'd let my college plans drop away after my brother disappeared. And why my high-school graduation two weeks ago was an obligatory formality, not remotely like a celebration.

"How long will you be gone?" Mom asked, focusing on the time element only and not on the person I'd be traveling with. This was an encouraging oversight.

"A week, maybe," I said. "Hey, would anyone like more stew?" I lifted the ladle and smiled at my parents.

My mother put her spoon down and blinked. *"A week?"*

And my father, who'd been studying the chunks of vegetables and meat in his bowl with mild interest until then, finally spoke up. "I'll take you to the other colleges. Which ones do you want to go to?"

For a second, I didn't know what to say. I hadn't anticipated my dad suggesting he'd take me himself.

"Oh, no, Dad. That'd be too much time away from work for you. I want to see a couple of schools in Wisconsin, Illinois and Iowa. And I have to visit on weekdays when the admissions offices are open. It's not a problem for Donovan to take me. He's already going, and I—"

"You're not traveling around half the Midwest with a boy," my father stated. "I should have a few days of vacation time. You and I can go in the next week or two."

"But that's *unnecessary*," I insisted. "Donovan is already going. He's leaving this weekend, and he wants to see a lot of the same colleges that I do. It would be silly to waste gas and your vacation days when we don't need to. Plus, you *know* him. You know his family. He's not some dangerous stranger."

"Where, exactly, will you be sleeping while you're on this trip?" Dad crossed his arms and stared at me. "At a campground? In some cheap motel? In Donovan's car?" He shook his head as if trying to dismiss the image this thought created. "No. It's not safe."

"A lot of the universities have inexpensive housing nearby. There are motels that are almost like youth hostels and small bed-and-breakfast inns that are practically on campus. I'll make sure we're somewhere safe. You don't have to worry."

My dad pushed himself to standing. "I don't have to worry?" He tossed his napkin on his chair and stepped away from the table. "We've already lost one child. We're not losing another. The answer is no."

Before I could stop him, my father marched out of the room. In the distance I heard the TV being flipped on and the end of the "CBS Evening News" broadcast. Walter Cronkite was saying, "And that's the way it is June 14, 1978," and my dad was saying nothing at all. He was, however, making a racket picking up and crumpling old newspapers, something he did when he was agitated.

My mom had that haunted expression on her face, staring down at what remained of her stew, as if looking into a very murky crystal ball. I could sense her pain tangling with her feelings of guilt. Not just over Gideon, but over me, too. Remembering all the things I hadn't gotten to do because we'd lost my brother.

"Maybe...you should go," Mom murmured, not meeting my eye but talking to me just the same. "It would probably be good for you to see some new colleges." She put her elbow on the table and rested her head in her palm, closing her eyes. Almost unwilling, it seemed, to let our gazes meet for fear she'd change her mind. "We've known Donovan for years. He's not a wild boy," my mom added. "He'll be responsible, won't he?"

"Yes," I answered very truthfully. "He will." And though I didn't say this aloud, to myself I added, *That's because he's not a boy. He's a man. And that makes a world of difference.*

"I can talk with your father about it later," my mother said.

I went over to hug her. "Thanks, Mom."

But, once I'd put the leftovers away and washed the dishes (Mom had gone to lay down for a while), I found my dad alone, sitting in a living room devoid of newspapers, and staring at a few family photographs on the wall. The TV was a low hum in the background, and he was clearly not watching it.

I sat down on the sofa near him and stared at the pictures, too. There were framed photos of when Gideon and I had been babies, then preschoolers, then high-school students. Black and white snapshots— one of our mom perched on a wooden swing and one of our dad in his Marine blues from his days in the service. Pride and duty shown in his eyes. A large picture of our parents on their wedding day. And another of the four of us from Christmas 1975.

All happier times.

"Dad, I'm going to be eighteen in just a few weeks," I said. "I know you're worried about this trip, and I can understand that, but you don't have to be. I'm not one of those hippy types. I'm not going to be taking chances. And Donovan is very careful. He's been trained in the military. I'll be safe with him."

"You'd be safer at home," my father whispered.

I nodded. That was true. I wouldn't deny it.

"Is there something going on between you and this boy?" he asked. "I know you both share a…tragedy. But is there anything else? Anything I should know about?"

"No. It's not like that." Also, regrettably, true. "We just—we just have a common goal."

My father took a deep breath. "Well, then, we could invite him along with us. He could be our guest, and the three of us could go look at colleges together."

I smothered a sigh. This wasn't working like it was supposed to. I'd known from the beginning that my mom would need some reassurance. I hadn't realized my dad, being the good man he was, would need far more than that.

"Dad, please listen to what I'm saying." I waited until my father nodded and, slowly, turned his head to face me. "It's important that Donovan and I go on this trip alone." I met his gaze and held it.

And my dad, who had a touch of heightened perceptiveness about him—even if it wasn't so strong a trait as mine and even if he rarely chose to harness it—got a glint of curiosity in his eye that I hadn't seen for years. For *two* years, to be exact. "Why?" he asked.

I paused and inhaled a few times. It was critical that I explained this right.

"There's really only *one* thing Donovan and I have in common… and it isn't college plans," I said, taking a chance that honesty was my only hope in getting him to really loosen his grip. "Only one thing we both desperately want to know. *One*. And, Dad, you know what it is."

I watched as my father's facial expression slid into something odd and almost indecipherable. He glanced at Gideon's graduation photo, then over at me, then back at the wall of pictures again. Dad's eyes focused on my brother's easygoing smile and, under his chin, his strong fingers carefully curled—hiding the grease-stained nails in his fist while the ruby-and-gold graduation ring flashed outward to the world.

"You know something new about them?" he whispered. "Your brother and his friend? You have a hint about why they left?"

I didn't want to answer this. Didn't want to raise hope if I couldn't be sure. But, in many ways, my father's intuition had just moved beyond his need for me to supply the words. There was a watery glaze to his eyes and a battle on his face between belief and fear, hopefulness and despair.

"I love you, Dad," I said instead. "Donovan and I are going to find out for *all of us* whatever answers we can."

After that, he didn't say anything more about it. Didn't argue or try to talk me out of leaving. He just murmured, "Do you need money? Anything?"

I shook my head and moved to hug him.

He tugged me toward him and held me tight, pulling me into his arms like when I was a toddler. I could smell the scent of his pipe on his clothing. I could hear his heartbeat through his thin shirt. And I could feel his tears on the side of my cheek. They mingled with my own.

ON FRIDAY night, as I sat next to Betsy in our town's packed little cinema and watched cartoon animations of the cast sing, dance and proclaim that "Grease" was the word, there were two thoughts that kept running through my mind, hindering my ability to concentrate on the movie:

One, I needed to remember to pack a few more snapshots of Gideon and Jeremy. The photo I'd taken of them to Crescent Cove was okay, but I knew I could find better images.

And, two, what was Donovan doing *three rows behind me*…and who the hell was he sitting with?

I'd expected to see him outside of the theater. On the sidewalk. Not inside, watching John Travolta flirt with Olivia Newton-John. And most especially not rumbling with laughter at some of the racy lyrics to "Greased Lightning" while the shrill giggles of the girl he was with distracted half the audience.

Then again, maybe *I* was the only one distracted by her. Betsy didn't seem to have a problem paying attention to the film.

My friend elbowed me. "I don't see why anyone would like that mean Crater Face dude. Not even Cha-Cha." On the screen, good-guy Kenickie was getting ready to race the bad Scorpion leader for their cars' pink slips. "He's sort of evil looking, isn't he?"

"Yeah," I agreed.

But, a few minutes later, when Kenickie got knocked out and Danny Zuko, John Travolta's character, was doing the racing, I found myself really liking that nasty metal-and-tire-cutting attachment on the bad guy's fast car. I fantasized about using something like that on the wheels of Donovan's Trans Am if he couldn't get that girl he was with to shut up.

Second choice was to pelt a few Milk Duds at her. I peeked inside my box of candy. Still had about four or five hard caramel-chocolate balls left.

Thankfully, the film finally ended and, when the houselights came up, I turned to get a good look at this person Donovan had brought along. She was tall—nearly the same height as him—blondish and, from the frequency of her laughter, easily amused.

I narrowed my eyes when I saw him put his arm around the blonde, grin and whisper something that made the other girl absolutely hoot at the hilarity of it.

Betsy nudged me. "C'mon, let's go."

I nodded my head in Donovan's direction. "Okay, but I have to talk with *him* for a minute before we get out of here."

My friend shot me a sideways glance. "With Donovan McCafferty? Why?"

I tried to explain in a couple of short sentences about how he and I were trekking to visit a few colleges together. "I just need to double check the time we're leaving tomorrow."

Betsy smirked at the display of lovey-dovey affection going on right in front of us as half the population of Chameleon Lake marched passed us and out of the theater. "Well, I'd ask you if something was going on between the two of you, enough so that he's driving you to a bunch of different campuses, but I think he's got his hands full already."

And in that second, I saw Donovan checking out the number of residents who'd walked down the aisle to the exit, marking the people who'd already seen him and the blonde together and had surely tagged them as a serious couple. He raised an eyebrow at me quickly and then turned his attention to his girlfriend of the night, saying something else that seemed overly intimate for the setting.

Which, of course, was exactly his intention.

But, even though I sensed he'd set this all up on my behalf—so there'd be no malicious gossip about us while we were gone, no more relationship questions from my friends or my parents—I was irritated by it. And even when the four of us had finally walked out and were standing face to face in the lobby, I still couldn't shake it.

"I really wouldn't have pegged you as a Travolta fan," I told him with mock sweetness. "I'll have to remember to bring my 'Saturday Night Fever' cassette along for the trip. We can listen to some disco on the drive."

He pulled the blonde—whom he'd introduced to us as "Vicky from St. Cloud"—closer to him and laughed. But I could hear the steel in his voice when he said, "You *young* girls…always so into silly fads."

I glared at him. I'd had more than enough of that *young girl* crap.

Before I could say anything in return, Donovan added, "So, about tomorrow, is eight a.m. too early for you? The sooner we hit the road, the sooner we can come back." He sent Vicky a look of longing that made me want to puke.

"Eight in the morning is *just fine*," I stated. "I'll be ready even earlier than that, but, you know—" I feigned a shrug. "*I'm* not going to be up very late tonight."

He waited to make a face at me until Betsy and Vicky were both looking elsewhere. A junior-high kid had spilled what remained of his buttered popcorn on the red carpet, and the knowing glance Donovan gave me during that temporary distraction left me with little doubt that he sensed my jealousy. And I *was* jealous. Maybe it was stupid, but I couldn't help how I felt.

"Well, we should get going." He squeezed Vicky's shoulder, and she nuzzled up to him. "Bye, Betsy," he said. "Aurora, g'night. See you tomorrow."

We waved them off—a braided ribbon of anxiety, frustration and something else churning deep inside my gut. I did, at least, have the satisfaction of hearing Vicky say to Donovan as they walked away, "Do you really think disco is a *fad?*"

I bit my lip to keep from laughing. Donovan was the living antithesis of anything remotely "disco," which meant I knew just how to make him suffer on the trip for taunting me so much tonight. I was in possession of *several* Bee Gees cassettes and, oh, I wasn't kidding about bringing them along.

"Do you have time to get a milkshake at Rudy's tonight, or do you still have some packing to do?" my friend asked me.

"There are just a couple other things I have to still add in," I said. *Photos of our brothers. Tire-slashing tools. Bee Gees music.* "But I can do that right before bed. It'll be fun to talk about the movie for an hour."

Betsy grinned at me. "It was great, wasn't it? I wish I could sing like Olivia Newton-John! And I would've loved to have lived in the Fifties with those cute poodle skirts and guys in leather jackets, going to drive-ins and sock hops…"

I listened to my friend rhapsodize about life two decades ago—although Betsy's current world couldn't have been more like her fantasy. It was still all about milkshakes, dances and frivolous movies. She didn't need to be in the Fifties for that. (Maybe just for the poodle skirts.) But Betsy didn't see it the way I did. Didn't see the pure simplicity of her life.

Over chocolate malteds, I let her chatter while my mind drifted ahead to the morning, to being with Donovan and to pressing on in the search for our brothers. Three obstacles down, zero left to battle…at least here at home. Who knew how many challenges were ahead once we were on the road, though?

At one point, Betsy mentioned how we'd run into Donovan, and my attention was fully engaged again.

"He seemed to really like that blond girl," my friend said unhelpfully. "It's good that he's trying to find happiness, you know. After everything."

She paused then sent me a goofy look, like one of the many we'd shared early on in high school when teen life had been amusing and uncomplicated. "Hey, do you think he's one of those guys who'll stop at payphones to call her five times a day?" She laughed at the mental image. "Or pick up souvenirs for her at every campus?"

"No," I said. That wasn't going to happen even if he *was* that type.

"Ha! I didn't think so. He seems so…moody. You know, serious and brooding sometimes, but then kind of funny and flirtatious." Betsy fancied herself liking "moodiness" in a guy ever since she'd read about Mr. Rochester in *Jane Eyre*. "Are you, like, excited about taking this trip with him and seeing the colleges?" she asked. "Or more nervous?"

"A little nervous," I admitted. "Mostly because the future is so… uncertain."

I studied my friend after I said that, knowing Betsy would understand the words but not look or listen for nuances. She wouldn't think beyond the obvious and, maybe, it wasn't fair to expect that of her. But I also knew she wouldn't probe further. Wouldn't ask for clarification or question anything I said in a way that wasn't light, breezy and as shallow as a cookie sheet.

It was a problem I had with people again and again in my life, even before Gideon had disappeared. There were too many situations others took at face value. A useful trait when I needed to withhold important information for safety's sake. A disappointing one when I hoped to form a truly genuine connection.

"Well, I hope you guys have a good time," Betsy said brightly, slurping the last of her shake. "He's kinda cute, but at least you don't have to worry about him coming on to you or anything. He'll probably spend half the trip mooning over Vicky."

"Probably," I said, smiling, though it hurt to do so.

Yes, it irked me that Donovan played these flirtation games with other girls, but the pain I felt didn't stem from that. I knew he'd been acting again. The ache went deeper. To my friendships in Chameleon Lake and the transitory nature of them. Yet another anchor, tying me to home, that had just been released.

THE NEXT morning came quickly and, like clockwork, Donovan pulled into our driveway at eight a.m.

My parents walked out of the house with me, shook hands with him and said soft superficial things that were in love's code:

Mom: "Drive safely." *We can't lose you, too.*

Dad: "Don't forget to take breaks." *Please stay alert.*

Mom: "Call us and let us know how things are going." *We need to be sure everything's okay.*

Both Donovan and I promised all of these. Promised we'd be very careful, check in every night by phone, not take chances. I had a list of emergency phone numbers and some money I'd saved up from work. Dad slipped me fifty dollars more, and Mom handed us a thermos with hot coffee, a couple of sandwiches and a few blueberry muffins for the road.

By silent agreement, my dad and I didn't let on to my mom that the trip was anything more than a routine college-scouting expedition. It was better that way, we both knew.

So, when Mom hugged me goodbye and said, "I hope you find the perfect campus...one where all your dreams will come true," my heart broke a little at her trust and hopefulness on my behalf.

And, when I met my dad's eye, I could barely contain within me the bursting love I felt for both of my parents and, though I hated to admit it, the surprising surge of anger I felt toward Gideon.

How could he be alive and not tell us? How could he keep hurting us *all* this way?

"I'll take good care of her," Donovan whispered to my dad.

"Just bring her home safe," Dad murmured back, both of them—I was sure of it—thinking I hadn't overheard them.

"I will," Donovan replied. "I give you my word." A pledge between two former military men that I suspected was stronger than law, or even life.

Chapter Six

Chicago, Illinois ~ Saturday, June 17

"CHICAGO'S NOT like Crescent Cove, you know," Donovan said, stating the obvious for at least the third time since we'd left Chameleon Lake that morning. "It's not some one-street backwater town where we can just drive through it and pick up clues about two random guys who were there a couple of years ago. We're flying blind."

"We're not," I countered, flipping to the middle of Gideon's journal and reading the *Chicago* page yet again:

Washer fluid
Antifreeze
Motor oil
Sparkplugs
Mercury switch

Radiator pressure gauge

I noted there was a slight ink change here.

Thursday, May 13, 1976
J & I in Chicago
M + 2, D - 9
Amy Lynn_____Best TV
show on Saturday
morning

"Look, I don't know the significance of all the details on this page, but I'm sure Gideon gave us some clues. I've been thinking about this ever since you figured out there were different shades of ink. On this page, the ink change is between the radiator pressure gauge and the date, and 'J & I in Chicago' is right underneath that." I paused. "There's something about all this that's been bugging me ever since I read it."

Donovan took his eyes off the road long enough to glance over at me. "What?"

"For Crescent Cove, it's possible our brothers were there on a Monday—a weekday—in the middle of the school year. Twice," I said. "I looked on an old calendar back home and Monday, April 19, 1976, the first time they went to Crescent Cove, was the day after Easter Sunday, and we had no school that day. The next time they went to Wisconsin, three weeks later, it was mid-May and seniors were skipping days all over the place. So, the guys could've been gone eight or nine hours that day without Mom, Dad or me noticing. Seven hours on the road, plus an hour or two visiting."

Donovan nodded. He was listening. Good.

I pointed to the journal. "But there's no way the two of them went to Chicago three days later, on a Thursday. They not only would have had to skip school, they'd have been gone half the night. It's eight hours one way. *Sixteen hours* roundtrip."

I shot him a significant look. "Jeremy and Gideon didn't go to Tulsa, Oklahoma on May twenty-sixth either—a Wednesday while school was in session. So the dates and the places can't be connected. Or, if they're connected, something about the listing is off somehow. The dates or places are wrong. Or the whole thing means something else."

He shrugged. "Yeah, that's because *none* of it makes any sense."

I flipped between pages in the journal and tried to decipher Gideon's hints. I wasn't about to tell Donovan this because he'd press me to try to explain, but I just couldn't shake the feeling that Gideon and Jeremy had been to *all* of the cities mentioned.

J & I in Chicago.

What did it mean, though, that I knew they weren't there on the date listed? That Gideon had deliberately written down a day that they for sure could *not* have been there?

"I'm going to figure this out," I told Donovan. "I'm not positive what Gideon was trying to tell us just yet, but I know this wasn't accidental."

"We're flying blind," he muttered.

"We're *not*," I insisted again. "Because I did figure out one clue that I think will be useful." I studied him as he changed lanes to stay on I-90, as the I-90/I-94 Interstates split just south of Madison. In less than three hours, we'd be in Chicago. He didn't argue with me or even bother to ask what I'd discovered, so I said, "Amy Lynn."

"You know her or something?"

"No, but it's what Gideon wrote *after* her name that gives me the clue. The line begins with Amy Lynn, but then there's a blank right after her name. Then there are the words 'Best TV show on Saturday morning.'"

"Okay." He smirked a little, clearly unimpressed but at least moderately humored. "So Amy Lynn is…what? Someone on a cartoon? A big fan of them? A character in one? Is there an Amy Lynn on 'Scooby Doo'…or maybe on 'Land of the Lost' or 'Shazam'?"

I shook my head. "That's just it. That's one of the reasons why I'm so sure Gideon is alive and giving us clues to follow. Because that line is an inside joke that no one outside of our family would know."

Donovan raised a single disbelieving eyebrow. "Because it means…?"

"Because it means 'dreams.' Gideon never woke up before eleven-thirty on a Saturday and didn't watch TV at all on weekend mornings. He always said, 'The best TV show on Saturday morning is my dreams.' So, I think this was his way of telling us Amy Lynn's last name without actually giving it to us."

"Why couldn't he? I don't see why your brother didn't just write the name down in his journal, too."

"Maybe it would be dangerous for her to talk with us. Or, maybe, it would be dangerous for *us* to be in contact with *her*—if someone bad knew about it."

"Amy Lynn Dreams?" he said, trying it out. He shook his head. "Sounds like a flower-child name."

"Well, when we get to the city, we'll look it up in the phonebook. Maybe…maybe we'll find her there and we can see for ourselves."

He continued to look dubious, but he didn't turn the Trans Am around, which I considered an encouraging sign. At least he was committed to getting us to Chicago, although every one of his nonverbal cues pointed toward his disbelief that we'd find anything at all useful once we got there.

I also sensed that, perhaps, he was *hoping* this would be the case. Then we could put this search behind us.

Because the day was so bright and the highways we were taking so busy with weekend travelers, Donovan didn't want to chance pulling over somewhere and setting off the last of the fireworks. "It's not remote enough," he said. "Plus, I don't want to get an out-of-state ticket—or worse—if we get caught."

So, the only stops we made were for gas and bathroom breaks and, briefly once, we made a visit to McDonald's to grab burgers, fries and shakes for lunch. The anticipation of the week ahead made the food roil uneasily in my stomach, but I figured it wouldn't do to faint from hunger later in the day, especially in the middle of a metropolis with three million people.

It was after four p.m. when we emerged through the sprawl of the western suburbs and entered the city of Chicago.

"Okay, we're here, Nancy Drew," Donovan said. "What now?" He rubbed his eyes and looked tired enough from the day of driving for me to take some pity on him and not slug him in the arm like I wanted to.

"Now we need to find a phone booth," I told him.

It took us a few minutes to spot one in the parking lot near a movie theater. I noticed that "Grease" was playing here as well, along with three other films. Imagine living in a place where *four* movies were shown every day. It was that type of thing I loved so much about life outside of Chameleon Lake. The incredible number of choices. The options paired with anonymity.

We parked and walked to the empty booth. "There's no directory," I said, pointing to the silvery chain where the phonebook had once been attached.

"Damn." He picked up the receiver and dug his hand deep into his jeans pocket, retrieving a dime. "Well, we can call the operator—"

I snatched the phone from his hand. "No. I want us to look up her name ourselves. I don't just want to be connected to her line without knowing anything about her. Her address, for instance, or if there's anyone else listed with her."

"Or if this person even exists," Donovan added sarcastically. "It could be that there's no one by that name anywhere in the city. I think the whole idea to come here was—"

"I already know what you think." I glanced across the street. "There's a gas station over there. Don't they usually have phone directories?"

He shrugged a halfhearted "yes."

Sure enough, when we asked the older guy behind the counter, he pulled out a thick copy of the phonebook and plunked it down in front of us.

I flashed the guy a smile and began flipping to the "D's" just as soon as he turned his attention to one of the other customers.

Dream, James P., 23 Park Ave W......... 324-5645
Dreamsly, Steve, 1556 Green Bay Rd 354-9091

Dreamson, Amy L., 653 Ashton St, Apt 301-C 467-8207
Dreamstrand, William & Gail, 21006 Michigan Ave 316-0866

Amy L. Dreamson. Amy Lynn?

I pointed at the name. "Pretty close to what I thought," I whispered. "I think this is her. It'd be too much of a coincidence otherwise."

Donovan made a doubtful face and glanced away.

I pulled a pen and mini notepad out of my purse and jotted down the address and phone number. "Thanks," I told the guy as I handed the big book back.

Donovan nodded at him, too, and bought a dollar's worth of Kit Kat bars. "Snack," he told me, though I was mystified that he could even think of eating right then.

We walked back across the street to the phone booth and Donovan unwrapped one of the candy bars and snapped off the first chocolate-covered wafer. He waved it in front of my nose, but I took a step back and shook my head.

"Suit yourself," he said, crunching the stick in half. "Want me to make the call?" He devoured the other half of the wafer in one bite and broke off a second one.

For the first time since I'd met him, he looked *young* to me. Like a ten-year-old kid chomping on his Halloween candy. And I got a hint of what he must have been like as a boy, on a day when he was happy and unfettered by life's burdens. There was a fun-loving recklessness lurking just beneath the surface, waiting to emerge.

"You look...preoccupied," I told him with a scowl. "I'll call the number."

He shrugged, as if not caring, and handed me a dime. But, as he gobbled down his third chocolate wafer, I understood the reason he needed a snack. I knew a nervous habit when I saw one. The tremor that ran through his hand as he watched me reach for the phone was a dead giveaway.

I punched in the phone number and waited—my stomach flipping—as it rang. After five long rings, someone picked it up. A woman.

"Hello?" she said with a voice that sounded younger than I'd expected.

I cleared my throat. "Hello," I said back. "May I speak with Amy Lynn Dreamson, please?"

There was a longish pause on the line, and I could almost feel the woman's hesitation. "This is Amy Lynn," she said at last, quietly. "May I ask who's calling?"

I swallowed. Hard. And Donovan, who was listening attentively next to me, stuffed the last of his Kit Kat into his mouth and swiped his lips with the back of his hand.

"Yes," I said, realizing suddenly that I hadn't thought out this next part when I envisioned myself contacting Amy Lynn. Didn't know what, exactly, to say.

I cleared my throat again. "My name is Aurora Gray. You and I have never met, and you may not know anything about me at all, but I believe you might have met my brother and his best friend. They… they, um, visited Chicago two summers ago."

There was another long pause. "What were their names?" the lady asked, and I couldn't help but detect a hint of dread in her soft voice.

"Gideon," I said. "That's my brother. And—"

"Jeremy," Amy Lynn whispered, interrupting. "Right?"

"Right," I managed to say. *Oh, God! So they really were here! When? Why?*

Beside me, Donovan was as still as if he'd been flash frozen.

"Yeah," the woman said. "They were here. Have you, um, talked to them recently?"

"No," I admitted. "They…they haven't been home since then. I was hoping you might know something about what happened that summer."

Amy Lynn's breath caught. "There are a few things I could tell you, but I'd rather not talk on the phone. Where are you?"

"In Chicago," I replied, my heart pounding. "It won't be a problem to meet you wherever or whenever you want. Are you free today? Tonight? Tomorrow morning?"

I needed to see her in person. To find out what she knew about my brother, of course, but also so I could study her reactions face to face. There were only so many signals I could read over the telephone.

"Are you alone?"

I shook my head, aware that my pulse was racing against itself and my throat had begun to clog up. Then I realized the lady on the line couldn't see me.

"No," I said, explaining that Donovan was with me.

"Jeremy's older brother." Amy Lynn stated this with a certainty that was both gratifying and anxiety producing. "I knew about him," she added. "Army guy, right?"

"Right."

Donovan, who was able to hear every word, not only looked as unmoving as a marble statue, he now looked as pale as one.

"Okay. He can come, too, but no one else," Amy Lynn said, giving me her address, which matched exactly the one we'd found in the phonebook, and suggesting we meet her there at six o'clock.

She paused and made a sound that was almost like a laugh, but a little strangled and uneasy. "I've been waiting to hear from you for a few days," Amy Lynn murmured in the seconds before she hung up. "Gideon said you might be coming."

THE DRIVE to Amy Lynn's apartment in the Portage Park neighborhood only took about twenty minutes, even with the busy Saturday-night traffic. Figuring out where 653 Ashton Street was, however, took twice as long as that and required Donovan to finally buy a city of Chicago map, because, God knew, he was too cool to even consider asking for directions.

But we did manage to get there with twelve minutes to spare and find one of the few available parking spots. We waited impatiently in Donovan's car until my watch read two minutes to six.

"Let's go in," he said, every muscle in his body so taut, he looked like he might snap.

The security in the four-story brick building was stronger than in most of the apartment complexes I'd seen in Chameleon Lake or even in Minneapolis/St. Paul. We couldn't just walk in and take the stairs up. We had to press a button to be buzzed into the lobby first.

Donovan knocked on the door to 301-C, his body language a study in rigidity and seriousness. I could tell this Amy Lynn person was taking her sweet time inside and checking us out. A shadow passed behind the keyhole, and a number of bolts needed to be unlocked on the other side of the heavy oak door before it swung even halfway open.

When, at last, it did, I got a good view of the woman who'd been on the other end of the line during our phone conversation. I had to admit my surprise.

I'd always considered myself kind of on the mousy-looking side, being of slight build and fair complexion, with longish light-brown hair that hung limp, just past my shoulders, unless I pulled it back into a ponytail. But Amy Lynn took "mousy" to the tenth power.

She was around twenty-five years old, painfully thin, with wrists so delicate and pale that the veins protruded. Her short, goldish hair was pixie-like in style, giving her face and features a look that reminded me of Peter Pan. Her eyes—clear, blue and wary—studied me right back.

I introduced myself and Donovan, using a well-honed super-calm voice and working to put this new person at ease. With the back of my palm pressed against his chest, I physically held Donovan in the hallway, keeping him from stepping forward into the apartment until Amy Lynn was ready to receive us.

She kept us waiting longer than I'd expected but, thankfully, Donovan took my lead and allowed me to watch Amy Lynn's reactions. He gave me time to carefully adjust my mannerisms until I felt the two of us girls were on a similar vibration. Until I could sense she was sure of us.

To my eye, Amy Lynn might have given off an air of timidity at first glance, but I could feel a resolute core beneath her fragile appearance. When she smiled carefully and stepped back to allow us to enter, I got the distinct sense that she was, in fact, choreographing every move.

Her first words to us weren't greetings. Instead, she said, "You both resemble your brothers." Then she turned to Donovan and added, "Especially you."

I watched him process this. While I didn't understand him so well as to be able to gauge half of his responses in advance, I knew him well enough to realize an inquisition was coming. Soon.

"How did you meet him?" Donovan asked almost immediately. He glanced at me for a split second, then back at Amy Lynn. "How did you meet them both—Jeremy and Gideon?"

The slender woman nodded and motioned for us to sit down. My insides twisted wildly at the thought of her parting words on the phone and the questions that were burning my tongue. I couldn't wait a second longer to ask, "And *when* did Gideon tell you we might be coming? *How* did he contact you?"

But the other woman shook her head slightly and said, "I promise I'll get to all of that. This—" She pointed at me then at Donovan then at herself. "This is all a little overwhelming for me, too. Just let me organize my thoughts so I can tell you both the whole story."

So, I was forced to bide my time, knowing it was too important a meeting to screw up with impatience. But that didn't mean I wasn't itching to hurry her along. And Donovan looked like he was about to jump out of his skin with restless anxiety.

I forced myself to sit politely at the edge of the sofa, a foot away from Donovan, acutely aware of the tension straining his leg muscles, the rigidity of his torso and the pressure of his fingertips as they dug into the cushion between us, surely leaving angry indentations in the thinning fabric.

But then, when Amy Lynn started to speak in a curiously measured and melodious voice, I began to lose myself in her story, as cleverly executed as if by a professional narrator.

"I've been waiting to tell someone about this for a long time," she said and, from my perspective, Amy Lynn did look more relieved than fearful. "In the spring of 1976, I'd just moved in with my new boyfriend, Patrick Bradley—everyone called him Treak—who was a couple of years older than me and a reporter for the *Chicago Tribune*."

She nodded at a copy she had of the newspaper on her coffee table.

"I was an actress back then, only getting small parts in small theaters, and while I liked to think my big break was on the verge of finally happening, I suspected my life probably wouldn't play out that way. That I wouldn't end up being *discovered* and landing in a Broadway show or in a Hollywood movie. More likely, I was on the fast track to being either a strung-out hostess at an adults-only nightclub or a married mom juggling three kids and a sheepdog." She laughed but I wasn't reading a lot of genuine humor in her expression.

"Anyway, I figured when Treak asked me to move into his south side apartment with him, this would be a better choice than doing lap dances at dive bars on Mannheim Road to pay for groceries, so I did."

Amy Lynn shrugged. "Back then, everybody who knew me called me by my stage name, Chelsea Carew. My parents lived in western Ohio, and I hadn't bothered to get a driver's license when I moved to Chicago because I didn't have a car. Since most of my work transactions were done 'under the table,' so to speak, I avoided stuff like filing income taxes and, because I was crashing on the floors or the sofas of other actors' apartments, my name never showed up on a lease. Turns out, the fact that I was pretty much an irresponsible adult probably saved my life."

Donovan was listening intently to her, and Amy Lynn, in turn, studied him carefully before continuing, her words something she seemed to weigh like fresh produce at the Grocery Mart.

"One day, about a month after I moved in, Treak came home all excited because he'd finally gotten a lead on a big story he was working on. Only problem was that he'd need to be gone—out of town somewhere—to work on it. I wasn't going to get to see him for at least a week. Maybe two." She looked at us and then away. "The first few nights he was away, he'd call me and we'd chat. Things still seemed normal, but then his digging led him to this little town in Wisconsin. Crescent Cove."

I inhaled a sudden rush of air, but it didn't help. Yet another link between my brother, his best friend and that Wisconsin town—it made me lightheaded.

Start here, Gideon had written.

I struggled not to slump back against the sofa cushions and cradle my head in my palms, but Amy Lynn noticed the change in me.

"Are you okay?" she asked.

I forced a nod. "Yes, please go on. So, you're saying your boyfriend followed some clues for a story and they led him to Crescent Cove?"

"Yes," Amy Lynn replied. "That's where he eventually ended up. We were talking less frequently by then. He'd call only once every few days and usually just for five or ten minutes. He was hot on the trail of something, and he was busy with it for hours at a time. Almost all day and well into the night. The last time he called me was on July 1, 1976. It was a Thursday afternoon."

Donovan bowed his head, bit his lip and then said, in a very stilted voice, "Do you mean that was the last time Treak called you on that trip? Or the last time you ever heard from him?"

"Both," Amy Lynn replied.

She let this sink in, belatedly asking if either of us wanted something to drink, almost enjoying the dramatic moment, I felt. Definitely a former actress.

But, much as I hated the skilled performance and the pregnant pauses used to great effect, I also strongly sensed that there was very little exaggeration in Amy Lynn's retelling. Sure, her delivery bordered on stagey, but the actress formerly known as Chelsea Carew didn't need to heighten the tension with unnecessary theatrics. The real story provided more than enough natural drama.

Donovan and I both declined a drink and pressed Amy Lynn to tell us what happened next.

"Sunday morning, about two a.m. on the Fourth of July, I got a phone call out of nowhere from these guys I didn't know. They sounded really scared, and just being shaken awake like that made me really scared, too. They told me I was in a lot of danger. That they had some stuff of Treak's and had to give it to me, but that I needed to get myself somewhere safer first."

She slanted an odd smile at us. "Of course, I thought they were wackos, and I almost hung up on them. But one of the guys started listing all kinds of things he knew about me because of their conversations with my boyfriend. And then he listed all kinds of things he knew about Treak. And he said—I'll never forget this—'I know you don't want to believe us, and I know you have to be freaking out getting this kind of a call, but we saw two men get blown up in an explosion tonight, and Treak was one of them. I'm sorry to be the one to have to tell you that, but I'll be even sorrier if you get killed, too, when I could've helped prevent it. So take what you need. Take anything with your picture or with your name on it. Any important documents. Then get the hell out of there, Chelsea.' And I listened to him," Amy Lynn said. "That was how I met your brothers."

I tried to digest this. I knew, even without Amy Lynn telling me so, that Gideon was the one who had been listing things during that phone call.

It was very much like him. I could picture all too well what had happened that night, at least from the point where there was an explosion at Bonner Mill—killing Ben Rainwater and the unknown man, who must have been Treak, I realized—and then Jeremy and Gideon racing out of Crescent Cove, stopping somewhere to call and warn Amy Lynn.

But I still didn't know what had set off that chain of events. Who had caused the explosion and why. Although, thank God, it didn't seem to be either of our brothers who'd done it—at least not on purpose.

Donovan seemed to be thinking through this chronologically, too, and he was a few steps ahead of me.

"If you left Treak's apartment, how were Jeremy and Gideon able to find you?" he asked. "How long after that did you actually meet them in person?"

Amy Lynn squinted a bit, remembering. "Well, I still didn't totally trust them then, but I knew there was only one place in Chicago I could go to that no one in my current life knew about. It was my friend Karen's place, and she lived on the far north side of the city. Unlike most of the people I hung around with, she wasn't an aspiring actress, and she wasn't someone who knew Treak and his small circle of friends either. She was a grad student at Northwestern."

"Living alone?" Donovan asked.

"Yes, she did. So, I told Gideon and Jeremy that I'd meet them on the Evanston campus that afternoon, just outside of the student union. School wasn't in session, of course, but there were always college kids roaming around, so I figured I could blend in with the crowd pretty well, especially on a national holiday." She paused. "I knew it was them the second I saw them, though. They looked real jumpy and they were the only two people on the lawn who weren't smiling."

"Did the three of you talk right there? At the student union?" I asked her.

She nodded. "We didn't go in, but we found a private area to one side of the building where we could talk without being interrupted and where no one would be able to hear our whispers. Gideon and Jeremy introduced themselves to me and showed me the business card they'd gotten from Treak. That's how they'd known which phone number to call. They showed me other papers of his, too. Some notes he'd taken on this story he was working on. I was pretty much a mess, though, and I could barely concentrate on what they were saying at first. I hadn't slept since they'd awakened me, and the fact that a guy I liked a lot, someone I was living with, might really be dead had just begun to sink in."

Just remembering that day made Amy Lynn look shaken and pale. I knew how she felt. Even two years later, whenever I thought back on that moment when we first suspected Gideon and Jeremy were *missing*, not just out having fun somewhere, I felt a dark wave of nausea.

"The whole day was as bizarre as it was scary," Amy Lynn admitted.

"It didn't feel real to me at all, even though I'd done what they said. I'd all but erased evidence of myself from Treak's apartment. I threw my clothes, photo albums, important papers and a few keepsakes—I didn't have much—into one large suitcase. Then I grabbed my playbills, a few 8-tracks and cassettes, Treak's address book and a gold chain with a St. Christopher's medallion that he'd loved because it had once been his grandfather's. The patron saint of travelers. I wish he would have worn it to Wisconsin," she said wistfully.

"Anyway, I stuffed those things in my bag, too, and took my purse, filling it with whatever cash I could find. I also raided Treak's private dresser drawer, where he kept a couple of emergency one-hundred-dollar bills. My secret worry was that Gideon and Jeremy were lying to me, and that Treak would come home that day and think I'd robbed him and then left him without even a note." She shuddered. "It was horrible to imagine how betrayed he'd feel, but that was only because I was avoiding trying to accept that your brothers might *not* be lying. But then, when I saw the two of them—"

"Yes?" Donovan prompted.

"Then the horror of it hit me hard. They seemed too frightened, both for themselves and for me, to be making it all up. I'd been around lots of actors. Good ones. Bad ones. Not even the exceptionally gifted ones could've pulled off that kind of fear."

Amy Lynn suddenly stood and started pacing around the room, her own very composed performance having begun to unravel at last.

"Turned out, Jeremy and Gideon weren't just here to tell me about what happened to Treak and this guy named Ben Rainwater," she said, "but they also wanted *me* to fill in some gaps for *them*. The part of the story they didn't know. Stuff about his reporter's life before he went to Crescent Cove. And, while I could give them a little more information, there were huge chunks I didn't know myself."

My head began to throb. A low but rising ache that started behind my eyes and pulsed outward. A sob I'd tried to contain threatened to come out if I didn't get more answers. But I had *so* many questions…I didn't know which to ask first.

"What did they say about Treak and Ben?" I said. "How did your boyfriend even *know* Ben Rainwater?"

"Treak didn't know him. Not until he went up to Crescent Cove," Amy Lynn replied. "At the time, all I knew about the story Treak was working on was that it involved some shady Chicago union stuff. Something about problems in the city because of the power struggles between the workers' unions—mostly the Teamsters—and the mob. Reporters were covering all different angles, but the one Treak was working on led him to a trucker from out of state. A guy from Wisconsin."

"From Crescent Cove," Donovan murmured.

The woman nodded. "Treak went up there to investigate, and he met Ben Rainwater after a few days. Ben was an amateur filmmaker, did you know that?"

We shook our heads.

"From what Treak said, Ben was just getting started. He'd bought an 8mm camera a few months before and was filming things for fun, whenever he had time, and trying to learn the best shots. He worked in his cousin's shop—some little grocery store, I guess—but filming was his passion. Treak liked him right away and said he was a natural behind the camera. Told me Ben was going to show him some film footage that he'd shot in and around the town." She paused. "That was our last conversation."

"I'm sorry," I whispered.

"Me, too," Amy Lynn said. She bit her lip and inhaled a few times. "Anyway, I came to the same conclusion that you're probably coming to now. That the filmmaker caught something on camera he wasn't supposed to see. Your brothers knew all about it. They'd seen the film, too. They were in Crescent Cove that weekend and they'd actually watched it *with* Treak and Ben. That film reel was one of the things they brought me, along with a few pages of my boyfriend's notes."

"Where is it? The film?" Donovan said, speaking softly but it came across as a demand nonetheless. "And what's on it?"

"It's in a safe place," she replied. "I only watched it once, by myself, a few weeks after they gave it to me. And I only half understood what I was seeing."

"Can we see it?" he asked, his breath shallower than normal. "Please?"

"Of course," Amy Lynn said. "I'd already planned to show you. But I'd need to borrow a projector. I might be able to arrange to do that tomorrow. The landlord is a friend of mine, and I know he has one, but he won't be home until really late tonight."

Donovan, quite clearly, didn't look like he could be that patient.

I was feeling my own frustrations rising. If there were answers to be had, I wanted them *now*. "You must have some idea of what your boyfriend was uncovering in Crescent Cove," I said to her. "Just from talking to our brothers and reading Treak's notes. It had to be something really big to put them all in such danger."

"Yes," she said. "So big that Treak didn't want to talk about it on the phone. So big that I had to pull the details out of your brothers. They were afraid to tell me more than they had to when they saw me because, in their opinion, the less I knew, the safer I was."

She peered out the window. "They made me promise on my grandmother's grave that I wouldn't contact the police or report Treak missing. That I would go back to using my real name, cut off contact with the people I knew from my actress life and stay away from Treak's apartment. That if the cops were to ever manage to piece together that Chelsea Carew and Amy Lynn Dreamson were the same person, I should deny knowing anything more about Treak's disappearance. I was just supposed to say that he was a jerk who'd left me one day and never came back. That I had no idea why."

Her expression turned hard as she stopped pacing and sank into a chair across from us. "I can't express just how difficult it was to try to absorb all of this that day. I'd taken the train up to my friend's place, and Karen let me in at six a.m. without any questions. But what your brothers were asking me to do was going to require me to explain at least a few things to her, and I didn't want to do that if I didn't have to. Especially if this was all so dangerous."

She massaged her forehead for a moment. "The Bicentennial fireworks were set for that night. It was a big deal, so I watched them with Karen and a few of her friends, and then I slept like the dead afterward because I was so exhausted. The next day was a Monday, but it was a holiday because the Fourth of July had been on Sunday. I couldn't stop thinking about Treak and everything that happened in the past twenty-four hours."

I remembered that weekend well. Gideon had been gone on overnight trips before, so my family didn't panic at first when he hadn't shown up for the big fireworks celebration. But when, after a whole weekend away, he wasn't there on Monday either, or on Tuesday…

Amy Lynn said, "The first time I could slip away was on Monday afternoon. I took the train back down to the old neighborhood—just to see if Treak's car was there. Maybe peek in the apartment and check for any last things I should bring along. But I didn't even go in the building. His Chevy was nowhere in sight, but there were three cop cars lined up outside, and I could see a couple of officers milling around inside his second-floor apartment as I looked up from the street into his front window. I hid in the shadow of the doorway of the apartment complex across the street and watched for half an hour as policemen went in empty-handed and came out carting boxes of Treak's files."

She shivered in the summer heat. "It was awfully strange that they'd shown up there so fast, taking his papers with them. And I knew then that your brothers had been right to warn me. To be scared. There was something really *off* about the cops raiding his place. Treak wasn't, perhaps, the one true love of my life, but he was an honest man. A dedicated reporter. And a seeker of the truth. Whatever the police were looking for, I didn't get the sense that it was to protect him."

Her expression pleaded with us to understand. She'd *cared* about Treak Bradley—as a friend and fellow human, if not as a lover. And I could tell he'd been kind to her when few others had. She was helping us because, even two years after he was dead, she still wanted to help *him*.

"Something about the intensity of the cops made me think that whatever the police were looking for wasn't just about him," Amy Lynn said. "I doubted he would've been important enough for that kind of attention and focus. I think they were looking for something else. Some dirt on someone or, maybe, a way to protect somebody or some group. I felt like I'd dodged a heck of a lot of trouble, thanks to your brothers, and I hoped that Treak's work wouldn't be in vain. Especially after I saw his obituary in the *Chicago Tribune* a week later."

She grimaced. "It read to me like a monstrous lie, and I don't know if that was the fault of the press or the cops. All I know is that the paper wrote he'd been killed in 'a car accident in rural Wisconsin' on Independence Day. That there were no witnesses but 'evidence at the scene' showed he'd been driving too fast and had collided with a cement divider. That there was an explosion and his body was badly burned, so much so that his grieving parents in Indiana were sent only his ashes. Now wasn't that convenient?" Amy Lynn's bitterness at this was impossible to hide. "I knew then that my old life had ended."

Yours wasn't the only one.

"Could we, maybe, take a look at his notes in a bit?" I asked. "I don't know if anything written in them will stand out as a clue, but it's possible Donovan or I might recognize something."

Amy Lynn nodded. "You can try. I'll pull them out for you later and you guys can see if you're able to make anything of them. To me, it was gobbledygook."

I glanced at Donovan. He looked beat. Like he'd gone twelve rounds against Muhammad Ali and was lucky to still be upright. Processing all of this new information was exhausting, I knew, but I still had a lot of questions. There were tons of things Donovan and I would need to know just to fill in a small portion of our brothers' story. I was about to ask my most pressing question—the one that made my heart rise into my throat just thinking about it—when Donovan abruptly jumped up.

"Anyone hungry?" he asked.

I stared at him.

Amy Lynn tilted her head to one side as if not quite comprehending the question.

He tried again. "I'm starving. Is there somewhere close to here where I could pick up a snack for us? Burgers, pizza, anything like that?"

"There's a Roma's on Cicero," Amy Lynn said, pointing out her window. "They've got Chicago-style hot dogs, sausage and Italian beef sandwiches."

"Okay," Donovan said quickly.

"Or—" She wandered into her kitchenette and peered into a couple of cupboards. "I have noodles. I could cook those up instead with a little tomato sauce and—"

"No," he blurted. "No, thank you. That's very generous of you, but I don't want you to go to any trouble." He paced the room like a caged baby Bengal. "How do I get to this hot dog joint?"

"It's a green-topped building—you can't miss it. It's just north of the Six Corners shopping area, where Cicero, Milwaukee and Irving Park Road all meet. A three-minute drive. Maybe a fifteen-minute walk."

"I'm just going to walk down there and grab a few to go. It sounds perfect."

I offered to go along but he immediately shot down that idea.

"What would you ladies like?" he asked. "You each want one? Two?"

Amy Lynn smiled kindly back at him. "One is plenty for me, thank you."

I didn't feel the need to eat anything, but it was obvious he was desperate to get out of the apartment and be alone. So I held up an index finger to signal "one" and said, "Thanks, Donovan." He sent me one of the most grateful looks I'd ever seen.

"Yeah, no problem. I'll be back in about a half hour or so." He was in the hallway before I could even say, "Okay."

"It's a lot to take in," Amy Lynn said to me, her voice gentle. "Why don't we take a break, too. You must be tired. Would you like some coffee? Wine?" Then she regarded me more intently for a moment. "How old are you, Aurora?"

"Almost eighteen," I said. "And thanks, but I'm fine. Maybe I'll have some water or something in a bit. I probably need to splash my face with it more than drink it, though." I laughed. "I want to be able to stay awake a lot longer, but I'm wearing out. It's been an action-packed day."

"Where are you and Donovan staying tonight?"

"Not sure yet," I admitted. "Honestly, we didn't get that far in our planning. We were just trying to figure out any information we could from my brother's journal." I explained how I'd guessed at what Amy Lynn's real last name was from the description Gideon had written next to her first name.

"Clever guy," Amy Lynn said.

"He was. I mean, he *is*." My hopefulness surged every time I thought about that, although there was a big "but" attached to it. But, if he was alive out there like I wanted to believe, even if he'd seen or heard something horrible, was it still impossible…still too dangerous…for him to come forward?

"You're clever, too, Aurora."

I mumbled, "Thanks," but I didn't feel as smart as I would have if I'd have just ignored the cops' dismissal of me and worked harder at figuring out what had happened two summers ago. I should've trusted my intuition from the start and not wasted all of this time. Time when Gideon must have urgently needed my help. A glance at the clock told me it was after eight p.m. already, and I realized I owed my parents a phone call.

"May I use your telephone?" I asked. "My mom and dad in Minnesota are expecting a call from me, but I'll reverse the charges."

"Go right ahead." The other woman pointed to the phone and left the room to give me a few minutes of privacy. The operator dialed my parents' number, asking my father if he'd accept a collect call from me, which, of course, he did.

"Hi, Dad," I said, filling him in briefly on our long driving day and our arrival in the Chicago area. "I've only got a couple of minutes, but I wanted to let you know that everything's going really well so far. We were just talking with someone who's familiar with the Northwestern University campus in Evanston, and we'll check it out tomorrow," I told him, which was kind of true. At least the first half of the sentence.

There was a long pause on the line. "Have you learned anything… new?" he asked carefully.

"Yes," I whispered. "It's…mostly helpful news, but I'll, um, find out more tomorrow. And we'll talk again then."

He asked how Donovan was treating me—if he was being "a gentleman"—and I couldn't help but laugh. "Oh, yeah. He's been fine, Dad. Don't worry about that. He just went out to get us some more food." *And to walk off some of his edginess and fear.* Then I changed the subject and told him to give my love to Mom, who was in the bath. I said that, really and truly, everything was okay. "Better than okay," I insisted.

It took another minute of assurances, but I was finally able to hang up. It was going to get harder, I knew, to pile on the falsehoods if our trip lasted for more than a week. Much more challenging to tell fractional truths as the chasm between what we were *really* doing and what we *said* we were doing continued to expand.

Even if my father knew enough to understand that a search for Gideon and Jeremy played a part in this road trip, he didn't know about the journal. He didn't know anything about Crescent Cove, Ben Rainwater, Treak Bradley or the Bonner Mill explosion. And I couldn't explain any of it over the phone, even if I'd wanted to.

Not only was it too chancy—he might tell someone he shouldn't—but I was also worried he'd react too strongly to the news that his son was most likely still alive. He was like Donovan that way. He'd slammed the door on any hope that my brother and his friend had survived.

When Dad had given his permission for this trip, all he'd really wanted was for our family to finally get closure on Gideon's death. To find out for sure what had happened. Why Gideon and Jeremy had left town. I knew my father had no idea I was tracking Gideon himself. Veering right onto the path where my brother had last tread and all but walking in his footsteps.

Dad would not like the potential danger of that—not one little bit.

Amy Lynn returned to the room. "I brought the notes," she said, setting a thin manila folder down on her small glass coffee table. She glanced at the telephone. "Everything okay?"

I nodded. "Yes, thanks. Just overprotective parents."

"I'd be overprotective, too, in their shoes," she admitted.

Donovan knocked on the door and, when Amy Lynn opened it for him, he strode into the room with a bag filled with warm hot dogs and fries. They smelled so good, I actually felt a pang of hunger.

He pulled out one Chicago dog for Amy Lynn, one for me and two for himself.

"Only two for you?" I teased.

"Only two left," he retorted. "I had my first one on the walk back. Good stuff."

I grinned at him and Amy Lynn, who'd been watching our exchange with interest, laughed a little. *She likes us. More than she thought she would.*

This feeling was confirmed a few minutes later when Amy Lynn said, around a mouthful of hot dog, "I know we're going to be up late tonight, talking and looking through these papers." She waved her hand in the direction of the manila folder. "And then there's the film reel we need to see in the morning. It's silly for you two to leave here and stay at some motel. I don't have a lot of space—" She glanced around her one-bedroom apartment. "But I do have the sofa, a sleeping bag and extra pillows and blankets. You could crash here tonight, if you'd like."

A few conflicting emotions flashed across Donovan's face. I wasn't sure what they all meant, but one of them was appreciation. And rightly so. Amy Lynn was being very generous to us.

But a tight feeling of jealousy strangled me a bit when I suspected that another of Donovan's emotions might be attraction. The pixie blonde was closer to his age than I was. And pretty, in a very delicate way. More worldly than the kind of women he ran into in Chameleon Lake. A woman who'd *lived* with a man before. Not an inexperienced teenager, like me.

If that was the case, though, Donovan didn't seem to dwell on it. Instead, he said to her, "Are you sure?"

I, however, knew our hostess's answer before she verbalized it. Amy Lynn had been watching the way Donovan and I had been interacting all evening and, to some degree, envying it. Her obvious relief at having unburdened herself of a dark, two-year secret must have buoyed her and made her want to continue our private party for longer.

So Donovan made one more trip downstairs—this time to check our parking space to make sure we could stay there until morning and, also, to retrieve our bags from the trunk of his Trans Am. Then the three of us got settled in for the night.

Amy Lynn was right about Treak's notes—they *did* look like gobbledygook. I recognized some of the squiggly lines as shorthand symbols, but I couldn't read them. I didn't have the kind of knowledge about the dead reporter that I had about my brother either, which was the only way I'd managed to decipher anything at all in Gideon's journal—and that had been written in standard English.

Still, I laboriously traced the three half-sheets of paper that had belonged to Treak and were his only remaining clues to us. Amy Lynn gave me some thin typing paper for the task, encouraging us to keep a copy but to be careful with it. And finally, when I was finished, I asked again the question that had been haunting me since I first made the phone call to Amy Lynn that afternoon. God, was it only five hours ago?

"How did you know we were coming?" I murmured, unable to tolerate the suspense of this even a second longer. "On the phone you said Gideon had told you to expect us. H-How did he communicate with you? Has he called? Stopped by in person?"

It was at that moment, when Amy Lynn tilted her fair-haired head in confusion again, that I began to realize that, no matter how many questions Donovan and I had already asked, there were a billion more still unanswered.

Amy Lynn must have realized it, too, because she didn't immediately reply. Instead, she went to a desk drawer and pulled out a couple pieces of mail.

She crossed back to me and held out two postcards that had been sent in envelopes. The first one had a picture of some weird cactus-like sculpture thing on the front and a Northern Arizona University "School of Art" logo. The smudged white envelope was sent to Amy Lynn at her friend Karen's place and postmarked *September 8, 1976, Flagstaff,*

Arizona. More than two months after the guys had disappeared. There was no return address.

On the back of the card, in Gideon's distinctive script, were the words:

Much worse than I thought. Be careful. Will write again if it's ever safe to share anything. G.

I pressed my lips together tight, remembering the "funeral" services we'd had for the guys just a few months after this postcard had been sent. Hard to believe we may have all suffered through that day unnecessarily and, yet, I couldn't help but hope that was the case.

Mutely, I handed the card to Donovan and I looked at the second one. The image on the front was of a row of painted Cadillacs, each stuck in the ground at about a forty-five degree angle. My brother was definitely going for "bizarre local attractions" as his correspondence theme.

This envelope was light beige, and the postmark stamped it as being from *Amarillo, Texas, June 12, 1978.* Dated less than a week ago! Again, no return address, but he'd sent it to Amy Lynn's Chicago apartment. How had he known where she lived now? The phonebook?

I held my breath as I read the words on the card:

My sister will probably be passing through Chicago soon. Why not show her a movie? G.

It, too, was in his handwriting, and it showcased both his sly sense of humor and his proclivity for enigmatic wording. Real proof that he was alive. *(Hallelujah!)* But, also, that he'd both planned this wild goose chase we were on and made sure it was being orchestrated in the way he'd expected.

Oh, Gideon, don't you understand? This hurts. Where are you leading us, and why this crazy game? You seem so close, like we might run into you around any corner, but yet...

It was all getting to be too much for me. The hope mixed with the confusion. The ambiguities I had to hold in my head and in my heart.

Ever since I'd found my brother's journal, I could feel my wall of pseudo-strength cracking. Piece by piece. The pain of him being gone had been so strong, so powerful, I'd forced it back...but I couldn't keep doing that. Not if he might really be out there.

A sob that had been lodged deep in my windpipe rose up and pushed its way to my lips, gashing through my defenses and shattering the silence in the room. I heard the pain in my own cry and it made me sink to the floor.

Donovan knelt beside me. He gently put his hand on my shoulder, comforting me, and then slowly wedged the second postcard from my grip, scanning the words once. Then scanning them again.

If I was having a hard time dealing with the vagaries of our brothers' behavior and the mysterious, hazardous situation they'd somehow found themselves in, I could only imagine what Donovan's reaction to the second card would be.

I found out soon enough.

He shook his head. "It's a lie," he stated. "This can't be real. And I'm gonna fucking *kill* whoever's faking it." Then he jumped up and stormed out of the room while I buried my face in my hands and wept for all of us.

It wasn't until over an hour later that Donovan returned for the night. He mumbled an apology, first to Amy Lynn and then to me, but he didn't offer any explanation of his whereabouts, nor did he want to discuss our brothers any more that evening. I could tell he'd reached his saturation point. Truth was, so had I.

All of us were exhausted anyway. During his absence, Amy Lynn and I had put together two makeshift beds—one for Donovan in a sleeping bag on the carpet, and one for me on the sofa. Tired as I was, though, I knew I wouldn't be getting much sleep.

It was destined to be a restless night for Donovan, too. I closed my eyes, willing myself to relax, but he was only a few feet away, and I could see him flipping, shifting, attempting to get comfortable on the floor. When, finally, he did drift off, he was still in an uneasy state—wrestling, no doubt, with the demons that were Jeremy's memory and his own latent guilt, and mumbling angry words directed, I sensed, at my brother. Something about Amarillo and that Cadillac Ranch.

In my case, my mind kept replaying the memorial service we'd had for our brothers when they still hadn't returned after several months and everyone—particularly the police—had presumed them dead. There had been the loud sobbing of some family and friends. The utter silence of others. Like me...and like Donovan. Our mutual grief stabbing invisible holes in the serene air of the church.

I remembered my parents holding hands, bracing each other for support. And I remembered Donovan's mom and stepfather, with a palm's span of light between them, the first noticeable fissure of what would eventually lead to their separation some months afterward.

I always knew I wouldn't have stayed in Chameleon Lake had it not been for Gideon and Jeremy's disappearance. But it occurred to me that I didn't know what Donovan would have done differently if this tragedy hadn't befallen our families. He'd left our hometown when he was eighteen. I seriously doubted he would have ever returned for more than a long weekend, even after he finished his stint in the service.

The chain of events sparked by our brothers' disappearance led to both of us being in Chameleon Lake almost against our will. My future plans had been murky, but they'd involved going away to college and moving somewhere larger, more cosmopolitan.

For the first time, I wondered what Donovan's dreams had been.

WE AROSE the next morning, not well rested but grateful for the day to begin, tiptoeing gently around each other as we felt our way through an unfamiliar routine.

"May I use your shower?" Donovan asked.

"Of course," Amy Lynn replied. "Let me get you a towel." Then, to me, "Aurora, can I offer you some toast or cereal? Coffee, tea or cocoa?"

"Oh, thank you," I said. "Just toast and coffee, please."

Such politeness.

It was like that until Amy Lynn deemed it late enough to patter down the hallway to her landlord's apartment. As good as her word, she asked to borrow his projector for the day and was soon spooling up a small, light-blue, plastic film reel with the word "Tribute" written in jaunty black permanent marker across the diameter. Jeremy's handwriting this time.

I glanced at Donovan to see if he'd noticed. He had.

To help out, he and I strung up a white bed sheet across one wall, attaching our screen with a few strong tacks from Amy Lynn's sewing drawer. But, as she turned on the machine and the film began threading its way through the projector, I couldn't help but think back to the last film Donovan and I had watched, just two days before. There would be no singing in this picture. No poodle skirts. And I doubted much humor.

But I was wrong—at least about that latter point.

There was no sound, save for the clickety-clacking of the 8mm Kodachrome film as it snaked around the spools and fed into the empty white reel, but Donovan and I watched the grainy images come into focus in color on the bed sheet in front of us. The first of these was stunning: Our brothers, running around outside somewhere.

My breath caught as I saw them both on our flimsy fabric screen. Laughing. Taking turns being in the frame and, then, pushing the other one out of it.

In the two years since they'd been gone, I'd caught up to them in age. They were now timelessly eighteen. As young as we'd remembered or, perhaps, young in a way we didn't *quite* remember…since our recollections were tinged with such heavy loss. We'd forgotten the rawness of their joy. Their shared streak of mischievousness. Their energy, which leaped into the room to dance with us.

Donovan cleared his throat. "You said Ben Rainwater—he was the one who filmed this?"

"Yes," Amy Lynn replied. "There are a few different segments to it."

We continued to watch as Gideon and Jeremy horsed around in the summer sunshine. I noticed their clothing. Both clad in old blue jeans, Gideon was wearing that distinctive red t-shirt of his with the white stripe slashing diagonally across the front. He loved that one. And Jeremy had on a sleeveless muscle shirt featuring a faded American flag and the words "Fort Monroe, U.S. Army" stamped above it.

I saw the softening in Donovan's eyes as he got a closer look at his brother's shirt, and I remembered how proudly Jeremy had worn this gift from his big brother. It'd been a birthday present, given to Jeremy after Donovan's first year of his enlistment.

But it wasn't until they'd set off the first firework that I realized Jeremy and Gideon's patriotic colors weren't unintentional. That the clothing was, in fact, a vital part of the message.

A few more seconds of goofing around followed and then, suddenly, it stopped. As if the "testing: one, two, three" stage had ended, and now the guys were going to get serious.

The camera turned its attention to a largish tag-board sign with the words, "In Honor of the Bicentennial..." written on it with the briskness of Jeremy's block printing. Black marker on a crisp white surface.

Then a second firework was launched. And a third. Ben's camera caught both of these explosions on film, capturing the powerful burst of sparkling light and smoke, if not the deafening sound.

Another tag-board message followed. This one read, "Happy 4th of July to our Military Heroes!" That board was removed and, in its place, Gideon stood with a smaller sign that said, "Dad." Jeremy squished his way into the frame with his own sign—one that read, "And Donovan."

Next to me, I heard Donovan make an involuntary, indistinct noise, but his eyes were fixed on our bed-sheet screen.

There were two more fireworks set off after that before we saw the final tag-board sign: "Our Country's 200 Years of Freedom...is Thanks to Men Like You!" Then each of our brothers saluted and lit a series of more visual fireworks, ones that had a few aerial bursts and rivaled the display the Chameleon Lake police and fire department hosted every year.

I stole another glance at Donovan. His eyes were moist and he was rapidly blinking, clenching his jaw so hard I almost expected to hear a molar crack. Was this the "fun thing" Jeremy had spoken to him about?

Regardless, neither Donovan nor I could speak while watching it, and if Amy Lynn had anything to say, she was holding her tongue.

But then the screen went dark. And the scene changed.

The laughing, cheering pair of young men we'd loved so much weren't in this shot. But their fireworks were. Buckets and buckets of them, labeled and carefully stashed on long shelves in what looked to be a backroom somewhere.

I shot Amy Lynn a questioning look.

"I don't know where that is," she said, sensing this was what I wanted to know. "But I'm pretty sure it's somewhere near Crescent Cove."

"It's a kind of storage facility," Donovan said and, then, the camera focused on a picture ID, which was face up on a small table by the entrance. "That's Ronny Lee Wolf," Donovan murmured.

There was no disputing it. "It is," I said.

The eye of the camera took in more of the room, swinging in an arc—sector by sector—until we were given a full three hundred and sixty degree view. And what we saw was that the regular fireworks and firecrackers we recognized from Ronny's store weren't the half of it. Alongside the shelving with the buckets of M-80s, quarter sticks and cherry bombs, was a different brand of firework. One I hadn't seen before. And, jeez, there was a lot of it. Enough to almost fill the rest of the room.

As the camera zoomed in on a box of them, I got a closer look. The casing was kind of like a tube—the type you might find at a hardware store for plumbing. A silvery color. Sturdy steel. Not quite...legal-looking. But I was hardly an expert.

Donovan was.

"Holy Jesus," he hissed. "Those aren't fireworks. They're pipe bombs."

The screen went to black again and, finally, spliced onto the end of the reel was the last segment of film with close-ups of a few remnants of those silver casings—blown apart into metal shards like shrapnel. Dirt and rubble lay all around.

Following this image, and zooming wider and upward, were exterior shots of a place I vaguely recognized but couldn't, at first glance, pinpoint. Then I did.

"It's Bonner Mill," I whispered.

Donovan was already nodding. "I know."

Chapter Seven

Sunday, June 18

IT WAS the film that began to change Donovan's mind about the trip.

I didn't know if the Bicentennial tribute played the bigger role or if it was the realization that Ronny dealt in pipe bombs as well as fireworks that sealed the deal…but, suddenly, Donovan stopped challenging my certainty that Gideon's journal was leading us to more information than the cops ever had or were willing to share.

I saw in his expression a slew of questions that had been raised in the past twenty-four hours, not the least of which was—if Gideon had really been in Amarillo, Texas just a couple of weeks before and if, in fact, no one had been forging his handwriting on those postcards—where the hell was Jeremy?

We asked, but Amy Lynn didn't know the answer. With her help, though, we were able to piece together a few additional tidbits about that Fourth of July weekend two years ago.

Our brothers had said to her that Ben Rainwater's cousin was involved, but she didn't know his name was Ronny until we told her. Our brothers also explained to her that there'd been more than one explosion at Bonner Mill, which, of course, Donovan and I already knew, thanks to the microfilm we'd read at the Ashburn Falls Public Library.

From Ben's film footage around the mill, Donovan and I concluded that the first explosion was caused by Ronny's stash of pipe bombs, which Ben had somehow caught on camera and spliced onto Gideon and Jeremy's tribute reel.

Amy Lynn explained that Ben wasn't done with his Super 8 project. He'd been doing a lot of filming in and around town and gathering more evidence against his cousin (related by marriage, not by blood) who, in Ben's opinion, had always played fast and loose with the law.

But, one of the most surprisingly things I'd heard was that, however shady Ronny Lee Wolf appeared to all of us to be, he wasn't the one actually setting off the bombs.

"Then who was?" Donovan asked.

Amy Lynn sighed. "Your brothers didn't know that."

"Then how did they know he wasn't doing it?" Donovan said back.

"Because of what happened next," she said. "Because of what they witnessed during the second explosion."

"Wait—did they know if the same pipe bombs caused both explosions? The first one that Ben filmed and also the one that killed Ben and Treak?" I asked her.

She nodded. "That's what they believed, but they'd just seen Ben's cousin in downtown Crescent Cove before they drove to the mill. He was strolling down the street. So, although the guy—Ronny, you said his name was—seemed to be involved in the storing and maybe even the manufacturing of these bombs, your brothers were convinced he wasn't lighting them personally."

Donovan was struggling to assemble all of these details. "How is it that our brothers even knew Ben Rainwater? What made them go up to Crescent Cove in the first place? I just don't understand." He scored his fingers through his hair. "What *exactly* did Jeremy and Gideon say about that?"

Amy Lynn rubbed the center of her forehead, as if trying to bring the memories back to the surface. "They told me they'd first met Ben Rainwater at a party in St. Cloud—I don't know how long ago—but that Ben invited them up to visit him and to make a film. Your brothers had gone to Crescent Cove once or twice before the Bicentennial, mostly to buy fireworks to bring home, they said, to keep for the upcoming holiday parties. But they also got together with Ben for drinks and shot some of the film footage. The guys went up on the Friday night before the Fourth, and Ben said he'd just picked up the developed reel with everything he'd filmed recently on it. On Saturday afternoon, they all met Treak at his motel in the next town over—"

"Ashburn Falls?" I asked.

"I suppose so," she said. "I remember Treak telling me how there weren't motels in Crescent Cove, so he had to stay somewhere else. Gideon and Jeremy were at a different motel, but not that far away. And Ben brought his film projector with him to Treak's place so the four of them could watch what he'd shot in the past week or two. Gideon and Jeremy were going to take their portion home with them—first to show Gideon's dad and, then, to mail to you, Donovan."

He nodded at this, but then glanced away in silence, either not willing or not able to speak.

Amy Lynn continued, "I guess Ben had his suspicions about his cousin's 'fireworks' supply already—he'd discovered the storage unit not long before Treak came into town and had snuck in there a few times to check it out—but Gideon and Jeremy recognized how powerful the pipe bombs really were and explained it to them. As for Treak, at least according to what your brothers said, he'd been digging up information all over the place. Ben's film confirmed a few details that he'd been investigating—it was all somehow connected to his big story—and he was desperate to go back to Bonner Mill with Ben. To shoot some more footage and to document whatever evidence of a bombing cover-up they could find."

Donovan massaged his temples. "So, Jeremy and Gideon went with them then?"

"No," Amy Lynn said. "Aurora's brother had some kind of car trouble. He knew they were headed into a holiday weekend, so he wanted to try to get the problem fixed as soon as possible. I guess he and Jeremy fiddled around with it for a while and knew they needed to get a car part from an auto shop, but Ben and Treak were impatient to drive to the mill. Ben didn't want to leave them stranded, so he loaned them his car—a white Oldsmobile Cutlass—so they could get the part they needed, while Ben and Treak went to the mill in Treak's Chevy. Your brothers planned to meet them there as soon as the car got fixed."

She started packing up her landlord's projector. "But they weren't able to fix the car. The part they needed wasn't in stock and, with the Bicentennial, they weren't going to be able to buy it until Tuesday at the earliest. So, they left Gideon's car at the motel and took Ben's

Oldsmobile into Crescent Cove, driving through the center of town and, finally, getting to Bonner Mill."

She fiddled with the white leader tape on the Super 8 reel then stared at us both for a long moment. "Look, I got all of this secondhand on a day that was the most awful one of my entire life…but I remember it. I remember exactly what your brothers said. That's what you asked for, right?" She met Donovan's eye.

He nodded.

And I said, "I know it's hard to remember all of this stuff, but it's helping us to understand. Just tell us what you know."

"Okay," she said. "So, when they finally got to the mill, it was getting dark and it was a woodsy area without much light. But they could make out Treak's car, so they parked behind it, and they noticed there was another vehicle in the lot. They could hear voices coming from inside the mill. At first, they thought it was just Ben and Treak talking really loudly to each other, but they soon realized there was a third man and that he was shouting at the other guys. Gideon and Jeremy hunted for a flashlight so they could see better outside, and tried to decide how serious the argument was. Bad enough for a fist fight to break out? Or bad enough that their friends might needed the help of the authorities?"

She paused. "They finally found a flashlight in Ben's glove compartment and got out of the car. When they did, they saw that the other vehicle had markings on the sides. It was a police car. They were worried about Ben and Treak getting in trouble for trespassing. Or, maybe, that it was illegal to film home movies in a privately owned building or something. But as they got closer, they heard Ben yelling at someone. And Gideon told me that Treak shouted that he had *notes* on the guy, and that the truth would come out."

She took several deep and steadying breaths. "The next thing they heard was a series of blasts. And, suddenly, Jeremy said they could see more than they'd wanted to because parts of the mill were on fire, and there were more explosions still happening."

Donovan put his head against his fist and closed his eyes. "Then what?" he whispered.

"Then they ran back to Ben's car just as the cop came racing out of the building—setting more bombs off behind him and carrying Ben's movie camera. Your brothers didn't get a clear look at the man's face, and they didn't think he got much of a look at theirs either. They said everything was in shadows. But he must have recognized immediately that Gideon and Jeremy were live witnesses to his crime. So, he lit a pipe bomb filled with gun powder and flung it at them. It landed just a few feet in front of them, on Treak's Chevy, and pretty much torched half the car."

My bottom lip was raw and bleeding from biting it. More dirty cops. I hated them all. "But, obviously, our brothers got away from that crazy policeman and made it here," I said. "He didn't try to follow them after that, did he?"

"Actually, he did," Amy Lynn said. "But they'd had a tiny lead on him and, eventually, were able to lose him. They didn't dare go back toward Crescent Cove, or even Ashburn Falls, though, because the cop probably got a good enough look at the car's make and model and very likely caught the numbers on the plates."

Donovan's jaw was clenched, but he was nodding. "The cop would run the plates with dispatch and Ben Rainwater's name and address would turn up. He'd figure out in no time, since he'd just killed Ben, that someone else had to be behind the wheel. Our brothers were so sociable. So open and friendly." He said it almost like it was an indictment. "In a small town like Crescent Cove, it would take less than ten minutes of talking to people at the bar to figure out that Gideon and Jeremy had been with Ben…to find out their names, what type of car they drove, where they were from."

"Right," Amy Lynn said. "So, of course, they were too afraid to go back to get their car or to even think about driving home to Minnesota. With Ben and Treak dead, they didn't have anyone they could trust in the area. They thought a cop as dirty as that one might keep trying to kill them or, if that didn't work, he might try to frame *them* for the Bonner Mill explosion. As it was, that cop somehow managed to get police records to show that Treak's car had been eviscerated in a 'crash' that I don't think ever happened…at least not if your brothers were telling me the truth, and I believe they were."

She shook her head angrily. "I really think your brothers were right to run. They didn't stop until they got to Milwaukee. That's when they called me from a payphone downtown. And where, I later learned, they stole the Illinois plates off a parked car at a motel before they left the city. To make themselves harder to trace that night."

I let out a long breath I'd been holding. Yeah. My brother and his best friend were clever that way. No one asleep at a motel would notice a missing license plate, at least not until the next morning. It would buy the guys a few hours of driving without worry and, since they were heading into Illinois, it would make Ben's car as inconspicuous as possible there. How many white Oldsmobiles with Illinois plates were traveling on those very same roads that night? Hundreds. Maybe thousands.

"So, the reason you have the film was because it was in Ben's car, right?" I said, already visualizing the events as they happened to my brother and Donovan's and how, with every mile they drove, Gideon and Jeremy must have discovered something new about their circumstances. Their many losses…and, yet, their few unexpected resources.

"Exactly," she replied. "It was in the trunk, along with one of Treak's folders. I guess he'd left it there when they were transferring Ben's film equipment to his car to take to the mill. From what Jeremy told me, Treak had a stack of folders in his trunk, too, which were blown up that night, as well as a bunch of notes that were still in his motel room. And I, of course, knew how many papers he'd kept in files in our Chicago apartment. The police carted out all of them before the holiday weekend was over, so I'd guess that anything Treak may have left at that motel in Ashburn Falls would have been confiscated almost immediately."

"Along with Gideon's car," Donovan added.

Amy Lynn nodded. "Probably, yeah."

Nothing just "probably" about it.

I'd always wondered why there had never been any reports about my brother's Ford Galaxie being spotted or recovered anywhere. I could only imagine how quickly his car could have been found and, then, made to "disappear." How much easier and without raising questions it would have been to simply complete Gideon, Jeremy and Treak's transactions in Ashburn Falls. To clean out their motel rooms, which most likely had already been paid for in cash. To have a duplicate set of keys made and to turn those in instead, dropping them in the outside box before check-out time the next day.

No one would think anything of it.

And if the names or descriptions of three out-of-towners were to come up later, well, sure, these men might have visited, but then they'd left. After all, who stayed around those parts for long if they didn't have to?

"What did they say they were going to do next, after they left Chicago?" Donovan asked. "Did they tell you?"

"Not in any detail," she admitted. "They both agreed that they'd wanted to warn me, given what they saw happen to Treak and Ben, and they wanted to get the hell out of Crescent Cove that night. But they were still feeling their way through the next steps. Gideon said they would've liked to go straight home, or at least call their parents. But they needed to figure out who was behind the bombings so that they didn't walk into a trap and get arrested for a crime they didn't commit, especially since they didn't have any alibis who were alive. They were afraid it wouldn't be safe yet—either for them or for their families—to head back to Minnesota. But they said what Treak was investigating had a Missouri connection as well as a Wisconsin one, and I could tell Gideon was curious about that."

"So they were going to drive there?" I flipped through my brother's journal. After Chicago, the next page didn't list a place that I recognized, but on the page after that were the words "Cardinal Town."

Ah, yes. St. Louis.

I showed the entry to Amy Lynn and Donovan.

"That may have been their next stop," she said.

Donovan made no comment about that. Instead, he asked, "Did they tell you anything more? Call you later?"

"Nope. They left the film reel and the notes folder with me that afternoon. Said not to share them with anyone else unless they gave the okay or said it was safe. But I didn't hear from them again until I got that first postcard from Gideon. And that was months later. In September." She shot Donovan an apologetic looked laced with something else. Longing? Regret? "I never got any notes at all from Jeremy."

But she desperately wished she had.

I knew this now, finally understanding something important about Amy Lynn. About why she kept looking so searchingly at Donovan's face. About why she'd commented immediately on his resemblance to his brother.

Yes, when Gideon and Jeremy met with her two summers ago, she'd still been in shock by the news of Treak's death and wasn't immediately ready to move on. But, in spite of it all, and in the months then years that followed, she'd thought about our brothers often. About Jeremy specifically. She'd been attracted to him. And—it was so clearly written on her face that I marveled at how I'd missed it before—she'd hoped he'd write to her again. Call her. Visit.

But he hadn't.

Why hadn't he?

Donovan wasn't asking her about that, though. Either he'd failed to see her signals or he was ignoring them. Neither reason would have surprised me. He did, however, bring up something I should have asked sooner.

"Aren't Ben Rainwater's mom and his sister here in Chicago?" Donovan said. "We were told by a few different people that they'd moved here."

Amy Lynn shrugged. "Maybe. I've never met them or heard from them. Chicago is a big city, which is why I can still live here. It's easier to hide out in a cast of millions than it would be to try to blend into a small town. I've never run into anyone yet who knew me as Chelsea Carew." She laughed mirthlessly. "Not that I was famous or anything. And I work behind a desk now, mostly stuffing envelopes and filing papers, so I don't meet a lot of new people."

I thought about this. Considering how Ben's cousin was the one storing the pipe bombs, even if Ronny didn't actually detonate them, maybe there was some fear on Jeremy and Gideon's part about ever contacting Ben's family and explaining to them the details of his death. Whoever was responsible for killing Ben may have been keeping a close eye on the movements of his immediate relatives.

Donovan looked like he had the headache from hell, but I watched him working to keep an open mind about everything he was hearing. What I'd intuitively accepted from the moment I found my brother's journal—that we'd been lied to by the police, that our brothers were still alive, that there was much, much more to this story than we'd ever imagined—was not as natural for Donovan to wrap his brain around.

So, I admired him for his efforts. For being willing to rethink something so fundamental about what he'd believed. For taking a pure leap of faith, however atypical of him. And for saying to me, "Well, Aurora, I suppose you want to go to St. Louis now, huh?"

AFTER WE'D said goodbye to Amy Lynn, thanking her for all she'd done for us—not to mention the kindness and trust she'd shown our brothers—and swapping contact information, we emerged into the dazzling sunlight of a hot summer Sunday and got settled in Donovan's car.

He pulled out his road atlas and plopped it into my lap. "You get to navigate on this one."

I flipped it open in surprise. Considering his ingrained aversion to asking anyone for directions, this was a sign of great progress.

He started the engine. "If we get lost, it's on your head, Nancy Drew."

I glared at him. "Stop calling me that."

"Nancy, Nancy, Nancy," he mocked.

"Oh, you're real mature," I said, but he continued with his mockery. I knew he needed an outlet, a little levity, something—especially after all the grave, life-changing information we'd just gotten. I was beginning to learn his patterns. He would need to munch on something, and he wouldn't be able to discuss anything seriously for a couple of hours at least. Good thing we had snacks in the car and a five-hour drive ahead of us.

"Fine. Be that way." I told him the first few turns, taking us past the big Sears on Irving Park Road and following the signs so we could merge onto Interstate 90/94. Eventually, since I wasn't afraid to read a map—unlike *some* people—I knew we'd meet up with 55 South, which would take us all the way to Missouri.

But, as soon as Donovan looked comfortable with the roads, I dug through my purse for the cassette I'd been saving for just such an occasion, and I popped it in. As the opening strains of the Bee Gees's hit "Stayin' Alive" came on, I had the satisfaction of seeing Donovan make a disgusted face and reach to turn it off.

I batted his hand away from the cassette deck. "Do you really think disco is a *fad?*" I said, mimicking Vicky from St. Cloud. Then I started singing along with the song's chorus. I'd heard the lyrics about, oh, *sixty thousand times* since the movie came out last year. I knew every word.

"Uh! God, stop that!" he said, half laughing.

"What's my name?" I asked him sweetly during an instrumental moment.

He shot me a dirty look. "Just cut it out."

I sang along with the entire second verse. Loudly.

"Hell, Aurora. *Stop.*"

"What did you just say my name was?" I asked. Then, more threateningly, "You do realize that 'How Deep Is Your Love' is coming up next, right?"

He made a gagging sound that I took as a precursor to his inevitable surrender. I was right.

"Your name is Aurora, but I will *strangle* you with the long threads of tape that I'm going to yank out of my deck in about ten seconds if you don't do it first."

I snapped the "Saturday Night Fever" soundtrack out of the player.

"If you call me Nancy Drew again, you can expect a full hour of disco hits. I can sing 'If I Can't Have You' and 'You Should Be Dancing' and more. All of them *a cappella*. And, yeah, that's a warning. Be scared."

The look he gave me was nothing short of scathing but, a few minutes later, when I was studying the Illinois map in the middle of the atlas, I caught him glancing at me and smothering a laugh.

"Who knew you'd grow up to be such a weirdo...*Aurora*," he said, emphasizing my name, of course.

"Oh, you're funny."

"I am, actually. But I guess it's been a while since I felt much like laughing."

I was surprised to hear him say that. Not because I didn't believe him—just because I didn't think he'd be quick to disclose something personal if he didn't have to. Something that might invite follow-up questions.

"It's been a rough two years," I said, stating the obvious. Making it easy for him.

"Yep."

For a while we rode along in silence. I wanted to ask him what theories he had about our brothers. If he finally believed me that Gideon was alive. What he thought it meant that we hadn't gotten any recent news at all about Jeremy. But Donovan still wasn't ready for that. I decided to look more closely at the atlas.

At one point, he peered over at me and leaned in close to read the map I was studying.

"Shouldn't your eyes be on the road?" I asked him.

"Well, you keep staring at that thing like it's the Holy Grail. Is there something coming up I should know about?"

In fact, yes, there was. I just wasn't ready to tell him about it yet because, to be honest, I hadn't entirely figured it out.

I was hoping reading the names of the upcoming cities in the atlas would help. I *knew* I knew something important. I *knew* I'd been given some solid clues at Amy Lynn's apartment to figure out a few new puzzle pieces. I just wasn't sure which pieces. So, I was sifting through my memories of what she'd said and what I'd learned—names, details, places and dates—trying to let my conscious mind catch up with my intuition.

"There's something here that I'm looking at but not seeing," I told him. "It'll help us if I can figure it out. And I know it's somewhere on these pages."

I tapped the Illinois map with my index finger and then waved my hand at Treak's notes and Gideon's journal, which I'd set on the dash. Before we'd left, Amy Lynn had given me the two postcards my brother had sent her, and they were sticking out of the small leather book, taunting me even more than Donovan had been.

What was I missing?

"What's on the next page of the journal?" Donovan asked. "You usually get some kind of weird clue from that. Why don't you read it aloud?"

I exhaled on a sigh. I'd scanned it back at Amy Lynn's and there hadn't been anything that'd jumped out at me there. But Donovan was looking at me expectantly and, if he was finally willing to discuss our search, I didn't want to discourage him.

Besides, staring at the atlas for fifteen minutes straight hadn't done me any good.

So, I opened the journal and shuffled through the pages until I got to the one right after "J & I in Chicago" but just before "Cardinal Town."

As usual, Gideon had his list of car thingies, chemical substances and directions for some automotive procedure—about half a page's worth—which I read to Donovan, even when it got a little embarrassing:

Draining the cooling
System:
1. Make sure engine is
cold then open
radiator cap
2. Find the radiator
drain cock under the
front of the car &
place a large pan
underneath
3. Drain radiator fluid
into the pan then close
drain cock

Donovan snickered next to me. "Do you have any idea what a drain cock is?"

I shrugged and tried not to look as awkward as I felt. "I don't care what it is. You told me you wanted me to read this out loud, so I'm reading."

He laughed openly. "Yeah, but I remember seeing this page when you first showed me the journal and I wondered then why your brother would've written down the steps for this. It isn't a tough procedure. Hell, the way Gideon loved cars, he probably learned how to drain coolant when he was ten."

"Well, I don't know why he did half the things he did," I said stiffly. "I'm sure he had a reason."

"If you say so," he said.

I returned to the page and kept reading:

4. Refill radiator with water; replace cap & run engine to circulate the water

5. Repeat

6. Add 1/2 water & 1/2 antifreeze to both radiator & overflow reservoir—fill to top

7. Leave off radiator cap; let engine run until radiator burps

Donovan found that line to be pretty darned hilarious, too, but I just ignored him:

> 8. Coolant level will drop—keep watch on temperature gauge
> 9. Refill radiator and reservoir so fluid is back to the top again, put cap back on
>
> 10. Put old coolant/water in a container & dispose at a service station

I paused. That was the end of the latest lesson in car mechanics and, just below it, the ink changed. It was really subtle—I had to strain my eyes to see it—but I knew as soon as I read the words underneath that I'd been wrong in thinking Gideon hadn't given us a place name on this page. He had.

"Listen to this," I told Donovan, and then I read him the last three lines:

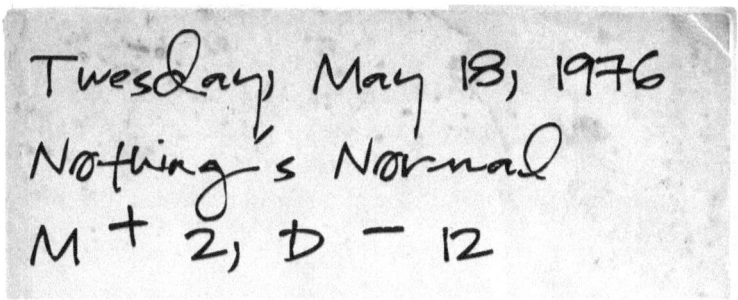

"So?" he said.

"So Gideon wrote 'Nothing's Normal' in the new ink section." I snagged the atlas, still open to the Illinois page, and pointed excitedly to a city in the middle of the state. "Interstate 55 runs right through Normal, Illinois. It's right here." I held up the map so he could see the black dot. "It's next to Bloomington. Then, further south on 55 is Springfield and, finally, St. Louis, just across the Missouri state line."

"And that proves…what? That they'd stopped in a place called Normal on their way to St. Louis?"

"Yes!" And, for a moment, I was relieved. I knew all along we were headed on the right path, but I still appreciated having these little acknowledgments of our progress along the way. Like getting to check the answer key in the back of my high-school algebra book. Even when I'd solved the equations completely on my own, I liked knowing I could double check just to be sure I got them right.

Then Donovan added, "In May?"

"What?"

"The date," he said. "It was May eighteenth. You told me on the way to Chicago that you thought either the dates or the places were wrong."

And my uncomfortable feeling of "knowing without knowing" returned full force. There was definitely another clue to find, and I was so close to it I could almost hear it whispering in my ear.

"No, it has to be July. If they met up with Amy Lynn in Chicago on

July fourth, they had to be in Normal and St. Louis after that." I flipped back a page in the journal. "We know for sure they were in Chicago on Independence Day, but the date written down on the page for their Chicago visit is May thirteenth—a Thursday in the middle of a school week. They couldn't have been in Illinois then. We know Gideon sent Amy Lynn a postcard from Flagstaff that was dated September eighth."

I pulled it out and reread the postmark on the back. "But, in his journal, the only reference I can find to Flagstaff is here." I skipped through several pages to get to the one where the city in Arizona was mentioned briefly. "It's on a page that Gideon dated June 22, 1976."

I returned to the *Normal* page and reread those last three lines to myself:

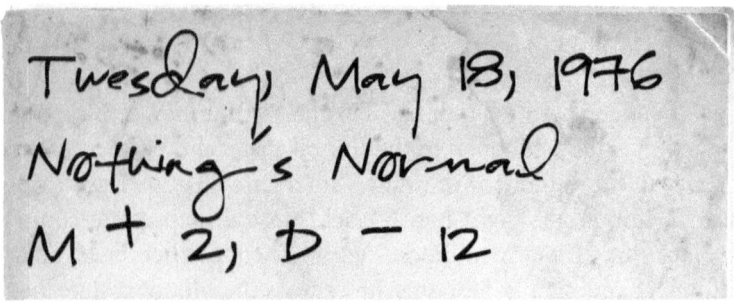

It was wrong no matter how I looked at it. They were not there in May, but in July. And not there on the eighteenth, but on the fourth or later.

Then, in a flash of recognition, I saw it. The pattern I'd been missing.

It was so simple, so obvious…once I had the key. And, just as I'd suspected, it had been right in front of my eyes the whole time.

"Oh, my God, Donovan," I whispered. "We just needed to read the equation."

He sent me a quizzical look. "Where?"

"At the bottom of every page."

I grabbed a pen from my purse and a piece of scratch paper from Donovan's glove compartment. On it, I wrote:

Normal, Illinois = 5/18/76 (date written in journal)
M + 2, D - 12
M = month, D = day

M = 5 + 2 = 7 (month = July)
D = 18 - 12 = 6 (day = 6th)
7/6/76 (real date of visit)

I read this to Donovan. "See? The M and D stand for Month and Day. We just need to make adjustments for that and we'll have the correct date that they were in each city!" I was kind of shouting, but I was excited. I showed him how it worked on the *Chicago* page:

Chicago = 5/13/76 (date written)
M + 2, D - 9
5 + 2 = 7 (month = July)
13 - 9 = 4 (day = 4th)
7/4/76 (real date)

And then, for good measure, I decoded the *Flagstaff* date:

Flagstaff = 6/22/76
M + 3, D - 14
6 + 3 = 9 (month = September)
22 - 14 = 8 (day = 8th)
9/8/76 (real date)

"Wow," he murmured. "That's really...clever. Good, um, code breaking. It'll be easy for you to figure all the dates out now." He looked impressed with my detective skills but, thankfully, he knew better than to call me Nancy Drew again.

I nodded happily and set to work on decoding each date in the journal. That unsettling feeling was gone, thank God. At least for the time being. And I was able to finally concentrate again on the still-unsolved mysteries within the journal—as well as those outside of it. Not the least of which was why my brother had gone to so much trouble to disguise where he went and when.

However, even as I was wondering this, my mind was spinning with possible reasons. Let's say someone else were to have found the journal before I did—or if, by chance, it was either lost or stolen later—*all* of the listed dates would be from *before* the "disappearance." It would be an odd object of Gideon's to find...but, if by chance he *wanted* people to think he was dead, the dates in the journal kept that possibility intact.

In fact, there was only one page where the current year, 1978, was written at all, just in the corner, and—to almost anyone else but me—it would be far too insignificant to dwell on:

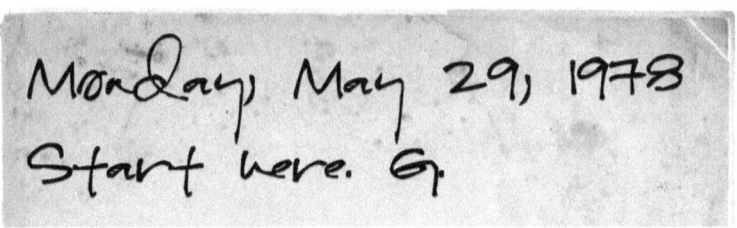

Monday, May 29, 1978
Start here. G.

I turned back to that section, rereading the entire page for the nine-hundredth time in the past two weeks, my mind focusing on all of the lines with numbers in them:

Zirconium powdery + 2
(+ o)
Monday, April 19, 1976
M + 1 (+ o), D + 10
(+ o)

I used the equation at the bottom of the sheet and applied it to the date:

Crescent Cove = 4/19/76
M + 1 + 0, D + 10 + 0
4 + 1 +0 = 5 (month = May)
19 + 10 + 0 = 29 (day = 29th)
5/29/76 (real date)

Only, this time the month/day pattern didn't work.

May 29, 1976 had been a Saturday. Specifically, the Saturday before Gideon and Jeremy's high-school graduation. It was the first day of a crazy week-long set of activities, both at the school and around town, thanks to the Chameleon Fest. I'd run through that social obstacle course myself just a few weeks ago. No way were they goofing off in Wisconsin then.

Plus, I remembered seeing them every single day of that Memorial Day weekend and each weekday leading up to their big graduation bash in St. Cloud on June fifth of that year.

So, no.

Donovan and I had always thought April nineteenth made sense as the real date our brothers went to Crescent Cove for the first time. On the next page, May tenth, it said they went there again, which also fit with what Jeremy had told Donovan in June 1976. I reread the lines with numbers on that page:

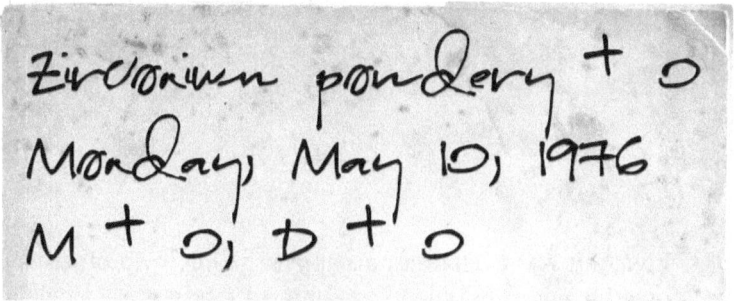

The month and day lines in the equation were both + 0, so there was nothing to add to the date, and the only other number on the page involved that chemical—whatever "Zirconium powdery" was—but that, too, was + 0.

I'd seen that chemical on the *Start here* page as well, but the number added was different. I flipped back and read it again:

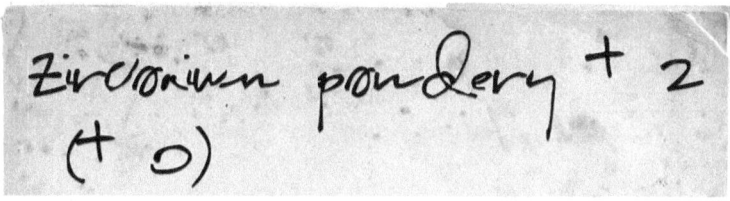

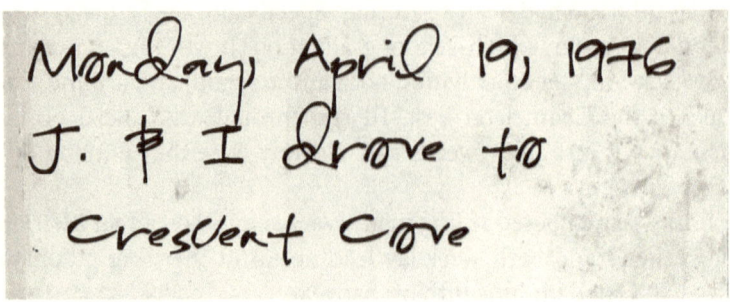

Ah. Now I saw the tricky thing Gideon had done. The ink change started just above the date. It wasn't *"powdery + 2 (+ 0),"* like I'd thought for so long. It was *"powder y + 2 (+ 0)."* With the y + 2 (+ 0) part written in that subtly different shade of ink.

Y = year.

M + 1 (+ 0), D + 10 (+ 0), Y + 2 (+ 0) was the equation for *both* dates on the page, not just one. I just had to split them up—almost like the reverse distributive property in math—and factor them in with the correct dates:

4/19/76 (M + 0) (D + 0) (Y + 0) = 4/19/76
4/19/76 (M + 1) (D + 10) (Y + 2) = 5/29/78

Granted, this was the hardest page to crack, but my brother would have known I wouldn't be able to rest until I'd solved every single part of the puzzle. That I prided myself on taking intuitive hops, skips and jumps.

"You're kinda quiet over there," Donovan said. "Everything still okay?"

"Yeah," I said, explaining what I'd figured out about the *Start here* page. "Gideon put a lot of thought into this."

He nodded. "Seems like it. But so did you as you've tried to solve it. I wouldn't have made half of the guesses you did along the way. I'm pretty sure no one else would have either. And—" He sent me a look that had only a hint of his usual mockery. "After everything we learned from Amy Lynn about our brothers and their visits to Crescent Cove and to Chicago, it showed you haven't been wrong about much. Well, at least not about the journal."

It was the way he'd phrased this almost-compliment that made me laugh aloud. "What? You're saying I *have* been wrong about other things?" I poked him in the side of his ribs with my fingers.

He responded by shoving my hand away—none too gently—and grinning.

"Tell me, Donovan, what, exactly, have *you* been right about?"

His grin broadened. It made my heart flutter with joy to see him smile again.

"Been right about a couple of things," he said.

"Such as?"

He lifted his right hand from the steering wheel and made a "V" with his index and middle finger. "Two big important things," he said. "And I'm not telling you."

"Oh, sure. Like you can just say that and have it be true," I told him in my most sarcastic voice.

"Believe me or don't. Doesn't bother me."

And I knew it really *didn't* bother him. That was one of the most maddening things about Donovan. Almost every experience affected me in some way, whether I admitted it aloud or not. But he—he was unfazed by most things. Aside from his responsibility to the few people closest to him, his commitment to his country and his sense of honor, he really couldn't be swayed by much. I wouldn't be able to goad him into revealing to me anything he didn't want to share.

So, I just shrugged. I closed the atlas and the journal. Stared out the window at the transforming landscape, which had been slowly mutating from city to countryside with each passing mile. But Donovan, in the driver's seat, looked too smug for his own good, and I couldn't let him get away with that.

When I opened my mouth next, the lyrics to "Jive Talkin'" just happened to come out. I thought I did a pretty decent imitation of the first verse.

Donovan didn't share my sentiments.

"*Stop* that horrible noise," he cried.

"I think this song is real catchy, and I'm gonna just keep sing—"

"No! No. But…if you stop, I'll tell you one of my two things."

I giggled like a little kid. See how powerful the Bee Gees were?

"Okay." I crossed my arms, closed my mouth and waited for the big reveal.

"The first thing I know I'm right about is that *disco sucks*. Trust me, it's a fad and the end is coming." He shot me a wicked glance. "Though not soon enough."

I rolled my eyes. "C'mon, that's not big *or* important. Doesn't count. Tell me the other one."

There was a funny twist to his lips and, for a second, I thought he was going to give in. Allow me to take a few steps deeper into his carefully guarded private world.

But, instead, he shook his head. "Nope. Not yet." Then, "When did you say you were gonna turn eighteen?"

"July first." I calculated what was left of the month. "In thirteen days."

He shot me a speculative look. "Well, maybe I'll tell you then."

Chapter Eight

Normal, Illinois

DONOVAN SURVEYED the tree-filled Quad in the heart of the Illinois State University campus with the careful scrutiny of an Army lieutenant before ripping an old flyer off of a nearby bulletin board. "This is not the 'Promised Land,'" he muttered, regarding the flimsy sheet of paper with his typical skepticism.

"No," I said in a disgruntled voice. Hey, I could do disenchantment as well as anyone. "But it is Bloomington-Normal. The *other* Twin Cities."

He waved the yellow flyer at me. "This thing says the Grateful Dead actually played a concert here, on this campus, at the Horton Field House back in April." He motioned toward the lush lawn and pretty foliage and raised his eyebrows at the absurdity. "Yeah, sure. Welcome to Deadhead Central."

I glanced around the Quad myself, taking in the laidback summer-school students weaving between the buildings or lounging idly under one of the trees. Donovan's "promised land" song reference made sense now, and I had to admit that, pleasant as ISU was, this wasn't a place that screamed out "musical hotspot full of generational trendsetters." People looked to the coasts for that kind of thing, not a cornfield college in Middle America.

"Think Jerry Garcia might still be hiding out somewhere in town?"

I said, getting the snicker out of Donovan that I'd hoped.

"Not unless he's having a secret psychedelic party with a bong and a side dish of acid at a local frat house." He pointed at the journal. "What did Gideon say about this place again?"

"It was the entry with the step-by-step directions for draining coolant." I grimaced. I wasn't going to read it all to him a second time.

"Oh, yeah," Donovan said, folding up the Grateful Dead flyer and pocketing it. "The one where the date in the journal said May eighteenth, but it was really July sixth."

"Exactly."

He nodded. "So we know the dates were added later and that they were fake. That the equations are the key to figuring out when the guys were really in these places. But what about the stuff that was written above it on most of the pages? The chemicals and procedures at the top? A lot of that information had to already be in there, right?"

"I guess so," I said.

"Do you remember your brother writing in the book during high school? Did he keep it with him out in the garage or somewhere private?"

I thought about this. I had no idea where Gideon had kept it, but I could remember a number of times when I'd caught him jotting down some notes inside of it. He didn't seem worried about me watching him in the midst of his journaling, though. If anything, he struck me as amused, particularly when I insinuated that the journal was some kind of tawdry record of his encounters with girls. He dared me with his sly smiles to ask him about it for real, no teasing involved. But I didn't. Not even once.

I'd never regretted my lack of curiosity on any subject more than this.

"He seemed pretty open about it, if that's what you're asking," I told Donovan. "No evidence of him keeping any serious secrets. Honestly, I don't even think he even hid it."

Not like I did with my diary.

Which, I recalled with a cavernous ache in the center of my chest, Gideon had found one summer in the tool shed, in that cedar box. But, for once, he didn't laugh at me. Didn't read through what I thought then was an interesting personal life. He just put the key back in my desk drawer and told me to hang onto it. That the box was a good hiding place for my diary, as long as I was the only one with the key…

Although, a few weeks later, after writing in my diary one evening, I realized I couldn't put it back in the box. I'd somehow misplaced the key again, and it was forever lost—or so I'd thought.

Donovan shrugged. "I don't know then. Still think it's strange that he'd write down so many easy procedures in that journal. Unless he was losing his memory and wanted to make sure he wouldn't forget them."

This struck me as an odd theory and one I couldn't quite wrap my mind around. "Do you really think that could happen? Is there any reason someone might fear getting amnesia at age eighteen?"

He paused and stomped on a discarded cigarette butt at the edge of the Quad. "No, not really. Not unless he was a war vet. Sometimes the shock and terror of battle can make an otherwise healthy man lose his memory, but Gideon wasn't a soldier. In fact, if anyone was anti-establishment…"

He shook his head. "I have no idea what the hell was going on in your brother's brain, Aurora. Or in my brother's, for that matter. But I do wonder if…*if*…they're really alive, where they are now and how we might find them."

We walked around the ISU campus for an hour more—reading signs, watching people, trying to make connections that weren't there or that we simply couldn't see.

"Well, we now know that ISU was Illinois's *first public university*," I said, parroting the words on a plaque we'd read, which commemorated this. "I don't know much else about it that's relevant to our search, though."

"Look on the bright side," Donovan said. "At least you won't have to make up details about college campuses when you talk to you dad tonight. You can tell him all about this one." He waved his palm at the, admittedly, eye-catching university tennis-court building—a place that looked like royalty might live there. It was, in fact, called Ewing Castle.

For a moment, my vision—clouded by the past—cleared, and I saw ISU for what it was: A large, well-respected university in the heart of the heartland. College students, warmed inside and out by the summer sun, were engrossed in their studies, their sports and their social lives.

They weren't trying to parse out bits of meaning from a grease-stained document.

They weren't obsessed with their family's recent tragic history.

They were daydreaming of their futures and brimming with the excitement and hopefulness of youth.

I felt a powerful stab of envy. But, when I glanced at Donovan again, none of my longing for a normal life seemed to register on his face. He either didn't want it...or he'd forgotten what it felt like to have it.

"Did you ever check out any colleges?" I asked him as we meandered back toward the Trans Am.

He made a show of hunting for his keys and unlocking the car door for me. But I recognized the motion for what it was—stalling—and looked at him, expectant, until he couldn't ignore me any longer.

"I didn't really think about it after Jeremy and Gideon disappeared," he said finally.

"But what about before that? You had to know when you first enlisted that you'd eventually qualify for the GI Bill," I said. "Knowing you were eligible for several years of free tuition had to make the idea of college at least a little tempting, right?"

"Just because you have the opportunity to do something, it doesn't always mean it's the right thing to do. Besides, when I enlisted, it was a long time ago. Everything was different back then."

I slid into the car and watched him mess with a couple of old receipts on the dash, but I wasn't going to let him off the hook that easily.

"No kidding," I said. It wasn't like I didn't *know* just how different it was between the Before and the After. "But c'mon, Donovan. You had to have had *some* idea of what you wanted to do with your life. If our brothers hadn't gone missing were you planning on being career military? Was there a subject you were hoping to study—if not at a university then at a technical college? A dream job? A rock band? A fantasy wife and kids?"

He snapped his head to glare at me then started the car engine. "Man, you're nosy."

I pursed my lips together, not feeling the slightest remorse for my inquisitiveness. I'd already spent five days traveling with the guy, if you counted our visit to Crescent Cove...and I did. For most of it, he'd treated me like a pesky little sister. Was it any wonder I was starting to act like one?

I crossed my arms and waited.

"Where are we headed?" he asked, driving a few blocks.

"On a one-way street to the Truth." He groaned and squirmed. "Be serious. If there's nothing else to do in Normal, I'm putting in some miles toward St. Louis. We need to get there, see if we see anything and then get home. We can't spend a month on the road."

"I *am* being serious," I said.

I didn't know what it was about that moment—maybe because we seemed to be at some kind of unmarked crossroads, or maybe just because I'd been so lonely for so long—but it was vitally important to me that he answer my question. I had to know something *real* about this guy who'd been sharing my strange journey. Something *true* about the person he'd been before our lives were forever changed. I *needed* that.

And I didn't want us to drive even one more mile in any direction until I could grasp some genuine fragment of his character...and see a little more of the unguarded man. It was usually almost too easy for me to read a novel's worth of emotions, frustrations and dreams on someone's face. But with Donovan? He wasn't as quick to let me do this with him.

"You had to have had a plan for your life," I whispered. "Once upon a time."

He let out a long, slow breath, and I could feel him, as well as see him, visibly try to relax. In no way was this working, but I appreciated even this small gesture. He was trying hard to wrestle with some demon from his past and, perhaps, the only thing that seemed clear was that it was a very old demon. I suspected it predated the summer of '76. It may well have predated nearly everything.

Donovan pulled into a parking space near the edge of the campus and let the engine idle.

"Once upon a time," he began, "I used to think it would be fun to be a car designer or an architect. When adults would ask me what I wanted to be when I grew up, that's what I'd tell them. Mostly, they'd just humor me. Nod at me. Say something insincere but nice. 'Sounds great, kid. You can do it.' Stuff like that."

I honed my perception onto his every movement, like someone trying to tune into a hard-to-reach radio frequency. He was telling me the truth—I knew from the steadiness of his gaze, the depth of his breathing, the mild tension of his grasp—but the twitches of pain at the corners of his eyes and mouth also told me this wasn't the whole story.

"Mostly?" I asked as gently as I could. "You mean there were some people who weren't as encouraging? People who told you that you couldn't do it?"

The stiffness in his fingers increased as he gripped the steering wheel more firmly, and the cord at the side of his neck jumped once or twice before he shrugged and said, "Yeah."

He glanced out the front windshield then over at me again. "Look, Aurora, my life was never much of a fairy tale, even before July two years ago. You know my dad left us. He was gone by the time I was six and Jeremy was three. My stepfather moved in when I was thirteen, and I've known warmer, sweeter drill sergeants. Can't say I was sad when he left, but I wish he hadn't chosen Jeremy's disappearance as the reason. Almost killed my mom to lose them both within a year."

"So you came back and stayed in their place." It wasn't a question. I knew this was what had happened.

He nodded.

"It's why I'm still in Chameleon Lake, too," I confessed, though that wasn't much of a secret either. Donovan had known years ago that I had aspirations of college. Heck, I'd told him my plans to escape our little town at our brothers' graduation party. He knew then that I was just biding my time.

"Is there anything more you want to see in Normal?" he asked. "If you want, if you think you might really consider this place for college, we could drive around for another hour or so. Pick up an application packet for you or something. Give you a chance to take a better look."

I studied the students milling nearby. Their Midwestern normalness—no pun intended—was almost jarring to me. It was the kind of campus that might have been of great interest to me a few years ago, but now it was too much like home. Too reminiscent of the kind of place filled with fun-loving, partying coeds that my brother might have gone to eventually, if ever he was ready to give up his passive fight against "the establishment."

I felt a heavy pang at what he'd lost. No doubt about it, it wasn't different enough here to keep me from remembering my past or where I came from. I might as well just stay in Minnesota and be somewhere that would at least make my mother happy.

"Nah," I told Donovan, motioning him forward. "That's okay. If I ever make it out of Chameleon Lake, I probably won't go much further than Minneapolis. It's not…not as easy to break away from home as I thought it'd be. Especially now."

"Yeah." He pulled out of the parking space and started driving south and west.

A couple of hours later and a hundred miles closer to St. Louis, we finally decided to stop for the night at a roadside inn near Litchfield, Illinois.

There were a few appealing restaurants there, and the town's oldest and most famous was The Ariston Café. I really liked the look of it, but the inn we chose a little further down the road had the advantage of being next door to a twenty-four hour diner and gas station, all owned by the same family, and we'd get a discount on our food and gas if we stayed there.

The sign on the motel boasted, "Ultra Modern! Air Conditioned! TV in Every Room!" and, most importantly, "Vacancy" with a handwritten "1 room left" scrawled on a chalkboard by the office.

Donovan said, "Let's take it."

He produced the fake gold wedding band from his bag and shoved it at me. Though I made a show of sighing and looking irritated, I slipped it on my finger and we checked in as Mr. and Mrs. McCafferty, paying in cash. Strange how quickly such lies could become routine. Then we walked over to their family diner.

There was nothing remarkable about our sodas or our burgers and fries but, while we were there, Donovan's attention snagged on something unexpected.

"Check out these placemats," he said, pointing to the laminated, multicolored, '50s-era cheesy things beneath our platters.

I slid my dish with my half-eaten burger aside and scanned the placemat. It looked like a vintage relic from the "Grease" movie's props department.

"Travel Mat" it read across the top. Then, "Scenic U.S. 66 Hi-Way" and, beneath that, was a line connecting the cities along the route, complete with recommended stops between Chicago, Illinois and Springfield, Missouri on the left side of the mat.

I noticed that Bloomington-Normal was listed on there. So was Litchfield. So was St. Louis. Certain motels, attractions and diners were highlighted with short descriptions. In another section in the lower right-hand column was an additional bit of information with recommendations for the segment of the route between Springfield, Missouri and Shamrock, Texas. There was a mention of Tulsa and another of Oklahoma City.

Donovan and I both flipped our placemats over at the same time. The travelogue continued with a new line of stops and attractions, this time including the featured places from Shamrock, Texas through to Los Angeles, California. And there were dots on the mat's map pointing to Amarillo, Albuquerque, Santa Fe, Flagstaff, Topock, San Bernardino and Pasadena.

The information receptors in my brain were pinging wildly with connections as I read these particular city names. Finally, something that might lead to something important. A clue at last that made the remaining entries in my brother's journal make a little more sense.

With my fingertip, I traced a few pen-and-ink sketches interspersed around the placemat, most likely to add decoration and to further entice potential tourists to visit: A St. Louis riverboat, Meramec Caverns, the Ozarks (all of those were on the Missouri side of the mat), a peculiar Blue Whale attraction somewhere in Catoosa, Oklahoma, the Cadillac Ranch in Amarillo, a steam train near Flagstaff and gold mines by another city in Arizona called Oatman.

I opened Gideon's journal, already knowing what I would find but just wanting visual confirmation. All of the cities mentioned within the journal's pages were listed somewhere on the placemat. Somewhere on Route 66. Not to mention that both of the postcards Gideon had sent Amy Lynn—one from Amarillo and the other from Flagstaff—were also places that could be found on the classic 2,451-mile westward journey.

Donovan verbalized what we were both thinking. "Where they were driving wasn't random." He ran his index finger along the highway, tapping the spot where the road met the ocean. "I don't know why— maybe it had something to do with what they'd learned in Crescent Cove or found in Ben's car—but, for some reason, it looks like they were following Route 66 toward California."

We both immediately went into investigative mode.

I flipped to the back of the journal and read Gideon's *Pasadena* page. But aside from the "M + 3, D + 7" code and the date (July 3,

1976, which really meant October 10, 1976), there were only a couple of phrases there (*Sunset ranger? One shield?*) and I didn't understand their significance. The previous *San Bernardino* page was of no help either. It seemed Gideon had set things up so it would be necessary to figure out his journal clues chronologically.

Meanwhile, Donovan began reading—with audible murmurs. He not only read the details on the placemat, but he expanded his search to take in the jauntily framed pictures on the walls and the decorative objects surrounding us.

I realized I hadn't really *seen* anything in the little restaurant that I'd looked at so far. I'd been tired when we sat down. Hungry. Unobservant. There were only a handful of other patrons in the joint, and none in the booths nearest ours, so we slipped out of our seats and studied our surroundings more carefully.

"Look at this." He pointed to a large Route 66 map tacked up on the wall opposite our booth. "There are dates showing the development, history and the decline of the 'Mother Road,' as they sometimes call it." Of particular interest to us was not the year the route was built (way back in 1926) or the famous novels, like Steinbeck's *The Grapes of Wrath*, that had featured tales taking place along its winding path, but the driving lines that showed the changes in the route. Some of them very recent.

"The original road began in Chicago and went to L.A.," I said, reading a blurb at the side of the map, "but things changed, even as recently as last year."

I showed Donovan the latest modifications to the route, trimming the eastern edge, so that the starting point of Route 66 was now in Normal, Illinois. Prior changes from 1974 had the western end of the road listed as Topock, Arizona. "So many people are now taking the faster, wider and better-paved four-lane Interstates, bypassing these little towns, that many parts of the route have fallen into disrepair. And it says here that the U.S. Government decommissioned the Chicago to Normal segment in 1977. That's probably why we didn't see anything on I-55 about Route 66 until after we passed through Bloomington-Normal."

"But Jeremy and Gideon were traveling in 1976, so the road was still mostly drivable, at least through to Arizona, although most people would have used the Interstates even then," he said. "I'm getting the sense that they didn't. That they took the original route."

I was getting that same sense.

My eyes were at last fully opening up to all of the Route 66 paraphernalia around us. It was more than just the placemats and the map. It was Perry Como singing "Get Your Kicks on Route 66" over the speaker near the cash register. It was the faded Route 66 design on the coffee mugs. It was all of the 1950s kitsch throughout the café, complete with that billboard-like scripting and certain pastel shades, which had colored that particular decade...a time when the route was in its modern heyday.

Times had changed since then. It was a part of American life that was romantic to think about—like Betsy did with her crazy love of poodle skirts, drive-ins and sock hops—but even the memories of that era were dying. Who wore poodle skirts anymore? Bell-bottom pants and tie-dyed shirts were in fashion. Fast-food restaurants had been new back in the Fifties, but these days they were tired old chains.

Driving across the country in a big convertible had been a great family adventure once, but we'd suffered through long gas lines in recent years and people didn't have the patience for that kind of travel. Who wouldn't just fly if you had to go so far? Or, if you drove, wouldn't you take the best and fastest roads?

And who had time for bizarre attractions like a Blue Whale or a Cadillac Ranch? After all, we had so much entertainment right in our own homes. *Four* television stations! How many people would really get their kicks by doing any of that old-fashioned stuff nowadays?

When I asked this question of Donovan, he just shrugged. "Maybe our brothers were sentimental about the past. Or they liked that old 'Route 66' TV show and wanted to be like the main characters—those two guys on it. I don't know."

It was possible that Jeremy had been intrigued with the old Martin Milner TV series, but I couldn't remember my brother paying much attention to it, even in reruns. Who knew the truth, though? Maybe he'd liked it more than I realized. Or maybe he and his best friend had had a particular reason for following the original route. Something that had to do with the trouble they'd gotten into in Wisconsin two years ago...and we just didn't know what that was yet.

The only thing I knew for sure was that we were following Gideon and Jeremy's trail down a fading patch of pavement that was quickly becoming outdated and abandoned.

It was an odd thing, really—not only had our brothers disappeared, but the road they'd been traveling down was experiencing the same fate. Fading from view right beneath our wheels.

Chapter Nine

St. Louis, Missouri ~ Monday, June 19

OVER THE next few days, Donovan and I slipped into an easy routine—one of driving, collecting details and following hunches that pushed us toward the next location.

Well, more accurately, *I* was following hunches. Donovan, despite his default setting as our resident skeptic, was following *me*.

"We know they were in Normal on July 6, 1976 and that they got to St. Louis a few days later on Friday the ninth," I told Donovan as he was chowing down a double scoop of chocolate frozen custard at Ted Drewes—a local spot that had been a recommended stop on the placemat.

I swirled the custard in my single strawberry cup and flipped through the next several pages of the journal. "Thing is, they were here for a while and I have no idea what they were doing. They don't get to the next city—Joplin—until Sunday the twenty-fifth. That's more than two weeks that are unaccounted for...unless they were just hanging out here. But why?"

"Maybe they were laying low like Amy Lynn said," Donovan suggested, around a mouth full of frozen custard. "Waiting to see if they were being followed. Or listening for news reports to find out if they were wanted in connection with the Bonner Mill explosion. I don't remember hearing about it in Virginia at the time, but maybe the blast made the regional news."

"Hmm. Maybe."

I didn't remember hearing about the Bonner Mill incident either, and I'd been living a lot closer to it. I was pretty sure somebody somewhere capped the story on that pretty fast. Based on what we'd found at the library near there, coverage had been minimal even in Crescent Cove and Ashburn Falls.

"Where would they be able to stay in St. Louis for so long, though? Gideon didn't have any friends here that I knew about. Amy Lynn didn't mention that they were going to meet someone. Do you and Jeremy know anyone in Missouri?"

He shook his head and ate some more chocolate custard.

I looked at the Route 66 placemat we'd snitched from that diner in Litchfield and scanned for any lodging recommendations that were listed in the St. Louis area. The only place mentioned was a motel called Coral Court.

"That's an infamous motel," Donovan said when I pointed it out to him. "It's a motor court but also known as a 'No Tell Motel.' I knew a few guys from the Army that stayed there once. Had special rates so you could rent a room for as little as four hours." He raised a brow. "And there was a well-known kidnapping case back in the Fifties where one of the murderers hid out there anonymously for a couple of days."

I opened my mouth to suggest staying there for a night so we could check it out, but Donovan anticipated me.

"No."

"Oh, c'mon. Gideon doesn't give us any clues that I can figure out about where they stayed when they were here. This sounds just like the kind of place that—"

"That your dad would kill me if I took you to," he interrupted. "Absolutely not, Aurora." He shook his head for added emphasis and pitched his empty custard cup in the trash.

I snickered. "Don't be such an old fogy. It's not like we're going to *do* anything there."

Seriously, it was all I could do not to shake him. He hadn't so much as given me a little side hug since we'd been away from Chameleon Lake, even when he was pretending to be my "husband." He probably thought if he held my hand or something I'd combust from his act of grand passion.

Considering my mockery, I expected him to say "no" again

right away, but he didn't. He just looked at me for a very long, very uncomfortable moment with an expression that was odd and unsmiling. Too inscrutable for me to read. God, I hated that.

"Get in the car," he said finally.

"Why? Where are we going?"

"To Coral Court."

"We're going to stay there?" I asked, delighted but surprised.

"No," he said, swiftly crushing that idea. "But if you really think it would help to see it, we should take a quick look at it."

The motel was located about a mile west of the city limits and, to my eye, it looked respectable enough.

"The only really weird thing about it," I told Donovan, "is that just the *sign* is coral in color. All of the units are gold. And they are very Art Deco."

It was set up kind of like duplex groupings. There were the rounded gold brick units with brown highlights, thick glass block window squares and private one-car garages where the guests could safely keep their vehicles. And, I supposed, their secrets.

I knew it would have been the perfect place for Gideon and Jeremy to disappear from the world for a couple of weeks. How they paid for it, I wasn't sure, but the rates had to be moderate and the anonymity offered was worth any extra charges.

"Maybe they were working while they were here, too. Getting extra cash for a few days' labor," I suggested. "Somewhere within walking distance. Something easy, like washing dishes at a café or cleaning windows."

Donovan said, "It's possible," but I could tell he didn't want to hazard any guesses.

After I'd had a half hour to wander around, he made me get into his car again and he took us back into the city, where he checked us into the same kind of mom-and-pop motel we'd stayed at in Crescent Cove and in Litchfield.

"At least one time on this trip we need to stay at a motor court," I told him. "So we can park your *obvious* Firebird Trans Am in a garage for a change."

He laughed and said with heavy sarcasm, "Yeah. When we need to hide from bad guys, we'll do that. Until then, the lodging is *my* choice."

About an hour later, we were in the downtown area, meandering past the shops and finding ourselves walking along the section of the Mississippi River that flowed through the city.

"The part that keeps tripping me up are Treak's notes," I told Donovan as we sat on a park bench near the famous Gateway Arch, our view of the St. Louis skyline obscured by the large trees and the taller city buildings near us. "Even if we can somehow translate the shorthand in those few pages, there has to be tons of stuff we're missing. Stacks of folders that got burned up in his car at Bonner Mill. Boxes that got carted away from his apartment in Chicago. I don't know how we're ever going to figure out a fraction of what Treak had uncovered, even if we somehow find our brothers and they're able to explain what they know to us."

Donovan shrugged. "Probably safer that way."

"Yeah, but what's the point of us being here then?" I snapped. "We'd be *safer* at home. Not asking questions. Not traveling anywhere. And then we'd have exactly what we had before—nothing."

I shook my head. "We need to keep searching for anything that might lead us to our brothers or tell us why they can't come back home. There has to be a new clue in the journal, in the decoded dates. Things that we'll be able to see now because of the extra information Amy Lynn gave us. I just wish Gideon would've given us a little more to go on in the first place."

He exhaled slowly but didn't speak. It was clear he didn't want to deal yet again with my familiar rant about how we needed to keep pressing forward. Going further westward.

On some level, despite being shaken up by the film our brothers made and despite all the proof we had challenging the presumption that our brothers were dead, I knew Donovan still believed we were better off turning all of this evidence over to the Chameleon Lake Police Department and having them lead the investigation.

But I strongly disagreed and he knew I'd argue with him. And, also, there were his growing questions about Jeremy.

He didn't openly say anything about it, of course, but I recognized it in the way he dealt with any new detail we'd gleaned in some way from Gideon. The postcards, in particular, bothered Donovan. Especially the one sent earlier this month.

My brother was being his typical cryptic self when it came to communication, but the fact that Gideon knew we'd be heading toward

Chicago meant he was confident in both his ability to orchestrate our direction and, also, in our ability to correctly follow along. I got the sense he'd almost been monitoring us. The natural question that arose was where were *Jeremy's* hints and clues? Had Donovan missed them, or had Jeremy just never sent any?

After a day and a half spent scouring old newspaper clippings and ambling down the streets of St. Louis in hopes of making some new connections, I asked Donovan to just get us to the next city mentioned in Gideon's journal—Joplin, Missouri—find us a place to stay and give me some space there to lay out all of my collected papers and notes. I had a few questions I wanted to get down on paper.

To his credit, he did this and without even too much grumbling.

While Donovan left for a half hour to scrounge up something that might resemble a dinner, I used the bed in our motel room to spread out every map, scribble of notes and sheet of paper we had in our possession—anything that had anything to do with our brothers—and I flipped over the largish construction-paper calendar on the wall to use the blank back side as my personal writing board.

When Donovan returned bearing Cokes, sliced turkey sandwiches and a bag of Oreos—"Dinner of champions," he informed me—I went through each item with him, one at a time.

"Okay, we've got the placemat that shows the Route 66 cities and famous attractions," I said. "Our road atlas, which shows the Interstates as well. We've got Gideon's postcards, Treak's notes and the journal."

I tapped the *Joplin* page with my index finger. "This entry is more promising than the St. Louis one because that only had some car parts at the top and, then, 'Cardinal Town,' the fake date and the equation on the bottom. Here we have at least a few more things written down, especially beneath the ink change."

The more I looked at my brother's journal, the more I was convinced my earliest hunch about it was right—that it was a parallel record. That Gideon had the original entries already in the book and, in adding notes beneath them, had found a safe and convenient place to record his journey with Jeremy. On this point, at least, Donovan didn't seem to question my instincts too much.

He picked up the journal and read the first part of the entry aloud:

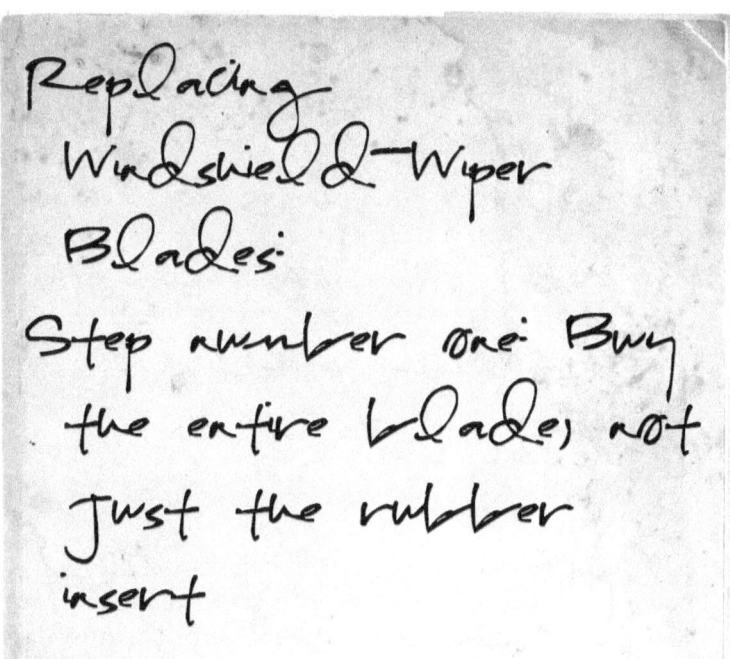

Replacing
Windshield-Wiper
Blades:
Step number one: Buy
the entire blades, not
just the rubber
insert

He didn't bother to hide his exasperation when he glanced my way. "Are you kidding? He wrote down *nine* steps for this—a job that's even easier to do than draining coolant. Maybe your brother was planning to teach a car-maintenance class to a group of kindergarteners someday."

I glared at him.

He ignored me, split open the bag of Oreos and continued reading from the point where the ink changed.

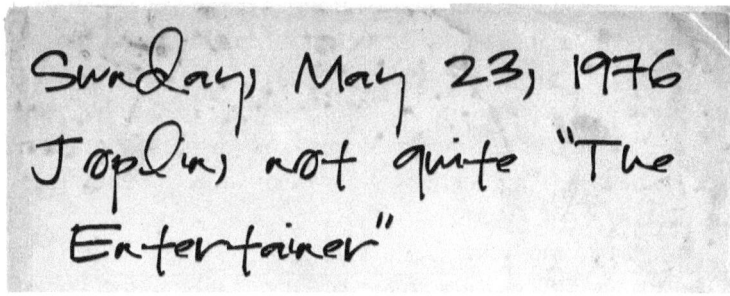

Sunday, May 23, 1976
Joplin, not quite "The
Entertainer"

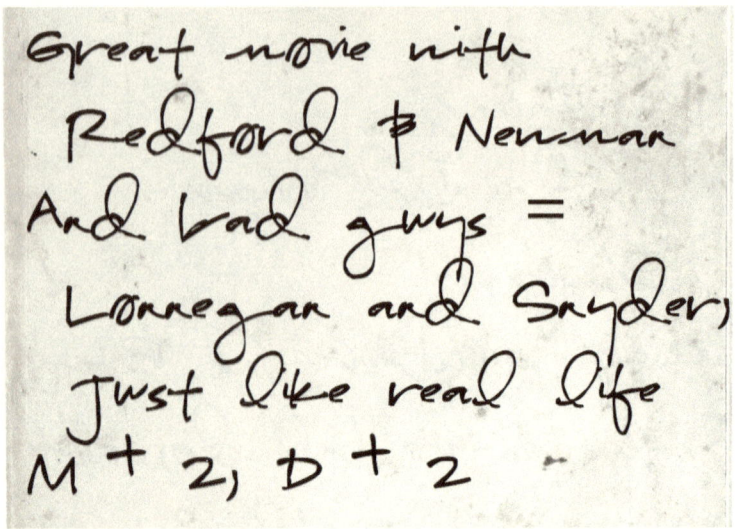

Great movie with
Redford & Newman
And bad guys =
Lonnegan and Snyder)
Just like real life
M + 2, D + 2

He looked at me blankly. "So, you think this is useful?"

I nodded. "We know the real date they were here was July twenty-fifth. May plus two months is July. Twenty-three plus two days is twenty-five. And then he makes three references to the movie 'The Sting,' so that has to mean something important." I knew I didn't have to explain to Donovan that "The Entertainer" was used as the musical theme for the film. It was so famous, even people who hadn't watched the Redford-Newman picture knew that.

He reached for a cookie, twisted it and ate half. "It was a good flick," he said, chewing. "Been a few years since it was out. You see it in the theater?"

I told him I had. "But I mostly just remember that Robert Redford and Paul Newman were con artists. It was a complicated plot. I don't remember who Lonnegan and Snyder were." Leave it to my brother to give us a clue like this. He'd loved that movie.

Donovan handed me the bag of Oreos and paced to the window and back. "One was a Chicago mob boss and the other was a corrupt police lieutenant. And there was a woman, too. Loretta. She was dangerous."

"Sounds like you remember it well."

He shrugged. "I saw it a couple of times. Once with a few Army buds. And I took Jeremy to it when I was home on leave. It came out around Christmas." He paused. "Jeremy laughed like crazy when Newman and Redford's characters pulled off their sting operation. Pretty sure he and your brother went to see it again."

"Yeah. I'm sure they did, too."

We didn't say anything for a few minutes after that.

"So what do you think he's saying?" Donovan asked. "That he and Jeremy were trying to con a bad cop and a crime boss?" He snatched the bag of cookies again and twisted another one open. "I wasn't getting that from what Amy Lynn told us."

"No, I didn't get that either," I said, "but it may have something to do with the story Treak was working on. He was from Chicago and, based on what we learned at Amy Lynn's, I really don't think Treak was one of the bad guys. She said he was investigating some mob-related stuff, so, maybe, he accidentally stumbled upon something like this."

Donovan made a weird face but he didn't tell me it was a completely stupid idea.

I reread the line my brother had written about the mob boss and the cop:

And bad guys = Lonnegan and Snyder, just like real life

"It's the 'just like real life' part that's making me think that," I said. "But he's also careful to say that Joplin wasn't quite 'The Entertainer.' Maybe it was a play on words to confuse people. We know he was following Route 66 and went through Joplin, Missouri. Maybe someone else reading it would think he was talking about Scott Joplin, though, the composer of the song."

Donovan ate another Oreo then rummaged through the bag of food for his sandwich and bottle of Coke. "Thirsty? Want me to open yours?" He had a bottle cap opener on his keychain and deftly popped the top off of his drink.

"In a few minutes," I said. "I want to show you the rest of this stuff."

He sighed. "Okay." He took a swig of Coke and plopped down beside me on the bed, scrunching the corners of my copied shorthand pages from Treak's notes.

"Careful," I said, rescuing them from under his leg. "We need to decode these. Like tomorrow. There's got to be a library in town that has books on how to read and write shorthand. Maybe we can puzzle it out while we're there."

"I'm always going to libraries with you…" he murmured.

"Yeah, well, that's because they're wonderful."

"Sure." He didn't sound convinced.

My temper ignited. "Donovan, you were willing to defend our country's *freedoms* when you joined the Army. But what's the use of having freedom of speech and freedom of the press if people don't have a place where they can read what others have written? If they don't have free public access to information? Libraries give that access to everybody."

He started humming "The Star-Spangled Banner."

"Oh, stop it."

"Only if you get off your soapbox, Aurora." He shot me an annoyed look. "I don't know how you're jumping to half of these conclusions, but fine. We'll go to the library—your little *utopia*—and you can look things up."

"Good. And while we're there, we need to check out what was happening in Joplin and along the westward course of Route 66 two years ago. Any news stories that might be connected with Chicago, Crescent Cove or our brothers."

He pointed to the construction paper calendar I'd flipped over. "What's that?"

"This is my list of questions—or, at least, the start of it. Things we need to know but don't yet." I read him what I'd written so far:

1. Who was the bad guy/cop at Bonner Mill—the one who killed Ben and Treak and who threw the pipe bombs at Gideon and Jeremy?

2. What did Treak find out that led him up to Crescent Cove initially and what information is in his notes?

3. Why did the Chicago police want Treak's files and who wrote the report that said his car was destroyed in an accident?

4. Who got rid of our brothers' possessions at the hotel and confiscated Gideon's car?

5. What kept Gideon and Jeremy from ever feeling they were safe enough to call home or send a letter to us to let us know they were okay?

"Can you think of a number six?" I asked Donovan.

"Not right now." He abruptly got off the bed and drank more of his Coke.

"If either of us thinks of anything else, we can add it later. There are lots and lots of little questions, but I think these are the biggest ones," I said. Which was a lie. I knew there was at least one huge question neither of us was willing to say aloud: *If we ever saw our brothers again, would they be the same as we remembered?*

Donovan said he'd "had enough detective crap" for one day, so we spent the rest of the evening unwinding and watching "Happy Days" and "Laverne & Shirley," just because it was Tuesday night.

The shows reminded me of Betsy and her love of the Fifties. I didn't feel that same sentimentality for any prior decade, but I wondered if— someday, in the distant future—I'd get all nostalgic about the Seventies. Look at it through rose-colored glasses. Think of it as an easier, simpler, more fun time.

Maybe, but that was hard to imagine.

THE NEXT day we arrived at the Joplin Carnegie Library with our mission laid out before us and I, for one, had no intention of leaving until we'd accomplished it.

"Impressive," even Donovan had to admit, taking in the three-story, four-columned entrance of the white edifice on the corner of Wall and Ninth Streets.

I couldn't guess at the style of architecture, but it looked like one of those ancient Roman buildings.

"And it's old," he added, pointing to a stone inscription that read: "The Gift of Andrew Carnegie. To the City of Joplin. 1902."

"Carnegie was a great supporter of libraries," I said. "He'd financed a lot of them. Unlike *you*, he was someone who believed in their importance, both to the individual and to the community."

Donovan cocked his head. "Oh, what a dreamboat," he said in full mockery. "Too bad you didn't know him personally. He would've been the perfect boyfriend for you."

I couldn't think of a snappy answer to that, so I just huffed and pushed past him on my way into the library and onto my quest to find the card catalog.

After a quick search of their nonfiction collection, I located several possible books on shorthand, needing only to narrow down which form Treak used in his notes—either the Pitman or the Gregg style— since both were widely used. In the stacks, I pulled out a representative copy of each and compared them to the notes I'd brought along.

"These two shorthand forms are similar," I told Donovan, "but if you look at the width of the Gregg characters, it doesn't vary. With the Pitman style, there are different thicknesses in some places." I pointed to Treak's notes. "I don't see any variation here, so I think he learned the Gregg version."

"Yeah, all right," he said, looking impatient. "Now what?"

"Now, we try to decode what Treak wrote. I'm going to sit over there." I indicated a small table toward the back. "Help me if you want. If you don't, that's fine. Go look at old newspapers or try to dig up any regional news from two summers ago or something. I'm going to need at least an hour for this. Maybe longer."

Donovan, no doubt realizing that decoding shorthand was a one-person job and he wasn't that person, meandered to another section of the library and left me in peace.

I spread out the pages I'd copied from Treak's notes and opened the Gregg shorthand book to the quick reference chart. Squiggle by tedious squiggle, I matched the lines on the notes with the corresponding sounds from the chart. I knew it wouldn't be exact, but I hoped I'd get close enough to figure out most of the words.

Eventually, Donovan strode back in to check on my progress. He squinted over my shoulder at the sheet of notebook paper where I'd been writing the words down as I decoded them. "What's a 'halchaney'?" he asked.

"I'm not sure," I admitted. "At this point, I'm just trying to get all the major sounds written down so I can look at Treak's notes as a whole. Then I'll scan for patterns, sentence breaks and anything that might be meaningful."

He ran his fingers along his hairline and, then, down his sideburns. Pausing. Thinking. Evaluating. "You like this kind of thing, don't you?"

"What do you mean? I don't know anything about shorthand," I said. "I know I probably should've taken it in high school, but it was an elective and I was pretty distracted my last couple of years, so I wasn't—"

"Not what I'm saying, Aurora." He crossed his arms and tapped his fingertips near each elbow, slapping the skin. "I meant the code part. The solving of the mystery. Your brother's journal with all its weird little clues. The big puzzle behind it. You like that sort of stuff."

He didn't say it like an accusation—not exactly—but it was clear he didn't share my interest in problem solving as a form of entertainment. I wasn't about to tell him how I used to love reading mysteries or the thousand times Gideon and I wrote in code to each other when we were kids. He already thought I was strange enough.

"Swear to God, Donovan, if you start in again on the Nancy Drew name calling—"

"Did I say anything about that?" He shot me an irritated look. "Listen, it was just an observation. Seems to me it's the kind of thing someone who should go to college would like. You know, it fits you. Shows you're bright. That's all." Then, before I could manage any kind of reply, he spun on his sneaker sole and said, "I'll be back in another half hour."

By the time he returned, I had most of Treak's shorthand symbols decoded into sounds, and what I saw on the page was starting to take shape into something almost recognizable.

"It seems like a list of names," I told Donovan. "See this first one?" I pointed to the word *halchaney*, which he'd seen before. "It looks like there's a space between the 'l' and the 'c.' So, maybe, it's actually *Hal Chaney*. The reason I think so is, also, because of what comes after it. There's the phrase *Americana Trucking*, like it's a company he owns or works for. And, after that, it's *Cres Cove, Chic, MO, TX, NM*, which I'm betting is 'Crescent Cove, Chicago, Missouri, Texas and New Mexico.' Does that make sense to you?"

Donovan nodded. "But Hal Chaney?" he said. "Why does that name sound familiar?"

"I don't know. Below it are some other names and places that follow." I whispered the full list to him aloud:

Hal Chaney - Americana Trucking - Cres Cove, Chic, MO, TX, NM
Vincent Leto - Chic
Rick Brice - Chic
Sebastian James - Chic
Timothy Wick - Americana Trucking, Jop, Amar
Billy Neville - Albuq
Julian Carello - Chic

"I've never heard of any of these people," he said. "They can't be famous. At least not to an average American."

"Maybe not. But for some reason they were important to Treak. We should check every reference source we can lay our hands on to try to figure out who at least a few of them are and what they do," I said. "Microfilm. Phonebooks. Newspapers. Periodical indexes. Anything at our disposal."

"Is this everything Treak had listed?" he asked.

I shook my head. "There was one more section." I showed him the last page. "It's mostly numbers, as you can see in this left-hand column. The shorthand words to the right vary, but each of them is a city. There were several mentions of Chicago and St. Louis, a few of Joplin and Amarillo, an Oklahoma City and an Albuquerque."

"All places along Route 66."

"Yeah."

"But no idea what the numbers mean?"

"Not yet," I said. They had to mean something, though, and the quicker I could figure out little details like these, the quicker we might be able to track down Gideon.

Donovan was staring at the list of names again. "I'm thinking the thing to start with is the trucking company because that, at least, gives us a jumping off point. We can look them up. See where they're based. Try to find something on Hal Chaney and Timothy Wick through them, since Americana Trucking was listed after both of their names."

Something tugged at my memory. I looked at Hal's name again and the places Treak had written after it:

Cres Cove, Chic, MO, TX, NM.

"Didn't somebody in Crescent Cove know a guy named Hal?" I asked.

Donovan remembered an instant before I did. "Kim."

"That's right. Our waitress at the bar. The desperate Cher-lookalike chick who was drooling all over you."

"What?"

"Never mind," I said. "Didn't she say her old boyfriend was a trucker? A guy named Hal. The one she'd moved to Crescent Cove to be with…"

"But then he left her."

"Or, maybe, he just *left*."

"Kim didn't say a last name, though. She might've been talking about another Hal," he said.

"Right. Because there would be *so many* truckers named 'Hal' in a town with a population of 949." I sighed. Donovan was so damn unwilling to let his mind take any leaps at all.

He jabbed my shoulder with his index finger. "Stop it with the snottiness. I'm just trying to make sure we don't overlook anything."

I shrugged. "Fine. Let's just go to the reference room and get started."

He followed me, though several paces behind, as I collected my papers and speed-walked through the first floor and the general reading room so we could enter the connected reference area. Just as I'd done at the public library in Ashburn Falls, I took a quick scan of the available staff members to gather impressions about them and to see which one might be the best to approach. Who looked both knowledgeable and trustworthy?

There was a white-haired librarian with a warm smile, and she seemed like a good prospect to me, but she was busy helping a group of four teenage girls find something. I heard one of the girls ask, "And can we get Donny Osmond's address, too?"

It was going to be a long wait.

There was a somewhat younger staff woman, but she had an angry crease between her brows and wore a grim expression on her lips. She was filing cards in the card catalog and gave off the distinct vibe that she didn't want to be disturbed.

Finally, there was a third librarian—the youngest of them all and a guy—who was filling out forms at the reference desk. He looked to be just out of college, so about Donovan's age. He had sandy-colored hair, circular wire-rimmed glasses that made him look studious, but also a playful grin tugging at the corners of his mouth. Cute. I made a beeline for him.

"Hi," I said, slightly breathless from my hike across the library. "I was hoping you could help me locate some articles."

He looked up at me. "I'd be happy to." He smiled, showing off his dimples. Wow. *Really* cute.

I smiled back just as brightly. I couldn't help it.

Then I felt Donovan's shadow over my shoulder and realized he'd finally caught up. I didn't need to look behind me to know that Donovan must have been scowling. The librarian's smiled dimmed a few watts.

"Uh, what's your topic?" Cute Librarian Guy asked.

"Oh, right." I took a quick glance at my notes. "We were looking into local trucking companies. The kind of routes they take. The kind of cargo they carry. The ones with the best safety records in the area."

He nodded. "Sure. I think I can get you started. Do you know the names of any of the companies?"

"Americana Trucking," Donovan piped up. "That's the first one on the list. Alphabetical, you know."

Cute Librarian Guy eyed him with curiosity. "Great. So, you're both working on this? Together?"

"Yes," I said cheerfully. "But it's really *my brother's* project." I hooked my thumb in Donovan's direction but kept beaming my warmest, most flirtatious smile at the librarian. I leaned in a little closer and lowered my voice. "He needs the help," I added, just like a snotty younger sister might.

This earned me a chuckle from Cute Librarian Guy and another flash of his dimples. He stood up and turned his back on us so he could grab one of the periodical indexes.

As soon as he did, Donovan jabbed me with his finger in between my shoulder blades. "Better be nicer to me, *Sis*," he hissed in my ear.

I snickered. "Just as soon as you do the same, *Bro*."

With the help of the librarian, we soon had a stack of material to sort through. It took us over three hours of digging and reading archived microfilm, but Donovan and I finally unearthed something worth saving.

In following the trail of Americana Trucking, we learned from an old Joplin newspaper clipping that one of the guys on Treak's list—Timothy Wick—had been an executive with the Missouri-based company. That was, up until two years ago when he was arrested for the "unauthorized shipping of explosive material" that resulted in "an unfortunate accident in Amarillo, Texas."

"Oh, God, Donovan. Look at the date."

"August 5, 1976," he read. "Was that…uh, when…?"

"Yes," I said. "That's when, according to the decoded dates in the journal, Gideon and Jeremy were in Amarillo."

"Shit."

We looked up another newspaper article, this time from a Texas paper. There weren't many more details, but we did glean a few new hints from the report:

On the outskirts of Amarillo, late Thursday, August 5th, tragedy struck as an Americana Trucking semi headed for Albuquerque caught fire and, due to the explosive nature of the cargo, was destroyed before the fire department could be called for help. The truck driver was missing from the scene, but the manager responsible for the shipment, Timothy Wick of Joplin, Missouri, is being held for questioning.

Donovan and I exchanged nervous glances.

"This isn't good," he murmured.

Then there was one final article, posted about a month later, with a follow-up to the story. It recapped what had been written before, adding that Wick had been jailed for illegally ordering the transport of boxes with explosives.

But that wasn't all.

The name of the driver was still being held in confidence by the police, pending further investigation, as there had been evidence of foul play. And the big mystery investigators had been working on was where the explosive material had been manufactured. It was rumored there were ties to Chicago mob activity, but the police didn't know for sure where the bombs had originated...

"Although *we* know," I whispered. "And so did Treak, Ben, Jeremy and Gideon."

Donovan crossed his arms. "Probably why Ben and Treak are now dead. And who knows what happened to our brothers as a result?"

"Yeah," I whispered.

Then, as if trying to win the Understatement of the Year Award, he added, "Aurora, if we keep driving west, we've got to be very careful."

Chapter Ten

Tulsa, Oklahoma ~ Thursday, June 22

WE'D BEEN in Tulsa for twenty-two hours…and arguing for a full fifteen of them. (But that was only because we'd slept for seven and neither of us talked in our sleep.) I'd managed to convince Donovan to enter the state of Oklahoma, but to say we did not see eye to eye on our next step since we'd gotten here would be an accurate deduction.

An even more accurate deduction would be to say that, less than a week into our trip, we wanted to have a lightsaber fight to the death like a Jedi Knight battling one of the Dark Lords of the Empire.

"What part of 'Chicago mob activity' makes you think poking your nose any further into this would be a good idea?" Donovan demanded, his voice rising. "Especially without police protection. Seriously, Aurora, you've reached the point of *crazy* with this road trip."

"You know we have to go to Amarillo. Not only did Gideon send Amy Lynn a postcard from there—just a few weeks ago—but that's where the Americana truck exploded. It happened when our brothers were there! God, Donovan, we've almost cracked this mystery. We're *this close* to finding Gideon and Jeremy. We can't stop now."

"Oh, yes. Yes, we can." He crossed his arms. "And you're wrong, you know that? We are *not* close to finding our brothers. They would have shown up if they'd wanted to be found. And we are *not* close cracking this mystery either. Not by a long shot."

He started pacing around the room. "With everything we find a partial answer to, there are fifty more questions that come up. Maybe Hal was our waitress's boyfriend and he was a trucker for Americana, bringing explosives from Crescent Cove to Albuquerque via Texas. But *why*? And how did the Chicago mob get involved? And what happened to Hal? And what exactly did our brothers witness? It couldn't have been an accident that they were in Amarillo at the very same time this happened, could it?"

He shook his head and gave his sideburns an agitated rub. "Listen to me. This is not some little hick-town scheme gone wrong. This is major stuff. Maybe with a crime boss, just like in 'The Sting.' *Just like real life*, your brother wrote. Remember?"

"I remember. And there was a dirty cop in Gideon's movie reference, too, if you're going to go that way with it. Police can't be trusted," I shot back. I shoved the journal at Donovan. "Look at this. We've got so much more information now, even if new questions have arisen."

He snorted. "You always say—"

"Gideon wrote on July 27, 1976, 'Tulsa with J.' And below that he wrote, 'Andy Reggio is OK, OK.' And finally he wrote, 'Bikes at 100N.' These are valid leads! Names I can look up. Places and things I can find." I was already pulling out the motel phonebook to search for this new name when Donovan all but ripped it out of my hands. He flipped to the R's himself, his jaw clenched as he studied the page.

"Reggio, huh?" he said. "Well, see for yourself. There is *no* Reggio listed in the Tulsa phonebook. Not an Andy or an Andrew. Not anyone with that last name. It's just another puzzle. Another stupid clue in code. The next part of some new game your manipulative brother, or whoever's impersonating him, is playing. And I've had enough." He waited until I'd looked at the phonebook page myself. He was right. There was no one by that name listed.

"Maybe it's unlisted—" I began.

But Donovan wasn't going to indulge me with any more conjecturing.

"People have *died* already. Other people are missing," he said. "Most, if not all, of them were doing illegal things. It's not our job to bring them to justice. We need to get back home and get on with our lives and our own jobs. If any more answers are out there—"

"*If?* Donovan, of *course* there are more—"

"Then the police can be the ones to find them," he said. "We've got something legitimate that we can give them now. A solid starting point. There's a storage facility with pipe bombs near Crescent Cove. There's probably a trucking connection with this Hal guy. Maybe that's how boxes of explosives were brought to Amarillo. These details ought to give some weight to our claims. And once they've cleared up that whole bomb mess, then maybe Jeremy and Gideon's story will naturally emerge. If they're dead—" He paused to gulp a few lungfuls of air and fight for his usual sense of control. "Then...then, I guess, they're dead. But, if not, they could safely come out of hiding then."

I chose to ignore Donovan's attempt at a dispassionate speech. Why the hell did I still have to struggle to get his help despite all of the evidence I'd gathered?

I gritted my teeth in frustration and returned my focus to the phonebook and the name while Donovan blathered on. Why wasn't Andy Reggio in there? I glanced again at the journal:

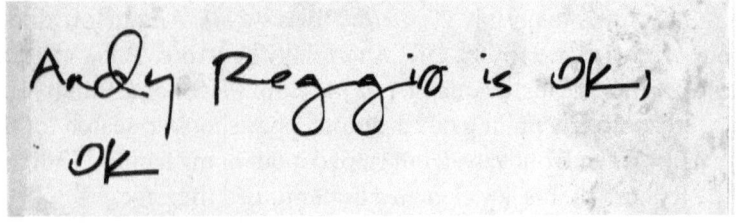

It was written under *Tulsa* but what if my brother meant that Andy wasn't only "okay," as in a person we could trust, but also that he was in Oklahoma City, Oklahoma...which would be the next big stop on Route 66? Maybe the front desk at our motel had an Oklahoma City phonebook. Or maybe we could contact the telephone operator there...but, if not, we were going to have to drive there so I could look this up in person. And, always, talking to people face to face was a better move.

Donovan may have set a limit on the amount of ambiguous information he could hold in his head, but I hadn't. I had to *know* the answers to these questions, even if they led to a thousand other ones. I had to *go* to Oklahoma City and Amarillo and maybe even Albuquerque. Following the trail that Gideon laid out for us had stopped being optional for me days ago.

"...so we'll leave tomorrow morning and we should be back home by Saturday night. Monday, after we're both done with work, we can go into the police station, okay?" he said.

"What? No! That's *not* okay."

"Fine. We can see if anyone's around on Sunday and, maybe, we'll—"

"I'm not going back with you, Donovan." I crossed my arms and held my ground as I watched the anger color his face. "If you want to drive home, you can do it. There are buses that go to Oklahoma City and Amarillo, and I can take one of them."

"For God's sake, Aurora! I promised your dad I'd *keep you safe.* There is no damn way you're staying down here without me."

"I'll tell him I insisted." I paused. "That I forced you to go. Or that I ran away from you. Whatever it takes." I glanced at the door. It wouldn't be too hard to do that for real. To sneak away in the middle of the night. Scary as hell, sure, but not complicated.

Donovan saw where I was looking and shook his head. "I won't let you," he said hoarsely. The look he gave me was almost as desperate and resolute as the way I felt.

A combination of emotions welled up deep in my chest. I fought it, or tried, but my heart and lungs were constricting. Breathing became harder and I felt those tears of aggravation—tears I didn't want to show anyone, to Donovan least of all—gathering behind my eyes, making it too difficult to see him in front of me.

"C'mon," I managed to whisper. "You know I've been lying to my parents about where we've been for the past six days. But what you don't get is that I've really been lying to them for *years.* Not just about this, not just about the search for our brothers, but about everything."

Donovan, of course, didn't really understand what I meant. He was focused on the trip, on his promise to my dad, on our safety.

"They're just lost in their own pain," he said, trying hard—I could tell—to be empathetic. "I haven't been able to tell my mom everything either. But whatever worry she's able to spare, she's spent it on me anyway. I know your mom and dad have to feel the same way, and I know you don't want to hurt them by worrying them even more."

"Of course I don't but, Donovan, don't *you* need to know where Jeremy is and what happened to him? Don't *you* have to find the answer?"

"Not if it'll hurt someone else too much. I mean, yes, I'm haunted by his disappearance and by whatever the cause of it was, but we know so much more now than we did. After watching that film at Amy Lynn's that he and your brother made—" He paused and I saw him battle with his own emotions and memories. "I...I felt better, you know? Their intentions weren't bad. It was just that they were in the wrong place at the wrong time. They had their reasons for what they did."

I massaged my forehead with my fingertips. Caught up as he was in preserving his positive mental image of our brothers, he truly wasn't getting any of this. At least not from my perspective.

"And that knowledge is *enough* for you?" I asked. "That feeling of everything being fine because you don't think Gideon and Jeremy set out to kill anyone or bomb any buildings? You can just stop looking now?"

"If Jeremy were still alive he would've contacted me," Donovan replied with complete and utter certainty. "So, yes, I found out what I needed to know."

I studied his face, realizing how different he and I were in this way. "But it's not all *I* need to know. And even if we weren't talking about a life and death situation involving people we love...even if we weren't talking about our brothers at all, it *still* wouldn't be enough for me." I bit down on my bottom lip to keep it from quivering. "I can't keep pretending that my problems are so straightforward, Donovan. Don't you see? No one understands me. My parents least of all."

He shrugged. "Everyone thinks that about their parents when they're growing up." He said it gently, softly, not *trying* to be condescending, but, nevertheless, unable to be anything else.

But I knew I didn't have typical teenager issues, like the kind most parents wrote to Ann Landers to ask about. *My daughter watches too much TV, Ann. What should I do to encourage her to read books instead?* The advice columns were filled with inconsequential crap like that.

No. As frustrated as I was with Donovan's overprotectiveness combined with his inability to grasp what I was saying, the problem wasn't just that he didn't see the connections I'd been constantly making...or comprehend the sheer *need* I had to figure out the clues hidden in Gideon's journal. The problem was my overwhelming helplessness in facing my true self.

I didn't know how to stop myself from *understanding too much.*

From perceiving too many signals. From being so aware that it hurt.

My life was a constant source of painful realizations. I craved an ignorance-is-bliss existence. I was envious of Betsy's sweet simplemindedness and Donovan's ability to turn perplexing problems over to others. I wished I could be as easily satisfied and as habitually transparent.

But, in my reality, I knew that wasn't anywhere close to the truth. That it might never be. For that to happen, I'd have to trust in another person more than I'd ever been capable of doing. Believe their perceptions were stronger or at least equal to mine.

And how could I explain to somebody that what gave me my identity was the *very thing* that kept me from sharing myself with anyone else?

I couldn't stop the tears from coming, hard as I tried to hold them back. Even worse, I couldn't seem to just cry softly, silently. No, I was sobbing. Loud, gasping moans and snivels.

Donovan looked at me in panic. I could tell he hadn't expected this. That he wanted to comfort me but didn't know how. To be honest, I didn't know how either.

"Hey, it's okay." He gingerly placed his palm on my arm, like a toddler might approach the petting of an unpredictable puppy—one that might nip his hand at any second.

But it wasn't okay. Really, how could it *ever* be okay?

"S-Sorry," I whispered between sobs, blindly reaching for the edge of the bed so I could sink onto it and hide my face from his searching expression.

I was aware of him moving around the room but, before I could figure out what he was doing, he was back in front me. He held a box of tissues that he'd found somewhere and pulled a couple of them out for me. I cried even harder into them.

He sat down next to me and, again, touched my arm with that awkward petting motion. "Aurora, it's going to be all right. I—I didn't think you'd get this upset."

I knew he didn't have a clue what had actually set me off, just that he somehow realized there was a much deeper issue at stake. Score one for his insightfulness.

"Look, if it means that much to you, I guess we can go to Oklahoma City for a day. It won't take that much time…" He paused. "Would that help? I'm not trying to be unreasonable or to make you mad. It's just that I think we're walking into really dangerous territory here and we should go back soon."

"I know you do," I murmured, wiping some of the biggest splotches of wetness away from my cheeks and blowing my nose.

This was hard. I hadn't been trying to get my way by bawling my eyes out, but Donovan didn't know that. I hated the thought of being one of those girls who manipulated guys with her tears and, much as I wanted to go (and *would* go) to Oklahoma City, I didn't want him agreeing to take me just because I'd turned into a human water faucet. I told him this.

He leaned in closer to me and smiled. "You're forgetting that I didn't just meet you for the first time last week, Aurora. You've never been one of those types of girls. If anything—" He abruptly stopped talking, leaned back and fiddled with the corner of the tissue box.

"If anything what?"

I saw a fleeting grimace, as though he hadn't wanted to reveal that much. But, nevertheless, he continued. "If anything, you've been too reserved with your emotions. Too careful. You're always watching people. Hardly ever letting on what you think of them."

He put the box down between us on the bed. "I remember how strong you were during the memorial service. You and I were the only ones who didn't lose it in front of everyone. I kept checking on you. Telling myself that if you could keep it together for an hour that day, so could I."

I exhaled and stared at him, not bothering to disguise my curiosity. During the service, I'd caught him watching me a few times, but I'd never had any idea that was what he'd been thinking then.

He tugged a little at my shirt, a playful maneuver that normally would've made me smile. "And remember that barbeque we had at school when Gideon and Jeremy were just starting their freshman year?"

I nodded. I'd been in junior high then. Donovan had been a high-school senior. But because they'd had a special event at school one night—some sort of "welcome" ceremony for the freshmen—he and I both had to go with our families.

"I remember the badly charred hotdogs," I said. "Unfortunately."

He laughed a little. "And I remember you with pigtails in your hair, sitting on the bleachers, taking in the whole scene. It wasn't a good night for me. Lots of stuff going on at home that I didn't want to think about. I'd thrown my jacket on a bleacher bench near you and just wanted to grab it, yank Jeremy away from there and go to Super-Tastee for burgers or fries or something. Anything edible."

In spite of myself, I grinned at that.

"But, before I left, I asked you a question," he said.

"Yeah, you did." I remembered every time Donovan and I had ever been alone. "You asked me what I knew about that high-school gym teacher, Mr. Morrigan."

"Right," Donovan said. "'Cause he was a dick. You'd lived in Chameleon Lake for longer than me. I figured you might know what his story was." He looked at me. "And you did. You knew about his divorce and all the small-town gossip that came with that. You told me as much in a sentence, but you told me something else, too."

He moved a little closer in again. "You studied him standing there across the football field, as if you were seeing him for the first time, and you said, 'He's trapped. Like a lobster in a boiling pot of water with his pincers rubber-banded shut. He's dying a slow death here and he knows it.' And when I really looked at him, I could tell you were right. You were only *twelve*, but you sensed all of this stuff about him—things I just knew no one had told you—all from a quick glance. And it wasn't like you had any bones to pick with him. It was pure insight. Amazing. And dead accurate."

I sniffled and he handed me another tissue.

"So, let's just say, that's not a quality I've seen in a lot of girls I've met. Or guys, for that matter." He pulled me to standing and waited until I met his eye. "We'll go to Oklahoma City, but not just because you're crying, okay? You've got good instincts and, I gotta admit, I've been reluctant to believe them. But I shouldn't have been. Maybe there'll be a solid clue over there."

He took a step forward and wrapped his arms around me in the first hug he'd given me since our brothers' graduation party in St. Cloud. It brought back a rush of memories. Some sad, but some pleasurable, too. I held my breath as he pressed his body gently against mine, only long enough to brush my bangs to the side and peck a tiny kiss on my forehead. Then he stepped back really fast.

"Minnesota is directly north, though, and I'm planning to head home just as soon as you're done with Oklahoma," he said. "We need to get back. We said we'd be home this weekend, and we will be."

"Maybe," I murmured.

"Definitely," he countered. There was an intractable degree of conviction in his voice, but I wasn't going to fight him tonight. I'd bought myself another full day of investigating, and I planned to use every second of it.

As he turned the TV on and flipped between stations, finally settling on CBS and a repeat episode of "Hawaii Five-O," I wiped away the last of my tears and, admittedly, felt better for having shed them.

It wasn't as though I thought Donovan really understood me or that the world suddenly made more sense than it had a half hour before. It didn't. But I appreciated his efforts to reach out to me and, most of all, I was grateful he wasn't afraid to try.

TURNED OUT, Andy Reggio's name wasn't in the Oklahoma City phonebook either—something I discovered about four minutes after we got into town. Fortunately, that hadn't been the only clue Gideon had given us. Seemed there *was* a place on 100 North Street that sold bikes. Motorbikes, to be exact. And I made Donovan take me there right away.

"In the market for a Harley?" a sales guy with a scraggly salt-n-pepper beard asked Donovan when we walked in together. I'd grown accustomed to being overlooked by most salespeople most of the time, either because I was with one of my parents and the store owners were trying to win them over, or because I was with a guy, like my brother or Donovan, and everyone knew they were the ones with the money.

Not so true in our case, though.

Donovan hadn't let me spend much of my own cash since we'd hit the road, so I still had a couple hundred dollars left. I wasn't planning to use it to buy a motorcycle, but Donovan, of course, looked intrigued by them.

"Maybe," he told the guy, skimming his fingers down the body of a sleek red one. "Man, she's beautiful."

The salesman nodded, looking half in love with the gleaming

chrome and scarlet body of a motorcycle that was curvy in all the right places.

I wandered away, hearing them delve into talk of horsepower, paint detailing and bike accessories. Meanwhile, I glanced around the shop, giving measured, deliberate attention to its wares. There were probably eighty-five motorbikes on display in a range of sizes, shapes and styles. All of them Harley Davidsons. The kind of place my brother and his best friend would have liked. It was a Route 66 "freedom on the open road" dream come true.

I imagined a slew of college guys, perhaps just having read *Zen and the Art of Motorcycle Maintenance*, bursting into the store and impulsively buying bikes to take the rest of their way westward. Something Gideon and Jeremy might have done if they'd had the chance.

And then there was this Andy person. If he was from anywhere in Oklahoma and was someone my brother had trusted, then they had to have crossed paths somewhere. Might have even been here.

"Excuse me," I said and, then, repeated it a little louder, having to interrupt Donovan and the salesman in the middle of a clearly life-affirming discussion about performance tires. "Do you know anybody named Andy Reggio? A...friend told us he might live in the area."

"Why, sure," the man said, scratching the bottom of his beard where it connected to his leathered skin. "Everyone knows Andy, but he's a Texas boy. Used to work here more, but he's got an elderly momma living in Shamrock, so he's gone a lot these days. Did see him on Tuesday, though. And he said he'd be in over the weekend."

"He's an employee?" My excitement rose at the thought. "And he's scheduled to work this weekend? Like, tomorrow?"

The sales guy shook his head. "Andy's hours ain't regular like that. He works on special repair projects mostly, but he's got a mailbox in the staff room and he checks it every day he's in town. So, if you wanna leave him a note..."

"Okay." I wasn't entirely sure what to say to Andy, but I figured it ought to be worth a shot trying to contact him. What Donovan and I had learned from Amy Lynn had been tremendous, and I couldn't help but get my hopes up that a conversation with Andy would be just as helpful.

The guy handed me a pencil and a slip of cream-colored notepaper.

"Put down the number where you're stayin' and he'll for sure get back to you. He's real responsible that way."

I shot a look at Donovan, who said, "Aurora, no. We need to get going. Why don't we give him our home phone numbers, and he can call us in Minnesota?"

I crossed my arms, shook my head and prepared for a stare down.

Donovan gave it his best shot, but I held out for longer. Finally, with a resigned sigh, he said, "Fine. We can stay at the motel down the block for tonight. *Just* tonight."

"Great!"

He chuckled at my burst of enthusiasm. "You get to write the note, though. I'll go check us in quick so you can tell him our room number."

It took me almost the whole twenty minutes he was gone to compose a five-sentence message, but it had to be written just right. Something anyone could read without raising suspicion. In a spurt of inspiration, I finally scribbled:

Hello, Mr. Reggio,

I think my brother Gideon and his friend may have visited your shop two summers ago. Do you remember them? Perhaps they've come back to see you since? My brother thought highly of you, and I'd love to hear about your meeting. Please call room #6 at the Prairie Pine Lodge tonight, if you're able, and thank you.

Sincerely,
Aurora

Donovan, who'd returned with the room key, okayed my note with a shrug when he read it. I'd purposely avoided mentioning anyone's last names, and I hadn't even given out Jeremy's first name. Amy Lynn had known exactly who I'd been talking about when I called her in Chicago. This Andy guy would have to bring some extra knowledge to the table before I'd believe we could trust him, too.

The call, when it came that night, wasn't quite what I'd expected, though.

"Mrs. McCafferty?" the weary front desk clerk asked when he telephoned our room at 10:37 p.m.

"Um, yes?" I still wasn't used to being called that, no matter how many times Donovan and I lied to motel clerks about being married.

"I hope I'm not waking you or your husband—"

I gazed at Donovan, who was sprawled on the bed, flipping with great amusement through last month's issue of *Seventeen* magazine, which he'd found on the nightstand. He sat up fast when I caught his eye.

"—but the lodge just received a call from a delivery service asking us to make sure you received your package. Should've been dropped off by your door tonight."

"At our door?" I asked. "Let me just check."

But Donovan jumped off the bed and raced me there, literally pushing my hand away from the knob and motioning for me to stay back. He first glanced through the peephole. Then he shoved aside the heavy curtains to look out the front window and, finally, spotting nothing yet that alarmed him, he cracked the door open—leaving the chain still on—and cautiously peered into the night.

A large, thick, light-brown mailing envelope leaned against the doorframe.

Donovan prodded at it a time or two with his fingers, then he snatched the package and pulled it inside the room.

"Uh, yeah. Thanks," I told the desk clerk. "We did receive it." I said a quick goodnight to the guy and hung up, watching as Donovan cautiously sliced the side of the large envelope open with his pocket knife. "What's in it?" I asked him.

"Papers. Lots of them." He showed me the stack of sheets he'd pulled from inside the package. There were a bunch of newspaper clippings, a few mimeographed pages of what looked like police reports and a neatly typed note paperclipped to the top of the stack. Donovan unclipped it and handed it to me. "You should read this."

I took it from him and scanned the page. It said:

Aurora,

Got your message at the bike shop tonight. Last time I saw Gideon, he told me that if you ever came looking for me that I should give you this packet. It has some info about what happened in Amarillo, and he said you'd know what that meant.

I really liked meeting both your brother and his buddy Jeremy and wished we all could've talked for longer.

It's late and I need to head back to Texas real early in the morning, but if you have any questions, just leave me a message at the bike shop with the direct phone number to wherever you're staying tomorrow. I can give you a call from Shamrock later in the day.

Andy R.

Donovan and I spent half the night going through the clippings page by page. Unlike the two brief newspaper announcements we'd read on the microfilm at the public library in Joplin, these actual pages were from several Texan newspapers, a few of them smaller, less conventional publications. They contained longer and more speculative passages about Americana Trucking and the Amarillo disaster in early August 1976. And though the information provided might have been less reliable than a mainstream paper, it did seem to fill in some possible missing gaps.

According to one clipping, the driver of the truck, whose name was still not officially released to the public, "disappeared after the incident, but a search of private Americana correspondence suggested that a trucker with a last name of Chaney was reported missing from work the following week."

Another clipping stated that "there was one man confirmed dead on the scene and, though the police would not verify the identity of the victim, a hospital source leaked his name to be Rick Brice of Chicago, IL."

There were mimeographed pages of police reports that showed this Rick Brice person as being "a former Chicago cop, wanted in connection with some still-unsolved labor union dispute that resulted in the mysterious deaths of two union leaders back in 1974."

"Can these be real reports?" I asked Donovan, who looked alarmed when he read what they said.

"I don't know," he replied. "Maybe. But how would your brother have gotten them?"

"I don't know."

Still, the name of the guy mentioned looked unsettlingly familiar to me and, when I flipped back through my translation of Treak's shorthand notes, I saw why. The name and place, *Rick Brice - Chic,* stared up at me from the middle of the page.

But that wasn't all.

There was another police report for Timothy Wick, that Americana

Trucking executive who'd gotten jail time for his involvement in ordering the explosives to be shipped to Albuquerque. The private report stated that he had "a verified association to Chicago crime boss Vincent Leto and to Leto's right-hand man, Rick Brice."

Guess whose name and city was right above Rick Brice's on Treak's note page?

Yeah. *Vincent Leto - Chic.*

Somehow all of these bad men—Leto, Wick, Brice and more—were connected. And somehow my brother had an important reason to be interested in them.

As soon as the bike shop opened the next morning—"Not 'til ten o'clock on Saturdays, dammit," Donovan muttered—we telephoned them and left a message for Andy to call us at the Prairie Pine Lodge.

"You realize this means at least one of us has to stay here all day," I told him. "We're not missing this call."

He was striding around the room like a wild animal held in captivity, but he nodded. "Dammit," he said again. "Why couldn't he have just come over last night? Talked to us then? He *had* to know we'd have a thousand questions."

"Maybe, maybe not." For the trillionth time, I flipped through the pages we'd gotten the night before, shaking my head. "We don't know what Gideon told Andy about Amarillo when he gave him these papers. Or when my brother gave them to him. It could've been a year ago. We don't know how well Gideon and Andy even know each other, just that my brother must have had a good reason to think him trustworthy."

"Well, we were supposed to check out of here by noon," he said. "You're right. We can't drive home until he calls us back, but that might not be for hours."

"Look, why don't you go out for a little while? Get some fresh air," I suggested.

"I don't feel comfortable leaving you alone here."

"I'll be fine," I said. "See if the desk clerk will give us a later check-out time. It's possible, if no one's waiting for the room, they might let us stay until three or four this afternoon."

He shrugged. "Worth a shot, I guess." He slipped on his sneakers. "I'll get us something else to eat, too." He tossed the now-empty bags of cookies and potato chips into the trash bin with a heavy sigh.

"Some fresh fruit, perhaps?" I suggested, given that we'd eaten nothing but junk food for the past twenty-four hours.

He laughed. "Yeah, okay. Some fruit…and maybe a couple of Kit Kats."

I smiled and watched Donovan close the door and, for my safety, lock it securely behind him. "Don't open this for anyone," he threatened from outside the room.

"I won't," I called back.

He might not be quick to think of healthy dining options, but he never stopped remembering his promise to my dad to protect me. And, on top of that, every night—unfailingly—he was a gentleman when it came to our sleeping arrangements. If we could get a room with twin beds, he opted for that. If we couldn't, he scrupulously stayed on his side of our double bed.

In an irritating way, he'd taken on the role of both father and brother for this trip. I sometimes wondered if he ever even saw me as that girl who had once kissed him at our brothers' graduation party. If he ever even thought of me as someone who would become a legal adult in just a week.

Donovan returned to the room long before the phone rang, bearing a bottle of orange juice, crunchy red apples and fresh chicken salad on sliced wheat bread. He also brought news of a new four p.m. checkout time and was in possession of two slightly melted Milky Way bars.

"They were out of Kit Kats," he informed me.

"Ah."

We passed the hours eating, watching snippets of various Saturday morning cartoons, playing a couple of rounds of gin rummy with a deck of cards Donovan found in the desk drawer and holding our collective breaths.

At 2:08 our patience was rewarded.

Donovan snatched the phone before the end of the first ring. "Hello?"

Through the tinny receiver and the stuffy airwaves separating Donovan from me, I could hear the strains of a distinctive Texan accent coming through the line. I heard Andy Reggio ask for me by name.

"She's here," Donovan said coldly. "But I want to talk to you first. I'm Jeremy's brother, Donovan McCafferty." There was a pause and, from what I could gather, a jovial greeting—enough so that when Donovan spoke again, his voice had warmed up about ten degrees. "Thank you," he said. Then, "Yeah, Jeremy was…" Another pause. "Yes, I always thought highly of them both."

I moved closer to where Donovan was standing so I might be able to better hear Andy's comments. It was much harder to read reactions when I only had a voice to go by, but I was going to try. Andy said something about how the three men had all met at the bike shop two years ago, just as I'd guessed.

"You said you saw Gideon when he gave you the papers," Donovan said. "Was it recently?"

"Oh, yeah, 'bout a month ago."

"*Really?* What about Jeremy? Was he there, too?"

"Nope, not this time," I could hear Andy say clearly. "Gideon was alone. He just stopped by the shop for a bit—first time we'd crossed paths since '76. When I asked about Jeremy, though, he said he expected to see him soon, but he didn't give out any specifics."

A look of pure hope bathed Donovan's face in a flash of light, effusing it in joy and amazement. It was an expression unlike any I'd seen him wear, at least for the split second that he allowed it to be shown. He covered his eyes with his palm, almost immediately muting the effect, or, perhaps, it was to prevent any tears from leaking out. He cleared his throat several times.

In almost a whisper, Donovan said, "We haven't seen our brothers in a long time. What do you know about the incident in Amarillo?"

I strained to hear Andy's response, and Donovan, finally seeing how hard I was trying to follow both sides of the conversation, yanked me close to him and shared the phone with me—putting the receiver between our ears, holding it tight.

"Not much more than what was in the papers," Andy confessed. "Though Gideon did hint he knew the rumor was true about the trucker being some Yankee named Chaney."

I glanced at Donovan and tugged the receiver just a fraction of an inch closer to my mouth before speaking. "Hello, Mr. Reggio. This is Aurora."

"Why, hello, Miz Aurora," the friendly voice on the line said with one of the thickest accents I'd ever heard. You know the kind—so strong you almost think it's fake. As a Minnesota native, it was hard to believe anyone could draw out their syllables for that long. "With you and Donovan, y'all can call me Andy."

"Andy," I breathed, "thank you for calling us back and for delivering these papers to us last night. Do you have any idea how my brother might have gotten ahold of the police reports? They seemed pretty... um, confidential and official, so I wondered."

"Don't rightly know," the Texan replied. "But your brother told me to hang onto them for ya, so that's what I did. He had a law enforcement friend, though, so maybe that was how he got 'em."

Donovan pulled the phone back toward his mouth and repeated, "A law enforcement friend?" He sent me a perplexed glance. "Do you know who, Andy? Or even which city this *friend* of his lived in?"

"Sure do," Andy's cheery voice boomed back. "Gideon told me about a cop from your hometown. Guy by the name of James—William James. I remember 'cuz Gideon mentioned him a bunch of times. Fact is, he told me if his sister were ever to be in Oklahoma and askin' for advice on what to do that I should tell her it was all right to call this police officer. Share the information in the envelope with him...but *only* him. Say there were details about the Amarillo explosion that Gideon had given to a friend to give to her and that she could bring those papers home to show him."

No way!

I couldn't believe this. It couldn't be right. I felt the blood rushing from my face at Andy's suggestion, but Donovan shot me a triumphant look. He said into the receiver, "So, Gideon specifically told you we could trust Officer James?" I knew he was saying this far more for my benefit than to clarify anything with Andy.

"Yep," the Texan said. "But, again, just *him*. You don't wanna be tellin' the whole entire police force about what you know just yet. Probably best to call him personally, at home on the weekend, maybe, rather than go in to see him. There'd be more questions and such if you were at the station."

I exhaled slowly, trying to control my desire to contradict everything Andy Reggio was saying. I snatched the phone from Donovan.

"Do you know how to reach my brother?" I asked Andy.

How was I supposed to believe we could trust any cop after

everything that'd happened? Maybe if the words came directly from Gideon's mouth…but still. It just felt wrong to me. In opposition to every one of my heightened perceptions.

"'Fraid not," Andy replied, a hint of sadness in his voice. "Would like to see him more often myself. Seems he moves around a lot. But," his tone brightened, "he told me if you needed proof that what I was sayin' was the truth, that I should tell you something only you would know, Miz Aurora."

I held my breath for a full fifteen seconds before I managed to ask, "What's that?"

There was a low chuckle on the line. "In your diary, when you and your brother were kids, he read about your first kiss."

"He never read my diary," I replied. "At least, he *said* he didn't."

"Ah, brothers do things like that," Andy said with gentle humor. "Sometimes they lie to their sisters when they're trying to protect them."

My distrust of Andy's opinion was growing by the minute. "Oh, really? What did he tell you?"

"Said the boy's name was Mike somethin'. Klausen, I think. You were fourteen. And you told your friends you liked his kiss, but in your diary you said he was as 'slobbery as a sheepdog.' Did I remember that rightly?"

My mind reeled. Truly, no one in the universe but Gideon could have known that. It was the *exact* phrase I'd used…and only in my diary. I hadn't even told Betsy my real reaction.

"One day, I hope I'll see my brother again," I told the chuckling Texan with a sigh, "so I can get even with him for that." I tried to joke about it, but it was just a flimsy cover for my shock. I was trembling from the inside out.

"Well, I wish you luck finding him," Andy said kindly before he hung up.

Donovan slanted me an odd look. "Mike Klausen was your first kiss? *That* bonehead—really?"

"Oh, shut up."

He laughed. "So, okay. We'll talk about something else, like how we now can tell all of this stuff we've found out on the road to Officer James."

"We don't know that for sure. I just—I don't think we should reveal everything, Donovan. I mean, Andy told us that Gideon said we could share the clippings and the reports from the envelope with Officer James, but what about the names in Treak's notes? Or Ben's film? What about Crescent Cove and the pipe bombs that Ronny Lee Wolf had stashed up there? What about Amy Lynn? We might be willing to take a risk and trust what Andy said, but I don't feel comfortable forcing that risk on Amy Lynn, especially not without her knowledge or permission."

I implored him with my eyes to understand. "Do you see the difference? It's one thing to tell the officer about information we got from Gideon. It's another to connect the dots for him and involve someone innocent."

I may as well have been talking to the chipped imitation-marble nightstand for all Donovan was listening to me. He was too busy, I could tell, striding around the room and feeling vindicated.

And stunned by the thought that Jeremy might just be fine.

And elated that my brother was on his side when it came to trusting the police.

And pleased that we'd be heading back home in less than an hour because, let's face it, I'd already pleaded with him to let us keep searching for Gideon, and this dead end—*contacting the police at home, for God's sake!*—was where it had led. I could no longer dream up reasons to keep us on the road.

"Let's just call Officer James right now," Donovan urged, "and give him the Cliff's Notes version. We don't need to tell him about Amy Lynn yet, but I don't see any reason to protect that slimeball Ronny. We can just explain that we found out about the pipe bombs in Crescent Cove when we went up there to get more fireworks. He'll believe that, since he caught us launching some this month. And then we can say we figured out from there that, somehow, Hal was hired to take a bunch of pipe bombs by truck to Albuquerque. Hell, maybe the officer even knows some of this already and—"

"But, see, that bothers me. Why, if Gideon felt that cop was so trustworthy, didn't my brother work out all of this himself with Officer James? If Gideon got the police reports from the officer and he shared what he knew about what happened in Crescent Cove, why didn't the police follow through? Why wasn't this case solved by August or September 1976 when these newspaper clippings first came out so our brothers could've felt safe coming home long ago?"

Donovan shrugged. "Aurora, I say this respectfully, okay? I don't want you to get mad at me, but think about it from my side. I know you love your brother, but he's a *big* game player. All these codes and hidden messages and crap… I realize he's a brilliant guy, and I always liked him, but I didn't have to deal with this side of him before. Maybe he's got a real good reason for doing every one of the things he did, but I don't think he needed to act like James Bond about it. He *likes* creating puzzles for you to solve as much as you like solving them."

He paused for a long moment, stroking his sideburns and looking mystified. "That's something your family is into, I guess, but mine isn't. This whole game has been wearing me out. I'm ready to be straight with the police about it all. To say what we need to say and then go home."

I acknowledged his words. He'd spoken them without a hint of harshness, but he was both firm and honest about his feelings. There was no way I'd get him to back down from that decision and, in trying to see things from his viewpoint, I could understand his frustration. He'd played along with Gideon's road-trip scavenger hunt for a long time already—a game that even I didn't know the rules to. A game we'd been struggling to learn as we went along.

Donovan had trusted me enough to decipher the codes in the journal and he'd cared about me enough to stay by my side no matter where those clues led, but I could see he'd reached the end of this particular highway, especially at a point where he felt we had a good reason to stop.

"All right," I said on a sigh, trying to exhale my paranoia along with all the air in my lungs. "Call him now. The sooner we can give him the info, the sooner he can start catching the bad guys, right?"

My instincts had always been excellent, but I knew I wasn't infallible. Maybe I'd misread some signals back home. Maybe I'd let my fear and anger over my brother's disappearance color my perceptions too much. Maybe, just maybe, we could trust Officer James after all.

Donovan's hand was already on the phone. "Thanks," he said to me a second before connecting with the operator and, in moments, getting the home phone number of Officer William James of the Chameleon Lake Police Department.

The phone rang three or four times before our hometown cop with the quick grin and the auburn hair picked up.

"Officer James," Donovan began, identifying himself immediately and, then, launching into a surprisingly eloquent explanation of where we were and much of what we'd discovered. I could tell that, though he was nervous, he'd also been rehearsing some version of this conversation since the first night I showed him the journal. He knew what he wanted to say.

Also, even though I wasn't sharing the phone with Donovan this time, I could hear the stunned silence through the line as the Minnesota cop tried to process what Donovan had just told him.

"You and Aurora Gray are all the way down in Oklahoma City, *right this very second*?" he asked, incredulous. "With documents that her brother—a guy we'd all thought was *dead*—gave to a friend of his to give to you?"

"Yes, sir," Donovan answered.

"And you think what you found shows a connection between the manufacturing of pipe bombs in a little Wisconsin town, some possible Chicago mob-related activity and a truck explosion in Amarillo, Texas?"

"Yes."

"Do your parents know your whereabouts?" the cop asked. "Does anybody up here?"

"No, sir," Donovan said. "We didn't think it was safe to tell anyone about this except you. But we're planning to start driving back tonight. It'll probably take us about sixteen hours but we—"

"No, son, don't do that," Officer James interrupted. "Don't drive back yet. Carrying around information like that is too dangerous. I think we can come up with a safer alternative."

There was a long pause while the cop thought about this and asked Donovan a series of new questions—lines from the police reports that the officer wanted him to read over the phone and details he wanted Donovan to share about what we'd seen in Crescent Cove.

Donovan was very forthcoming with the information we'd uncovered ourselves, but I was thankful he did as he'd promised and left out our visit to Amy Lynn's apartment. He also minimized any hints that Gideon had, in some way, been orchestrating our discoveries. Probably because the officer wouldn't have believed us anyway.

I heard the cop ask for the second time, "You didn't actually *see*

Gideon Gray, did you? Or your own brother Jeremy?"

"Unfortunately, no, sir," Donovan replied.

Though I couldn't see his expression, I could almost feel the officer's relief that we weren't admitting to consorting with ghosts in Oklahoma. But I would've given a lot at that moment for just one five-second glance at the cop's face and hands. Being sightless like this, there was so much information about the conversation that was unknown to me.

"Well, now, if this is all what you say it is, and if we can locate those explosives in Crescent Cove, we might just have a major bust on our hands," the cop said. "You and Aurora will be heroes when you return, but I don't want you to leave there just yet. And I don't want you to talk to anybody else about this until we're sure we can nail the bad guys."

We heard the sounds of shuffling pages in the background, as if Officer James was flipping through something thick, like a phonebook. It must have been a road atlas, though, because he added, "Looks like you're only about two hundred and fifty miles from Amarillo, Texas, and I have a trusted fellow officer who lives out that way. I won't tell him anything yet, but it'll be helpful to have a good man on our side. I want you to drive to Amarillo and stay at the Cactus Flower Inn on the outskirts of town. Should take you about four and a half hours. You're in your red Trans Am, Donovan, right?"

"Yes. We took my car."

"Good. It's a fast one. But drive the speed limit." He laughed. To me, it sounded a little forced, but I appreciated that he was trying to keep things light.

"Here's what I'll do," he added. "I'm going to go to Wisconsin right now, check out the situation in Crescent Cove and then I'll give you a call late tonight or sometime tomorrow morning. When we've got the evidence in hand, we'll take the next step. I can set up a meeting for you with my friend. Someone who will not only be able to protect you while you're there but who has access to all the records on file and can reexamine the crime scene, if needed, until I can get down to Texas myself."

"What about our families?" Donovan asked. "They're expecting us home this weekend."

"Well, if town gossip is correct, everyone in Chameleon Lake thinks you two are out scouting colleges in Illinois and Iowa—" the officer said.

Donovan winked at me. *Did we know how to start an effective rumor, or what?*

"—which was what I thought, too, until this afternoon." Officer James let out a long breath. "So, why don't you just give your folks a quick call and say you need a few extra days. That the admissions department of a campus you're visiting won't be open until Monday, and that's why you have to stay a little longer than you'd expected. Okay?"

"Okay, sir."

"And, remember, this is very sensitive information you two have. You need to be very careful and not discuss this with anybody else. Not even family yet."

"We won't," Donovan promised. Then, when he hung up, he said to me, "So...it looks like we're gonna get to go a little farther on Route 66 than I thought."

Chapter Eleven

Amarillo, Texas ~ Saturday, June 24

WE MADE the calls home to our parents and, also, to our bosses about our delay, and we assured everyone that all was well.

Dale was furious with me, of course, but he was at the store with customers when I called him, so he was limited by how much of a jackass he was willing to be in public. Through gritted teeth, he threatened me with "a talk" when I got back and no more vacation time for the rest of the year.

I just sighed and said, "Sure." It wasn't worth the high long-distance rates to argue with him.

The conversation with my parents was trickier, though. Mom and Dad were genuinely concerned about us, but I'd gotten so good at lying to them about how "fine" and "safe" we were that I'd begun to believe my own fabrications. Never a good idea.

It was 8:40 p.m. when we spotted the Cactus Flower Inn. There were exactly two other cars in the parking lot and the "us" in "Cactus" kept flickering in neon green. I'd expected someplace louder, bigger, flashier—or at least more centrally located. But it was a very quiet Saturday night at the edge of Amarillo and the silence taunted me with its artificiality. It was almost defiant.

Donovan shrugged when he got out of the car. "Well, we're here."

"Yeah."

"Why don't we check in and then…I don't know, go for a drive or something? Maybe see the town. I think most of it is over there." He pointed westward, where a hint of the setting sun still colored the horizon with a thin streak of orange. "Officer James said he wouldn't call us until late tonight or tomorrow."

"Okay," I said again, agreeing to the drive.

Not sure what I thought yet about the cop's plan to talk to us again by phone, though. He still had to get himself to Crescent Cove and find Ronny Lee Wolf's storage facility. We didn't tell him how we knew to look for it—just that he should—but Donovan and I were both aware that it'd been two years since Ben Rainwater filmed the insides of the place. Maybe it was on tribal lands and not accessible. Maybe the contents changed. It might even all be gone by now. We'd have to wait and see.

As for our evening, it turned out Amarillo was, in fact, bigger and more active than we'd been led to believe by our sleepy introduction to it. The lady at the front desk handed us a stack of "attractions" brochures along with our room key when we checked in.

"Y'all might wanna catch a bite at The Big Texan Steak Ranch, if you're hungry and you like meat," she said with a smile. "And on the other side of the city, right along Route 66, there's the Cadillac Ranch. It's a pretty famous landmark."

I thought of my brother's second postcard to Amy Lynn and nodded.

We thanked her, dropped our overnight bags in the room and headed into the heart of Amarillo.

With darkness having fallen over the city and the lights all around, I was finally beginning to see it as the largest Texas town in the north of the state. After driving through the Interstate-40 business district, I had to admit I wasn't sure why Officer James had specifically told us to stay at the Cactus Flower Inn and not a motel nearer the city center.

"He really has us on the fringes," I said to Donovan.

"Yeah, it's an odd choice, but he probably knows what he's doing," Donovan said, giving the cop his vote of confidence yet again. "Maybe it's a place he's stayed at before and he liked it. I just hope—" He hesitated.

"You hope what?"

"That us going through all of this won't be for nothing. That it'll make the world safe for our brothers." He exhaled. "I just haven't wanted to let myself believe…you know, that Jeremy might still be out there. Alive. Unharmed. That I might get to actually see my kid brother again."

"I know." I'd believed Gideon and his friend might be alive for much longer than Donovan had, but I, too, wondered what it might be like to simply see and chat with my brother once more. Wondered about it all the time, in fact.

"Hey, there's that place." He nodded toward a bright yellow building with blue trim that said *The Big Texan* on the side. "Hungry?"

I pulled out the large advertising card the motel lady gave us about the steakhouse and read a bit about it. "Not hungry enough for The Texas King," I told him.

"What's that?"

"Their famous 72-ounce sirloin steak, served with salad, shrimp cocktail, baked potato and a dinner roll. It's free if you can eat the whole thing by yourself in an hour. Otherwise, you pay for it."

"I've got an appetite, but I don't think I could finish all that tonight," he admitted. "Maybe just a steak sandwich or a burger?"

"Sounds good."

Inside, it was more like a three-ring circus than a typical restaurant. So many people, so many sizzling steaks hissing on the grill. In the center of the main dining room there were a couple of lumberjack-like men going for The Texas King challenge. One of them looked red and overheated from the colossal meal, and he seemed to be slowing down. The other was munching steadily, like he'd polish off everything on his plate but the silverware and lick the dish clean, too.

We were seated at a table for two near a wall that had the stuffed head of a heavily antlered beast above us. Just a buck, but it looked scary hovering over our heads that way. Like it might attack at any moment.

I glanced uneasily at it as we ordered our sandwiches—or, rather, "steakwiches"—and glasses of iced tea. Donovan opted for mashed potatoes and I got a side salad just to be contrary. Not that lettuce made that big of a statement, but it at least made me feel better that I wasn't just blindly following along with everything he did.

I could tell he was still riding high on his victory, being right, in his opinion, about trusting Officer James and handing over our findings to an authority figure. Just because I wasn't openly arguing with him, though, it didn't mean I was convinced that was the best move.

He glanced around the large room, his gaze resting on a picture that showed the outline of Texas. "Didn't think we'd get this far south and west," he said. "We're a long way from central Minnesota."

"That we are," I had to agree, sidestepping any commentary on the first part of his statement because, of course, I *did* think we'd get this far away from home. I'd begun imagining myself trekking along the same route as Gideon ever since I saw all of the locations listed in his journal.

Donovan seemed to sense the direction of my thoughts. "You got the journal with you?"

I nodded. I kept everything with me in my tote bag—my brother's journal, the two postcards, the envelope Andy delivered to us, Treak's decoded notes, the Route 66 placemat and any other scrap of paper with helpful information on it. I was a walking, talking card catalog for anything remotely important that we'd discovered.

"Did you want to look up something?"

"Maybe just check to see what he'd written in the days after Amarillo—" he began, but he was interrupted by a loud cheer. One of lumberjack guys had finished his steak.

I grinned at the challenge winner and, then, at Donovan. "Still time to go for it."

He grinned back at me. "Nah," he said, and then he muttered something almost too low for me to hear. I could have sworn he said, "Not what I'm hungry for…"

I shot him a sharp look. "What?"

But he didn't answer me or even meet my eye. He just reached for the journal I'd pulled out and flipped through a bunch of pages until the waitress brought us our meal.

Finally, sometime later, on the drive back to the motel, I worked up the nerve to ask him, "So, do you miss Vicky?"

"Who?"

"You know, *Vicky*. From St. Cloud. That girl you were with just last week at the movie?"

"Oh, yeah. Sure. She's…nice." He studied me from the driver's seat when we stopped at a light. "Why are you asking about her?"

"Well, I just, um, wondered. If you missed talking with her. If she was someone you're going to go out with again after we get back. That's all."

He shrugged. "Don't know. It's taking us longer to get back than I thought it would."

True enough.

I guess I hadn't given much thought to the specifics of Donovan's dating life, although I always supposed he'd had a fairly active one. Girls were drawn to him because of that moody, flirtatious, bad-boy thing he had going, but I didn't remember seeing him with any one girlfriend for long. Couldn't help but wonder which girl had been *his* first kiss… not that I'd ask. His expression didn't invite further questioning.

From the second we walked into our room at the Cactus Flower, I felt something was different. Even before I saw it.

It wasn't anything I could pinpoint precisely—not a sound or a scent—just the oddest sensation that a few nearly invisible things had changed in our absence.

"Something's not right," I told Donovan, who was staring at his camouflage duffle with a perplexed look.

He squinted at me and then again at the duffle. "I think…someone rifled through my bag."

I watched him unzip it and poked cautiously through several of the items inside.

"Nothing important is missing," he said. Then he clarified, "Nothing is missing at all, as far as I can tell. But I'd left it unzipped before we went out. It may have been searched."

The contents of my bag showed subtle signs of having been sifted through as well. My clothing was jumbled—and I was a conscientiously neat packer. The bag itself was positioned a few degrees differently than I'd remembered and a number of other items in the room sat at angles slightly askew from how they'd been when we left.

"A dishonest maid looking for easy cash, maybe? Or some other staff member who overheard us talking to the lady at the front desk and knew we'd be out of the room?" I suggested, but I couldn't quite make myself believe it.

We'd stayed at a lot of motels and never had anything like this happen before. Dressed in our old t-shirts and jeans, I knew how youthful and unexceptional we looked. Maybe we'd never been as inconspicuous as I'd have liked, but we just didn't give off the vibe of people who carried items of much monetary value. Motel workers had to have a sense about things like that.

"Maybe," Donovan said. "But I still don't like it."

I didn't want to have to bring this up, but it seemed foolish not to mention the possibility. "Any chance our hometown cop might be behind this somehow? It's a strange thing to have happen to us…and he's the only one who knows we're here."

Donovan glanced around the room, considering. "I don't know," he murmured. "I really don't, but I don't like it." There was a long pause. "Do you have everything you need from the car?"

"Yeah."

"Good."

In a few swift motions, he locked the door, latched the chain and pushed the small but heavy wooden table in front, blocking anyone who might even consider entering. Then, he made sure the window was bolted shut from the inside and, in utter silence, did a comprehensive check of every cubic foot of the room.

After he returned from investigating the bathroom thoroughly and checking in closets and behind the shower curtain, I got as far as asking, "Did you find anyth—" before he shushed me.

"Everything looks fine," he said, narrowing his eyes and nodding toward the small notepad and pen near the motel telephone.

I picked up both and handed them to him.

He wrote:

Don't say anything about your brother or mine tonight—not unless Officer James calls. If he does, say as little as possible out loud. Just a precaution in case the person who came in the room wasn't a maid.

He let me read that segment first and waited until I nodded. Then he wrote:

You and I can go somewhere early tomorrow so we can talk outside the room. And we won't stay here a second night—that's for sure. But I think we're okay for now. I've secured every possible point of entry, and I didn't find any bugs. Still, it's not impossible that someone's listening.

Bugs?

The idea sent a tremor of panic through my body. I hadn't thought us important enough to even consider that.

And every possible point of entry?

I could see Donovan's military training coming out. He'd gone into full protection mode and, I had to admit, I appreciated it. But realizing there might be a need for this level of security was what was beginning to seriously scare me.

I nodded at him again. "So," I said with feigned cheeriness, "I'm just going to give the front desk a quick call to thank that lady for recommending the steakhouse. Great food."

"Okay," he agreed warily.

"And I'll see if maybe my, um, *mom* tried to reach us while we were out."

"Oh." Understanding dawned on his face along with another just-watch-what-you-say look. "Good idea."

He clicked on the TV and flipped through stations, waiting impatiently as I checked in with the chipper desk clerk, who confirmed that, no, she hadn't directed any calls to our room and there weren't any messages for us. No news yet from Officer James.

I can't say I was actually worried about the cop's wellbeing, but a deep sense of foreboding tangled with concern in my gut. Why hadn't he tried to contact us yet? Was he having trouble finding Ronny's storage unit and the stash of pipe bombs? Had something happened to him on the way to Wisconsin?

I shook my head to let Donovan know we hadn't missed any calls, and he responded with a sigh. I could see the sweat beading up on his forehead, which he swiped away with the front of his t-shirt.

With the window closed tight, I was grateful we at least had a room fan. It was going to be a hot Texas night and this sure wasn't the kind of place that offered air conditioning.

Donovan turned the fan on high, but I could tell his attention wasn't on the heat. He kept glancing distractedly between the door and the telephone. Not a sound came from either, however, and, eventually, we had to give up the wait and get ready for bed.

When the lights were out and we were both lying on top of the sheets, twisting in hopes of finding a cool spot, he flipped toward me and brought his body closer than he ever had at night, especially in bed. I looked up at him, startled, as he crossed the midpoint between us for the first time.

I couldn't bring myself to pull away. My mind went blank, my pulse began to race and I held my breath.

He drew himself nearer to me until his lips were just a hair away from my left earlobe. "Don't be afraid of anything tonight," he whispered. "I'm going to keep a close eye on everything until we hear back from the officer. You don't have to worry."

"Thanks," I murmured back, willing my heart to stop pounding. It was so loud, I was sure he could hear it. "I'm not worried."

This was, of course, a rather gigantic lie, and I was sure Donovan knew that, but he just said, "Good," and he slid back to his own side of the bed.

We said our goodnights and each turned to face the opposite direction—Donovan staring at the door and me at the phone. Honestly, I doubt either of us got more than three hours of sleep. Morning couldn't come soon enough.

When it did, though, Donovan was the first to rise. At 5:23 a.m. he made another thorough check of the room and then peered through a slit between the front curtains to gaze outside.

"How does, um, everything look?" I asked.

He gave me a thumbs up and then motioned for me to get dressed. On the notepad he scribbled:

Let's go for a quick drive so we can talk. Take everything with you. We don't want anyone going through our stuff again.

I nodded, slipped on a t-shirt and a thin flower-print skirt in the bathroom and grabbed my tote and overnight bag. Donovan moved the table away from the door and quietly unlocked it. Then we both jumped in the Trans Am.

"God, I feel like I've been holding my breath for hours," he admitted once we were out on the road.

"Me, too." I exhaled and then inhaled deeply, rolling down the window and greeting the day. It was a bright, beautiful Sunday morning in Amarillo. Quiet and still. Donovan's car was one of the few out at this early hour.

"How are you holding up?" he asked me. "Did you get any sleep?"

"Not a lot. You?"

He kind of laughed. "Hardly any. I kept hoping Officer James would call, and I'm sure he will soon. Probably not *this* early, though." He stared hard out the front windshield.

"What if we don't hear back from him?" I asked.

"You mean today…or ever?"

I exhaled. "Neither option is all that promising, but I meant today. How long are you willing to hang around Amarillo and wait?"

"Until Tuesday at least," he said. "If he hasn't called us by that afternoon, maybe we should check with the police department at home. Make sure nothing's wrong. They'd know by then."

"All right."

Donovan drove us through the city again, which looked like a different place during the day—as did most cities, I supposed—and he got us back on Route 66 on the other side of town.

Ah, yes. The famous Cadillac Ranch awaited.

It wasn't even six a.m. so, of course, the site was abandoned, but I found myself admiring it in spite of its strangeness. Donovan and I parked on the shoulder and leaned back against his Trans Am, gazing at the display in the distance for a couple of minutes.

It looked just like Gideon's postcard.

I counted ten Cadillacs of various years and models, upended in the ground so only their tailfins were fully visible. Who thought up weird stuff like this?

"Odd," I said finally.

"Genius," Donovan replied. "Look at that lineup. A '48 Club Sedan all the way up to a '63 Sedan de Ville. Right in a row." He gazed at it with the same level of admiration that I reserved for leather-bound first editions of literary classics.

I tried to imagine I was staring at a shelf with rare copies of novels by Austen, Brontë and Dickens. Even so, I still wasn't feeling the same zing of excitement about it that he did. But, then, unlike Donovan, I'd never worked on a car nor had that kind of love affair with a vehicle.

I wasn't surprised my brother had been drawn to this site, either, but it made me wonder if he'd left any graffiti for us to find on one of the cars. He'd been here less than two weeks ago.

Donovan boosted our bags out of the backseat and transferred them to the trunk for safekeeping and so we could leave the doors unlocked and the car windows rolled down without worry. Even this early in the day, we knew it was going to be a scorcher.

"Let's go take a closer look at it," he said.

We meandered across the dusty field. Once we were standing next to the cars, I began examining the words spray-painted on the sides of every Cadillac. While I didn't find anything that struck me as being a coded message from Gideon, I found a few phone numbers for a "good time," if ever I wanted one, and lots of names of people who were once "here."

I caught up with Donovan, who was walking the length of the display, examining each of the Caddies stuck at a forty-five degree angle and appreciating something about every one of them.

"Which is your favorite?" I asked.

He patted the one he was standing next to with reverence. "This baby. The '59 Coupe de Ville. She's a beaut."

I'd probably never get over the way guys talked about cars, motorcycles and boats as if they were female but, given how just seeing this car put Donovan into an instantly better mood, I wasn't going to be quick to criticize.

As we turned to head back to the road, though, we noticed a patrol car pulling up behind ours. Donovan's smile vanished like light in a black hole, and he quickened his pace.

The Amarillo cop was inspecting Donovan's car when we reached him, and he gazed at us both with the expectancy of an authority figure.

"This Trans Am belong to you kids?" His voice was serious and his eyes shaded by the low brim of his police hat. Made it hard for me to read his expression. And, with the way the sun was glinting, I couldn't see the name on his nameplate or the specifics on his badge.

Donovan nodded. "It's mine, Officer. Is there a problem?"

"You got your driver's license with you, son?"

I sensed some hesitation on Donovan's part, but he pulled out his wallet and handed his card to the man.

"*Donovan McCafferty,*" the cop said slowly, as if trying to pronounce a foreign phrase. "From Minnesota."

"Yes, sir."

Then the cop turned his attention on me. "And what's your name, young lady?"

"Aurora," I said. And, since I could tell he was waiting for the rest, I begrudgingly added, "Gray."

He nodded. "Just the pair I was looking for." Then he handed Donovan back his license and broke into a friendly grin. "My buddy, William James, has been trying to reach you two since last night.

Finally called me this morning and said to be on the lookout for you at the Cactus Flower Inn or driving a red Firebird Trans Am around town."

He extended his hand to Donovan to shake it, which he did. To me, he just touched the brim of his hat. "Good to meet you. I'm the chief of police here in Amarillo, but you can just call me Sebastian."

"Officer James tried to reach us last night?" Donovan asked. "When? We were out of the room for a little over an hour, but we were there the rest of the evening. And this morning, too, until about thirty or forty minutes ago. We were just about to head back."

Sebastian shrugged. "Said he had some kind of problem getting through. Anyway, I've got you two covered now. You don't have to worry."

A pair of motorcyclists drove up and parked several yards ahead of our cars. One of the guys pulled out a camera and began snapping shots of the Cadillac Ranch.

The officer glanced at us and then at his watch. "We should sit down, talk about some of those materials you have. Papers and such. But we're close to where the truck accident happened. It's just a coupla miles down that country lane there." He pointed to a dusty side road that branched out from Route 66. "Thought you might want to see it."

As he spoke, I was urgently trying to get a decent read on the guy. There was something familiar about him, but I was good with faces and knew I'd never seen his before. His accent wasn't Texan—no hint of any kind of a drawl—just a cloak of big-city-ness about him, despite the down-home casualness of his manner. An affectation, I could tell, designed to put others at ease.

Donovan expressed an interest in going to the site, but he was quick to suggest we drive there separately from the cop.

"No problem at all, kids," Sebastian said, and I could tell he was genuinely pleased with our acceptance of his invitation. There was something at the site he must have really wanted to show us. I was just relieved the cop hadn't insisted that we ride with him in his squad car.

My uneasiness returned, though, when we got there and I realized what an isolated stretch of pavement we were on. Route 66 hadn't been crawling with vehicles this early in the morning, but I knew an occasional traveler would buzz by—like those bikers.

This spot where the accident happened looked like it might not see any traffic at all in three days. Which left me wondering, what was a *semi truck* heading to *Albuquerque* doing out here on this nearly abandoned country road anyway? Making a special delivery, perhaps? But there were no buildings in sight for miles…

"Donovan," I whispered as he parked behind the cop car. "I don't think this is a good—"

"—idea," he finished for me. "I know, I know. You don't like cops. But this is a man of the law and a friend of Officer James. I think we should at least give him a chance. If his behavior starts getting bizarre or something, we can just leave."

"But even Andy Reggio said we should *only* share the papers with Officer James. No one else. And I find it really strange that he said Officer James tried to call us last night. *Someone's* lying—our hometown cop, this cop here or that desk clerk lady. Maybe more than one of them."

There was a slam and we both saw Sebastian get out of his squad car. He strode toward us with purpose. As Donovan and I slid out of the Trans Am, I watched the cop pull off his police hat for a second and brush back his brownish red hair with a sweep of his fingers. A practiced movement that reminded me very much of our own cop back at home.

That and the hair color.

The facial features and the build, too.

The lack of a southern accent.

And, of course, the choice of profession.

This time, when I got close enough to Sebastian, I focused all of my attention on his badge. I could make out his number—729—but it took me a few moments of solid concentration to finally read his nameplate. When I did, I almost gasped.

JAMES.

Sebastian James. His name was on Treak's list of bad guys.

The Amarillo cop was grinning again, standing shoulder to shoulder with Donovan, his hands on his hips, with the right one fingering the top of his gun's holster.

I tried to catch Donovan's gaze, but he'd slipped into that military-like hierarchy of respect that men often do. Sizing up each other and falling into rank accordingly.

Donovan, who was so willing to defy authority in a host of

mundane ways—driving way over the speed limit, providing alcohol to a minor, buying illegal fireworks—and whose notion of personal security usually rivaled that of a presidential bodyguard, had failed to question the motivations of a potentially very dangerous man, all because Donovan saw him donning a badge and wearing a uniform he trusted.

To me, that nameplate offered the final bit of convincing evidence that this new cop was not only someone Treak had been worried about, but that Sebastian and William James were somehow related. They weren't merely "buddies."

But I couldn't pull Donovan aside to tell him this. Not with Sebastian leading him around by the elbow, pointing out the exact location of the truck explosion and sharing what he said he saw when the police arrived at the scene two years ago.

"It was a fiery mess," the cop told Donovan. "Quite a sight."

"Did you ever figure out what caused the accident?" I asked in an attempt to pull the two of them apart just a little. "Or even what the truck was doing out here on this deserted road? I'd think the driver would have wanted to stay on Route 66 or have taken I-40."

The cop glanced my way in surprise. "Maybe he needed a rest stop."

"Wouldn't there have been more options available for him along either of those two main roads?" I replied, but I wasn't thinking it through before I spoke. I wasn't prepared for Sebastian to look at me with such interest after I'd said that. The first male stranger in a long time not to discount me just because I was a girl.

Suddenly, that didn't seem remotely like the triumph I'd hoped.

"Why, that's a very curious question, miss. Where are the documents that brother of yours collected for you, by the way?" he asked. "I'd like to take a look at them."

"Back at the motel," I lied.

He smiled at me—a cold, bloodless smile—and I could now see something I'd missed before: The barely suppressed contempt he held for people in general and, in particular, for anyone who got in the way of something he wanted.

"Now, we both know that ain't true." In one smooth motion, Sebastian pulled the gun out of his holster, cocked it and pointed it at Donovan's heart. "You'll tell me, won't you, son? Where are those papers?"

Donovan sent me a look of distress mingled with disbelief. "We... we put them somewhere safe..." He paused as Sebastian raised the gun to Donovan's forehead. "But we'll get them for you."

"Yes, you will," the cop said with chilling confidence. "I already checked your motel room. Last night *and* this morning." He shot an assessing glance at the Trans Am. "They're not on the seats or on the floor of your car either, so that leaves the glove compartment or the trunk."

"Why are they so important?" I asked, trying to keep the panic out of my voice and distract Sebastian long enough to give Donovan a moment's breather. "The papers were mostly newspaper clippings that anyone could collect," I said, hoping I sounded reasonable and not on the verge of hysteria, which was how I felt. "And, as the chief, you could've easily gotten those two police reports yourself. What's so special about the copies we were given?"

Sebastian continued to stare at me with a combination of amusement and mystification. First he chuckled, and then he full out laughed. "Nothing at all, little lady. It's the people carrying them that's the problem. *You two.*"

He waved his gun in a reckless arc between Donovan and me. "I want them out of your car before I burn the both of you inside of it. Don't want the investigators who'll arrive on the scene later today to find any document fragments that might connect the two of you with what happened in August of '76." He waved his gun again, and I held my breath.

"Thought we had that story put to bed once and for all. Can't have it all resurrected again now, can we?" He glanced at each of us and then answered his own question. "No. You would've done better to mind your own damn business and not come poking around like your fool brothers did. Couldn't believe it when Willie called me yesterday afternoon and told me the two of you were on your way here," he muttered.

So, Sebastian had known our brothers and, from the way he described what he planned to do to us, I more than suspected the truck explosion had been no accident, and he'd been right at the center of it.

Officer James had called Sebastian yesterday, not this morning, which meant our hometown cop had lied to us for sure about what he said he was going to do. He'd promised he wouldn't contact his "friend" until after he checked out the storage facility in Crescent Cove and talked to us again. I found myself wondering if he'd even gone to Wisconsin and how deeply he'd been involved in what had happened to our brothers two years ago…

I saw these same alarming realizations wash over Donovan's face, too, along with a look of regret.

"So, how are you and Officer James related?" I asked, hoping I'd throw him off guard a little. "Brothers?"

Sebastian raised an eyebrow. He didn't stop pointing his gun at Donovan, but he did at least take a small step away from him so he could turn and get a better look at me. "Think you're pretty smart, don't ya?" he said.

Donovan blinked and mouthed, "What?" at the same time that Sebastian added, "First cousins. And best friends as kids." He sent me a sneering look. "Blood, you know, is very thick."

I nodded. "Yeah, I know."

At this, Donovan cleared his throat. "So, are we correct in understanding that your, uh, cousin didn't try to call us at all last night? That he's in on all of this?"

"Willie got your call and, then, immediately called me. Just like he was supposed to. Told me where you were staying and when you'd be there. Helpful having relatives who know how to follow directions." He grinned, but it was like ice cracking. "Isn't it?"

My mind raced as I tried to reinterpret this new information in light of everything that had happened. Andy Reggio had *said* that Gideon had *said* that we could trust William James. Which one of them had been lying to us? Or, was it possible that they, too, had been fooled and were each passing along what they thought was the truth?

Donovan was looking a little less than relaxed with a gun so close to his left temple. Even so, I could tell his brain was whirling as well, trying to reframe all of the events given what we'd just heard.

"You two, stand over here," Sebastian commanded, pointing us toward the side of his squad car with the tip of his gun. He opened one of the back doors and pulled out a large red five-gallon gasoline can. "You're about to have a little car accident," he said sarcastically, setting the red can down between our two cars and unscrewing the cap. "Perhaps an exploding gas tank after you run into that big telephone pole."

He glanced at the thick wooden pole nearest us and shrugged. "It happens." He prodded us again with his gun. "Now get me those papers, and I do mean *now*."

When it came right down to it, everyone probably thought they were too young to die. Even if they'd already lived sixty, seventy or eighty years. But I wasn't even eighteen yet. I'd never traveled abroad, not even to Canada or Mexico. I hadn't tasted champagne or caviar— and I'd probably hate them both, but I wanted to know for sure. And I was a virgin.

I really *was* too young to die.

My gut twisted in terror and, for all of my natural perception and logic, I had no idea if there was any reason to hope we'd get out of this alive. But there was one thing I was positive about: I was going to fight Sebastian with every ounce of strength I had.

Sebastian marched us over to the Trans Am and told Donovan to unlock the glove compartment. I noticed that, while Donovan appeared to be complying immediately, he actually took his time with this task. I'd seen him move twenty times faster before, but he was a clever guy, and I sensed he was trying to give us a few extra seconds to think.

I hoped I could do my part with a different kind of delay tactic. "Is this what happened before?" I asked the cop, working hard to come across as respectfully afraid of him and a touch impressed. "Two years ago? Were you the one who set up the explosion?"

"I was." He smiled like he was proud of it. Like it was one of his life's crowning achievements. Good. That meant this was probably the best strategy under the circumstances. Knowledge was power.

I bobbed my head contemplatively. "But why?"

He threw an annoyed glance in Donovan's direction, who had just unlocked the box and was sifting through the old insurance cards and a few car-related papers stuffed inside, pulling each item out and laying it on the dash, one at a time.

"Because that little prick was gonna talk," he told me. "Hal Chaney. The driver. He wanted more money. He'd done jobs for us in Chicago and St. Louis, but this was the farthest south he'd gone for a delivery. He was starting to understand the scope of our operation. And when your brothers got ahold of him, they just inflated his already enormous and greedy ego. Made him think he was owed more than he was getting for the tiny job he was doing."

"So, you destroyed his truck and killed him before he could rat you out," I said. "Right?"

"Right." He shoved me aside, reaching into the car and grabbing a handful of papers off the dash. "What the hell is this? A receipt for a new tire?" He crumpled the thin yellow sheet and tossed it onto the pavement.

"But the driver's body wasn't found," I said, watching in desperation as the cop threw more of Donovan's papers on the ground. We were running out of time. "Did you bury him out here?"

Sebastian grunted in anger and frustration and smacked Donovan's bicep with the side of his gun. "Those documents damned well better be in the trunk," he threatened. Then, to me, "You ask too many questions, little girl, but you know what? There are a few things it pleases me to tell you before you die. Number one, you can stall all you want, ain't nobody gonna find you out here until it's too late." He sent me a villainous look.

"Number two, I put that bastard's body in the trunk and took it back with me to Chicago. It's where I lived at the time. Getting promoted to chief out here was my prize for a job well done." He patted his badge. There was that unmistakable pride again.

"And number three," he said, pulling me in front of him so I was standing next to Donovan behind the Trans Am. He pointed the gun at both of us and motioned for Donovan to unlock the trunk. "I'm gonna enjoy seeing the life drain out of your bodies, the way it did with Hal and with that stupid fuck, Jeremy."

Next to me, Donovan's motions stilled. He turned slowly to face Sebastian, betraying no particular emotion, but his silence all but screamed the pain he was feeling.

The cop laughed. "Oh, now you're taking me seriously, huh, big guy?"

"You? *You* killed my brother?" Donovan whispered.

Sebastian grinned. "Sure did. My buddy Rick wrestled him to the ground right about there." He pointed to a patch of pavement seven or eight yards away. "And I shot him in the head. Dead and gone in under a second." He snapped his fingers to demonstrate just how fast.

I fought to keep my knees from buckling under me. Sadness, regret and a tidal wave of anger swept across my body and left me gasping for air. *Damn that evil bastard! How can hateful people like this exist in the world? How can Jeremy be gone?*

All of those feelings of helplessness I'd felt before the trip came rushing back. I wished I could believe Sebastian was lying about killing my brother's best friend, but none of his nonverbal tells indicated that. I glanced at Donovan to see how he was handling this news, my heart reaching out to him, even though I was too afraid to make a move and touch him.

Donovan swallowed several times before he spoke again. "Where's his body? You take him back to Chicago, too?"

"Nope." Sebastian nodded once in my direction. "Her brother did a number on Rick, snatched Jeremy and took him somewhere." He shrugged. "Never did get that sonovabitch Gideon. He drove away with a few cracked ribs, a bullet in his side and two tires that were going flat by the second. But, by the time I could get up off the gravel and get into my car to chase him, he was already gone."

"Off the gravel? Did Gideon punch you?" I asked.

"Aw, now don't you go getting any bright ideas, missy. You ain't gonna take me by surprise like that. Not this time." He shot one bullet into the air and I jumped half out of my skin. "Now, both of you turn around and *open the goddamn trunk*."

Scared as I was, I understood something critical in that second: Sebastian didn't want to shoot us.

Not because he had a soft spot of humanity anywhere in his cold, evil body, but because if there was any proof our deaths were caused by anything other than internal injuries from a car crash and burns from an explosion, there was no way the incident could possibly be ruled as "accidental" by the handful of investigators and evidence technicians that would come later.

Someone honest—at some point—would notice gunshot wounds on our bodies. The paramedics, the trustworthy members of the fire department or the police force, certainly the coroner wouldn't miss those, even if we were badly burned.

And Sebastian didn't have the luxury of just removing our bodies from the scene because, after what had happened in this exact spot two years ago, it would be viewed as too coincidental. Draw too much notice in Amarillo. As would a second mysterious disappearance of two siblings from the same two families back in Chameleon Lake.

So, because he had to be careful about how he killed us and because he needed us to be alive and relatively unharmed before he trapped us in our car...we had at least one small temporary advantage.

Before I could in some way signal this realization to Donovan, he opened the trunk and motioned to where the last five of the Crescent Cove fireworks were carefully wrapped and stashed in that box. Grabbing my tote, he pulled out the package Andy Reggio had left for us and handed it to me to hold up to show Sebastian, then I saw him unwrap and stuff all but one of the leftover firecrackers into my bag.

"We've got your papers," he called to the cop. Then, to me, "Here, *I'll* give them to him, Aurora." He snatched the envelope out of my hands and thrust the tote at me. "Get in the car."

I took my bag, surprised Sebastian wasn't objecting but, even though his gun was still trained on us, he was several feet away, listening to something. A buzzing sound in the distance that took me a few seconds to identify.

Motorcycles.

"Get in the car," Donovan said again, his voice low and urgent. He pushed me toward the open passenger side door.

Sebastian glanced over at us, fury washing over his face when he saw that I'd moved from the spot he'd placed me, but we could all tell that the motorcycles were fast approaching.

This distracted Sebastian. He instinctively lowered his gun and, for a moment, hid it from view. No doubt contemplating the consequences of being seen out on a deserted road with two people who'd likely be reported dead fairly soon.

It wasn't a long reprieve, but it was long enough for Donovan to jump in the Trans Am—trunk still wide open—and start the engine.

We heard Sebastian swear and shoot at our car, bullets hitting the open trunk door and one smashing through a side window as the cop came sprinting toward us.

Donovan hit drive, spinning gravel and running into the red gasoline can, knocking it over.

"Here, take this!" he shouted at Sebastian, flinging the envelope out his window toward the cop but holding it upside down so most of the papers escaped into the safety of Donovan's lap instead of leaving the car.

Sebastian reflexively grabbed for the envelope, but it took him only a split second to realize it was empty. Before he could react, though, the motorcyclists—the same two guys we'd seen back by the Cadillac Ranch—buzzed by on their bikes.

Wearing bandanas, helmets and lots of leather, their features weren't easy to distinguish, but I could tell that one biker was white and the other black. They both lifted their hands in a friendly wave to all of us as they drove slowly past.

Sebastian apparently ceased to care anymore if anyone heard his gunshots. As Donovan tried to get his car back to the road, Sebastian tossed the envelope to the ground and fired again at us, this time managing to get a shot through the front windshield.

I saw Donovan wince, blood leaking through the sleeve of his shirt. His left shoulder. The one closest to the window. Even so, before I could blink, he had his lighter out and he lit the cherry bomb in his hand, lobbing it at the cop, and getting close enough to make Sebastian stumble backward when the powerful firecracker exploded. He pressed the lighter into my hand. "Light one and throw it near the gas spill."

I pulled out the first firework I touched from inside my tote—a very illegal quarter stick—and did just what Donovan told me. The gasoline fumes made it detonate even before it hit the pavement and, boy, was that explosion impressive.

From my side window, I could see that the motorcyclists had stopped their bikes and were turning them around.

Sebastian gasped and ran toward his squad car, trying to rescue it before the blazing fire followed the trail of spilled gas and reached his engine.

"Now light one for me," Donovan said, having managed to turn the Trans Am around far enough to get onto the road, headed in the direction we came. Back toward Route 66. "And hang onto the steering wheel after you do. As soon as I've thrown it, light another, okay?"

"Okay." Breathless, I followed his instructions exactly.

Even with a wounded arm and using his non-dominant hand, Donovan had good aim. He threw the first lit firecracker at Sebastian's front tires, taking one of them out, and the other at the cop himself. It didn't burn him to a crisp the way I would have liked, but it did singe the driver's door enough to get him to swerve to the other side of the road.

By the time we reached the Route 66 intersection, we could no longer see Sebastian behind us and the magnitude of what had just happened was only beginning to be absorbed by my whole being.

My mind had known for several minutes that we were in grave

danger, but my body was only just starting to understand. As much as I tried to stop it, I was visibly trembling from the top of my head to my toenails.

"He almost killed us," I cried.

"Yeah, I know," Donovan said. "How many fireworks do we have left?"

I peered inside my tote, my hands shaking so hard I could barely keep it open. "Just one."

"Okay." He looked steely, determined and…bloody.

I leaned forward just far enough to see how much blood had been coming from his left shoulder. It was dripping everywhere. "Oh, God, Donovan! We have to get you to a hospital right—"

With his other hand, he waved me off. "It's just a flesh wound, Aurora. Relax."

"But you're bleeding—"

"Yeah. That happens when someone shoots a .357 Magnum at you." He turned onto Route 66 heading westward and sent me a grim half smile. "I'll be fine. It's mostly from the broken glass. I'll be even more fine once Sebastian is out of the picture forever." He studied me in silence. "Are you okay?"

"No! He almost *killed* us!" I repeated. "And why are we going west? It'll be miles before we get to another big city, and we need to take you to an emergency room."

He shook his head. "No, we need to get the hell away from Amarillo. I'm not going back from where we came."

"But we still have the key to our room at the Cactus Flower Inn," I said, which for some irrational reason seemed important to me. There were so damned many loose ends in my life.

Donovan just laughed humorlessly at this. "If you're really worried about that, we can mail it back to them from Albuquerque."

"Albuquerque? Jesus, Donovan! We can't go that far. That's got to be almost *five hours* from here. I really, really want you to see a doctor right now. I mean it. And then I want us to head toward home. It was a very bad idea continuing on this far. I'm so sorry." I choked back a sob and the profound guilt of responsibility. "Please, if you won't turn back on Route 66, at least go north."

I grabbed the atlas and flipped frantically until I saw a map of the Texas panhandle. "Th-There's a good road coming up. See? Route 385.

We can take it north up through Oklahoma, Colorado, Nebrask—"

"We could, but we're not going to," he said. "I didn't want to take this trip. You know I didn't, but—"

"Donovan, I said I'm sorry, and I really am, for *all* of this. I should've listened to you. If we'd just stayed in Chameleon Lake, it would've been safer. It would've been—"

"A lifetime of never knowing the truth," he finished for me. "Stop apologizing, Aurora, and hear me out. I didn't want to go on this trip when you first suggested it. Once we started, I didn't want to stay on it any longer than a few days. But I'm glad we did. I'm glad you talked me into it—your first instincts were right. And, in spite of everything, I'm glad we learned all that we have so far."

"I think we've learned more than enough now, though. Back there, almost all I could think about was getting away from Sebastian. But a part of me kept worrying about our parents, too. About how they nearly lost their remaining children today. We can't do that to them. We need to get back home safely before anyone else gets hurt." I glanced at his still bleeding shoulder. "Or gets hurt even worse."

"It's not safe at home right now. Officer James is there."

"He is but—" I stopped.

But nothing.

I didn't know what else to say about him. For the life of me, I couldn't understand how Gideon could tell us to trust him. Unless Andy Reggio was the one lying to us. Or Gideon had been fooled by our hometown cop. Or Officer James himself had meant well but, somehow, had been manipulated by his cousin.

Since we didn't know which scenario was the right one, though, I was at a loss.

"It has to be safer for us to deal with the devil we know," I said finally. "Even if Officer James is as crooked and ruthless as Sebastian, there has to be a good, honest cop that we can trust somewhere in Minnesota or Wisconsin. Someone who will help us and protect us and our families."

Donovan raised one disbelieving eyebrow at hearing these particular words come from my mouth. "That's what I'd thought until about an hour ago. But now...now everything's different."

With the immediate danger gone for the moment, I could see him struggling to process the anguish of Jeremy's death all over again, knowing with certainty that it had been his worst-case scenario. As senseless, terrifying and painful for his sunny kid brother as Donovan had feared. And that, of all people, Jeremy didn't deserve such a tragic fate.

But there was also suddenly something different about Donovan. Perhaps that same certainty of knowing what had really happened helped him in some small way. Helped him channel his anger and grief.

"I won't be able to rest until that bastard Sebastian is locked up for life or, preferably, dead," he told me. "We'll be able to deal with Officer James better once his cousin is put away. Until then, we're staying out on the road."

Just before the point where Route 385 North branched off from Route 66 West, Donovan pulled onto the side of the highway long enough to let me look at his shoulder. He was right. The cuts were mostly caused by flying glass, but a few of them were deep and I suspected a bullet had come awfully close. We cleaned out the wound with a little drinking water, and I hunted down a couple of bandages I'd packed in case I got a foot blister. Never would've imagined I'd be using them for something like this.

"Hold still," I said, trying to keep his shoulder steady by reaching for the warm, taut flesh at the base of his neck. His muscles flexed under my touch, and I tried to shake away the desire to stroke him there.

"Just put the bandages on, Aurora, and let's go."

I burned a little under his gaze, he was so close. His emotions still so raw and visible on his face. "Fine. But the first store we see, I'm buying some antiseptic and gauze for your shoulder," I told him. "Plan to stop soon."

He nodded as he pulled away from me. He stuffed his bloody t-shirt into a corner of the trunk, put on a fresh one and, again, told me not to worry.

"I'll be fine, and so will you," he insisted. "No matter what happens, I'll protect you. I promise."

Despite my pleading, however, he refused to turn right onto Route 385 and drive north.

We argued about it some more—honestly, probably close to three hours on and off—as we pushed further westward. At one point, Donovan tried to distract me by switching between radio stations in search of songs that were especially annoying or overplayed.

"Hey, could we get any luckier?" he crowed, tuning in to the Captain and Tennille singing "Muskrat Love."

When I groaned, he said, "What? You don't like it?" He flipped through a few more stations, passing by some decent ELO, Billy Joel, Jackson Browne and the Carpenters in favor of David Cassidy's "I Think I Love You."

"Donovan..."

"Oh, c'mon. I know you like this one. I saw that cheesy Cassidy poster you used to have up in your room. It's not still there, is it?"

When we got back home—*if* we got back home—I really needed to rethink my room.

When I didn't immediately answer, he laughed. It was strained, but he seemed positively determined to keep our conversation light.

"Once all of this is over, I'm going to take you to hear some *real* music. No Bee Gees disco shit or stupid teenybopper stuff by those Cassidy brothers. I think Shaun is even worse than David." He scowled. "You need to go to a *rock* concert. The Rolling Stones. The Steve Miller Band. Bob Seger. Bad Company."

"After eight straight days of traveling with you, I know all about bad company," I retorted, doing my best to play along with him.

He rewarded my effort with a small grin. "Guess I set myself up for that one."

When the musical teasing stopped and silence descended on our car again, though, my fears seeped back in. Seeing the green "48 miles to Albuquerque" sign up ahead didn't help.

Donovan, who'd been much quieter for the past half hour, looked cautiously at his rearview mirror and then his driver's side mirror before passing a small flatbed truck.

I figured, by this time, it was too late to convince him to head home, but in a last-ditch attempt to suggest we get off the beaten path, I said, "I've never been to Colorado. Have you?"

He shook his head.

"I hear it's beautiful with the mountains, trees and lots of...nature and stuff. Maybe we could go for a couple of days. Just to take a break from everything. Think about what we should do next."

"Aurora," he said, his voice patient but unyielding, "you, more than anyone, know we need to get to the bottom of this. Going west on

66 is our best chance of finding out what happened. So is reading the rest of your brother's journal, given everything we know now. We need to look for more clues in the cities Gideon went to and, maybe, we'll catch a lucky break and either find him or piece together the rest of this puzzle."

He checked his mirrors again, his expression tense, then he sped up and passed two other vehicles.

"It's easier to disappear in a bigger city than it would be in the great outdoors. We want to blend in with the crowd until we have a few more answers. Besides—" He glanced uneasily in his rearview mirror one more time. "We're being followed."

Chapter Twelve

Albuquerque, New Mexico ~ Sunday, June 25

FEAR PUT a stranglehold on my chest. "Are you sure?" I whispered. "How do you know?"

Donovan didn't say anything for almost a full minute. Then, "It's those same bikers from back in Texas. They've been on our tail for the last hour."

I tried to come up with a reasonable rationalization. "Well, 66 is a main road. It's either this route or I-40, if you want to go west, right? They were tourists snapping pictures of the Cadillac Ranch back in Amarillo when we first saw them. It's not unusual that they'd be continuing on toward Albuquerque."

"It is if they talked to Sebastian after he shot at us and now he's got them looking for us, too. It is if they're more than willing to pass other drivers, but they refuse to pass *us*." He checked his mirrors again and frowned. "If I slow down, they slow down. If I pass one car, they pass one car. If I pass two cars, they do the same. It's not a coincidence."

"What are we going to do?"

"Well, first, we're going to get into Albuquerque. Then, we're going to lose them."

He was focused, serious and determined to do exactly what he said he'd do. Until we'd driven into Amarillo, I'd only gotten a few glimpses of Donovan as the coolheaded military man that he'd become during his years away from Chameleon Lake. After watching him get us away from Sebastian, though, I suspected Donovan had been downplaying this side of himself, containing it to whatever mental compartment he stashed his Army memories and training.

But I'd seen these traits come out a few times in the past twenty-four hours, and he seemed increasingly ready to jump into taking stronger and more evasive action with each new incident. I'd had no choice but to be very self-reliant these past two years and hadn't realized how much I would appreciate his expertise and his partnership. How much I would admire the former and, almost immediately, come to count on the latter.

Over the next thirty miles or so, I saw that Donovan was correct about the motorcyclists. Sometimes he'd slow down. Other times he'd speed up. No matter what he or any of the other motorists on the road did, though, the two bikers maintained the same distance between themselves and us. It was eerie.

True to his word, as soon as we hit the Albuquerque city limits, Donovan was on a mission to lose them. He took a right down a big street named Juan Tabo Boulevard and, when they followed, he made a quick left onto Buena Ventura Road. The bikers didn't miss a beat. Wherever we turned, there they were, too.

Donovan shot me a resolute look. "Keep your seatbelt on" was all he said as he cut a labyrinthine streak through the heart of the sprawling downtown.

The Sandia Mountains cradled the arid city in its majestic purple haze, but it was hard to think about the desert beauty for long with a pair of dangerous strangers just a few car lengths behind us.

After slipping through a series of deeply yellow stoplights—with the bikers always managing to follow—we finally caught a break.

Donovan crossed the railroad tracks at Lomas Boulevard, red lights blinking and bells ringing in warning, just seconds before the gates came down. We were on one side of the tracks, the bikers back on the other—with a freight train between us. And we were free…at least for the time being.

"Wow." I breathed out some of the shallow air I'd been barely holding in my lungs. "That was some really great driving. Thanks."

"You're welcome, Aurora." A thin smile played at his lips as he glanced first at me and, then, down the street. He drove a convoluted route though several more city blocks in silence before saying, "Remember in St. Louis how you wanted to stay at one of those no-tell motel motor lodges with a garage?"

I nodded.

"You're gonna get your wish tonight."

THE MOTOR lodge Donovan chose for us was called Sandstone Suites. The sixteen-unit complex was near the intersection of both I-40, which was east-west, and I-25, which was north-south. We could, according to him, drive in any cardinal direction at a moment's notice.

"But, if I have my way," Donovan said, as he closed the unit's garage door behind the Trans Am, "we won't be driving *anywhere* for a few days."

I knew he was serious about going incognito for awhile in, perhaps, the same way our brothers had done when they were laying low in St. Louis. It wasn't just what Donovan said that gave away his intentions, though, it was what he did.

Making me hide out at a corner grocery store while he checked into the motel.

Claiming for the first time on the trip to be a single guy traveling alone.

Telling me he'd listed his name on the registry as "Joseph Walters" (which was really his grandfather's name).

Paying by cash, of course, not by check.

And quickly stocking up on medicinal supplies as well as nonperishable, ready-to-eat food items at the store before hightailing it back to Unit #12.

Oh, and then there was the 32-ounze bottle of golden whiskey that he just bought and plunked on the table next to the TV.

"In an hour, I'm not gonna be able to drive anyway," he informed me, as he poured himself a generous serving of the alcohol in one of the motel's Dixie water cups. "You can have some, too, if you want. I won't tell your parents." He put only about an inch of liquor into a second paper cup and handed it to me.

"Thanks," I said. "I think."

"Here's to Jeremy and Gideon." He raised his cup in a toast and waited for me to do the same before he downed every last drop of the amber liquid in his.

I took a tiny, dutiful sip, but it was still enough to leave me coughing. "St-trong," I managed.

He chuckled and poured himself another triple shot. "That's the idea."

I eventually finished mine, but I didn't ask for a refill.

It was early afternoon when Donovan had his first few whiskeys—with a peanut butter and jelly sandwich as a chaser—but these were far from his last drinks. He was walking that razor-thin line between wanting to numb the pain and, also, knowing he had to be alert enough to handle whatever situation might arise next. But danger was unpredictable. There could be a lot of hours to kill between boredom and terror.

By the time night fell, Donovan had found a seemingly happy balance between the pain-free wave of drunkenness he sought and the overly mindful sobriety he needed.

"Hey, hey! Look what's on," he hooted, pointing at the television.

ABC. "The Hardy Boys/Nancy Drew Mysteries." Great.

"Very funny," I said.

"We should watch." He turned up the volume and sprawled himself across the center of the bed. But when I studied him, laying there in his current state of willful inebriation, he scowled at me. "Oh, don't look at me like that. There's room for you here, too." He patted the right side of the mattress with a small grin and added, "*Nancy.*"

On any other day or at any other time, I would have made a face and shoved him in the chest, probably calling him a few names in return.

But this wasn't that day or that time.

In fact, as I sat down beside him, I found myself increasingly worried about his wellbeing.

By implicit agreement, we hadn't talked about either of our brothers, what we'd heard from Sebastian or the fact that we'd nearly been killed that morning… We both knew we were *going* to talk about it all—no doubt at great length—but Donovan had a dash of Scarlett O'Hara's attitude about him ever since we'd walked into our no-tell motel and locked the door behind us. He'd made it clear that we'd deal with all of that *tomorrow.*

So, instead, we snacked, we drank and we watched Nancy Drew try to solve some kind of a case involving a "whispering" statue.

"The statue's not really whispering," Donovan confided, having turned the show into something of a personal drinking game. He said "bottom's up" and slugged his whiskey every time any of the characters mentioned Nancy's boyfriend Ned.

I wasn't watching the episode half as closely as I was watching Donovan, but even I could tell everything was not what it appeared to be in the world of Miss Drew and her friends. Bad people got away with their crimes, at least for a while. Good people were sometimes in the wrong place at the wrong time. The sleuths trying to figure out the caper often thought they'd drawn the correct conclusion, only to be proven wrong in the next scene. It was starting to feel a little too much like real life.

"Bad timing," I murmured, as Nancy and the gang discovered another victim, moments too late, but I was thinking of Gideon and Jeremy filming that tribute clip up in Crescent Cove. I wasn't sure of the chain of events that originally led to them meeting Ben Rainwater at some party in St. Cloud, but the tragedies that followed surely could've been prevented if our brothers hadn't visited Wisconsin that weekend.

"It's a bitch," Donovan agreed, his eyes never leaving the screen, but I suspected he knew I wasn't talking about the show.

While he finished out Nancy Drew, then lost himself in a repeat episode of "The Six-Million Dollar Man" and, later, the Sunday Night Movie, I mentally reviewed what we'd learned that day about the summer of '76.

I pulled out the notes I'd decoded back in Joplin from Treak's shorthand pages, and I studied them as if seeing the words for the first time:

Hal Chaney - Americana Trucking - Cres Cove, Chic, MO, TX, NM
Vincent Leto - Chic
Rick Brice - Chic
Sebastian James - Chic
Timothy Wick - Americana Trucking, Jop, Amar
Billy Neville - Albuq
Julian Carello - Chic

Of course, the name "Sebastian James" now jumped out at me like a Fourth of July sparkler burning in my hand. I hadn't guessed there would be any relationship between him and Officer William James at home—it was such a common last name—and I hadn't thought I'd meet anybody named Sebastian in Amarillo. Treak had listed the man in question as being from Chicago...which had been true two years ago.

But, in reading through all of this again, I realized Sebastian might have given away even more information than those details. He told us "his buddy Rick" had been involved in Jeremy's death. And I remembered from one of the newspaper articles that "Rick Brice" had been found dead at the scene. So Sebastian's friend must have been the *same* Rick as the guy on Treak's list—a man also from Chicago—which was a significant tie between them.

In the papers Gideon had given to Andy to give to me, I clearly remembered reading those two police reports. Rick Brice was a former Chicago cop who was wanted in connection with some unsolved labor disputes. A couple of union leaders had died a few years ago, and he was most likely the reason.

I checked the papers just to confirm that recollection and also dug up the report on Timothy Wick, the Americana Trucking exec who'd ordered the shipment of the explosives. That report had shown a direct connection between Wick, Chicago crime boss Vincent Leto and "Leto's right-hand man," a.k.a. Rick Brice.

Sebastian told us he'd started out in Chicago and had gotten a "promotion" to a higher police position in Texas as a result of putting a cap on the truck explosion and the news stories that followed. To get a kickback like that, someone with a lot of clout—like, perhaps, a major mobster—would need to pull a few strings with his "associates" in that town. Sebastian's buddy Rick was high up in the mob, but on the run from the law. Bet it helped to have someone still involved with the police force as a friend...

Somehow Rick and Sebastian both ended up in Amarillo, trailing Hal and our brothers and killing both the trucker and Jeremy. And, while I couldn't prove it yet, I got the distinct sense that one of these two dirty bastards was the "cop" responsible for gunning down Treak and Ben, too.

When Gideon and Jeremy were cornered on that deserted road,

my brother did something to distract and hurt Rick and Sebastian, but it was too late to save Jeremy. Gideon got his friend's body away from there, though, despite being shot himself. Where he went after that and whom he turned to for help with his injuries, I had no idea.

But, while there were still plenty of missing pieces—like how Rick Brice ended up dead in Amarillo, who Billy Neville and Julian Carello were or why the Chicago mob was transporting pipe bombs halfway across the country—the picture was becoming clearer.

Donovan, not surprisingly, didn't want to chitchat about any of these revelations just then. Thanks to the assistance of his golden liquor and a steely determination not to think too much, he held himself together through a full night of TV and even a few hours of sleep. But, sometime around two a.m., I woke to the sounds of him retching violently in the bathroom.

I sprang out of bed and sprinted to the door that separated us. "Donovan, are you okay? Can I get you anything?"

"I'm fine. Just sick. Go back to bed."

"How about some water?"

"There's water in here." He ran the faucet as proof. "Sorry to keep you up…I just—" I could hear more coughing and heaving. "I just need to be alone right now, okay? I'm…I'm gonna take a shower."

"Okay," I said. "But, really, if you need anyth—"

"I don't. Thanks. I'm *fine*."

Yeah, right. Because I *always* thought people were *fine* when they were gagging their guts out in a motel bathroom in the middle of the night.

I stepped away from the door but didn't get back into bed. Instead, I sat down in a chair close to the bathroom and just listened.

Donovan had polished off half a bottle of whiskey that afternoon and evening, which would make almost anyone sick. I wasn't sure, though, if the alcohol was also responsible for the sobs I heard, despite how well they were being muffled by the running water.

After fifteen minutes, the shower stopped and I jumped into bed, closing my eyes and pretending to sleep. Donovan still didn't come out for a while, though. He spent a long time brushing his teeth, gargling with mouthwash and thoroughly drying off. When finally he did emerge, he was wearing only his thin pair of shorts—discarded was the t-shirt from before. He slipped back into bed without putting another one on.

I let him get comfortable and waited to see if he'd fall asleep. He didn't.

With a sigh, I abandoned my charade of sleeping myself and turned toward him. "How are you feeling now?"

He'd been staring up at the ceiling, but he glanced over at me for several seconds—his eyes moist, his jaw tight—and shook his head.

Despite his recent shower and his lack of a t-shirt, he was sweating hard. All over. The perspiration dotted his forehead and cheekbones. It glistened on his neck and bare chest. He'd taken off the bandages I'd put on his flesh wound earlier in the day, so dark-red scabs slashed across his otherwise smooth shoulder, and beads of wetness were surrounding them, too.

"It's not the liquor that's the problem, is it?" I asked.

He shook his head again. "No." It came out as a rasp.

"I'm—I'm so sorry about Jeremy."

"Yeah, me, too. I'd hoped so much…but I knew he wouldn't still be alive and not…not let me know somehow."

I heard another sound, one originating deep in his throat, like an injured mammal fighting against his own agony. Donovan flipped away from me and curled inward upon himself.

That sense of helplessness I despised came upon me again, like a suffocating veil in the darkness. God, there was almost nothing I hated more than that feeling. I had to try to do *something*. To be of some comfort to him. But all I could see was his back and his lacerated shoulder.

I took a breath and slid toward his side of the mattress. Kept sliding until my chest was against his spine. Then, careful to avoid the site of his wound, I snaked my arm around him, spooning him. Cradling him even tighter when he entwined his fingers with mine and when the silent sobs wracked his body.

Eventually, the sobs stopped and his breathing slowed, though he didn't let go of my hand, and I didn't pull it away. I, too, drifted into sleep for a couple of hours. Wasn't sure when, exactly, his position changed. Just that the next thing I remembered was waking up with my head against his bare chest and his arms embracing me.

I snuggled closer and whispered, "It'll all be okay."

He murmured something back, kissed my forehead lightly and said, "Thanks."

I nodded, pressed my lips against the vee of his neck—which was very warm but no longer damp—and kissed him lightly in return. It was a simple exchange. Not so terribly different from the night I'd been crying in Tulsa and he'd tried to console me.

But then I looked up at his face. And, in the same moment, he looked down at mine. Somehow, without either of us thinking about it, our lips met in the middle.

It was just a soft kiss—at least at first. An act borne more out of a need for comfort and gratitude than out of passion.

But then it changed.

Then it was no longer this innocent, nonverbal sign of friendship and support. There was suddenly something much more powerful connecting our bodies to one another. A force that had always existed between us. I'd known it was there for years, but it had lain mostly dormant.

To be honest, the strength of this feeling scared the hell out of me—I'd begun to lose myself in his kiss—and I knew if it continued for even ten seconds longer, Donovan would never be able to forgive himself in the morning.

So, I pulled away.

Donovan instantly stopped touching me. "Oh, Jesus…Aurora, I'm sorry."

"It's okay," I said quickly. "Really." I gave his arm a reassuring pat and scooched back to my side of the bed.

He slid himself as far to the other side as he could go and collapsed against his pillow—staring at the ceiling again as if watching a fiery meteor shower in the night sky. The sweat started to return to his brow. He groaned and covered his eyes with his palm. "I'm not…myself. I'm not—"

"I know. Don't worry about it." I faked a yawn. "We need more sleep." I twisted away from him and tried to still every one of my limbs. I only allowed myself to take quiet, shallow breaths until I knew he was asleep again.

But no matter how motionless my body may have appeared on the outside, my insides were careening wildly, threatening to give me and my deepest secrets away.

Donovan and I had just *kissed*.

I knew better than anyone that it didn't mean anything to him—

especially since alcohol had been involved. But just the fact that it had happened, and that I'd felt what I felt while it was happening, was enough to throw me into a disorienting whirl.

It wasn't just about my attraction to him. Those feelings had always been there. No, it was also about what I told my dad before we'd left on the trip. My lie to my own father. My insistence that there was *nothing* between Donovan and me other than a desire to find out what had happened to our brothers.

I guess I'd never expected that Donovan would let down his guard long enough for anything to actually occur between us. And, now that he had, I was confused.

Were my feelings for him *real*…or just a product of being a romance-hungry American teen growing up in a lustful generation? And what were his feelings toward me? What would he think of me the next day when he remembered my behavior from tonight? He might only be twenty-three, but he was already such a man of honor. Too much of one to ever take advantage of me, even a couple of years ago, before any tragedies had taken place, and back when I was practically throwing myself at him in the middle of a wild party.

Yet, here he was tonight—sad, emotionally distraught and under the influence—and when he moved to kiss me, I didn't immediately stop him.

I kissed him back. And I enjoyed it.

Sure, eventually I pulled away, but I hadn't wanted to, even knowing how he'd later consider this all to be his fault. That he'd try to take responsibility for it, like he did for everything.

I'd been acting smug and superior toward him ever since I first showed him the journal, just because I was more intuitive, but, in so many ways, he'd proven to be the more mature person of the two of us. It wasn't because he was older but, rather, because he lived by an unshakable code of conduct. Firm guiding principles. Ethics that wouldn't waver, even in the face of tragedy and injustice.

WE WOKE up to a clear, hot weekday morning in Albuquerque—as deceptively bright and unthreatening as the morning before in

Amarillo—but look at how wrong we'd been about that, huh?

I was exhausted still. Donovan was, of course, more than a little worse for the wear, but he was making a heroic effort to get back to a healthy equilibrium after his whiskey bender.

He scrubbed his face with his palms, ran his fingers through his dark hair and looked at me with concern. "Morning," he said. Then, after gulping down a few Dixie cups of tap water, "Um, Aurora, last night—"

I used his pause as an excuse to jump in. "Yeah, I know you were pretty sick. How are you feeling? I hope you're not too headachy today, but we can take it easy if you are. I'm not sure what you feel like eating, but I think simpler and plainer food is better, right?" I didn't wait for him to answer. "And maybe you'll want to take an aspirin now and a nap later. I know you didn't get as much sleep as usual."

He glanced at me warily. "Yeah. Aurora, about that—"

"Oh, and we should really go over some things in the journal," I babbled. "A few new words or phrases might stand out more for us now."

He exhaled, walked up to where I was standing by the edge of the bed and put his hands on my shoulders. "We'll do that today, I promise. But first, I just wanted to apologize for yesterday. All of it. The morning and all the danger I put us in. The afternoon, the evening and especially the middle of the night. I was just…I don't know…for some stupid reason I thought the alcohol would help take the edge off, but it didn't really work that way. And then I kept waking up a thousand times and waking you up along with me."

I put my index finger up to his lips. "Been drinking," I said, parroting his words from the night of the graduation party. "I understand. I really do. Nothing happened last night." When he shook his head and opened his mouth to contradict me, though, I added, "Nothing you need to worry about, okay? Please, Donovan. Please don't."

He still looked like he wanted to continue debating this point, but I was determined to put an end to any further apologies. Especially since I should be the one apologizing for most of it.

Instead, I pulled out Treak's notes and reviewed with Donovan what I'd noticed when I reread them last night. Then I opened up Gideon's journal to the Albuquerque/Santa Fe page and read it aloud:

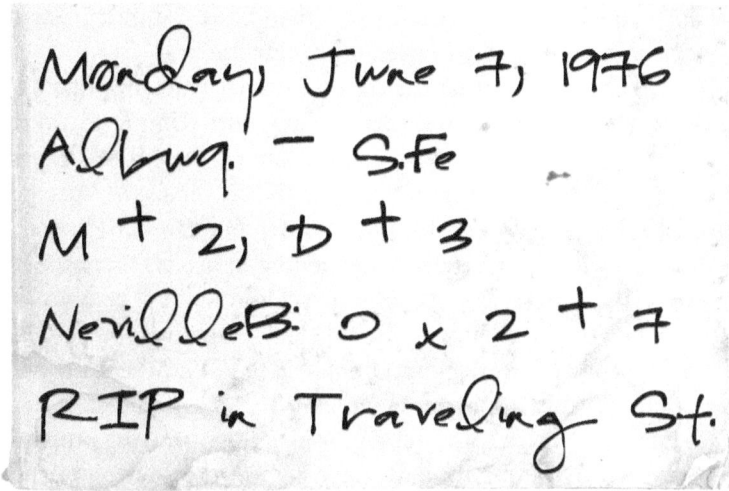

"So, the date, when run through the month/day equation, is actually August 10, 1976," I said. "Five days after the explosion in Amarillo."

"And 'NevilleB'? What's that?" he asked.

"Treak listed a 'Billy Neville' in his notes, and he was from Albuquerque, so that's my best guess. As for the numbers following the name, I'm not sure. Zero times two is zero. And zero plus seven is seven. So maybe the number seven has some meaning in connection with this Neville guy."

But Donovan was staring at the page with an odd expression. "I know you're better than me at this stuff, but could the zero times two equal a double zero with the seven added onto the end? So it's actually 007?"

Instantly I saw what he saw and knew he had to be right.

"Wow, yeah," I said. "That's it for sure. It's exactly the kind of thing Gideon would write." Then I thought about it. "I just don't know why. Is Billy Neville some kind of spy? Someone who's British? Or does it refer to something else from the Bond films?"

He shrugged, but I couldn't help but notice that he looked fleetingly proud of himself for having cracked one of my brother's little codes.

As for the final line—*RIP in Traveling St.*—neither of us had any idea what that meant specifically, but I felt justified in fearing that the "RIP" probably had something to do with Jeremy.

Donovan may have been thinking exactly the same thing, but

he willed me with his eyes not to verbalize it. So I didn't. Instead, I confessed something that had been bothering me.

"I hate that we can't trust the cops we know personally. I hate that we don't know who the 'good guys' are anymore. Until our brothers disappeared, I always thought we could count on the police to uphold the law, but it feels like they're more often the criminals. At least when it comes to this case." I knew I sounded bitter, but I couldn't help it.

Donovan sighed. "Whatever's happening here feels more like war than crime, Aurora. With an act of war, a soldier's moral compass isn't set to true north. Depending on the side you're fighting on, you'd label one act as 'justice,' if it was your troop doing it, and the same act as 'terrorism,' if it came from your enemies."

He had another cup of water and took a few steadying breaths. "I didn't get sent to 'Nam, but I had friends who were there and lived to talk about it. And my grandpa fought in World War I, dropping depth chargers on enemy U-boats. These were all good and honest men here at home. Heroes, in my book. But to the other side—to the Viet Cong, to the Germans—they were monsters. In war, no one is totally good. Everyone loses."

I nodded. What he was saying made sense. Gideon and Jeremy had been doing something patriotic, yet Jeremy ended up dying senselessly. And even though it appeared that Gideon managed to survive, it was only in body. Nothing of my brother's prior life remained. He'd lost his best friend, his family, his home, the world as he knew it, the future he had planned, however casually... None of this was fair, but we all knew war wasn't known for its fairness.

"We still don't know the whole story, though," I said. "After our brothers fled Crescent Cove, what led them to Texas in hopes of uncovering the truth? Sebastian said they'd been talking with Hal. Stirring up trouble, in Sebastian's opinion. Were they ignoring what they knew to be the *safe* thing in hopes of doing the *right* thing? Were they *trying* to be heroes?"

He wrinkled his nose and gave his head a shake. "That's my point. In an act of war—foreign or domestic—there's no standard or unquestionably 'right' side. It all depends. Could Gideon and Jeremy always clearly read their moral compass? If so, would we agree with their choices? I don't think we can say." He sort of smiled at me. "I mean, are you always sure of what your moral compass says? Are you positive you're acting the *right* way? Doing the *right* thing all the time?"

I felt my face begin to flush as I remembered our kiss from the night before. Had I been doing the right thing? Had I genuinely been comforting Donovan…or had I been taking advantage of his weakened state?

I mumbled something noncommittal and changed the subject.

"I still think we should head towards home again. Maybe not drive all the way back to Minnesota, but get within striking distance." I pointed at the journal. "I suppose if we search, we might find somebody in Albuquerque named Billy Neville, but I don't think there was anyone on Treak's list who wasn't a big crook, a nasty killer or both. I don't want to take a chance on running into somebody else who might start shooting at us."

But Donovan was already pulling out the phonebook and flipping to the Ns.

"Neville, B.J." the listing read. "157 Greenleaf Cir." And there was a phone number, too, that I didn't even bother to memorize.

"But I don't want to find him," I said again, more insistently. "I'm scared of these people, Donovan." *I'm scared of what they might do to me…and especially to you.*

Never before had I felt the weight of my mortality so strongly. The consequences my life—or death—would have on other people that I cared about. It wasn't about giving up the search. I just knew I had to be grown-up enough to take my loved ones into consideration.

"I know," he said. "Me, too." He blew out some air. "But we're not going back home. Not yet. And I can't spend another day in this motel, so I have an idea. I think we need to take a little field trip today."

"To where? The grocery store?" I glanced at the bags and boxes of food on the table that we'd both rummaged through all day yesterday and had half eaten. I was, admittedly, pretty sick of Ritz crackers and beef jerky. "Or maybe the library?"

He laughed. "No. I think we need to go to Santa Fe."

"I thought you didn't want to drive anywhere for a few days. That the point of being at this motor lodge was to hide the Trans Am in the garage."

"It is," he said, thumbing back to a reference page in an earlier section of the phonebook—one with a timetable of some kind and a bunch of multicolored routes listed on it. "That's why we're going to take the bus."

Chapter Thirteen

Santa Fe, New Mexico ~ Monday, June 26

DRESSED IN clothes that were as understated as possible, Donovan and I caught the first bus heading northeast to Santa Fe.

He was wearing a plain white t-shirt, blue jeans and a dark-colored baseball cap. I was in a pale-yellow t-shirt with khaki shorts, but that hadn't been my first choice.

"Isn't that shirt, maybe, too…pink?" Donovan asked me when he saw my original outfit.

In spite of everything that had happened in the past twenty-four hours, I burst out laughing. "Are you kidding me? You're telling me what I'm wearing is—oh, how should I put it—too *conspicuous*?"

He shot me a sheepish grin, acknowledging the irony, but he only said, "Just change it. It's nice and all, but a little, um, bright."

I snorted, but I put on the pale-yellow one anyway.

The bus ride took just over an hour with stops, but everyone onboard seemed like fairly normal people. A collection of melting-pot Americans. Lots of grandma-looking types with woven handbags, moms with little kids on their laps, working men of various skin tones and ages—reading their newspapers or their paperback novels or catching a light doze before their stop. Though Donovan and I both lacked the deeply tanned skin of many of the passengers, I felt we blended in with the group reasonably well.

When we got to downtown Santa Fe, we nimbly hopped off the bus and embarked on a city exploration adventure that lasted several hours. Gideon's journal hadn't given us much to go on. He only mentioned that he'd been in Santa Fe and Albuquerque on the same date—August tenth—which had been a Tuesday two years ago.

I vowed to keep an eye open for any street that might be called "Traveling St." or, maybe, a roadway that had something to do with travel. Planes? Cars? Buses? Trains? Something that might explain Gideon's "RIP" clue.

But nothing we encountered rang any bells and, from what I could tell, the only thing I was sure about when it came to Santa Fe was that this was a city of ninety percent artists.

There were sculptures and paintings and pottery and handcrafted jewelry in just about every store. More vibrant reds, oranges and golds than a string of summer sunsets. More splashes of turquoise, indigo and silver than the falling dusk on the night of a full moon.

"Hey, can I see your ring?" Donovan asked suddenly, after we'd walked by probably our twenty-seventh jewelry shop.

I handed him the gold-colored Cracker-Jack-like band he'd given me to wear during motel check-ins and check-outs. We'd been so preoccupied lately, though, that I'd forgotten to take it off for several days. When I pulled it off my left ring finger, it left a greenish residue on my skin. I tried to rub it away.

He saw my finger and said, "Sorry. You shouldn't be wearing this junk. I didn't think you'd have to have it on for this long."

I succeeded in getting some of the green ickiness off, but I could still see a line. I felt almost marked by it. "That's okay. It'll go away when I wash my hands next." I hoped this was true.

He pointed to a Burger King, nestled in a cluster of eateries, farther down the block. "They've got bathrooms there," he said. "Hungry? Wanna grab a couple of burgers?"

"Sure."

We walked most of the way together, but Donovan wanted to duck into an art shop that specialized in framed posters of classic cars. He told me to go ahead. That he'd meet me there in a few minutes.

"Take your time," I said. "I'll get the burgers for us." And when he moved to pull out his wallet, I took several steps away from him. "No, Donovan. You've covered most of our meals on the trip already. Let me buy this one." I scurried away, not waiting for him to give his consent.

I almost regretted telling him to take as long as he needed because our meal was starting to get cold by the time he got there. I'd already washed my hands twice and ordered Whoppers, French fries and Cokes for both of us (I was starving), and I'd been waiting impatiently for about ten minutes more before he finally walked in the door. But he was smiling, and it was nice to see that for a change.

Sometime after I'd finished my burger but before I'd eaten all of my fries, he pulled a little white box out of his pocket and set it on one of the paper napkins in front of me.

"Take a look," he said, grinning.

I lifted the lid. There was a gold ring inside with a small but lovely round-cut ruby on top. My birthstone. "What did you…" I stopped speaking. I was at a loss for words.

"Do you like it?"

"*Yes.* Yes, it—it's beautiful."

I lifted it out of the box. It reminded me of Gideon's graduation ring, but it was tinier, more delicate. I hadn't ordered a graduation ring myself but, if I had, I probably would have chosen something similar to this. What did it mean that Donovan had gotten this for me?

"Try it on."

I slipped it on my finger, and it was a perfect fit. "How did you know—"

His smile broadened. He produced the Cracker-Jack prize ring from his pocket and dropped it into the white box. "You'd sized it for me by wearing this old one. You should have a ring that doesn't turn your finger green," he said. "This new one's 14-carat gold."

"Donovan, you shouldn't have gotten me this. It's too expensive, and I don't need—"

"It wasn't very expensive," he insisted, "and, anyway, your birthday's this weekend, right? Happy eighteenth, Aurora."

I didn't know what to say to that. I somehow managed to mumble, "Thank you. This is such a surprise. I really didn't expect...anything."

"You're welcome. You deserve something nice. Something that'll last." His voice was smooth and confident when he spoke, like that of a family elder. But, when our gazes met, he seemed to get a little boyish and fidgety. He abruptly got up, tossed the used wrappers and table garbage in the trash and excused himself to use the bathroom.

I slowly finished my fries, glancing every other second at the new ring adorning my left hand and wondering if there was anything significant about this gift from his point of view. Anything more to it than simply being an incredibly pretty and very thoughtful birthday present.

EVENTUALLY, WE had to admit that all we were doing in Santa Fe was wandering aimlessly around town, shopping and eating. Nothing we'd seen had jumped out at us as far as being relevant to our brothers, so we hopped on the bus again and headed back to Albuquerque.

It was a pleasant return drive. Donovan and I, though not uneasy with each other, rode back to the motor lodge in silence. He was sitting on the aisle, studying the facial features of our fellow passengers. I, in the window seat, did that for a few minutes, too, before turning my attention to the New Mexico scenery.

We passed a handful of family restaurants, a Chrysler dealership, a church named St. Christopher's, a bunch of roadside fruit-and-vegetable stands and a sprawling K-mart.

Beyond the evidence of capitalism, commerce and community, however, were the mountains on one side and the stark but stunning desert on the other…the burnt edges of which rose up to meet the horizon. How odd to technically be in my native country and, yet, to feel as though I were traveling in a foreign land. It was at once both unsettling and invigorating.

It wasn't until we were getting ready for bed late that night that something we'd seen during the day registered on the canvas of my consciousness.

"Remember how Amy Lynn told us that Treak had a medallion of a saint?" I asked Donovan. "It was the patron saint of travelers, right?"

He nodded. "Yep. St. Christopher. Why?"

"Because Gideon wrote on his Albuquerque/Santa Fe page 'RIP in Traveling St.' and I thought it was Traveling *Street*. But what if it was his abbreviation for Traveling *Saint*? We passed by a St. Christopher's Church on the way home. Could Gideon have maybe taken Jeremy's body there?" Then, as gently as I could, I added, "It had a small cemetery."

The light in his eyes dimmed visibly at my words, but he took them in and nodded. "Yeah. That'd probably make sense. He would've had to have done something with the body." He glanced vacantly at the window. "I guess we could go back to it tomorrow. Check it out."

That night, Donovan didn't get wasted on whiskey, take a shower at two a.m. or cry soundlessly over the death of his kid brother—but neither did he sleep well. He tossed and twisted and breathed unevenly. At one point, he started sweating again, but this time he just gulped a cup of water, took his shirt off, threw it across the room and attempted to quietly get comfortable in bed. He never did manage that.

In the darkness, with him turned away from me, I studied the silhouette of his body—admiring the contours of his muscles, the thickness of his wavy hair, the *otherness* of his form.

A part of me felt guilty for taking mental energy away from the danger we were in and letting myself daydream about Donovan and me…together. My attraction to him was a luxury I knew I couldn't afford. Not with a killer still on the loose and a thousand unanswered questions remaining.

But I justified it by telling myself that my fantasy of kissing him again—when we were both completely sober and wide awake—was a harmless stress release, not unlike my fleeting but vivid daydreams about Roger Moore in "The Spy Who Loved Me" or Warren Beatty in just about anything.

I glanced at my new ruby ring, still finding it hard to believe Donovan had thought to buy it for me, and my heart filled with a jumble of conflicting emotions. I made myself promise that my whimsical romantic scenarios would be contained to the night. That I wouldn't entertain any such girlish silliness come morning.

But making vows was easy. Keeping them had always been much trickier.

It had been forty-eight hours since we'd ridden in the Trans Am. Both of us knew we were taking a chance by pulling it out of the garage and driving in the open again.

As forcefully as I'd once worked to keep Donovan heading west down Route 66, I was now doing everything in my power to get him to abandon it. Problem was, the stubborn man just wasn't listening to me. Not about that. Not about anything.

"Donovan," I began, as he jingled his car keys impatiently in our room, motioning for me to hurry up so we could leave. "Are you *sure* you don't want to take the bus to the church?"

He shook his head. "The next one that stops near there isn't for three hours. I read the schedule. Besides, I had enough of the bus yesterday. I want my own wheels."

"But your 'own wheels' are really recognizable." Not to mention that the car now had a busted driver's side window, a number of bullet holes and a huge crack in the windshield.

"I'm not the only person in town driving a red Trans Am, Aurora." He rolled his eyes. "Not even a damaged one. It's been two days. Anyone following us would have thought we'd traveled on by now."

"That's right. It's already Tuesday, and we've been gone from home for *so* long. I realize it might be too dangerous, with Officer James there, for us to go back yet—or for our families—but why don't we check out of the motor lodge, make a quick stop at St. Christopher's and then go just a little further north?"

Donovan didn't immediately answer, so I made yet another plea for Colorado. "It's not that far, but it's at least away from here and the roads they might expect to find us on. If someone like Sebastian or those bikers are still searching for us in Albuquerque—or if they have people on the lookout for your car—they wouldn't be as likely to spot us there."

But what seemed to me to be a perfectly logical and utterly responsible compromise had no sway with him.

"We're driving the half hour to this place, walking the grounds once and then picking up some lunch. I'm sick of crackers," he informed me. "If anyone wants to find us that bad, they can damn well do it. Now, let's go."

As we slid into the Trans Am, I was reminded that Donovan had taken a different approach to all of this from the beginning. When it was still possible to ignore thinking about Jeremy and Gideon's choices and their fate, he did. Back then, he felt he couldn't do anything about it, so he just avoided it all. But when that changed—when the situation became real, present and tangibly dangerous to us—he had a lower tolerance than most for burying his head in the sand.

If I didn't think I knew better, I would have suspected him of calling out "yoo-hoo" to our enemies. He'd had time at the motor lodge to mentally regroup. He seemed ready and refreshed. And, now, it was almost as if he was trying to flush the bad guys out of the desert shadows and into the light. Hoping to engage them in battle somehow. Clearly choosing fight over flight.

This worried me.

St. Christopher's was a tiny Catholic church, much like the thousands of singular little chapels along America's roadsides. Not really belonging to one community or another but, somehow, accessible to the residents of all of them. To anyone, really who was willing to make the drive.

Being just off the fairly busy I-25 had to have helped the parish in drawing the interest of strangers. They did, at least, have the benefit of drive-by traffic, I thought, as Donovan took us down the long gravel driveway and parked in the nearly abandoned back lot, away from the Interstate. Cars, trucks and buses could be heard zipping by but, as we walked around the old, small but well-constructed building to the cemetery behind the church, it felt plenty secluded to me.

As far as I could tell, there wasn't a mass in session then and we saw no parishioners strolling the grounds. Donovan and I each wandered around independently, reading the names on the tombstones and trying to figure out if any of them looked like something that might be Jeremy's final resting place. I hadn't thought much about it, since neither Donovan nor Jeremy spoke much about religion, but their family was Catholic. My brother would have remembered something like that.

"There's an unmarked section over here," Donovan said, his voice more tense than it had been a few minutes earlier. "They've got a bunch of graves with no names. Just metal crosses."

I swallowed the lump in my throat as I walked to where he was standing. There was no way to know if our hunch was right and this was where Gideon brought Jeremy. No way to guess in which grave Donovan's brother might be, even if we were correct. So, I did the only two things I could: I said a prayer under my breath for Jeremy and for all of the unknown souls resting there, and I reached out to Donovan and put my hand on his shoulder, so he'd know he wasn't alone.

We stood there for a long while, not saying anything. Finally, he took a step away, breaking our connection.

"So...what are you in the mood to have for lunch?" he asked.

I shrugged. "I'm not really hungry."

"Me, neither," he admitted. "Although, if we were anywhere near Johansen's Diner, I could probably go for some Sandvik's stew."

I chuckled a little, remembering our meal there before we drove to Crescent Cove. It seemed like a lifetime ago. "Yet another reason to start heading toward home."

"Should've guessed you'd say that."

"Donovan, it's not that I want us to just slip back in to our old lives and forget all of this ever happened. I know I never could, even if it were totally safe to go back. But I'm starting to think we've reached the end of the line. That there might be more to discover but, maybe, we just weren't meant to discover it."

The two of us started walking back toward the parking lot.

"I'm convinced my brother is alive, but he's a ghost. He's had a hundred chances to cross paths with us, but he doesn't want to be found. And, while I'm sure there's an excellent reason for that, it doesn't change the fact that he's...lost to me."

I inhaled deeply. The pain of this loss was still so strong sometimes that it blocked my ability to breathe.

"I don't want to give up searching for our brothers or looking for the answers to our questions," I said. "But, if Gideon wants to be off the grid, and if Jeremy's really...gone, then we can't do much for either of them. We can only help the people we love at home who are left."

He nodded. "I know. I just—I guess I hadn't realized how much I hadn't wanted to let my brother go."

"Yeah." I bowed my head. "That's the part that's hardest for me, too. That, somehow, we have to move on, even though we don't have all the answers. That we won't get the neat and tidy ending where the puzzle is solved. Where everything is clear and it all makes sense."

I never thought I'd reach a point where I'd even *think* something like this but, after everything Donovan and I had been through, it was true.

"Would've been nice, though." He smiled at me. "Hey, how about we just go back to the motor lodge and talk about our options. Maybe there's something we can do that we're overlooking. I just think—"

Suddenly, he stopped walking, grabbed me and shoved me behind him.

Standing half a parking lot away from us was one of the bikers that had followed us from Amarillo. The African-American one. We hadn't seen him drive up. Hadn't heard his motorcycle. But there it was, about four feet from the Trans Am, and he was standing—helmet off, legs crossed, arms taut and holding a gun in each hand—in front of Donovan's car.

"You two are gonna want to stay right there," the leather-clad biker warned, an unmistakable edge to his deep voice, as we all watched an unmarked, beige sedan pull into the lot and park. Sebastian James stepped out of it.

"Oh, shit," Donovan muttered.

Sebastian, out of police uniform but still managing to look officious and menacing, lifted his palm in a wave to the biker. "Thanks for the alert," he called to the other guy. Then he turned his attention to us. "Convenient of you to come to a cemetery," he sneered. "Ain't that just perfect...did you two pick out your plots already?"

Donovan tensed, but I could tell he was preoccupied with thinking through possible escape routes. He motioned for me to stay behind him and a little to the right. As far out of direct range as I could get from the two other men.

Before either of us could answer, we heard the sound of a motorcycle coming down the drive. The second biker. This guy, the Caucasian one, didn't even bother to take off his helmet. He just jumped off his bike, nodded in acknowledgment to Sebastian, then to the other biker, who handed him one of his guns. The white biker then took his place in the triangle of evil that surrounded us. Three against two. And all three of them were armed.

Sebastian grinned at those odds. "You're not going to get away from us this time," he said, taking a couple of steps forward. "Too bad these fine men and I didn't know we were all on the same team back in Amarillo. We could've gotten rid of you there."

Both bikers laughed at this, and the white one seemed especially mirthful. He slapped his black-leathered knee and, in the same motion, swiftly raised his weapon at us. Some kind of revolver with an extra-long barrel.

Under his breath, I heard Donovan murmur, "He's got a silencer."

The black biker pointed his gun in our direction, too, and then all of the men took several steps forward, closing in on us from three sides.

I reached ahead of me and grasped ahold of Donovan, putting my hands around his waist and, despite his resistance, pulling myself forward so we were standing side by side.

"Get back behind me, Aurora," he whispered, his voice urgent but too low for the others to hear. "I'll distract them. You run."

The men stepped closer.

"No," I said. "I'm staying with you."

He gazed at me worriedly, an expression that held more than a touch of affection and infinite sadness wrapped up in it. Then he put his arm around me and hugged me close, still trying to shield my body with his.

The two bikers shared a glance. The black guy nodded at the white one, who finally spoke. "I've been waiting a long time for this," the white biker said to us with a heavy Southern drawl. It struck a familiar chord. I knew I'd heard it recently, but I was too scared to place it.

His biker buddy nodded in agreement, and Sebastian, who'd pulled out his weapon and had it aimed it at us, chuckled and said, "Me, too."

I took a deep breath, certain it was one of my last, as the helmeted biker cocked his revolver. But then, in a movement even swifter than his earlier one, he swung the gun so the barrel pointed at Sebastian, and he fired twice.

The smile disappeared from Sebastian's face. He fell to the ground like an extinguished cigarette butt—almost as soundlessly as the muted bullets that had been shot at him. No doubt about it, he was dead.

Very much dead.

Donovan and I stood motionless, our mouths open, as the white biker returned the gun to the biking pal who'd given it to him. "Meet you back at the station," he said to his friend, saluted us and then strode over to his motorcycle. He hopped on it and promptly drove away.

The black biker that remained behind held his hand up at us in a gesture of peace. "Aurora Gray and Donovan McCafferty," he said, taking a few steps toward the fallen cop and studying the body from a couple of angles. "I'm sorry I was unable to introduce myself earlier. I'm Albuquerque police detective Billy Neville. My undercover partner and I have been monitoring your movements and trying to protect you two ever since we'd gotten word of your arrival in Amarillo. But I'm afraid we'd underestimated Sebastian James when we were there. We didn't think he'd make his move so fast." He paused. "This time, we made sure we had home court advantage, though. Glad we were able to stop him."

I had no words in response to this.

It was all I could do just to try to comprehend the little information he'd given us as he began to lug Sebastian's dead body toward the parking lot, muttering, "There's gonna be a lot of paperwork to do on this one..."

So, *he* was Billy Neville? My brother's "007" from his journal? His name had been on Treak's list, too, and *no one* on that list had been good news.

Donovan's thoughts must have been hovering in the same vicinity as mine because the tension in his torso didn't diminish at Billy's introduction. Still, he cleared his throat and was able to accomplish what I hadn't been able to do: Ask a direct question.

"The biker who just shot Sebastian," Donovan began slowly, "and who tailed us from Texas to New Mexico alongside of you—he was your undercover partner?"

"Yep," Billy said. "But, in a way, you already know him." He beamed a brief grin at us. "His name's Andy Reggio."

Chapter Fourteen

THE NEXT couple of days were a hazy, disorienting blur on one level but, simultaneously, they brought more clarity and enlightenment to our brothers' disappearance than Donovan and I had ever hoped to expect.

And, for the first time since our road-trip adventure began, we felt we'd finally found an ally.

In the forty-eight hours following the shooting, we were under Billy Neville's constant protective care and, as such, treated like royalty when it came to our safety and wellbeing. At the police station, where we spent the majority of those hours volleying questions and responses back and forth, we were made more comfortable and secure than if we'd been visiting dignitaries.

Not that Donovan and I weren't both extremely suspicious at first.

"How did Andy Reggio start working with you?" Donovan asked Billy that first afternoon, distrust cutting sharp edges into his tone. "No one, including him, ever said anything about him being a cop. Just that he'd worked in that motorcycle shop and had an elderly mother in Shamrock."

I nodded and crossed my arms, agreeing emphatically with Donovan's skepticism. "And why did he leave after he shot Sebastian? Why didn't he stay and help you with the body?"

Billy had used Sebastian's own car keys to open the back of that beige sedan and, with Donovan's reluctant help, tossed Sebastian's body into the trunk before anyone at the church could come out and ask questions.

The forty-something Albuquerque police detective didn't get flustered or defensive during our inquisition, though. He just took a deep breath and said, "There's a good reason for all of this, and I'll explain everything I know. Afterward, if you're able to answer some of my questions, too, I'd really appreciate it."

We agreed, though it was with a heavy dose of caution.

"To start with," Billy said, "Andy Reggio isn't a cop, but he's a man with many talents. After I met Gideon, I brought Andy into this case as a civilian to do undercover work. He has a way with people and is capable of getting information from some sectors of the population that I cannot. Since I'm stationed out here in New Mexico, I can only travel so far, but Andy's much more mobile, and he was willing to move around—"

"You talked to my brother?" I asked. "When? Why?"

"I only talked to Gideon in person one time, Aurora, and I'll get to the details of that in a bit. Andy has been the liaison between me and Gideon ever since then, whereas I've been the one who's primarily in contact with the FBI. I've got a couple of good friends there. The case they needed help with involved a major operation that had crossed a number of state lines but had begun in the Midwest. Specifically, in Chicago. There are a handful of bad seeds in the police department there with mob ties and, also, in a few places across the country. The Feds have wanted to put a stop to them for a long time."

"There are a *lot* of bad seeds, not just a handful," I said, unwilling to be fully trusting of the man, despite the fact that every vibe I'd gotten from the officer sitting in front of us had been consistently genuine.

Again, he didn't get mad or become aggressive. Instead, he said gently, "Aurora, not all of us cops are bad. Most of us are not. But, yes, there *are* some—certainly more than we'd like—who are motivated to do illegal things by greed, ambition, excitement or sometimes fear. They get caught up in dangerous, unethical ventures, and they either can't or won't get themselves out of it. For me, helping protect the innocent in these circumstances was where I knew I could be of service to my country."

I tried to remain unmoved by this declaration. "When and why did you meet my brother?" I asked again.

"We met after Sebastian James shot him," Billy replied. "I'd heard about the truck explosion in Amarillo and, from my underground sources, figured out someone had escaped from the scene, what kind of car the man was driving and which direction he was headed—turned out to be right into Albuquerque. I waited at the eastern edge of the city and then cornered Gideon as he came into town. His car had a couple of hastily patched-up tires, he was bleeding out of his right side and, in the backseat—" He shot a sad, apologetic look at Donovan. "In the backseat was Jeremy's body. It took some convincing, but I eventually persuaded Gideon that I was one of the good guys."

Donovan, who had learned his lesson about believing the words of shifty cops, continued to appear indifferent to Billy's thoughtful statements. But I could tell by his posture and by the pained look in his eyes that he wished he could take the police detective at his word. I could also sense that some part of him had still been holding out a tiny bit of hope that Sebastian had lied about killing Jeremy. Donovan didn't welcome Billy's confirmation of this bad news.

"So, Andy had been lying to us on the phone," Donovan said, with no small degree of accusation. "All those things he talked about, saying he'd asked Gideon how my brother was doing…he knew Jeremy was dead from the beginning. And he told us he'd only seen Gideon twice—in the summer of '76 and then in May of this year. Sounds like they'd had much more contact than that."

"Andy was undercover, playing a well-developed role, Donovan. His only objective was to pass along those documents to you from Gideon—which I'd helped them compile—and to get you and Aurora to contact William James," Billy said. "It was critical to the building of our case that we established proof of a criminal link between Sebastian James and his Minnesota cousin."

"Why? Didn't you already know they were criminals? Sebastian James *killed* Jeremy. And his cousin—" I stopped.

True, I'd always distrusted Officer William James and had suspected he'd been a dirty cop for the past two years, but it had been an intuitive thing for me. I couldn't put my finger on why, exactly, he'd seemed so deceitful, despite his youthful hipness and general popularity. Yet, even *I* had doubted my own perceptions when my brother—via Andy—had said it was okay to trust him.

"Sorry," I said. "I think, maybe, we need you to start earlier than meeting my brother. Go back to the 'bad seeds' and explain how this all started. Please."

Billy Neville nodded.

"There was a Chicago journalist," he began, "named Patrick Bradley. Your brother called him Treak. Treak Bradley had been working to crack a big story that involved a vendetta between a crime boss by the name of Vincent Leto and a corrupt union leader called Julian Carello. We're talking about two major scumbags here, but they're powerful ones who've evaded the law for years, all while threatening each other and retaliating violently whenever they could."

Billy poured himself some coffee and, after offering us a cup to each of us, continued. "In late 1974, Carello stole Leto's mistress at the time, and Leto responded by murdering a couple of Carello's union heads, with the help of Leto's henchmen, Rick Brice, who'd been on the city's police force back then. Carello did some nasty stuff in return and framed Brice for it, which resulted in Brice eventually losing his badge."

I remembered a few hazy details about union problems in those police reports and nodded at the officer, encouraging him to continue.

"In 1975 and '76, there was a full-scale war going on between them. Carello's car and house in Chicago were bombed a number of times, and some of Carello's 'business interests' in other parts of the country—including many holdings in cities along Route 66—went up in flames, too. Leto was a master of union intimidation schemes. While he focused most of his attention on Carello, there were other high-ranking union officers and business owners that were under attack by him as well. Leto needed a steady stream of explosive material that was cheap, easy to make and couldn't be noticeably traced back to him."

"So, he went out of state to get it," Donovan said. "To Crescent Cove, Wisconsin."

"Yep. He financed a fireworks factory not far from there." Billy flipped open a box of Girl Scout cookies. "Thin Mint?"

"Thanks," I said and, to be polite, I took one. Donovan took three.

"The journalist was a bright guy," Billy said, "and he picked up a few patterns the other investigators had missed. He noticed a link between some of the out-of-state bombings and deliveries by the Americana Trucking company. Especially odd because fireworks were being shipped to some states that had their own big suppliers. And there was one driver whose name kept showing up again and again."

"Hal Chaney," I supplied.

"Exactly." Billy downed several gulps of coffee and popped a chocolate-mint cookie into his mouth. "Addictive, these things," he said with a wink. "You want another one?"

I shook my head. Donovan took three more.

"Hal was *not* such a bright guy. He wanted to be taken more seriously and paid a higher salary for the jobs he was doing," the cop said. "But he didn't understand just how far over his head he was or how expendable the mob would consider someone like him to be." Billy sighed. "And he screwed up a lot of lives and jeopardized the FBI's covert investigation because of his idiocy."

"How did he mess up the investigation?" Donovan said. "Because of his demands?"

Billy bobbed his head. "While Treak was working on the Wisconsin pipe-bomb angle, which the FBI didn't know about at the time, the government agents were tackling the problem from the corrupt union and dirty cop side. They'd been tracking the progression of union-intimidation bombings throughout cities along Route 66 and had suspected Vincent Leto of spearheading most of them. I'd been recruited by the FBI to act as a potential player in the game. Letting the word out through established undercover agents that I was a police officer who could be bribed."

"And they tried to bribe you?" I asked.

"Yes. Eventually, I was contacted by one of Leto's men and offered money if I'd be the cop who'd scotch the details of the investigation in my department and keep the state out when the explosives were detonated. The target was going to be a housing development on the outskirts of Albuquerque. I agreed. My Fed buddies and I were going to be ready to take down the operation when the shipment got here... but it never did."

"Because word got back to Leto that Hal Chaney was going to talk, and Sebastian James killed him," I guessed.

"Yes, Aurora."

"But who killed Treak and that filmmaker, Ben Rainwater?" I asked him. "And who confiscated Gideon's car and the files in Treak's apartment?"

"It took us some time to piece all of that together," the cop admitted. "Your brother was the one who'd helped us a lot with that leg of the investigation. When we matched the description of the man Gideon and Jeremy had seen up at that burnt-out mill in Wisconsin—"

"Bonner Mill," Donovan interjected.

"That's right. When we compared his observations to our records and showed him a photograph, it turned out to be Rick Brice," Billy said.

"I knew it," I murmured.

The police detective shot me an interested look. "How? How could you have guessed that?"

"From Treak's notes. I narrowed the names down from there."

"You have some of his notes?" he asked.

I pulled out the shorthand pages I'd decoded back in Missouri, but I didn't want to explain how we'd gotten them.

"Don't worry," Billy said. "Gideon told me and the core members of our team about Amy Lynn Dreamson and the few items he'd left with her. Her whereabouts are top secret. No need for anyone besides our small circle to know, unless absolutely necessary. It's safer for her that way." He studied the sheets of paper I'd handed him. "I was going to arrange to get the film back for evidence but, from what Gideon said of the notes, we didn't think there would be enough useful information on those few pages to bother retrieving them." He looked at them more closely. "You decoded these?"

I nodded.

"My name's on here…"

"Yeah," I said. "That's why we weren't all that anxious to meet you."

He laughed—a good-natured chuckle—and put his hand lightly on my shoulder. "Oh, Aurora. I'm hoping I can make you change your mind about that before too long."

In spite of ourselves, both Donovan and I did, actually, change our minds about Albuquerque police detective Billy Neville. By the end of that very first night, he'd won us over, earned our trust and did the near impossible—made us believe once again that police officers were truly there to serve and protect.

Over the course of the next day or so, as we continued to exchange information with Billy, we realized that Treak had dug up many of the correct facts, but he'd picked up on the whisperings of his underground contacts and believed the mob party line about Billy being on the wrong side of the law.

"Explains why your name was on the list with that bastard Sebastian James," Donovan said. "And why Sebastian said at the church that you were all on the same team."

"Yes. I'm sure Treak Bradley would have gotten around to investigating me eventually, but it helped that I lived so far away. He was a good enough reporter that he might have discovered the truth and blown my cover." Billy topped off his mug of coffee—I'd lost count of how many cups he'd had since yesterday, but it was probably close to twelve—and then he broke open a bag of pretzel sticks for us.

Holding his pretzel like a cigar, Donovan asked him about the sequence of events. "Where did Sebastian James and his cousin come in? And how did Bonner Mill play into everything?"

"From what we've figured," Billy said, "Bonner Mill was first targeted because of a union labor dispute. It wasn't a site Julian Carello had a hand in himself, but the Bonner family was an ally of his, and Leto probably offered his help in creating trouble for them. The second blast was the night Rick Brice killed Treak Bradley and that Rainwater kid."

The cop paced to the window and back, rubbing some sweat away from his deep brown forehead and sighing. "We know Brice had been sent up to Wisconsin to deal with Treak. The journalist had gotten nosy and had hit too close to the truth about the source of the pipe bombs, tying it to the fireworks manufacturing and transportation. Knowing it would be easy for a shipment of fireworks to conceal the illegal explosives. By that time, Brice had already had to turn in his badge, but he was high up enough in the mob himself that he had a few cops in his pocket. Many were in Chicago, like Sebastian James, but also a few others scattered here and there, including a fellow by the name of Paul Earling, the police commander in Ashburn Falls."

"Is that how Rick got the squad car that night?" I asked.

Billy nodded. "The population of Crescent Cove is too low for them to have their own police department, so they hire out officers from surrounding areas to patrol and investigate—like Earling. He was instrumental in 'losing' some critical evidence and paperwork in regards to both of the Bonner Mill explosions. He was most likely the cop who confiscated Gideon's car and all of your brothers' belongings at their motel in Ashburn Falls. One dirty cop in a small police department can do a *lot* of damage," he said with disgust.

"Any chance some of those Crescent Cove and Ashburn Falls people are related?" Donovan suggested. "We knew that Ben Rainwater was the cousin of Ronny Lee Wolf, but was there any special connection between them and this Earling guy? Or between any of them and Hal the truck driver?"

"We've done a lot of checking into Earling's background," Billy said, crunching on a pretzel. "The three of them—Earling, Wolf and Chaney—weren't relatives, but they were friends. We think that it was through knowing Earling that Hal Chaney got the job with Americana Trucking. And Ronny Lee Wolf was moonlighting at the fireworks factory. He was the one providing the extra explosive material in Chaney's shipments. So all three of them were definitely working together."

I finally reached for a pretzel stick. "So, Rick Brice came up to put a stop to Treak Bradley's investigation, but he ended up finding out about Ronny's cousin, Ben Rainwater, who was on to his relative's bad deeds. And then both of our brothers showed up, too, and got themselves involved with Ben, Treak and this whole mess."

"Exactly. Gideon and Jeremy were on the good side," Billy said. "When they got away, it created a huge problem for Brice and Leto. That's where Sebastian James came on the scene."

Billy spent the next hour and a half bringing us up to speed on Sebastian, his background and his motivations. Started out a working-class city boy from a big family who'd gotten into a lot of scrapes with the law as a teen. But, like an atheist who'd finally found religion, Sebastian discovered the police academy and, for a while, pursued it with fervor. Worked his way up to lieutenant.

Only the zeal began to wear off after a while, and the extra perks he could get by cozying up to Rick Brice and his mob buddies began to outshine the luster of his badge. He took some bribes under the table, looked the other way more than once and wasn't above fudging a few documents when required.

When word reached him that the two witnesses who'd gotten away were Minnesota boys from Crescent Cove, though, he knew he'd hit payday. Sebastian got himself a meeting with Leto and proudly told the mob boss that he had a connection there. His younger cousin, William James, was on the force in that little town and, with some cash to grease the wheel, good ole Willie could be "persuaded" to help them out.

I found myself hating Officer William James with every single fiber of my being. Even more than I had during his phony "investigation" of Gideon and Jeremy's disappearance.

Billy must have seen the steam coming out of my ears because he was quick to try to reassure me. "Don't worry, Aurora, we're going to get him. We've only been holding out because we're hoping to snag some of the bigger fish, too. Truth is, the extent of William James's involvement was part of what we didn't know for sure until after you and Donovan started following the trail your brother had set up in the journal."

I needed him to explain that. "Are you saying the journal is something you and the FBI were involved in writing, as well as my brother?"

"No, that was all Gideon's idea. He told me he couldn't figure out how it was that he and Jeremy were tailed to Amarillo. They'd hidden out in St. Louis for a couple of weeks, just waiting to hear the news reports. At the time, they were most worried that they were going to be wanted in connection for that second Bonner Mill blast, but the story didn't even make a blip on the news. The few reports they found attributed it to a furnace explosion. They got ahold of some local Minnesota newspapers and discovered the only things out on them were missing persons' reports. People with information were supposed to call the police. Since they didn't know how much danger they were still in and they didn't want to put the lives of their families in jeopardy, they called William James."

Donovan swore under his breath.

"Then Officer James, who'd already covered up any evidence that might have led to the police tracking our brothers to Crescent Cove," I said, "called his cousin and let Sebastian know where they were."

"That's right," Billy said. "Gideon had explained to William James that he and Jeremy didn't really know what they'd stumbled onto but that it was a major operation. They wanted to make sure the few members of the Chameleon Lake Police Department protected their parents and siblings. They asked the officer to let their families know they were okay, but to keep their reappearance quiet until they were sure they really weren't being followed. They told him about driving Ben's car and gave William James enough information to initiate a real investigation of the Bonner Mill explosion. Your brothers also said they'd call again in a couple of weeks to check in on how everything was going from his side. To see if it would be safe to return."

Donovan took out his anger on a couple of pretzels but didn't say anything.

"What happened then?" I asked.

"Then Gideon and Jeremy told William James they were heading toward Texas because, in having the time to think about everything Treak had disclosed to them, there were some hot spots along the way—Joplin and Amarillo, for instance. Places to which the journalist had told them he was following truck shipments. So, they wanted to check these cities out for themselves. And, knowing what they did about explosives, they also wanted to see if they could figure out from talking to the locals what was really going on with them. You can imagine how much the mob wanted *that*. But your brothers were friendly and resourceful. They were good at getting information. Somewhere along the way, they ran into Hal Chaney and tried to talk some sense into him. Tried to be heroes and bring him back from the dark side."

"But he went in the other direction," Donovan said. "Wanted to blackmail the mob into giving him more money."

"You got it." The cop reached to refill his coffee mug yet again and muttered, "One of these days, I'll stop living on caffeine and snack food." He rifled around until he found his box of Girl Scout cookies. "But not today."

Billy told us much, much more after that, confirming details we already knew to be true—that Sebastian James and Rick Brice hunted down our brothers in Amarillo and were responsible for burning up Hal's truck. That Sebastian killed the foolish man who was driving it, then he murdered Jeremy and shot at Gideon.

The Albuquerque cop also explained something we didn't know, that Gideon was the one responsible for killing Rick Brice.

"Sebastian said that Gideon 'did a number on Rick.' Those were his exact words. He never said anything about my brother killing him," I said.

And even though I knew what a piece of scum Rick Brice must have been, I couldn't help but hurt for my brother. Feel his shock at what he'd had to do. Gideon had a laidback, peace-loving soul. As a kid, he'd had a contradictory streak—imagining himself as a superhero or a battleship commander or a proud Marine like our dad—but he hadn't ever really wanted to harm anyone. He was a lover not a fighter.

The police detective nodded. "That was how Gideon got away. He'd stolen a stick of dynamite and a pipe bomb from Hal's truck before Rick Brice blew it up. After Sebastian killed Jeremy, Gideon lit them both, and threw them—one at Brice, the other at Sebastian—half expecting to blow himself up in the process. He told me, by that time, he didn't care. That a part of him had died that day, alongside his friend. He just wanted to stop those two bad men once and for all. The blasts killed Brice and knocked out Sebastian. Gideon was thrown to the ground, too, but he managed to recover faster, even with a gunshot wound to his side. He got Jeremy's body in the car and drove away." Billy sent a half smile my way. "Your brother was a lot tougher than he looked."

"I guess so," I whispered. Then, because I just had to ask, "Is there any way I'll ever be able to see him again? Any time when it'll be safe enough for him to come out of hiding? When things will get cleared up enough so he can come home?"

Donovan came over to stand by me and to lend his silent support as Billy thought about my questions. The Albuquerque cop who'd been so kind to us looked very uncomfortable in that moment.

"It's not quite as simple as all of that," he began. "At some point, maybe Andy can explain it to you. Maybe be an intermediary of sorts between you and your brother. But I can tell you this…Gideon is still very concerned with the repercussions of returning home." He fiddled with his snack and his coffee.

"He needed some serious medical attention when he drove into town. He might have died without it, and I was able to get him cleaned up and bandaged on the sly. And, Donovan, as you and Aurora guessed, we were also able to privately bury your brother at St. Christopher's. I wish there had been a way to get help to them both sooner."

Donovan's face was shuttered against emotion, but I could tell he appreciated knowing this. Knowing that his brother's body had been laid to rest by a caring policeman and by Jeremy's best friend.

"The problem for Gideon is that, while he's still alive, the mob's interest in him may not go away, and anyone near him could likewise be in danger," Billy explained. "He's seen death firsthand already. The mob doesn't know how much he knows about their operations, and we don't know how much Rick Brice and Sebastian James told Vincent Leto about Gideon before they died."

"So, even though Rick and Sebastian are dead now, they may have passed the torch to someone else?" I said.

"Typically, mob crimes are very bad, but their cover-ups can be even worse. Gideon's afraid, and not without reason, that they might use his family as leverage to get that information out of him. But if he stays away from all of you, you'll be safer from Leto and his associates. If, in the view of the mob, you and your family were convinced Gideon was dead, he couldn't have been in contact with you. Therefore, he couldn't have told you anything."

I gulped back my frustration. I understood this, but I still didn't want to hear it. "What should we tell our parents, though?" I asked. "Is there anything we can say? Any fragment of explanation we're able to give them?"

Billy's face filled with compassion and I felt Donovan's arm reach around me.

"I don't know yet," the cop said. "But we'll work on that. I promise."

What he told us we could and should do, however, was get out of Albuquerque for a few days while the police and the FBI worked to wrap up whatever they could at this stage.

"Don't go too far away," he said on Thursday morning, "just far enough that any of Leto's thugs, who might be lingering in this area, can't find you. We still need to arrest William James in Minnesota and Paul Earling in Wisconsin and piece together what the two of them know. We're compiling as much evidence as we can and making sure it's airtight. We may not be able to make the world secure enough for Gideon to resurface, but we'd like the two of you to feel safe returning home to Chameleon Lake. I can tell you, having proof that William contacted Sebastian after you two called him was one of the linchpins to this segment of the investigation. We have verifying phone records, so we'll definitely proceed with his arrest. Fingers crossed we can prosecute a few mobsters while we're at it, too."

Donovan nodded at Billy in approval before glancing at me. "You keep talking about Colorado, Aurora. You wanna go there for a couple of days?"

I thought about it but, then, remembered something that made me say no. "My brother sent Amy Lynn a postcard from Flagstaff, Arizona. Guess I'm curious to know why he liked it so much. How about we go there?"

Chapter Fifteen

Flagstaff, Arizona ~ Friday, June 30

WE MADE an adventure game out of our explorations.

Donovan got to choose five sites to visit on the Northern Arizona University campus and another five in the city of Flagstaff, and I got to do the same. Not surprisingly, there was zero crossover.

"You don't have Heritage Square—the *historic* downtown—as one of your city sites?" I said, looking up from the reference materials at the NAU library that we'd been using to gather our visiting choices.

He read through my list. "And *you* don't have Lowell Observatory? It's where Pluto was discovered." He smiled. "I'd have thought you'd want to get to know the planet of your ancestors."

In spite of myself, I laughed along with his corny joke. Then I elbowed him. Hard.

But the truth was that I was reveling in the silliness of our conversations this afternoon, and I could tell Donovan was, too. It was a nice change to get to kid each other about goofy, normal things... and not to have to talk about explosions or mob retaliations or the disappearance and death of siblings.

As always, I loved being at a library. I loved the promise it offered. The gift of learning. How it was a bastion of possibility in an uncertain world. Really, I loved *everything* about it and just wanted to drink up the information so readily available to everyone. Weigh it in my mind and attempt to make sense of the Earth and its people.

Much as I'd been focused on my brother and our family's tragedy in the past two years, I hadn't been completely oblivious to how our nation's self image had been changing. Gideon used to yak about it all the time. The way any economic or social crisis led to citizens questioning the system. Like how the shock of Watergate or the Vietnam War left Americans doubting the depth of their patriotism or wondering whether capitalism really worked. There was a persistent fear that other countries might be winning "the race"—whichever one the press was most concerned about that week.

But I never felt any such fear within these four walls. In a library, there was always hope, a sense of fresh discovery and the comfort of being surrounded by the wisdom of the world's brightest minds.

So, while Donovan had been across the room, sifting through Flagstaff brochures and skimming a few city maps, I'd scribbled my own lists and had gotten to watch the college students filter in and out of the building. I'd seen them poring over their summer-school textbooks, flipping through newspapers and periodicals or just reading novels for fun—a cool, shaded and relaxing oasis from the late June heat.

It must have been pure heaven.

But I had things to learn, too, and quite a lot about this new region. I'd never been anywhere close to the Southwestern U.S. before and hadn't even read much about Arizona. Between Donovan and me, we'd figured out that there was a ski resort seven miles away, tons of hiking and biking trails and a hopping downtown area with frequent concerts, movie showings, restaurants and art fairs.

Flagstaff was also just an hour and a half from the Grand Canyon, two to three hours from the Painted Desert, Sedona and Phoenix and about four hours from Las Vegas. If this had been a vacation, we would've had our week booked with sightseeing.

But it *wasn't* a vacation. It hadn't even been a college scouting trip. Still, finally getting the chance to wander around a university town and act like a typical teen for a couple of days was quite a change of pace. I was enjoying it.

One of Donovan's campus choices turned out to be the Old Main building, so we left the library and headed toward it. The outdoor walkways that crisscrossed through the college were especially lovely for strolling. The city was in the middle of an enormous ponderosa pine forest, as well as at the base of the San Francisco Peaks. Gorgeous trees, breathtaking mountains and a clear blue sky. I was getting lightheaded from the beauty of it all.

When I told Donovan this, though, he laughed loudly.

"Or, maybe, you're feeling lightheaded because of the elevation," he said. "You're not used to walking around at seven thousand feet."

"Well, you're not either," I retorted.

"I know." He put his arm around me and gently squeezed my shoulders. "I'm a little lightheaded, too."

He didn't remove his arm until we reached the reddish brick building with the coppery roof and had to walk through the front door. Elevation or not, with Donovan's arm around me like that, I was pretty breathless by the time we got there.

Old Main was a collection of offices, museums and an art gallery. I pulled out Gideon's postcard and scanned the gallery for the weird cactus-like sculpture that had been on the front of the card, but I didn't see it there.

After that, we meandered to one of my campus choices, NAU's School of Art. It was the department that had been stamped on the postcard, and I was curious to look around. Again, lots of interesting artistic creations, but no weird cactus thing.

"The displays rotate regularly," one of the School of Art instructors said kindly. "But we photograph some of our most popular pieces and have them available as postcards. See?" She pointed to a rack full of images featuring amazing and innovative art projects—from pottery to paintings, jewelry to sculptures.

Sure enough, the one Gideon had sent to Amy Lynn was there, mixed in with thirty or forty others. It was strange to see a pristine version of that same postcard. No bent corners. No smudged ink. No hidden meanings or implicit hopes.

Donovan saw me looking at it and came to stand beside me.

"You interested in studying art?" he asked.

I shook my head. "I'm not very artistic. But it's cool to look at what some people can do with their hands. The gifts they have."

"Yeah."

Out of the corner of my eye, I caught him glancing quickly at his own fingers. Hands that had fixed a thousand vehicles, held scores of weapons, lit and defused explosives and, no doubt, were capable of building great things.

I thought of what he'd told me he'd once wanted to do—be a car designer or an architect—and wondered what it would take to convince him that fresh starts and second chances were as much for him as they were for anyone.

And, well, while I was at it, I guess I needed to convince myself of the same thing.

Courage. It wouldn't be the real thing if we weren't scared, right?

I took a deep breath and decided to take my first truly brave step, at least when it came to Donovan. I reached out my hand and I put it in his.

He held onto it and, for the longest time, didn't let go.

THE TWO of us spent the remainder of the day and most of the night in a state of contented aimlessness.

Sure, we wandered around town, as well as the NAU campus, and took in the lovely scenery but, really, we were just waiting to get the high sign from Billy Neville that it was all clear for us to go home.

We'd talked to our parents and, hopefully, lied to them for the last time about why we still weren't back in Minnesota. Our excuse du jour was some simple car trouble that needed a couple of days to repair, but it would only be a short delay and we'd soon be able to leave "Iowa." (They had no idea we were actually in Arizona.)

I sensed my dad didn't entirely believe our tall tale, but I was praying Billy would give me something I could tell him to ease the acute loss he and my mom had felt for so long. More than even that, I was hoping nothing would come up to prevent Donovan and me from returning to Chameleon Lake.

However much I'd wanted to get out of that little town and meld into the big wide world, I also wanted it to be on my terms, not as a reaction to some band of criminals.

"I'm going to grab an admissions packet tomorrow," I told Donovan, still feeling guilty about lying so much to my parents. "If Billy says it's okay to tell them we were in Arizona, I'll at least have a little proof that we really looked at a college."

"Not a bad plan," he said. "Otherwise, we can stop at the first college town we get to in Iowa and you can pick up a bunch of brochures and applications there. And, oh—" He tapped his temple, remembering. "Somewhere in my car, I've still got that yellow flyer about the Deadhead concert in Normal. Proof you were on an Illinois university campus, too."

I burst out laughing. "I'm sure if my parents were worried about me going away to school, that would ease their fears completely."

He smiled. "Well, yeah, okay. Maybe not."

At one point in the evening, our conversation turned to Gideon's journal, specifically, the later entries. My brother had completed the entire Route 66 journey, with all of its quaintness, unique attractions and powerful ideals of freedom.

In 1976, he'd been in Flagstaff on September eighth, Topock on September twenty-sixth, San Bernardino on October second and Pasadena on October tenth—making references to things we still didn't understand and could only speculate about in our little roadside motel room.

"Do you think 'sunset ranger' is a person, place or thing?" I asked Donovan, referring to a phrase on the *Pasadena* page.

He shrugged. "No idea. But I think the important thing for you to remember, Aurora, is that your brother is still *alive*. Somewhere out there—" He waved his palm in a westerly direction. "Gideon's okay. Living his life. Being protected by Andy Reggio and Billy Neville. And, even though you didn't get to see him in person, he *contacted* you... with his journal. You know he's out there and he cares about you. That's a lot to know."

I *did* know that, yes. But I felt deeply for Donovan, not having that, too.

He told me a little bit about his plan to go back to St. Christopher's Church near Albuquerque someday soon, just to find out from Billy where exactly Jeremy's unmarked grave was located. He wanted to be able to say a real goodbye to his little brother.

And it occurred to me then that it was more than just a sibling-to-sibling relationship he and Jeremy had shared. They were brothers, of course, but, in many ways, I realized Donovan had also played the part of a father figure during all those times their real dad or their stepdad wasn't there for them.

I remembered my little "act of courage" from earlier in the day.

Holding Donovan's hand. It was nice, but it was nothing like the courage he'd shown in the face of so many challenges and losses. I could do better, be braver, too, even in the face of mine.

We were laughing about something we'd seen on TV and eating Good & Plenty candy from the box before I finally worked up the nerve to talk with him honestly about my feelings.

"We met each other a long time ago, Donovan," I began. "But, until we went to Crescent Cove together, I didn't know you very well. I sort of thought I did—" He grinned at that. "But I really didn't," I continued. "You're not the guy I had that girlish crush on two years ago. You're someone I really care about. Someone I've been really lucky to have traveling beside me through all of this craziness. I'm so grateful to you for being the talented, generous, honest man that you are."

Tears began to well up in my eyes as I spoke. I felt them there, but they weren't out of sadness. So, I blinked them away, patted his left shoulder gently—above his bandaged wound, which was healing but it still had to hurt—sniffled once and stepped back from him.

He set the box of pink and white licorice candies on the side table and flipped off the TV.

Then he came back and stood in front of me.

For too many seconds to count, we just looked at each other. Body heat radiated off of him and warmed my skin without him even touching me. But then he broke through. He reached out, pulled me to him and bent down to kiss me.

There was not a drop of alcohol involved this time. No taste of grief either. Just pure emotion, and the happy oneness you feel when you live for a moment in the actual *present*. Not in the past, with all of its has-beens and regrets. Not in the future, with its expectations and projections.

Just here. Just now. Just us.

He wrapped me up in his kiss, cradled me in it, like a cactus leaf holds a precious droplet of rain. And afterward, we walked outside in the dark, hand in hand, as the clock raced its way to midnight and June turned into July.

"Happy birthday, Aurora," Donovan whispered as we wound our way back to our motel.

I smiled, pleased he'd remembered.

He'd already given me a gift, of course—the beautiful ruby ring from Santa Fe, which I never took off my finger—but the real present was him telling me in words what his actions had already shown. That he liked me a whole lot, too. That, in fact, he'd been attracted to me for far too many years, but had just considered me off limits, mostly because of my age and because of the friendship between our brothers and because of his concern that I might want or need a different type of man. One who was more academic and bookish than he'd ever be.

"You asked me in the car, after we left Amy Lynn's, what those two things were that I knew I was right about," he said. "Do you remember the first one?"

"You told me, 'Disco sucks,'" I said with a laugh.

"That's right! Disco *does* suck and we can't get rid of it soon enough." He wrapped his arms around me and leaned me up against the door to our motel unit. "But I didn't tell you the second one. It's that I knew from the day I met you, Aurora Gray, that you'd grow up to be a beautiful, strong and extremely intelligent woman. Someone who'd be irresistible to me someday." He paused. "I really didn't want to think about that when you were twelve, though."

I kissed him first this time, giddy as I was with happiness and unable to contain it. "But I'm eighteen now," I told him.

"Yes," he agreed. "Yes, you are."

We finally fell asleep sometime after three a.m., having spent the wee hours talking, making out and confessing the little things that had attracted each of us to the other. The qualities we appreciated. The times we were driven a little nutty with jealousy, too. (This applied more often to me than to him, but I was pleased to hear that my flirting with the Cute Librarian Guy in Joplin had ticked him off.)

"Oh, good," I said. "I'd been trying so hard to irritate you."

He laughed deeply at that and acknowledged he'd had fun teasing me with all the waitresses on the road and especially with Vicky from St. Cloud. "She wasn't even *kind of* my type, Aurora."

So, of course, we were exhausted. We woke up late the next morning, and only because the phone was ringing.

Billy Neville.

"The good news," he said, "is that we've taken several positive steps in the right direction. This case has been on the FBI's radar for years, so they were ready and eager to start making arrests—they just wanted to be able to do it in three states at once."

The police detective told us that Ronny Lee Wolf squealed on his contacts and sources like a trapped pig when he was busted for his part in the storage and distribution of the pipe bombs. The selling of illegal fireworks was a lesser charge, but he'd be facing that, too, thanks to the involvement of the ATF.

And, between Ronny and the crooked police officer, Paul Earling, the manufacturing leg of the bomb operation—which had taken place in the basement of a fireworks factory several miles outside of Ashburn Falls—was exposed as well, implicating a number of Vincent Leto's other associates in the process.

"The FBI's got quite a number of additional witnesses and pages of evidence against Leto," Billy said. "Enough to detain him for a while, but he's been clever about distancing himself from the actual bombings. The Feds are confident, though, that they'll be able to get him one way or another now, indirectly if necessary, through tax and real estate records or through knowing the direction of the money trail and some of the people he paid off. Like William James."

Turned out, our hometown cop also squealed pretty fast when facing charges of bribery, tampering with evidence, hindering an investigation and colluding with his cousin on three homicide attempts and one murder.

William admitted that his snazzy yellow VW Bug had been given to him as a "gift" from Leto for his help two years ago in masking Gideon and Jeremy's whereabouts from the other Chameleon Lake police officers and for telling Sebastian James that the boys were headed to Texas in Ben Rainwater's car. William had expected Sebastian and Leto to produce another comparable present for the information William had given his cousin regarding the location of Aurora and Donovan.

"He didn't know Leto had been apprehended and was facing a life sentence in prison," Billy told us. "And he also didn't know his cousin was dead. Which may be very good news for the two of you."

The police detective explained that William James might not have realized that Sebastian had found us in Amarillo or that we'd figured out the connection between the two of them.

"We think Sebastian might not have even told any of Leto's people in Chicago that he was searching for you in Albuquerque," Billy said. "I'd intercepted Sebastian when he got into town, told him my partner and I had been following you and gave him enough insider information to convince him we were all on the same side. I think he wanted to present his discovery and silencing of you two to Leto as a done deal."

Billy said the bad news was that he still didn't want us to leave Flagstaff yet. There were plenty of mob men waiting to jump into Sebastian James's and Vincent Leto's shoes, and he wanted to make sure we'd be reasonably safe before driving out of town.

But he told us he'd give us another call the next day. Said it looked promising that we might be cleared to head home by the end of the weekend, so we could be back in Minnesota for the Fourth of July.

Donovan and I both noticed that the Albuquerque cop didn't mention yet what we'd be able to disclose—or *not* disclose—to our families. The burden of the information I'd been carrying and keeping from my parents was weighing on me a lot, and I knew Donovan had to be thinking similar thoughts about his mom.

However, we pushed those worries aside for a while and spent the rest of my official birthday ambling around the NAU campus, which was still pretty charming and lively, even for a Saturday in summer. Then we hung around downtown Flagstaff, had a cozy dinner at a tasty Mexican restaurant near the Orpheum Theater and strolled along one of the tree-lined trails, hand in hand. Eventually, we wound up at the motel again for an evening of "Starsky & Hutch" followed by "The Love Boat."

The ABC television lineup had me chuckling to myself a little. So, the crime drama needed to be solved first before we got to enjoy an hour of romance, huh? Not that TV Land was usually anything like my real life but, tonight, I decided to make it so.

I clicked off the tube after the second show ended, put my arms around Donovan's neck and kissed him, holding nothing back. Finally allowing myself to get lost in the beautiful contradictions of him. Hardness and softness. Darkness and light.

We ended up on the bed, which wasn't difficult since it was right there, next to us. And we continued kissing but, unlike last night, we didn't break apart every few minutes to chat or laugh about something. And we didn't eventually just fall asleep.

It was getting more intense by the minute. I could almost count the number of seconds ticking until I knew Donovan would play the gentleman card and pull away. When that happened, I was ready for him.

His breath came in ragged puffs as he jerked back from me and stared at my lips, my cheeks, my eyes. "This is…um, we're…I mean, it's too—"

"Passionate?" I supplied. "Powerful?"

"Yeah. Yeah, that." He swiped a few beads of sweat off his brow. "We should really cool it, or else…"

"Or else?"

"Oh, don't pretend you don't know what I mean," he said with a laugh. "Believe me, it's not that I don't want to. I *really* want to. But, we shouldn't. You're still—"

"I'm still what? A kid?" I shook my head. "But I'm not anymore, Donovan. I'm eighteen. A legal adult. And I know exactly what I'm doing. Here. With you."

"That's bullshit, Aurora. You do *not* know." He smiled at me, his heart and soul in his dark brown eyes as he reached to push a few strands of hair away from my face. "Maybe someday you'll really want to, but I don't think tonight's the night."

"*You* don't think so, so it can't be true, huh?" I teased him. "Tell me something—is your only fear that you don't think *I'm* ready?"

He nodded. "But it's a valid fear. I'm five years older than you. A few months from now, maybe you'll go off to college in the Twin Cities or somewhere, and you'll meet someone else…and wish you'd waited for him."

I listened to what he was saying, and I could see those possibilities for what they were: The excitement of the unknown. The daydreams we have of a shiny future, untarnished by the pain of the past. The promise of an uncomplicated romance.

But I didn't want the unknown.

I didn't crave girlish daydreams or anyone else's vision of my future.

And I didn't trust anything just because it was uncomplicated.

I rested my head against Donovan's chest, and he held me there for several long moments, thinking—I was sure of it—that I'd come to my senses. That I agreed with his reasoning.

Well, he was wrong.

I pulled back and smiled at him. Confident I knew my own mind. Prepared to take responsibility for every one of my own actions.

"If you don't want to sleep with me tonight, Donovan, just say so. But let it be *your* decision about how *you* feel, not a projection about *my* choices and *my* emotions. Because I already know what I want." I paused to make sure he was listening. "I chose you a long time ago. I'm not going to regret anything, no matter what happens after we leave here."

He swallowed a time or two and studied my expression for what felt like an eternity. "I think you're maybe a little on the insane side to care about me so much, Aurora Gray."

"Maybe I am," I said lightly. His wallet was on the nightstand, and I reached over to grab it. He watched me with interest as I rifled through a few of the leather folds until I found what I was looking for. I held up the foil packet with the rubber inside. "Had a feeling you might have one of these."

"Oh, yeah? Your intuition tell you that?"

I shook my head. "I had an older brother, remember? I learned a thing or two about guys from him."

"Ah," he said. I heard him draw in an uneven breath. "Are you sure?" he asked. "Because I can only keep fighting you—fighting *us*—for so long."

"Donovan, I've never been so sure of *anything* in my life." And I meant it.

He slipped away, turned off most of the room lights and, finally, climbed back into bed next to me.

Then he half grinned and said something I truly hadn't expected.

"I'm putting my heart in your hands tonight," he whispered. "Be gentle with it."

I AWOKE on Sunday morning to find Donovan's arms encircling me. I snuggled closer to him, enjoying the scent of his very warm, very male body beside mine. Remembering the way he'd touched me, skimming his fingertips against the side of my neck and down my shoulder. And then further still—between my breasts, my thighs. Pulling me nearer.

Holding me tighter. Pressing into me, our bodies joining together in a union that felt destined. Magical.

My stomach growled, disrupting the memory and breaking the spell.

Donovan blinked open his eyes and laughed. "I'm starving, too," he admitted.

And, so, reluctantly, we began the day.

As Donovan showered and shaved, I smiled to myself, reliving even more images and sensations from the evening before, as if it were a romantic movie playing on a continuous loop in my brain. As long as I lived, I knew I'd never be able to explain how much being with him last night meant to me. Truly, I was *happy*...contented in a way I hadn't thought possible. A near miracle, actually, for someone like me who lived so much of her life in her mind, rather than in her body.

I wriggled and stretched in bed, slowly working my way up to a sitting position. Still, I wasn't quite ready to step out of my cozy cocoon or leave the afterglow of the night completely behind me yet.

So, I reached for yesterday's newspaper, which was on the side table, trapped underneath our half-eaten box of Good & Plenty. I nibbled on a few licorice candies to quell the hunger pangs as I thumbed through the pages of the paper, at least until I came to my favorite section—the puzzles.

Growing up, Gideon and I used to fight over who'd get first crack at this page in our daily newspaper. I often got to it soonest because I tended to wake up earlier than my brother did. Sometimes I'd start with the crossword, other times the cryptoquote. If I really wanted to annoy him, I'd tackle the word jumble. That one was Gideon's hands-down favorite.

For old time's sake, I began unscrambling the individual words in the puzzle before me, rewriting the clues into a disordered constellation of letters on the edge of the page and trying to imagine them anew. As words that were surely familiar but, as yet, unseen.

And, suddenly, I *did* see something. Something that made me bolt out of bed.

I couldn't say for sure which of my word doodles was the one that sparked my insight, just that I wrote and rewrote a completely different pairing of words in the newspaper's margin. A duo that had nothing at all to do with the puzzle on the page.

Then, with my pulse sprinting, I reached for the phone.

"I'm sorry for calling so early on a Sunday," I said to Billy Neville, "but I need to speak with your partner, Andy. It's important. Could you please ask him to give me a call here?"

"I can try," the police detective said. "What's this about, Aurora?"

"I think you know," I told him. "And thank you—for all you've done."

Not even ten minutes later, the motel phone rang.

I smiled and said, "Hello?"

Then I listened to Andy Reggio's heavy Texas drawl as he told me that he'd just gotten a call from Billy. "Said you wanted to speak with me?"

"Yes," I replied. "You know, you almost fooled me with the anagram. Same ten letters, just jumbled into a different name. I hadn't expected that, but I guess I should have...considering *you* were involved."

Suddenly, the faux accent disappeared and I heard a rueful chuckle on the line.

"I think you did really well figuring out so much, Sis," my brother said. "And, by the way, sorry to be a little late with it, but happy birthday."

Chapter Sixteen

San Bernardino, California ~ Tuesday, July 4

WITH BILLY Neville's help, we had a short but incredibly joyful family reunion in San Bernardino, California just two days later.

It was the Fourth of July.

We called my parents and asked them to fly down—not telling them the reason, just that it was important—and, of course, they came.

Donovan, Billy and I met them at the airport, and Gideon, who'd been on the road somewhere in Southern California, drove his motorcycle to the secluded picnic site Billy had reserved just for us that day.

The moment when Gideon took off his helmet and ran toward Mom and Dad, the world stopped spinning for a second. And then... everyone cried. Both of my parents. Me. Gideon himself. Donovan. And even Billy Neville.

My brother looked different. There were some similarities, of course. His build hadn't changed too much, although I could tell he was more muscular and a bit broader than he'd once been. His skin was tanned and starting to approach leathery. Like a California boy, rather than a Minnesota son.

His hair color was noticeably lighter, and he sported a beard I'd never seen before. He no longer wore his ruby graduation ring. Honestly, at first glance, I might not have recognized him. (After all, I *hadn't* when he'd been clad in biker gear in Amarillo or at the church cemetery in New Mexico.)

But his voice—without that phony "Andy Reggio" accent—was the same as always. And when he smiled at me again and hugged me close, I knew I'd gotten my big brother back.

There was nothing insignificant about the day. It was as if we all fully understood what a rare and precious gift this moment was and knew better than to waste a single second.

We conversed as a whole group but, also, in smaller, intense configurations. Billy, my mom and Gideon. My dad and me. Gideon and Donovan. We grouped and regrouped all day long.

My parents needed the most time with my brother, of course—both alone and, also, with Billy, who could so expertly provide explanations of the case. The police detective filled them in on what had happened over the past several years and, in particular, all of the events that took place involving their children.

I was relieved not to have to hold that secret anymore, and I could tell this was exponentially true for Gideon.

Even so, Billy still insisted upon strict confidentiality as we moved forward. He invited my parents to discuss anything else with him at any time but, despite the fact that William James seemed to be operating alone in the Chameleon Lake Police Department and the other two fulltime officers there had been cleared of general suspicion, Billy and the FBI preferred to keep their circle of confidants extremely small.

Donovan and I were told we were free to return home.

Gideon's safety was much less assured if he went back, but Billy told me privately that the final decision was really up to my brother.

"There will always be a risk," he said. "But I think the choice for Gideon is more complicated than that."

I didn't really understand what the police detective meant, though, until later, when I finally got a half hour alone with my brother.

I asked him a few of the questions I hadn't been able to on the phone: *What made you so certain I'd correctly follow the clues in the journal? Were you trailing us from city to city to make sure? Now that this is all over, will you come back home?*

He answered each of them, but in his own meandering and somewhat mysterious way.

"You're my sister, Aurora," he said with one of his flash grins. "You think I wouldn't remember how persistent you could be when you wanted to figure out something? I lived with you for sixteen years."

But then the deeper truth emerged. He confessed it had been his instincts that had saved his life in Amarillo, along with a little knowledge of explosives. He'd been only a few perceptive seconds ahead of Rick Brice and Sebastian James. "Still not quick enough to save Jeremy," he lamented, but it was enough for Gideon to get away, even though he'd had to kill a man to do it. The experience changed him, and he was reminded of the intuitive gift he knew I possessed.

"Once I'd sort of gotten my head together again, I tried to come up with a creative way to help Billy—and the special unit of the FBI—so we could get those bastards." he said. "And I remembered the journal."

It was, as I suspected, an object he just happened to have with him in his backpack when he and Jeremy took Ben's car to Bonner Mill. Slowly, months after the incident in Amarillo, the idea to use to journal took hold. He came up with the coded messages, wrote them down, brought the journal up to Chameleon Lake and planted it in the cedar box where he knew only I would find it.

"My main concern was to keep you safe, even as you worked to solve the puzzle," he said. "I knew, though, if anyone would be capable of skirting danger while piecing together the clues, it would be you."

And so, yes, he tracked our progress whenever he could. In Wisconsin, Illinois, Missouri and Oklahoma for sure. "Not nearly well enough in Texas," he said with an apology. "Sometimes you and Donovan were faster than I'd expected. In fact—" He paused. Studied my face silently for a few seconds and glanced at Jeremy's big brother, who was having a private discussion with my dad. "I didn't know for sure that you'd even involve Donovan until the two of you went to Crescent Cove together. I thought it was at least fifty-fifty that you'd go it alone."

"No, I needed his help," I admitted. "I did from the very first day." Then I pulled out Gideon's leather journal, which had been my constant companion for the past month and my touchstone of hope, and I offered it to him. "Would you like to have it back?"

He traced the butterfly on the cover with his fingertip and smiled at me. "No. See, the journal was always meant for you, Sis. That's why I thought of you whenever I looked at it. Some of the pages at the beginning were my own notes, but I'd been writing down car maintenance procedures in it to give to you after you graduated and moved into the big wide world. I knew you were going to be a very independent young woman, and I figured you might wanna know stuff like how to change the oil in your car," he said with a laugh.

He told me a little more about what his life had been like since that Bicentennial weekend—the regrets he'd had, the challenges he'd confronted, the hours he'd spent alone on his motorcycle just thinking. He'd become "Andy" after Billy saved his life. My brother described how he'd actually begun training as an agent himself for the past year. Being taught the proper procedures. Learning how to shoot a gun. Strengthening his undercover guises. Putting his natural talents in science and mechanics to work, along with his social skills.

And he explained, too, that he'd been given some unusual opportunities and privileges as part of Billy's special undercover team. Like getting to be the one to take down Sebastian James in Albuquerque.

"But wasn't it hard for you to kill somebody, Gideon?" I asked him. "Even someone that bad?"

"Not as hard as it probably should've been," he replied. "Besides, I did it for Jeremy. And for you and Donovan, too."

However, he also told me he was at a personal crossroads. If he wanted to continue on the agency path, it would take more formal schooling. A degree to earn. A set of rules to follow. A lifestyle to accept.

"There would be all of that settling down, grown-up stuff. Health insurance, income tax returns, being part of the system," Gideon said with an involuntary grimace. "Billy's been great and my FBI mentor has been real cool, too. They say I'm an asset to my team and my country, and I want to help them—I just don't know if that's the life for me. And I don't think I can just go back to how things were before I left Chameleon Lake either. I'm no longer that same guy. I need to be... more free than even the old Gideon was. But I also wanted to make sure you and our folks were just as free first."

Until then, I'd never really seen the powerful struggle my brother would have to face within himself, probably for the rest of his life. The dichotomy tugging between his beliefs and desires. He possessed an inherent contradiction in his nature so strong, it created an unsolvable conundrum. Not only was I utterly unable to resolve it, but neither was he.

It was interesting. I couldn't be sure if Gideon was destined to be more of an antihero than a hero. More of a vigilante than a trained secret agent. I think he equally liked the idea of both.

But the one thing that was crystal clear to all of us on this memorable Independence Day was that—however much he loved Mom, Dad and me, and however much he respected Donovan, Billy and his agency friends—Gideon would be making his own decisions about his future. And he'd take as long as he needed to do it.

The day ended too fast, in darkness, as night ushered us out of the park and pointed us toward our different destinations.

My parents, Donovan and I were all flying back to Minnesota together early the next morning. Donovan was going to leave his Trans Am at the airport in San Bernardino until he could make the return trip to Albuquerque to say his final goodbye to his little brother. Billy was headed back in his own car to New Mexico that night. And Gideon (a.k.a. "Andy" from that point onward) was riding west on his motorcycle.

Before we all disbanded, Donovan lit the last firework we'd gotten in Crescent Cove. I heard him whisper, "This is for you, Jeremy," and we all watched it light the sky with a hot, quick flash and a boom. We were grateful for our country but not blind to the fact that freedom came with sacrifice and, sometimes, with losses too painful to name.

Donovan and I were no longer quite so young after our trip ended, and I, at least, didn't feel nearly as inconspicuous in the eyes of those who loved me. Having had to fully face death, I think we both felt we could now truly live.

Regardless, it was time for all of us to finally move on.

Chapter Seventeen

Chameleon Lake, Minnesota ~ Wednesday, July 5

IT MAY have been only nineteen days since I'd last set foot in my hometown, but it might have been a decade for how differently I felt when my parents, Donovan and I drove back down Main Street.

Donovan squeezed my hand in the backseat, out of view of my parents, before we dropped him off at his apartment on Sixth and Main. My mom and dad had thanked him a dozen times already—for helping to find Gideon and for taking good care of me—so, in a way, there were no other words left to say but, "We'll see you soon." A phrase all of us repeated like echoes in a canyon.

I walked into my bedroom and collapsed on the mattress, my tie-dyed bedspread feeling soft and comforting after nearly three weeks of scratchy motel coverlets. David Cassidy stared back at me from my wall. I snickered.

When I worked up enough energy to pull myself to standing, the first thing I did was march over to that poster and tear it down.

The next thing I did was go to the Grocery Mart.

Dale was feverishly happy to see me. Not because he was glad to have me back, of course, but because he'd had to save up almost three weeks' worth of bile toward me and couldn't wait to begin spewing it.

I let him get as far as "You have some nerve, Aurora Gray, to neglect your work responsibilities here just so you could go *joyriding* around the Midwest—" before I strode past him and into the backroom, letting the door swing closed in the middle of his rant. I didn't have many personal belongings in my work cubby, but I liked the "Addams Family" thermos I'd stashed there and fully intended to eat my last unopened package of chocolate Hostess Cupcakes, too.

I grabbed both of those, waved to Sandy, who was watching me with growing admiration—especially after I gave my still-hanging puce-colored apron the finger—and pushed my way through the door and back into the store again.

Dale was still pitching a fit in the middle of the canned foods aisle. I caught a glimpse of three shelves of tuna and winced.

"Don't think you can just ignore me when I'm talking to you, young lady. I'm your boss and I—"

"You're not my boss anymore, Dale," I said very loudly and very clearly, causing the few customers in the shop to pause and watch us with interest. "I quit. Bye now."

And as I left the Grocery Mart, I felt the fresh summer air fill my lungs and the world of possibility opening up to me again.

Freedom.

BETSY CAME over that night.

"Mrs. Larrabee overheard you at the store today," she said with a giggle. "She told my mom she was just 'minding her own business, buying some eggs and milk' when you came in and 'damn near gave Dale Geiger a heart attack.'" My friend grinned. "Good for you, but why'd you quit now?"

"Because it's time," I replied. I told her a highly modified version of my "college scouting trip" and said that the experience convinced me I really should go away to school. "Still not sure exactly where or when, but it's going to be sooner rather than later."

She nodded and worried her bottom lip a bit. "Well, maybe this won't be necessary then." From a brown paper bag she was carrying, she drew out a small, flat, gift-wrapped package. "You were away on your birthday, so I couldn't give it to you until now. But I hope you like it."

I peeled off the wrapping paper and found a very pretty set of stationery. Light pink with my first initial embossed in glossy white on the left corner of every page and on the back flaps of each matching envelope.

"Thanks, Betsy. It's really lovely and so thoughtful of you. I can't wait to write on it."

"I just wanted to make sure we kept in touch after I left for U of M next month," she said. "You know, be pen pals." She gave an apologetic laugh. "But, if you're maybe gonna be in the Twin Cities, too—"

"I won't be there," I told her quickly. "I'm not planning to stay in state. I think I need a total change of scenery, actually, so I'll definitely need this." I held up the stationery and then patted it against my heart. "And I should probably get some for you before you leave. If I write, I want you to be able to write me back."

She hugged me. "I'll always write back to you, Aurora."

"Good," I said. "I'm counting on that."

THE NEXT couple of days were a series of readjustments, resolutions and decisions—for my parents as well as for me. All of us were feeling our way through this new world of having Gideon back but not quite back, and being thrilled about it but not able to share the news with anyone aside from each other.

Gossip was buzzing around town about the recent arrest of Officer William James, but word on the street didn't even hint at a connection to my brother's disappearance. It was all about the dirty cop's "shady financial transactions," which wasn't untrue…just not exactly the full story.

My dad pulled me aside Thursday afternoon. "I still don't know what to say about any of this." He was, I could tell, completely torn as a parent between wanting to lecture me for putting myself in such danger and wanting to praise me for having pulled off far more than I'd promised him before I'd left. "It was such a risk, Aurora. But—"

"But it was worth it," I finished for him. "It really was."

The rest of the world didn't have to know any of the details, but our family did, and we finally had the closure we'd all sought. At least most of it.

Knowing this one-ton weight had been lifted off all of our shoulders gave me the courage to add, "I've been thinking a lot about the fall. I have an idea for school that I'd like to share with you and Mom tonight."

He agreed, but as he hugged me, he whispered, "I talked to Donovan when we were in California. I could tell he cares about you a lot." He pulled back a little to study my face. "Am I right that it's mutual?"

I nodded. "Very much so."

My dad nodded back. "Well, I can't fault your choice. He's a good man."

"I know, Dad." I kissed his cheek. "I've spent a lifetime watching you. I know how to recognize the best ones."

THAT NIGHT, I pulled out the Northern Arizona University admissions packet and went through it with my parents, telling them about the buildings I liked on the campus and the natural beauty surrounding Flagstaff.

"It's not exactly close to home," I admitted, which was something almost too obvious to utter aloud, "but if they accept me, it would be a college I'd love to go to next year. This September, if it's not too late. January, otherwise. Either way, I've been thinking about maybe moving there…soon. Getting a job somewhere in the city to earn money for classes. The only downside is how far away I'll be from you."

My parents shared a look that told me in half a second all I needed to know. That they loved me, but they knew the time had come to let me go.

I knew that time had come, too.

With tears brimming in her eyes, but a genuine smile on her lips, my mom said, "Why don't you apply there, sweetheart? Send it out this week."

My dad agreed. "If you liked the place so much, that's where you should study. It's only a two-hour flight away. Not so far." He put his arm around Mom's shoulders and squeezed. "Won't that be a great state for us to visit during winter?" he asked her.

She nodded. "And maybe your brother will be able to meet us there sometimes."

I didn't say so, but that very thought had crossed my mind as well.

A few hours later, my mom motioned me into the kitchen while my dad was occupied watching the ten o'clock news. She looked fifteen years younger now that she knew Gideon was alive but, still, I could see she was worried about him. About whatever unforeseen hazard might befall him next.

"Do you think he's really okay?" she asked me. "Your brother… out there on his own? He said he'd keep in touch with us in some way or another, but I just don't know what to expect from him now. Everything's changed."

I agreed this was true. "I think he's still figuring out for himself how he's going to handle his next steps. It'll probably be a lot easier for all of us once he does."

Because, really, it was Gideon's willingness to live in relationship limbo that I had the hardest time wrapping my head around. I understood his need for freedom, but not his *lack* of need for connection. I suspected he enjoyed the secrecy surrounding his life too much. His personal mythology of being some kind of rebel *with* a cause. A lone ranger on a motorcycle, riding west into the sunset, final destination unknown.

A *sunset ranger*? Perhaps that was it. With *one shield*—the windshield on his bike. A man on the open road who didn't have to answer to anyone.

It had been such a huge cathartic moment seeing our mother getting to hold her son in her arms again. Her baby boy she'd thought she'd forever lost. But even being in the center of that, Gideon hadn't fully realized the price we'd all paid for his choices—right or wrong.

I would always love and admire my brother, but I simply didn't believe a man could fancy himself to be truly heroic while leaving the people he loved (and who loved him) in the dark. Not even if he thought it was for their own good.

"I hope that's the case, Aurora," my mom said. "With all my heart, I do." Then she hugged me so tight I didn't think she'd ever let me go.

But she did. And with a mother's unwavering love in her eyes.

THE NEXT morning, I went to visit Donovan at work.

"Heard you walked out on Old Man Geiger," he said to me in the garage, wiping some grease off his fingers with a cloth and sending me one of his half grins.

I'd missed seeing Donovan. Missed being around him. It was so strange to have gone two and a half *days* without talking with him face to face after we'd spent almost every second together for weeks.

"Yeah, I'd had enough of the store." I paused. "Um, can we talk for a few minutes? Alone?"

"Sure." He motioned me into the back office and closed the door securely behind us. Then he winked at me and snapped the blinds shut, too. "What d'ya have in mind, Aurora?"

I felt myself blushing. "It's not like that," I said, just because I knew it'd remind him of the day I came here to show him the journal. Knew it would make him laugh a little.

He did, and then he pulled me into his arms and held me close for several minutes before either of us said another word. I could feel the comforting pulse of his heartbeat through his white t-shirt.

When we finally stepped apart, I asked him how he was doing, how his mom had taken the news, what his plans were for going back. I knew he'd be leaving soon. When we flew home from California, my parents had purchased a one-way plane fare for me back to Minnesota but, because Donovan's car was still in San Bernardino, they'd gotten him an open-ended return ticket. It was just a matter of time before he used it.

"She handled it better than I thought," he said. "But, you know, it was hard. Both of us wished the outcome had been different."

I nodded and tried to push away the sadness. Jeremy had been like an extended family member to me—he'd been around so often. But I knew any pain I felt about his death paled in comparison to Donovan's loss of his brother or their mother's loss of her youngest son.

"I'm still glad we know, once and for all, what had happened to him, though. Your intuition steered us well. Often onto very dangerous roads," he added with a smirk, "but they led to the right places."

I bowed my head, acknowledging the truth of it. I may have

guessed the correct path more than once, but I'd also been stubborn and reckless far too often. "You know I couldn't have made it through any of this without you, Donovan."

"Ah, I think you'd have been all right…but we made a good team," he said. Then, "I'm leaving for California tomorrow morning. My mom's not fond of long car rides, so she's just gonna fly in and out of Albuquerque. I'm planning to fix my car in San Bernardino, drive out to meet her flight in New Mexico on Tuesday, then we'll both go to see Billy Neville. And, later, Jeremy."

He told me he'd spoken alone with Gideon about his brother. Had gotten some insight into Jeremy's final days. Donovan said Gideon had even apologized for misleading him into thinking Jeremy might be alive when he was playing his "Andy Reggio" role. That he'd been so focused on helping Billy nail Sebastian and William James that he hadn't realized the emotional wringer he'd put Donovan through.

"Anyway, I think saying goodbye at St. Christopher's will help," he said. "Then my mom can fly back here, and I can drive home."

"Will you take Route 66?" I asked.

He shook his head. "That'd take too long. It'll be I-25 North, I-80 East and I-35 North. But—" He smiled at me. "Although this drive is something I need to do alone, I'll miss your company in my car on the way back. Maybe not your singing—"

I laughed and slugged him lightly on his chest. He let my hand linger there for a moment before covering my fingers with his and pressing them against his heart. I hoped this was a good sign, given what I was going to ask him next.

"You know, I'm going to apply to college after all," I told him. "In Flagstaff. I really liked it." I paused. "Even though we were only there a few days, it has a lot of happy memories for me." And I held his gaze for a long time, making sure he understood that this was because of *him*. "It's new and different. Feels like the right place for a fresh start. But what I'm really hoping is…that you'll come with me. Will you, Donovan?"

I held my breath, waiting for his answer, my heartbeat on pause as he considered my question. My hand—still in his—rested hotly against his chest.

Finally, he pulled all of me close to him again and whispered, "No."

Disappointment crackled through my body, and my spirit

crumpled like a dried leaf. "Why not?" I managed to murmur.

He stroked my hair and pressed his lips to my forehead. "I will *always* be here for you, Aurora. But you should go to Arizona. You should try out college on your own. Be free for a while of everything and everyone. It's something you need to do. I love you too much to want you to limit any part of your life because of me. And, for now, I still need to stay in Chameleon Lake."

I wasn't ready to give up on this. *He loved me!* That had to count for something. "For how long? When do you think you could leave?"

He shrugged, sadness sliding across his face. "I don't know. A few months. A few years. I don't have an answer to that yet, but I need to make sure my mom's all right. And you need time to see if...if I'm really the man you want to be with."

I drew an uneven breath and rubbed the gold band on my ruby ring to give me strength. Whenever I stayed calm and paid careful attention to my inner voice, I always felt things would somehow be okay. It was harder than usual for me to do that this time, but I was just going to have to trust in what I knew deep in my soul to be true.

"I still don't regret a single thing that happened between us," I told him, wiping away a tear that had escaped and slipped down my face. "I love you, too, Donovan McCafferty, and that's not something that's going to change just because of time and distance. I know you think it might, but I know my heart. I believe in us. I believe we were meant to be together. And I believe my instincts wouldn't let me think so for a second if what we had wasn't real."

He tightened his grip on me and we kissed—long, slow and so completely—it was like we'd fused on a cellular level. Then we pulled apart and he said, "I'm never as certain about *anything* as you seem to be but, for the record, Aurora, I know my heart, too. And I hope your intuition is right on this one."

"Time, which changes people, does not alter the image we have retained of them."
~Marcel Proust

Chapter Eighteen

Los Angeles, California ~ Sunday, July 1, 1979

FROM THE shoreline I watched the sun, radiant in its shimmering cloak of orange, greet a rolling wave with a kiss and slowly sink into it. I could almost feel the ocean's embrace. The passion of opposites—fire and water—finally becoming one.

It had been an interesting year. Challenging in so many ways. Moving to Arizona. Starting classes at NAU (I was leaning toward library science. Nobody was surprised by this.) Only coming home for Christmas and for a couple of weeks early in my summer vacation. Not seeing my parents for months on end. Or Donovan.

None of us saw Gideon either, although he did send a couple of very enigmatic postcards, hinting he was still trying to decide which ribbon of highway he should ride his motorcycle down next. I suspected he'd pop in and out of our lives like the bubbles in a champagne glass for decades to come. Always keeping us guessing about what he did professionally, where he might be living, why he required such an extreme form of freedom.

I sighed and wrapped my arms around myself, imagining my brother giving me the hug I needed. But the connection and touch I craved wasn't so easy to satisfy, and the waves were crashing closer to my feet, splashing my toes with droplets of water that were too far away from the sun to be warm.

I jumped back, stumbling a little on the wet sand with all of its unevenness and stray seaweed. But then I heard the voice I'd been waiting for—hoping for—all year long.

"Hey, Birthday Girl. Watch your step."

Donovan.

I swiveled toward him and he caught me in an embrace so fierce it brought tears to my eyes. Or maybe it was because I was finally feeling his breath on my cheek again. Or hearing the deep strum of his vocal chords when he whispered my name. Or inhaling his scent as he pulled me even closer and kissed me. A union of salt water and body heat. Ocean and sun.

When I could gasp enough air to speak, I brushed away my tears and chided, "I've been waiting *forever* for you. I thought you'd never get here."

He pointed toward the parking lot of the beachside hotel that he'd chosen for us to meet at tonight. Even from this distance, I could spot the distinctive crimson gleam of his Firebird Trans Am. "It was a hell of a long drive from Chameleon Lake, Aurora."

We both laughed at that. A journey far longer than the sum of its miles, that was for sure.

"Yeah, I know," I said. "But I'm so glad you came."

This, too, was an understatement of massive proportions. Our plan was to celebrate my nineteenth birthday on the Pacific Coast—just for a few days, so we could finally see the city of Pasadena and the western end of Route 66 together—and then we were both heading to Flagstaff in Donovan's car. To work at our summer jobs in the city. To start classes in the fall. My eager second year of college. His tentative first.

Truly, I could barely stand the anticipation. Of wanting this future. Of wanting to begin this new journey with Donovan. No matter where the road led us.

"You have all your stuff with you?" I asked him, squeezing his hand and tugging him toward a trail that led away from the shore—a different one than I'd taken on the way down here. I wanted every step we took together, from this point forward, to signal the forging of a new path. For both of us.

Donovan nodded and hugged me as we walked toward the hotel. "Everything I need."

Acknowledgments

Jane Austen once wrote, "What strange creatures brothers are!" That may be true, but they are also amazing and generous creatures, and I've been blessed with a fabulous brother and brother-in-law, both of whom were instrumental in the drafting of this story. I'm indebted to each of them for the different ways they contributed to my manuscript.

Although all mistakes in writing are mine alone, I was extremely fortunate to be able to ask my brother-in-law Brad, a 30-year-veteran of the police force and a retired deputy chief, hours upon hours of questions about the guns and ammunition cops used in the late 1970s, what their communication tools were like back then and the methods they employed to conduct their investigations. Truly, if cluelessness had a face when it came to correct police procedures and topics like "ways bad guys can explode things," it would have been mine. But I loved learning so many fascinating details from you, Brad, and I'm very appreciative of your expertise and wisdom.

As for my brother Joe, let me just say that no sister on the planet has been luckier than I've been in having a sibling who is so consistently thoughtful, classy and smart. I've admired you for as long as I've known you, Bro. You're one of my heroes.

Some books take a village to write and publish; this one took a metropolis...

Thank you to my wonderful Chicago-North RWA friends and critique partners—especially Karen, Lisa and Laura, to whom the book is dedicated—for all the editing you did on this novel. Erika Danou and Simone Elkeles, my appreciation to you both for your early feedback on the opening chapters, too.

Huge thanks to my lovely friends Catherine DePasquale, Anita Mumm and Therese Walsh, who took the time to critique this project at various stages and offer such valuable suggestions. An extra dollop of gratitude to Sarah Pressly-James for not only reading the book but for helping me find the perfect title! And another one to Lexi Ryan for sharing so many insights on this story, being tremendously supportive throughout the publishing process and letting me include a novel excerpt here, too.

More thanks (and unlimited bottles of wine) to the members of the fabulous Glenview Book Club for their feedback and heartening enthusiasm, particularly: Dori Barbeau, Claudia Bianchi, Janet Conlin, Marcie Dixon, Terri Guercio, Chris Lama, Lisa Lockett, Megan Lockett, Fran Mazur, Marty Mazur, Allison Vevang and Beth Weigel. I love chatting about books with you ladies and always look forward to our delightful evenings together.

Endless appreciation to the Austen Authors and the entire JA community, as well as to Deb Haupt, Debbie Hoffman, Karen Karris, Jakki Leatherberry, Margie Longoria, Monica Perry, Joyce Twardock and all of the warm and generous librarians, reviewers, bloggers and friends—online and off—who've supported my novels for years, no matter what the genre. Couldn't have done it without you!

Special thanks to Sarah Hansen for your gorgeous cover design, and to Emily Mah Tippetts for your magical work on the manuscript's interior, especially the way you brought Gideon's journal to life. The two of you made the book look beautiful.

And my deep gratitude, too, to all who help maintain historic sites, like those along The Mother Road/Route 66, and who strive to preserve for future generations this famous American highway with its unique connection to our country's past.

Most of all, hugs and kisses to my family for being there for me every day through this rollercoaster ride of publishing. Special thanks to my dad for answering so many of my chemistry questions, to my husband Jeff for reliving the Chicago of the 1970s with me and to my son for being open to experiencing our own Route 66 travel adventure. I'm incredibly grateful for you all.

"Music is the shorthand of emotion."
~Leo Tolstoy

Soundtrack of the Story

"Stairway to Heaven" by Led Zeppelin

"Who Are You" by The Who

"Pinball Wizard" by The Who

"Dance With Me" by Orleans

"Life in the Fast Lane" by The Eagles

"Band on the Run" by Wings

"Love the One You're With" by Crosby, Stills and Nash

"More Than a Feeling" by Boston

"Hitch a Ride" by Boston

"Let Me Take You Home Tonight" by Boston

"Wheel in the Sky" by Journey

"Rock and Roll All Nite" by KISS

"Grease (Is the Word)" by Frankie Valli

"Greased Lightning" by John Travolta & the Cast of "Grease"

"Stayin' Alive" by The Bee Gees

"How Deep is Your Love" by The Bee Gees

"If I Can't Have You" by Yvonne Elliman

"You Should Be Dancing" by The Bee Gees

"Jive Talking" by The Bee Gees

"Promised Land" by The Grateful Dead

"Get Your Kicks on Route 66" by Perry Como

"The Entertainer" by Scott Joplin

"Summer Breeze" by Seals and Crofts

"Running on Empty" by Jackson Browne

"The Fuse" by Jackson Browne

"Saturday in the Park" by Chicago

"Muskrat Love" by The Captain and Tennille

"I Think I Love You" by David Cassidy

"Sweet Talkin' Woman" by ELO

"Only the Good Die Young" by Billy Joel

"Goodbye to Love" by The Carpenters

"Da Doo Ron Ron" by Shawn Cassidy

"(I Can't Get No) Satisfaction" by The Rolling Stones

"Roll Me Away" by Bob Seger and the Silver Bullet Band

"Abracadabra" by The Steve Miller Band

"American Pie" by Don McLean

"Nobody Does It Better" by Carly Simon

"Tonight's the Night (Gonna Be Alright)" by Rod Stewart

"Born to Run" by Bruce Springsteen

"Ventura Highway" by America

"Don't Look Back" by Boston

"A Man I'll Never Be" by Boston

"Rock 'n' Roll Fantasy" by Bad Company

"Goodbye Yellow Brick Road" by Elton John

About the Author

Marilyn Brant has been told she writes with honesty, liveliness and wit (descriptors she's grown terribly fond of) about complex, intelligent women—like her friends—and their significant personal relationships. Although her favorite pursuits undoubtedly involve books, she proves she's not just a literary snob by confessing her lifelong fascination (read: obsession) with popular music, especially from the '70s and '80s, most flavors of ice cream and a variety of sensuous body lotions/oils.

As a former teacher, library staff member, freelance magazine writer and national book reviewer, Marilyn has spent much of her life lost in literature. She is the *USA Today* bestselling and award-winning author of eight novels to date and, recently, the Illinois Association of

Teachers of English (IATE) selected her as their 2013 Illinois Author of the Year.

Her debut coming-of-age/new adult novel, *ACCORDING TO JANE* (Kensington, 2009), featuring the ghost of Jane Austen giving a young woman dating advice, won the Romance Writers of America's prestigious Golden Heart Award and the Booksellers' Best, and it was named one of the "Top 100 Romance Novels of All Time" by Buzzle. com. Her second novel, *FRIDAY MORNINGS AT NINE* (Kensington, 2010), was a Doubleday and Book-of-the-Month Club pick in women's fiction. And *A SUMMER IN EUROPE* (Kensington, 2011) was featured in the Literary Guild and BOMC2, and it became a Top 20 Bestseller in Fiction and Literature for the Rhapsody Book Club. The Polish translation of the novel was released in June 2013.

She's also a #1 Kindle and #1 Nook bestseller, who writes fun and flirty romantic comedies, like her stories in *THE SWEET TEMPTATIONS COLLECTION*, that involve sweet treats and large doses of humor. *THE ROAD TO YOU*—a coming-of-age/new adult romantic mystery—is her latest release. Be sure to look for more romantic fiction, coming soon!

Marilyn currently lives in the Chicago suburbs with her family. When she isn't reading her friends' books or watching old movies, she's working on her next novel, eating chocolate indiscriminately and hiding from the laundry. Please visit her website: www.marilynbrant. com.

Other Award-Winning Novels by Marilyn Brant

According to Jane
A young woman who is good at academics but struggles with finding true love gets two decades of dating advice from the spirit of Jane Austen.
New Adult/Coming-of-Age/Contemporary Romantic Women's Fiction.
For mature audiences.

Friday Mornings at Nine
Three married suburban moms contemplate whether they wedded the right men in this deeply thought-provoking relationship drama.
Contemporary Women's Fiction.

A Summer in Europe
A woman goes on a grand international journey of self-discovery with her eccentric aunt and their lively Sudoku and Mahjongg Club.
Humorous/Romantic Women's Fiction/Travel Adventure.

On Any Given Sundae
A shy dessert cookbook writer and the guy she had a crush on as a teen—an ex-football player turned hot-shot restaurant owner—must run an ice cream shop together for the summer.
Light and Steamy Romantic Comedy.

Double Dipping
A dedicated second-grade teacher fights the school's handsome and inscrutable new financial director to reinstate a much beloved fall festival.
Romantic Comedy with a Dash of Mystery.

Holiday Man
A love story told over a year of holidays between the lady owner of a scenic small-town inn and the big-city businessman who frequents the place just so he can see her.
Sexy Romantic Comedy.

The Sweet Temptations Collection
An anthology containing the complete trio of Wisconsin-set romantic comedies: On Any Given Sundae, Double Dipping and Holiday Man.

Pride, Prejudice and the Perfect Match
A modern, Austen-inspired story between an ER doc and a single mom who meet on an Internet dating site—both with motives other than the hope of meeting their perfect match.
Sweet Contemporary Romance.

Pride, Prejudice and the Perfect Bet (coming 2014!)
The course of true love doesn't run smooth when it comes to a wealthy flirtatious bachelor and a not-so-angelic psychologist in this lighthearted sequel to 'Perfect Match.'
Sweet Contemporary Romance.

All I Ever Wanted: An Abbott Springs Anthology
Four modern romantic novellas written by four different authors that all take place in one small town during the weekend of their community's annual winter festival.
Steamy New Adult Romance.

Sneak Peek

Wish I May by Lexi Ryan

I'm so excited to share with you a little about Lexi Ryan's sexy new adult romance, *Wish I May*, as well as an excerpt from the story. It's coming out soon, and I hope you'll enjoy it as much as I did!

About the Book

I grew up wishing on stars.

My father taught me to believe…in destiny, in magic, in happily ever after. Dreams were my scripture and the starry night sky was my temple. Then Mom stopped believing, left him, and took us with her. At the age of sixteen, I cashed in my dreams to pay the rent, pawned my destiny to keep my sisters together.

Now, seven years later, I'm returning home, grieving the death of my mother, and settling my sisters back into the life Mom threw away. I never intended to stay. I don't want to deal with my father, who is so invested in the spiritual world he forgets the physical. I don't want to face William Bailey, whose eyes remind me of the girl I was, the things I've done, and the future I lost.

This would all be easier if Will hated me. As it is, I have to hold my secrets close so they won't hurt him more than they've already hurt me. But he wants to be in my life. He wants what I can't bring myself to confess I sold. He wants me.

I find myself looking to my stars again…wondering if I dare one more wish.

Excerpt from *Wish I May* © Lexi Ryan

"Seriously? You're lost?" He pauses a beat. "In New Hope?" His tone suggests that I've gotten myself lost in a paper bag. And, okay, New Hope *is* pretty damn small, but I haven't lived here in seven years, and it's changed a lot. The good areas are all rundown now and the factories are closed, and the vast expanses of open land by the river have been developed into fancy neighborhoods with yuppy McMansions so ostentatious I can practically smell their oversized mortgages.

"My GPS keeps trying to get me to drive into the river."

At least that wipes the scowl off his face. "Yeah, GPS systems haven't kept up with the developments around here real well." He rubs the back of his neck and the movement sends the muscles in his arm and shoulder flexing. Between his sweaty muscles and my memories, I'm pretty sure my panties have disintegrated, and I'm pretty sure he knows it.

I clear my throat and resort to asphalt-gazing again. How hard is it to put on a shirt? "If you can point me in the right direction, I'll get out of your hair. I'm sure I'm the last person you wanted to see today."

His grunt has me looking up at him again. Those blue eyes, those crazy blond curls. That mouth. "Cally…"

I sink my teeth into my bottom lip as our gazes tangle. He takes a step toward me, and he's so close, I have to lift my chin to keep my eyes on his, have to curl my fingers into my fists to keep from touching him—sweaty and solid and so damn gorgeous.

I wait—for him to tell me how horrible I am for what I did to him, for him to ask me why I did what I did. I don't know what I'd say. In the shadow of my mother's death, it's hard to imagine that, once, leaving New Hope—leaving Will—seemed like the worst thing that could happen to me. I was so wrong.

But he doesn't ask and he doesn't move away from me. His gaze dips to my lips for the briefest moment, and the way my body responds to his nearness, even all these years later, even after…everything…it only confirms what I suspected.

After seven years. After the lamest breakup in the history of breakups. After breaking his heart and dismissing my own, I'm still very much *his*.

Coming in October 2013!

This paperback interior was designed and formatted by

www.emtippettsbookdesigns.blogspot.com

Artisan interiors for discerning authors and publishers.